BY CHARLES

CHARLES BUKOWSKI

REACH FOR THE SUN

SELECTED LETTERS 1978–1994
VOLUME 3

EDITED BY
SEAMUS COONEY

BLACK SPARROW PRESS
SANTA ROSA — 1999

Black Sparrow Press books are printed on acid-free paper.

LIBRARY OF CONGRESS CATALOGING-IN-PUBLICATION DATA
Bukowski, Charles, 1920–1994
    Screams from the balcony: selected letters 1960–1970 (Volume 1) /
Charles Bukowski ; edited by Seamus Cooney
    p.   cm.
    Includes index.
    ISBN 0-87685-914-7 (paperback)
    ISBN 0-87685-915-5 (cloth trade)
    1. Bukowski, Charles—Correspondence.   2. Poets, American—
20th century—Correspondence.   I. Cooney, Seamus.   II. Title.
PS3552.U4Z48   1993
811'.54—dc20   93-36411
[B]   CIP

VOLUME 2
Bukowski, Charles, 1920–1994
    Living on luck: selected letters 1960s–1970s (Volume 2) /
Charles Bukowski ; edited by Seamus Cooney
    ISBN 0-87685-981-3 (paperback)
    ISBN 0-87685-982-1 (cloth trade)

VOLUME 3
Bukowski, Charles, 1920–1994
    Reach for the sun : selected letters 1978–1994 (Volume 3) /
Charles Bukowski ; edited by Seamus Cooney
    ISBN 1-57423-088-3 (paperback)
    ISBN 1-57423-089-1 (cloth trade)

EDITOR'S NOTE

Like volume 2 of the Bukowski correspondence, *Living on Luck: Selected Letters 1960s–1970s*, this selection begins with some newly available letters which properly belong by date in its precursor volume. The vast majority of the letters included, however, date from the 1980s and 1990s.

The letters I was in a position to select from are by no means all that Bukowski wrote—just those which have become available in library special collections, which have been kindly furnished by their recipients, or which survive in carbon or photocopies kept by Bukowski himself. Many additional letters were doubtless written which may well turn up in time.

When Bukowski acquired his Macintosh IIsi as a Christmas gift from his wife in 1990—his delight in it, despite its frustrations, is well conveyed in some of the letters that follow—he found it easy to keep copies of outgoing mail, and, knowing that his correspondence was of value to collectors and libraries and that it would be eventually published, at least in part, he made a habit of sending duplicate printouts of his letters to his publisher John Martin (not always fully identifying the recipients, who were often simply private readers). These conditions explain a certain disproportion in the temporal distribution of the samples in the pages that follow. Moreover, the ease of entering with a few keystrokes not only the date but also the time of writing explains the occurrence of a time in the date line.

The most frequent correspondents, on the evidence of these letters, are a sympathetic and supportive editor, William Packard of the *New York Quarterly* and—as one might expect—his main publisher, John Martin. Next in frequency are letters to another congenial editor, Jon Cone, and to a fellow poet, Gerald Locklin.

I have selected roughly half of the material available to me. Long explanations of his betting methods occur several times and are only sampled here. Detailed responses to specific poems by some of his correspondents are likewise omitted, since without the text being discussed they would be hard to follow. A very few personal complaints that might give unnecessary offense to living persons have also been omitted, but literary judgments have not

5

been softened. Bukowski often expressed his willingness to stand by what he had written.

Date formats have been standardized, except for a few instances preserved to give the flavor of Bukowski's occasionally imaginative ways of dating his letters.

Salutations (generally a simple "Hello") have been omitted, with rare exceptions, as have closings, again with occasional exceptions retained to give the flavor. Bukowski's characteristic closings are "hold," "sure," "uh huh," and—to John Martin always —"your boy."

All underlinings, block capitals, etc. for emphasis have been regularized to italics, except when they occur to add additional emphasis after previous underlining. In such cases we use small caps.

The editorial "[*sic*]" is added chiefly in places where a reader might otherwise suspect a typographical error. Occasional brief explanatory notes or corrections are similarly in italics between square brackets. Insignificant spelling errors have been silently corrected, but some slips have been preserved when they seem to convey a flavor of Bukowski's impromptu composition.

Acknowledgments

The editor and publisher are grateful to the recipients and the owners, institutional and private, of the letters here printed, who have furnished copies, supplied information, and (when necessary) given permission to reprint. These include, as well as the individual addressees:

University of Arizona, Special Collections
Brown University, Providence, John Hay Library
The University of California, Bancroft Library
California State University, Long Beach,
    Special Collections
The University of California, Los Angeles,
    Special Collections
The University of California, Santa Barbara,
    Special Collections
The State University of New York at Buffalo, Poetry/Rare
    Book Collection
The University of Southern California,
    Rare Books Collection
Temple University Library, Special Collections

A section of photographs follows page 156.

—Seamus Cooney
Kalamazoo, 1999

6

REACH FOR THE SUN

Selected Letters 1978–1994

Volume 3

• 1 9 7 8 •

[To William Packard]
July 16, 1978

Back from Germany. West to a racetrack there and a couple of castles. Racetrack had no toteboard. My whole method of play revolves around the toteboard. The castles were cheaper. The last issue of the *NYQ* was the best—#21. People are getting to write more and more like I do.

Packed them in at the hall at Hamburg, 1200 with 300 turned away. Drank 2 bottles of wine and sang it to them. My German editor told me no writer of books had drawn such a crowd since the fellow who had written the book "Mein Kamph" (spell?). Newspaper and television interviews. Saw myself as tv newscast ... American writer arrives ... I wave off questions, snarl answers, look mean and hungover, hair in eyes, looked *authentic* somehow.

Anyhow, I'm back here where it's quiet and Mailer and Capote and Vidol (spell?). Working on a book about the trip. Some guy took 3,000 photos. I'm not sure I can do it but have begun to beat the ribbon, first 25 pages done. May go to Paris in September for the French boys. May not. May turn into a complete shit. May not.

That's it. 96 degrees here. Sitting in my shorts. Have fixed these poems for your eyes for better or worse. 96 degrees here.

Smoking Sher Bidi's from Jabalpur, India and caressing the good German white wine, Bernkastel Reisling (spell? O, I can't), Brooks too Broad for Leaping, you know ...[1]

Bukowski's daughter was 14 years old in 1978.

[To Marina Bukowski]
September 6, 1978

Hello Marina:
Happy birthday.
Enclosed an m.o. Get yourself something. You know best. There has been a great deal to do around here, writing and otherwise. Leaving for Europe on the 16th, will be back in 3 weeks plus. Meanwhile, I've got to learn to speak French, haha, and German, haha. Will probably not get to see you until I get back.

I hope going back to school is not too tedious for you. I never liked it.

o.k.

[To William Packard]
December 31, 1978 10 p.m.

I am sitting in this place in San Pedro, strapped with mortgage payments because my tax accountant says it's a good thing. "Look, man," I told him, "you don't understand writers. This thing is going to kill me." I've got this old desk here and I can step out on this balcony and see the harbor lights. Much trouble here—fell into the fireplace drunk the other night, really got scalded and tore a few muscle sheaths. My girlfriend put cat

---

1. Cf. A.E. Housman's poem, "With Rue My Heart Is Laden."

10

medicine on my side ... 2 trips to Europe this year. last one I am sitting in Paris and my French editor says, "you want to go see Sartre?" No, I tell him. I got up and got shit-ass drunk on national French tv before 50 million Frenchmen. I am having Henry Miller luck in Europe; well, not Henry Miller luck, say one-quarter Henry Miller luck ... novel, *Women*, finally out. trying to do a screenplay to be directed by Barbet Schroeder, writing short stories for *Hustler*, trying to change my luck at the racetrack. I like San Pedro, the blacks, Mexicans, whites, all mix without much trouble or tension—so far. I mean, since I've been here. Europe is clean and quick and a dollar there buys about what a quarter does here. The whores of Paris lovely, lovely ... I've got to do another 15 years of good, hard writing— let's see: 58 and 15 equals ... well, best not to think about that ... Met a guy at the track the other day. "Man," he said, "we sure miss you down at the post office! you were really funny, man!" the "funny" he was talking about were those sounds I was making from the cross ... Got your card. Packard, I don't know where the fuck your love is ... O.k....

p.s.—I guess you've moved by now and this will be intercepted by a batch of Porto Rican pimps. O.k., they'll like it. I do too.

●

11

• 1 9 7 9 •

To William Packard]
June ten 1 nine 7 nine

[* * *] took some mushrooms earlier that I paid $25 for, hardly anything. Thomas Hardy. Thomas Mann. You know, you can have most of the Tommies. And a lot of the Edgars too. you know somebody I think of now and then: Knut Hamsun. he ground it out, fat novels and thin, mostly fat, and when the fat ones hold up, that's the real score. I never read anything of his that he failed at. there are men who are simply fucking landscapes—like Sibelius. I got my new 1979 MGM[*sic*] and on the way to the track I often slip in a little Sibelius and listen to him over the front and back speakers, sun roof open, I get ready for the tote board, I play the horses like most men play chess and I usually win, it helps the writing and it helps the appetite and it's nice to have decent pocket money so Linda Lee and I can eat at Musso's and stock up on good German riesling, yes. (Havemeyer 1977 Berich Bernkastel.)

in the mornings, hungover, I lay with my ass up to the sun in a big yard full of fruit trees and berries and I let the others worry about my soul. that's their job; my job is to get along with my 17 private and personal gods and so far we are all voting for the same thing, though what it is we are not too sure of. [* * *]

13

[To William Packard]
July ending, one97nine

Here's a few more and the plan is now to go into prose a bit; I slide back and forth between those two prosties, prose und poem, I don't know why more people don't give themselves relief like that.

Lucked it again, passed up reading poetry with 21 American poets, 21 Italians, in some town over there. I mean, when you get at least 42 poets reading, somebody is going to get sick, and they did (the audience, I mean). One long time famous American poet began his chanting and got vegetables in the face when he wasn't quite ready to eat them. I'm told the others fared as badly. Here in America the poet simply gets away with reading too much bad and contrived shit and the audience is used to swallowing it. It's about time somebody told these that the game is up. The sad thing is that most (but not all) poets who gain some fame begin with some bombast, originality, guts, then quickly accept their role, become teachers, leaders, lookers into mirrors. I don't understand why they don't understand that to remain alive is more difficult than to be alive in the first place.

wait. I'm out of wine. have to so downstairs. ain't that something? I have a stairway to go down. And I never forget it, each time. stairway. I am doing it, going down it, good luck, refrigerator there, open it, chilled gong-high glory in bottle, bravo, but just a moment of it, anything can happen. now wait ... I'm back, I get letters from the young. some say I've saved their lives. it's not so. if it were, I wouldn't be interested ... how do you do it? they ask. what can I do? what did you do? I basket the letters. I can't help them because I don't know.

what I did, what I do wouldn't help them. I still need help. I am as confused as I was when it began. nothing has been solved.

my woman is good, she is a good one but I tell her, you must go talk to your friends. she says, is it another woman? and I tell her, no. but women need to be set free into space now and then or they'll claw you to death. they don't mean to. but they do.

we are all too precious. we are all too terribly precious. and

14

we are all looking for the hero (or the heroine) and there just aren't any. I like a cat asleep upon the rug. That's best. If you can have a cat and you can have a rug. that's best. and one more drink....

[To William Packard]
October 25, 1979

Back from Canada. Vancouver. Hall held 500. 680 drunks showed up. We played classical music over the speakers. I had a bit to drink in the afternoon, then came out and threw it at them. I drank 3 bottles of red wine during the reading. You know, if I can't be entertained I'm not going to entertain them.

I fooled them again. Party afterwards, more booze. I danced, kept falling down. I make an excellent fool; in the days of the kings I never would have been unemployed.

I don't remember much. But I got the money. 1000 plus air and expenses. Linda says they got me back to the hotel and into the elevator and I demanded another bottle. After they left I staggered about the room, finally fell and cracked my head open against the radiator. Great gash in skull. Blood everywhere. It looked like a murder sex orgy had been in that room. Linda cleaned it up in the morning. Nice town, Vancouver. I still can't comb my hair. But great part happening now. Picking at this long scab. Really living. Poems enclosed.

[To William Packard]
November 27, 1979

Well, we all approach the dreaded season. I've been climbing up this Christmas–Happy New Year cross for some time now, and it doesn't get any better. One New Year's I just went to bed and cut the lights and pulled up the covers and stayed there, phone off the hook and not drinking. It was my happiest New Year.

Won 9 races in a row the other day, that's 9 firsts, and that's some going you know, none of them favorites, On some days there is total control, you drive the freeways better, you do everything better. Then the other days arrive when you even fear the check-out girl in the supermarket.

Too many nights now with movie people who talk about camera angles, and producer directors who go to baseball games with Jack Nicholson, kissing his ass, trying to get him to act in their movies when they should really be kissing the ass of his agent. Rich girls laying on the backs of sofas with nothing to do. All very dangerous and swampland territory. I suppose they must be better people than I make them but I can only see that they drink from morning to night, sleep four in a bed, are always on the telephone or preparing food. It's good to get back here with my two cats and Linda Lee and to turn on the radio and drink the petite sirah and inhale the quiet walls.

seasons gratings,

●

• 1 9 8 0 •

[To John Martin]
June 14, 1980

There have been too many visitors and now Linda tells me that "mother" is coming soon. I am curious as to why people visit each other when there is hardly time to do the singular and necessary things, and one of the most necessary things is to do all the shit and trivial things to keep the gross and mindless forces from murdering you, and the other necessary thing to do is to do absolutely nothing, glorious spaces away from all things—it's kind of an easy breathing and if you don't get that no matter what else you do nothing can take form. But people don't seem to need this last. They need "togetherness," this legendary humanity of triviality; they need to sit in chairs and chatter away the hours. I feel uncomfortable doing this; I feel like a turd doing this; I feel violated; worse than this, I feel bad. And I know that the only way to shake them is to act like a "prick." So, most of the time I am ingested and the visitors leave fulfilled. Where do they get all this time to wallow about in and to piss away? To me, each minute is a guarantee against loss; I've had hours, years murdered working for other men for their benefit. Don't *these* have this background? Has it always been a welfare, roll-down the hill blind yawn? I mean, what's there to *say* in a room together? What's there to do? So they want to *go* somewhere. They are interested in things. We go. What a burning of garbage. I don't need movies, jazz clubs, fish

17

shows. "How can you be a writer?" one of my women once asked me, "you're not interested in anything."

Why must I like what they like? Does this make me inhuman? And if I am inhuman why must they try to humanize me? Where are *my* rights? Must I always act like a "prick" in order to obtain them (my rights)? Every now and then when one of them overencroaches (that's a beautiful word) I've had to say "enough" and they always leave wounded as if the guilt were mine, as if there were something that I lacked. I never knock on doors. What do they want with me? And each one that is gotten rid of is replaced by another. The world is full of the lonely and the lonely are full of poison. I have never been lonely. One of the finest things for me in all my life has been to close a door and to be in a room without anybody else about.

After this long string of visitors I actually became ill—chills, fever, my legs weakened, I could hardly walk. it was them, too much of them. I was sick for a god damned week. I'm not trying to act like a precious and delicate soul, John. One of my X-Women got it best—Stella—she drank scotch through her nostrils and could smoke up a room with her Pall Malls in 30 minutes but she knew something, she said, "Don't people *realize* you're a fucking *recluse*?"

That's one of the best things I like about our relationship: you leave me alone and I leave you alone and we do what we have to do. I regret very much that I bothered you while Linda was on her night-run trip. This was non-professional and weak; the next time there is trouble I will concur with the inside of my own dome. You were helpful then, thanks, but in the future it will not be needed. Things go in waves, fall up and down, but then we get past that and into our own clear. That's good, that way. But if Barbara ever starts swinging from the vines, feel free to call. I owe you one, and I have this vast backlog from the chamber of horrors that might make you laugh when you need to laugh. o.k.

Henry Miller. I didn't feel much when he went because I've been expecting it. What I liked is that when he was going he went to paint and what I've seen of his things are very good, warm, hot color. Not many lives like his. In his writing, he did the thing like that, when nobody else was going it, doing it. He

18

cracked the hard black walnut. I always had trouble reading him because he would leave off into this Star-Trek contemplation sperm-jizz babble but it made the good parts better when you finally got to them, but frankly, I usually gave up most of the time. Lawrence was different, he was solid all the way through but Miller was more modern, less artsy, until he got into his Star-Trek babbling. I think a problem Miller caused (and it's not his fault) is that when he hustled and pushed his stuff (early) he has made others think that that's the way it is done, so now we have these battalions of semi-writers knocking on doors and hustling and proclaiming their genius because they have been "undiscovered" and that the very fact of non-discovery makes them sure of their genius because "the world is not ready for them yet."

For most of them the world will never be ready; they don't know how to write, they are simply not touched by the grace of the word or the way. Not those I have met or read. I hope there are others. We need them. It's pretty fallow, around. But even like those who come around with their guitars, I've found that the least talented scream the loudest, are the most abusive and the most self-assured. They've slept on my couches and puked on my rugs and drank my drinks and they have told me, continuously, of their greatness. I'm not a publisher of songs or poems or novels and/or short stories. The battlefield has an address; to beg of friends or girlfriends or others is masturbation against the sky. Yes, I'm drinking very much wine tonight and I guess I'm dizzied with the visitors. Writers, please save me from the writers; the conversation of the Alvarado street whores was much more interesting, and more original.

Don't worry about the novel.[1] Let me do that. If it comes, it comes. I have a feeling that it will. Next thing I need is an outline so I won't write it and then find back in chapter 9 I left out a scene that was the best of them all. Besides, by cracking [sic] out poems in between, it tightens the skin of the work to come. I made a mistake in letting it out that I am possibly into novel #4. There's this one fellow I am affiliated with on another

---

1. *Ham on Rye.*

score and when he phones the first thing he asks is, "How is the novel coming?" You know, this novel is not a task, it is not something to be done. It's between me and me, and that's simple enough.

Henry Miller. A damn good soul. He liked Céline like I like Céline. Like I told Neeli Cherry, "the secret is in the line." And I meant one line at a time. Lines containing factories and a shoe on its side next to a beercan in a hotel room. Everything is there, it flashes back and forth. They are not going to beat us, not even the graves. The joke is ours; we pass through in high style; there's nothing that they can do with us.

Joe Stapen in 1980 was, in his own words, "a recently divorced psychiatrist in Denver who enjoyed poetry but came late to Bukowski."

[To Joe Stapen]
December 28, 1980

[* * *] I went to a madhouse once, as visitor, and remember walking about the grounds laughing with my girlfriend, we couldn't stop, I think it was because we sensed that we could be crazy, especially me. I can't describe the mood—it was just joyous being crazy and not being bothered about it, and I picked a flower and held it high in the air and waved to people and we couldn't stop laughing, waving and laughing as the faces stared back sedately. But getting inside, seeing the patients, it got strange, dark-hued, it got flat, it seemed stale, drab and senseless. The boys and girls were comfortable, just like blocks of wood. Nobody was flying over the cuckoo's nest, they were sitting in it. Of course, maybe the violent ward was more entertaining. I didn't try for it. Then I met one of my readers there. In a way, that's better than being in the New York Public library.

I get many of my letters from people in madhouses and jails and some from strange people out of them. What they say, mainly, is that I have given them a reason for going on: "Since you are so fucked-up, Bukowski, and still around, there is a chance for me." But I don't write to save people; I dislike most of them. I feel best when I am totally alone. I've tried to answer most of my letters, especially from people in the madhouses but I found that an answer just brings another letter, a longer one and a stranger one. And more and more letters come and there just isn't time to answer them, not with the racetrack and the drinking and fights with the woman and then just *writing* itself, for me, for money and for me.

Like, I don't know what to say to you. I put the words down and I forget them. Somebody once asked me what my theory of life was and I said, "Don't try." That fits the writing too. I don't try, I just type, and if I say any more than that, I'm trying.

Like right now I'm drinking this Concannon petite sirah, vintage 1976 and listening to classical music on the radio and I've got this capitalistic silly itch to shape a poem or something like that.

I wish you luck with your people and luck with yourself. Nothing, of course, has never fit right and the truly contented man is the insane one. There'll never be an out for us. Just endure if possible. Sometimes I watch my cat sleeping night and day and this teaches me more than all the books and all the past. Other times it doesn't help. Meanwhile, there's some wine, and the itch.

●

• 1 9 8 1 •

[To Louise Webb]
January 9, 1981

I know you think I'm a son of a bitch for not keeping closer touch, but you know how that happens—give a man a touch of fame and he's too busy watching his own ass in the mirror to remember the real beginnings.

You probably still have your emphasemia (spell?) but I always figured New Orleans was luckier for you than any other place. Whenever I saw you there I figured you belonged there rather than the other places. Jon's been gone a long time but both of us know what good things he did for both of us. [* * *]

With me, it's about the same. Still drinking, typing and playing the horses. I live in a big house now. It's not paid for but I live in it. First time I've ever had all this space. A good place to die, I guess. Finally living with a woman who isn't a whore. She's religious but most women are. Not much I can do about that. It's her business.

My luck's good in that most of my fame is in Europe. Over there I can't walk the streets. Here it's good. I can live a normal life. Especially in San Pedro. Old harbor town full of working people, Mexicans, Blacks, Yugos. My neighbors don't bother me. I have 3 cats and much ground out front. I grew some stuff last year—now it's all weeds. Got to get it cleared out. This house is screwed up. Had a handy man here, did his own

23

plumbing and wiring. Got to pay somebody to straighten things out. Got to keep writing for the plumbing, the wiring and the mortgage. Really not that. It still feels mad and clean to sit down in front of this thing...

You ever come west, do visit us. phone [* * *]. We have an extra bedroom and we drink good wine. Linda knows about you. We've got one copy of *Crucifix* and one copy of *It Catches* left. We show them to people when they come by and they marvel at the artistry of the bookwork, as they should. [* * *]

[To Louise Webb]
January 20, 1981

Well, I don't have an agent... not in the U.S. and I don't know of any. It would be great if you could get "Four Steps" done into a movie but, my god, it's difficult. I wrote a screenplay, *Barfly*, a good year or so ago and the director who wants to do it knows many people personally—producers and the works—but no luck, and I think it's a good screenplay. I wish I could help you but I don't know anybody.

Yes, I got cooled by W.C. [Corrington] some time back, a long time back. I was broke and asked him if he might send me the letters I had written him for some archives a university wanted for $$$. I told him that he had written me that whenever I wanted the letters I could have them. He said he never recalled writing a letter like that. He told me to send him that letter and he would mail the letters back to me. I sent the letter. (I should have xeroxed it). Nothing. Silence. Well, you know...

About the movie people—sometimes a guy will buy an option for the rights to a work, say for a year. They will pay almost nothing for the option and then try to re-sell the work to somebody else for a profit. I shouldn't call these types "movie people," they are more like the suckerfish of the universe. Be careful of them, they will glad talk you and get your hopes up

24

for nothing. But often if they have a good work for cheap, they can't get rid of it because they are so personally obnoxious. I'm not saying your fellow is one of these, only that he might be. [* * *]

[To John Martin]
February 4, 1981

Thanks for the rundown on the books. It's nice to see my children doing so well. It's especially strange and lucky that the old books are still moving too. I'm not partial to any of them, old or new. I like them all.

I got myself depressed on the novel when I told you I was going to re-write the whole thing. I can't do that, it's too much like working for the post office. What I will do is to re-write certain portions I didn't like or that read without verve. Then if you want to publish it you can go over it then for syntax and get a bit of the grammar and spelling but don't make it *too* smooth. If there is anything good about my writing it *is* the roughness, the quality of *not* being literary. But it's good of you to straighten out the few kinks that might just be too sloppy. My thanks, plenty.

I've done a few drawings for the proposed new book of poesy[1] but ran out of paints. I use the little tubes. Next time I go to Standard Brands I'm going to load up.

I've been a little low down lately. I can write poems no matter how I feel, good or bad. But to write prose, I can't feel bad and it's better if I feel pretty good. Things will lift soon, I'm sure.

---

1. *Dangling in the Tournefortia.*

[To John Martin]
April 16, 1981

The Linda situation will probably go into a continuance. If not, I can scramble eggs with the best of them,

Pity the poor writer, he not only attracts madwomen, he not only destroys his liver with drinking, he also has no Union (except in Hollywood) and few working rights and/or benefits. Stuck with his sickness for the word and usually having contempt for the business world he is left with nothing but to trust the others, and leaning on that, he is usually taken.

Your $250 bimonthly check which would break down into 6000 a year would probably make me eligible for food stamps. This doesn't so much reflect my ability as a writer as it does Black Sparrow's limited distribution. B.S. may print books as rare as diamonds and gain a literary reputation but not many people are buying diamonds these day, percentagewise. You probably make more on selling my works overseas (the right to publish), selling paperback rights and other similar rights, plus your cut of overseas sales than you do on paying me B.S. royalties. You can't miss.

Why an author derives no payment on the publication rights of his own creations (and other related rights) has always seemed unfair to me. This has been caused by writers being writers and not businessmen, and all the editors tell them is, "This is the way it has always been." Then the dear little writers, as their talents dwindle, as most talents must, watch their royalties dwindle likewise, and since royalties are all they have (had) upon some distant tabulation from some distant place, they become more than bitter, end up in mental and charity wards or as suicides.

It has always been the popular concept for the writer to starve, go mad, suffer, suicide. I think it's time for the editors and publishers to starve, suffer, go mad and suicide. I think it's time the writers got fat guts and drank champagne for breakfast. I think it's time for the writers to sleep with the golden girls of kindness.

They won't, of course, they are too interested in getting the god damned word down as the world breaks down their last door. I am too. I hate this haggling. I'd rather be at Del Mar watching them break out of the gate, with the lady sunning herself at the beach and the wine getting chilled in the motel room, and the portable typer under the bed. I don't like to haggle. The publishers drove Céline mad, pissed H. Miller off. There are, were, countless others. We never get our dues but if we only got half of them we'd feel fine. One of Perkins' editors may have rearranged Thomas Wolfe but Wolfe was there to begin with. What is often called the writer's self-pity is only his tabulation of society whose honor is milk thin. Sour milk thin.

By the way, when I phone you now and then when there's a jam here, it's not that I expect advice or solace, it's only an old habit gotten out of working the factories and the p.o. and all the other places, a subconscious calling in *sick*, meaning I won't be able to work for a while. It seems ingrained. It's a mistake. A good man is best when he works out of jams alone. 0-and-two doesn't mean crap. You can crack the next one over the wall. I'm back at the plate.

[To Al Fogel]
April 22, 1981

Hardly anybody makes it at the track—besides the plus 15% take other things conspire—horses in trouble, fuckers fail to break out of gate, jock is drunk or having trouble with his whore, all the dismal x-factors that can break the best of horse-playing souls and minds in half.

I've gotten hot, I've averaged a string of $100 days just betting ten win on one horse each race and I've gone along like that for 3 or 4 weeks in a row and then, bingo, it doesn't hold, I'll lose $15 or I'll win $15 or the day will come when I'll only cash one ticket.

And that 30 minute wait between races can make anybody sick in the head—surrounded by dullards talking out loud about nothing they don't know. These lonely-hearts gather at

racetracks because nobody can stand them anywhere else.
[* * *]
I guess I go to the track because it's like getting in the ring and slugging it out with some son of a bitch. Something is learned but I'm not exactly sure what it is. I guess it beats growing a patch of gladiolus. Maybe. And to go to a track on a Saturday, Sunday, holiday, opening or closing day just shows how close to suicide all of us are.

Gerald Locklin is a college teacher and a prolific author of books of poetry from small presses.

[To Gerald Locklin]
Augy two, 1981

Hello Lock:
You've got to know, every time I come over those bridges to Long Beach and I'm with Linda Lee (we're on a part-time basis: she needs to *expand*) I start in:
"Hey, maybe we're gonna see Locklin, maybe he's standing in front of some bar."
"You gonna start that again?"
"Maybe when we go to the Glider Inn we'll see him sitting at some table drinking beer with some whore."
"I'm sure we will," says L.L.
I stick my head out the window and yell: *"Hey, Lock!"* ...
I like San Pedro. It's a good place to hide, close to Hollywood Park, Los Alamitos. You're not going to find a bevy of poets sipping espresso anywhere along Pacific and/or Gaffey. There are some drawbacks: not a decent eating place in town and the liquor stores often close at 9:30 p.m. But since I buy by the case and have 3 or 4 bottles hidden around, I'm always all right. There's a sense of relaxation and easiness around here that you don't find in too many places. I like it.
The films, yes, mainly the Ferreri (spell?) I'd like to see. Gazzara can act and he's got good eyes. We'll see ... I've met

28

any number of movie people, mainly through Barbet Schroeder, cameramen, directors. mostly the European crowd, who I think get film down closer to where actuality is, except now and then they come on with some so called avant-garde stuff which I remember seeing some 40 years ago in the Art Movies in New York City … On the Godard subtitles: I can't speak French and I was surprised that he gave me credit. What happened is that a Frenchman translated the script into English and then I took the English script and Americanized that. But, on the other hand, Godard used one of my poems for a movie scene and I don't get credit for that, except one night we were drinking and he handed me this batch of francs, so that is cash, not credit, o.k.

There have been some cameras around looking at me and I'm not exactly sure what this has to do with creation, except that they are poking at what is left of the Chinaski soul. It's not good stuff but when I get drunk enough I don't mind. Then I can talk, then I can say things. But too much exposure is death, so I knock off a good 50% of it, and soon may stop it all. Recently turned down $2,000 to give a poetry reading because my gut is turning from this hanging from a limb and being poked at. You put a piece of paper in the machine and you type something on it. That's the essence; all the other crap is the bleed, and when they bleed you long enough and you sit down to that sheet of paper and nothing comes out, the old yea-sayers will be the first to leave. So it's best to leave them first and to get back to the mechanics of doing. Horses, booze and the typer. Anything that gets in the way of that is deathly, including women, and *especially* including women. The longer I manage to stay away from women the better I feel. Last night at the quarter horses I'm on the 2nd deck when I see this redhead with the ass and tits that I used to know, all that red hair in long fire, I see her walking up to a betting window alone. I run downstairs and bet the remainder of the night on the first floor. No more: that sticky web of madness is for the more hardy.

Besides, she was not a nice person.

Wormie [*Wormwood Review*]? Well, to me it's the only lit mag. I mean, when I get a copy I can go right to the crapper and read it while I'm shitting and I can jump into the tub or into bed and read it. I don't have any trouble with most of the poems and when I'm finished I want more. I can't say that about any other mag. When I read them I get a headache, I get sleepy, I can't turn the pages, I can't believe the stuff they get off with, 19th century posing as the poet, stuff that is so terrible that it is unbelievable, it's like a joke that doesn't work, again and again, and they keep telling it over and over. Malone has the editor's eye, that's all there is to it...The *New York Quarterly* had a great format, and about 40 percent on the poems but they are in the process of folding even though they tell me it's not true. All I know is that it's been a couple of years since they've come out and that they're sitting on 25 or 30 of my accepted poems, but I'll live, I'll write some more.

New York City? I could only last 3 months there. It's a hard place to be without money and when you don't know the territory and you don't have a trade. That was 1944 or 1945, so maybe it's a nice place now, only I'm not going to try it.

Politics? Politics are just like women: get into them seriously and you're going to come out looking like an earthworm stepped on by a longshoreman's boot.

Well, I've got an American Express card, a Visa and a BMW but I still write, and writing has always been a pleasure to me, a non-work item, it's as easy as drinking so I usually do them both together. I hear from other writers how *hard* it is to write and if it were that god damned hard for me I'd try something different. I had my longest writer's block last month—7 days, and most of it was caused by *people* getting in between me and the machine. Martin of Black Sparrow told me, "I've got so many of your poems on backlog that if you died today I could bring out 5 or 6 more books and all of them would be good." Of course, he's a fan. Maybe only 3 of them would be good.

I've turned down several free trips to Italy, France, Spain. That's just more *interviews*, Gerald. I'm about on page 240 on *Ham On Rye* (novel) which means it's just about done. Then a bit of re-write and then the 2 year wait for publication. That's all right. It was just 1970 that I quit the post office, and it's been a good fast glorious bang bang bang, and if I die right now I will have known that it was a real good cheap thrill.

There might be some new good writers around. I hope so.

But I no longer read books. I read the newspaper, the race results, boxing matches. I've got *on* tv, pretty bad. I look forward to the Hearns-Leonard fight. Notice I've reversed the order of the names and also look for the fight to end that way. Duran was just a fat man. When Hearns hits Leonard, L. is going to get swatted by a lean thin man with a mule's hoof at the end of his glove. Leonard's got guts though and style. Whoever wins is really going to have to earn it.

rivers of good wine to you,

[To Gerald Locklin]
Augie what 8? 1891 [August 8, 1981]

Well, you know, the ladies, when they start asking for "air" I give it to them. I am one of these strange fuckers who finds great pleasure in being alone. I also find pleasure the other way. So, which ever way it goes, I'm functional.

I've really liked some of your poems where you have taken this problem by the horns, er tits, and with humor, style and courage—have put it where it is. Neither of us hate women. We just don't like to be bluffed out of a poker game ... [* * *]

[To Joe Stapen]
Augie, what? ate, 1981

Well, now you can stand up in that class and holler "Bukowski" but it isn't going to do any good. The fix is in. The poetry fix is centuries old, that's why the form is practically lifeless.

I was invited up there[1] for a two week stretch to do something or other to the students or for the students. One of

---

1. I.e., to the Naropa Institute.

the lady teacher poets, from New York, I believe wrote me and invited me up.

I wrote her back thanks but that I couldn't do that sort of thing.

Then I got a letter from Ginsberg inviting me up. I sent back the same message.

Joe, you know when I don't come up when a woman calls I'm not going to come up when something else calls.

I've seen it happen again and again. Somebody starts writing poetry, they get some renown and they end up teaching others how to write poetry. They begin by railing against society and then end up on the same power trip.

How can I tell anybody how to write? Most of the time when I sit down at this machine I don't know what the fuck's coming out. And to bring poetry to people, to try to show them what it is, that's not needed. If the poetry is good enough and strong enough they are going to find it. The fry cook at your local cafe is going to be talking to the dishwasher about it.

We don't need poetry writing seminars, we need poetry writers; we don't need discussions, we need a few people hacking it out, typing, getting it down. And we need less snobbery and less poetry gang-factions.

p.s.—the Italians hot for my bod word now. mucho sales on translations over there. Marco Ferreri (spell) has finished directing full length movie, *Tales of Ordinary Madness*, Ben Gazzara acts as Chinaski. They shot some scenes in Venice, Calif. I got drunk with Ferreri and Gazzara, good fellows both.

but this is of the past, it's done, it's the fourth novel now, *Ham On Rye*, page 244. Ought to be finished in a couple of weeks. Then I'm going down to join the San Diego zoo.

●

• 1 9 8 2 •

Mike Gold edited Smoke Signals *from New York from 1980 to 1982.*

[To Mike Gold]
[1982]

I'm pretty burned out right now, just off the flu, in from the track, opening the first bottle of wine. Yes, just got new *Smoke Signals*, looks dashing and lively. I'll give it a go, bit by bit. Like to read while crapping, bathing or in bed. Note the bit on d.a. levy. We had a correspondence going, he ran a little book of mine, a long poem, *The Genius of the Crowd*, printed on envelopes as pages. He told me, "They'll read this and still won't understand what you're saying." Those Cleveland cops were squeezing him, for no reason at all. I never met him, but I feel his suicide came too early, maybe not for him but for a few others. His writing was just beginning to evolve. In those days most of the littles were fairly structured and snobbish. When Blazek and d.a. came along with their mimeos it gave a few of us some working room, and I don't know whether we wrote more letters or more poems or more critical articles (ranters really). Sometimes the poems and the letters crossed into one work. It was all right, we played it loose, and it was as exciting a time as I can remember—factory workers and bums playing with the word. I even put out 3 issues of a mag

33

myself.[1] I tried to make my rejects as gentle as possible but some of the responses I got from these were pretty rife and ripe. And shitty. One fairly famous lady poet of that time wrote back after a reject: How can you reject me? What the hell do you know about writing, Bukowski? Where have you been published? You're nothing but a drunk and a lecher!" Well, I was but... Then she went on to list her total publications, books and mags and all the places she had read at.

She had no style, cousin, and I felt that her writing showed it.

I could never see how being an oft-published poet could give that person a feeling of being elite. The poets are among the lowest of the breeds—outside their form. And often in it too. For instance, I am a lot more in awe of a plumber than a poet. The plumber can really do me something useful and not get the fat head about it. Also, 9 times out of ten he's a better person to drink with too.

[To Louise Webb]
January 27, 1982

It's been a long time since the old days. Remember the bathtub used up for space for book pages? And cool Jon and excitable Lou, and me sucking on beer.

I hope it's going o.k. for you. I always think of New Orleans and you as one.

I'm drinking about as much as ever but I seem to feel all right most of the time. No feeling in my left thumb and my liver is probably gone, don't want to think about it. As long as I can sit here and type, that's enough. I am still with Linda Lee and the 3 cats, Butch, Piranna (spell?) and the Manx. The Manx came to the door almost dead one day. We took him in, fattened him up, then a friend came by drunk and ran him over

---

1. Bukowski edited and published *Laugh Literary and Man the Humping Guns* for three issues beginning in 1969.

with his car. I saw it. The cat just stared at me as it was happening. We took him to the vet. X-rays. He's not a Manx at all. Vet says somebody cut off his tail. Also he's been shot, pellet still lodged and he was run over, once before—mend of backbone in x-rays He's also cross-eyed. Said he'd probably never walk again. Now he's running, tongue hanging out, cross-eyed. He's a tough crazy.

Is Corrington governor of Louisiana yet? After he went to Hollywood I never heard from him again. Speaking of which, I got drunk with Marco Ferrie (spell?) and Ben Gazzara. Ben is acting in *Tales of Ordinary Madness* directed by Marco. Taken from some of my short stories. But there's something I don't trust about celluloid. I guess it's an old superstition but I get the idea, still, that it kills people. Marco Ferrari, though, seemed a natural and ordinary guy, kind of like a dock worker. He seems to have retained his humanity.

San Pedro is a great little town. The blacks and the whites and the Mexicans seem to mix all right with very little trouble. at least, I haven't seen any of it like up in L.A.

You seem unhappy with your job. I know it's hell to work for somebody else, it seems senseless and endless. I worked until I was 50, that was eleven years ago. I just decided to let it all go on the writing, I was going to go crazy or suicide the other way anyhow. I got lucky. I wish to hell you could get lucky or maybe feel better.

luck and love,

[To Gerald Locklin]
March 14, 1982

[* * *]The novel, *Ham on Rye* should be out in the summer, says big John. That means Fall?[1] You ever read about my upbringing you'll know why I've been all these decades trying to straighten the kinks out, and am still working on it. The book

---

1. Published on July 28, 1982.

begins with the first thing I remember seeing in life and ends around where Pearl Harbor was bombed. (By the way, it looks like Japan is winning the war ...)

When you consider Fante wrote *Bunker Hill* dictating it to his wife while he was blind and amputated, you've got to know he's circled his field. Went to see him at the hospital recently and he looked pretty bad. He'd just come out of internal hemhorrhaging (I've done that too but can't spell it either). Anyhow, there he was talking about his *next* novel.

I tried to put into his ear that he should write about what had happened to him regarding his own personal and terrible luck but I don't think he will. It would make one hell of a story, you know, how people begin to treat you when you're no longer quite like they are. Well ... [* * *]

[To Gerald Locklin]
May 9, 1982

and I still haven't paid my fucking income taxes, or filed ... I have this tax accountant in Utah and he phones me drunk on cognac (spell?) and tells me he's working on my case, and how are the horses running?

Hello Lock:

"Lock." "Hey, Lock, ya locked in? haha, ha!"

I can see you now in grammar school listening to that crap; you had no choice but to become a writer. Have you ever noticed that all good writers have strange-sounding names or names that relate, in a sense, to something else?

I sure gotta thank ya for sending *By Land, Sea & Air*.[1] I read your stuff straight through whenever I get it. Sometimes when I'm wading in the dogshit blues and one of your books comes along I get lifted right up and out. Your stuff has this even tenor, it just keeps coming along. Of course, there's always

---

1. Published by Maelstrom Press, Long Beach, 1982.

a favorite. With these it came when I was reading "role model." I got that quiet gleeful feeling as I came down to the end of it. Catullus (spell?) couldn't have done any better. a poem like that is something that helps defeat the drag of the centuries.

Glad you used my blurb.

On *Home Planet News* or whatever it's called, I feel that rag's a fake. I think they just like to get submissions and play doll house with them.

Let an old man give you some advice. You know, man, that beer can kill you quicker than anything. You know what it does to the bladder, that amount of liquid just ain't supposed to pass on through the body, not even water. I know it makes for better conversation and keeps you out of alley fights behind the bar (most of the time) but the beer headache and the beer heaves are deathly. Of course, there's nothing like a good old beer shit. But a good wine will add ten years to your life as compared to drinking that green stuff out of the bargain pitchers. I know you prefer the bars and that when you ask for a glass of wine in a bar the tender reaches for this large dusty jug with a splash of dark coagulation hanging to the bottom, which is pure poison. I guess you just gotta go with the beer in the bars. The trouble with bars is that they're just like racetracks: the dullest and the most obnoxious go there. Well, hell, forget it. I'm drinking this here wine and rambling...Just one thing I'd like to ask you? What can a man do about women? When you first meet a woman she seems to show that she is different than the others but then when you get in deep with her she suddenly reverts and becomes *exactly* (with very minor variations) like the one which preceded her and the one which preceded that one and the one that...

This letter doesn't call for an answer, chappie, because there ain't none.

[To John Martin]
July 15, 1982

just a note upon the enclosed.

This man thinks a man gets fucked by women because he is "rich and famous." It does bring them around but a man gets fucked because he decides to get fucked. I once thought fucking was a magic and desirable thing. Most often it's just hard work to help the ego.

What makes a man get fucked is his "availability." Long before I became "rich and famous" I just sat round drinking wine and staring at the walls. How I quite made it, I don't know. But I was always around. One night I screwed 3 women in the same night because they were all staying at my hotel room. It's just a matter of being there and feeling like doing it for the hell of it. I wasn't a writer then, I was a drunk. The reason I stopped screwing at one time in my life is because I just didn't think it was worth it. Then I met Linda King and she got me into my old wasted habits again but she was so screwed-up with the sex thing that I had to laugh all upside and bottomside up about it—all the positions, all the tricks, all that crap. I went through it, and I was there and I wasn't there. Then after that busted I decided to do a little research. Which just meant jumping into bed and fucking women because they really want to do it, I think worse than men. So I did my research. And wrote a book.[1]

But this guy here has it all wrong, as most have it that way. Evidently he has problems of where to put his pecker and is envious of one who has put it in many places and at many times. He doesn't know. The poor fuck more than the rich because it's the only recreation they can afford.

It's like one of my women said in the old days, "You may not have much money but you're always around..."

The problem with judging another man is that it is always, almost always, done from your perspective. We are not, thank the devil, all alike.

———

1. *Women,* 1978.

[To Al Fogel]
Augie 6, 1982

[* * *] Sorry if I'm short or seem short with you sometimes. I have a lot of women troubles no matter which one I'm with. To begin with they don't believe that horseplaying can be a science just as beautiful as setting off an A-bomb or playing a great game of chess. They just want you to tell them how nice their hair looks and to slam that thing into their center. I don't mind doing that, it is just when they become mindless and babble about nothingness. Like Saturday Night Live. Or some god damned movie. "I make my own movies," I tell them. They don't know what the hell I'm talking about.

so you know, even as long as I've been around I come up short and maybe lay some shit on a guy like you who knows that the only fight is the use of the mind and the way against almost impossible odds. I'm sorry and I apologize. It's a deal. I'm sending back your checklist.¹ Send me anything you need signed. To me, a guy like you knows a hell of a lot more about life than the first 5,000 I follow on the freeway to seek whatever action is going. [* * *]

listen, man, I get pissed. These god damned cunts don't know who I am. Sometimes I think of this guy Roger [*Rodney*] Dangerfield, he's been around, and his humor comes from a driven reality of being and he has some line like, "listen, I demand a little bit of respect around here!" They don't give it to him. What he's really talking about is his damned family, his damned woman, they fuck up his money in large ways, large cars, large stupidities, they don't know the fire he's burning from or the way. But shit, man, they never do. [* * *]

Ham on Rye is out. now you'll know why I'll bet on anything but the human race.

---

1. Al Fogel, *Charles Bukowski: A Comprehensive Checklist 1946-1982* (Miami, FL: Sole Proprietor Press, 1982).

[To Gerald Locklin]
November 1982

Have been on a drunk and gambling kick, lucky the gambling has paid off quite well but the liver and pancreas are a doormat for the foot of death, along with what's left of the kidneys and lower intestines ... [* * *]

I'm honored that you're using *Ham* in one of your classes but only because it's you doing it. But I don't know what you can do with it. Like if you asked me anything about *Ham* the best answer I could give you is, "I don't know." [* * *]

Give us more women poems. You are the master. And you aren't afraid of them. A most refreshing thing when they've got most of us running because it is a seeming and intelligent thing to do? We must fight back or the world will be almost fag and almost lesbian. All right.

Let me know if you have any new books out and where to buy them. Yow.

[To Gerald Locklin]
December 2, 1982

you still leaning against the '49er? I got enough of the bars about 20 years ago. now I like drinking alone. Hemingway said that was the sign of a true alky. I don't mind being an alky except I get sad for what's left of my liver. but at the age of 62 I figure each day I go on I've beat the odds. I'm drinking now. maybe that's why I'm carrying on like this. like the guy at the bar next to you telling it all. what dull little fellows. they want somebody to talk to. that's one reason I got out of those places: lonely people are boring.

About the women poems, you show much guts and insight there; nobody could write like that unless he lived it.

The problem with the ladies (one of the problems) is that they don't realize we often attack ourselves too. Everybody is afraid of being mentioned as being not too good a person. Hell, there *are* some women who are bitches; there are some blacks, male and otherwise who are unsavory; there are browns like shits and yellows like malaria, and there *are* some Jews who act like Hitler said they did. There is *everything*. Since women's lib everybody is yelling, saying, you can't *say* that, you can't write that about us say the browns, the blacks, greens and the blues ...

About the *only* one you can write about without rejoinder is the white American male. He won't complain. He won't even care. Which, to me, says one *hell* of a lot for the white American male.

That's us, Jerry, heee, hee, hee ...

About people who write about other writers they think they once knew, other writers who have gotten lucky or good or both, these types just want a tie-in ... "I was with Norman Mailer when he got drunk and pissed in his hat ..." Of course, these types have a right to write anything they want to, their own and only problem being that they can't write too well. I really don't care what they write about *me*: the more vicious and untrue it is the better my books will sell and the further away from the breadline I will be. The worst thing you can do is to respond to these or mention them by name. When a dog barks at you, you don't bark back. Well, sometimes when a *dog* does, I do ... but you know what I mean. [* * *]

•

• 1 9 8 3 •

January 6, 1983

Thanks for the clippings ... So we have a play which distorts me and then reviews which further distort, and so it will always be ... I greet you with a beer after pulling in $525.00 at the track today.

It really doesn't matter what they say as long as I can go on typing, and I keep the people out of here; Linda is by a couple times a week, otherwise all I see are the track faces. I read where Steinbeck was eaten up by visitors; well, if you allow that, you will be eaten. I never liked crowds, even when I was starving.

Note that I'm described as "a very rich writer." I've never heard anybody else described as such, although there are many with more $$$$ than I have. Where these boys get such figures as me making $200,000.00 in one year in Germany, I don't know. Was Mailer ever described as a "very rich writer"? or Bellow? or Michener? People are always pointing things out about me: I'm a drunk or I'm rich or I'm something else. How about the writing? Does it work or doesn't it?

It works for me because it gives me something to do at night and a way to pass the time as time gets down closer to the nub. I guess I sound like a crank but it appears that people more gossip about me than anything else, much of it is word of mouth without factuality. Some women hate me as a "sexist" who have never read but excerpts of my work. Everything gets a little bit sick. A woman got off a plane once and told somebody, "Charles Bukowski is dead." It was taken as fact. I got a nice obit in one of the lit mags. Just today I got a letter in the mail from Amsterdam from a lady who says she has heard that I will be there in February. I didn't know this. She goes on to tell me what's best to drink there and so forth ...

Of course, all this doesn't matter but I can't help noting and it gives me an unclean feeling. Thank god I'm low enough on the totem pole so that the *National Enquirer* doesn't fuck with me.

But all in all, the typing is going all right and that's what I go by: if I can still feel the joy and verve of letting it go then I know they haven't gotten to me. Shapes keep changing but it's still a fight to stay clear of the muck and the swamps and the pits and the traps just like it was in the factories, in the post office. I always liked one thing old Ez said: "Do your work." That's the cure to everything. And you know that, and I know that you're doing your work, just like another old guy Gogol once said, "Laughter through tears."

Note they call me a "beat writer of the 50's." oh my oh my.

All right, we'll just have to out-endure them, as per usual.

[To Gerald Locklin]
January 16, 1983

[* * *] A couple of nights ago Linda King phoned me and told me in a cackling voice that she was going to write a book about our affair and that she was going to use some of my love letters to her. I wished her luck.

People will be that. In a recent article in *Reader* this guy says something like, "Bukowski has now been domesticated by his latest wife and is now happy and so his best writing days are most probably behind him ..."

Maybe there's *another* Bukowski but this one doesn't have a wife, this one lives alone most of the time. In the same article this guy states that Fante continues to write at his home in

Malibu. Fante's in the hospital legless and blind and the Fantes are about to have their home possessed for payment of hospital bills.

I think a lot of this misinformation gets about at gossip sessions. One so-called poet comes up with something and another so-called poet assumes that it's true.

Thanks for sending the review of Fante. I'm sure Joyce will read it to John and it will really give him a high when he needs one. You've certainly done your homework, teach ...

I agree with you that the earlier work is the best. After that he softened up his work for the *Sat. Ev. Post* and other journals of that ilk. And the movies—well, that's like masturbating day after day and then trying to get it up when the real thing arrives. But Fante was poor, the books weren't selling. Sure, a factory job would have left him with more but he didn't know that. It seemed better to dine at Chasen's and Musso's, meet Faulkner, Sinclair Lewis, so forth ...

The Catholic thing in Fante's work never bothered me because I was never sure whether he believed or had just been tossed into the Holy ditch. I never asked him. I know when I was a kid the whole Catholic thing seemed very funny to me, rather a circus. It was something to do when there was very little else to do, although those 10 a.m. Sunday masses were *hell*. I got out when I was 12 or 13 and when the priest walked up many years later to give me The Last Rites down at the County Hospital I told him I no longer believed that sort of thing. "Once a Catholic always a Catholic," he told me. "That's not true," I told him and he took a walk. [* * *]

[To Al Fogel]
February 5, 1983

Thanks for short story and mention of the Buk within. But I hope your old lady really doesn't boil you for reading the Buk. I no longer have an old lady, I've set her free to do her bidding since I think she finds me restrictive. I don't want anybody around who thinks I am putting the lid on them. She was never around anyhow and now that she's not around at all, I'm sure we both feel better.

[* * *] Just finished a short story tonight called "The Jockey," which I think is one of the best things I've done of late.[1]

You sound a little loose-ended in your last letter. To me you sound like a guy who's been out of the action lately and whose edges are drooping.

I realize that we all need an occasional rest from the gambling war pit. It can finally grind you. Sometimes I've taken a little day or two off and I've accomplished many things. And there's nothing like wasting a couple of days doing nothing. And when you go back into the bloodpit you're really ready.

By the way, I'm onto health foods. Take all the vitamins. Only eat fish or fowl. Fresh produce. Juices. One reason I do this is because I drink heavily and there is my gambling schedule. on top of all this there is my writing disease. Just let me tell you, Al, the worst thing is red meat. This is why many people can't walk, need canes, walkers in their sixties, need to be operated upon for stones and so forth ... Lay off *salt*. Pepper is not as bad as they say. *sugar* is. Stay away from milk and cream and especially *cheese*.

It's true that most healthfood people are not likeable. They are usually nuts in other ways and are seldom loners or self-contained. I don't like them. But don't let that get you away from the fact that they are right about nutrition. They just make too much of it.

[To Louise Webb]
February 12, 1983

It's always good to hear from you even though I know you are still mad at me for writing a certain short story about you

---

1. Collected in *Septuagenarian Stew*, 1990.

and Jon, but it was too good to resist, and you must understand that I have, still have, the love for both of you, here, now and later.

Maybe it's better you got out of the French Quarter. And if you want it back, it's still there. But like you know, the cities are getting uglier and uglier and the people look, and are the cities. [* * *]

Your love for Jon was beautiful and holy. I always marveled at it, the almost maddening purity of it, the total, not almost, purity of it. Jon was a very lucky man: you brought him a gift that few men in our time, in our day, ever get.

Please feel as good as you can. You should, you should.

Larry "Ratso" Sloman was editor of National Lampoon *and author of* Reefer Madness *(1979) and* Thin Ice *(1982).*

[To Larry "Ratso" Sloman]
May 7, 1983

Thanks for the book [*Thin Ice*]. I especially liked the conversation of those Hockey Pucks. Although you probably jacked it up a bit. Some of the language is delicious, wish I had writ it, ya.

These poor guy skate, drink, fuck and make money but they know it's going to end and the smartest of them stick a little into the old stocking.

But like they say, at least they got a *taste*, they got out of 8 to 5 and the breadline.

Good book, baby, but I still think I'm prettier than you. Ah well, no matter, we got something else? What is it? I dunno.

Next time you're boning and they're riding top-deck stick your finger up their ass and whistle the star spangled banner, they'll come in a minute.

[To Gerald Locklin]
August 13, 1983

[* * *] Here are the answers to your questions. I re-enclose your letter so you'll see which answers are to which questions. I'll take them in order.

1. I write a short story a month for *Hi-times*. Started a novel called *Streetwalker*, junked it. Rolling into another called *The Fool*. If it carries itself along I'll finish it; if it becomes rote, or hard work, I'll junk it too.

2. I don't know the $$$ breakdown on fiction vs, poesy, but looking at the reprints of past editions, I'd say it's about equal.

3. Yes, I've gotten letters and phone calls from a large circulation sex-oriented mag I used to write for. I sent them something but they said it was too much, even for them. So I didn't bother any more. Large German mag asked to see something, so I sent them the same story ("The Hog") but they didn't even respond... I guess I use this story to get rid of people. I don't like to slant my material. I like a column, a regular outlet somewhere where I can bust loose. Everything else is too tight, too stupid.

4. *Barfly* sits, as bar flies do. It might work into something some day. It's not a bad film script, it's just that many people with money think a barfly is not worth putting up on the screen. Of course, the producers are wrong, but they usually are... On *Tales of Ordinary Madness*, I didn't recognize the poet as anybody I ever knew. He was such a friendly fellow, smooth mug, and he never got so drunk he fell through a window or anything like that. His insanity was drab. It was just an Italian idea of an American poet, and they owe me money. That's probably another Italian idea, that I don't need money. What's a poet?

5. It feels good to write all of it. Once you sit down in front of the typer it's like you're watching a movie, a good one. Sorry, but it's all the same: poem, story, novel, I'm happiest at finishing interviews so I can get back to the writing, the bottles the racetrack.

6. Yes, I drink when I write fiction. Why not? I like things to be entertaining. If *I* feel entertained at this machine maybe somebody else will feel that way too... The typewriter is the

48

only way; it seems to make it official as it splatters out of the brain. Sound, action ... music on the radio ... picking up the wine glass ... smoking ... What a love affair! Never any arguments here.

7. Summer 1984? If I'm alive it will still be the same: the poem the story, the novel. If there has been a change, let's say it's this: I'm inventing more, taking less from my actual life. I get tired of myself and I'm sure others must too ... Of course, I think more of death but nothing comes through. It's a burnout. I'm ready to die, it's nothing. But you know, typing feels so good, and sitting in my shorts drinking at night, looking out the window. It's fine ...

8. People like to ask me, "Did that really happen to you?" And I used to tell them. Now, I don't. I think it's good for them to wonder. O.k., then, *most* did and what *didn't* should have.

9. No. I haven't been sued, mostly, I think, because I haven't exaggerated upon the actuality of things. I know that this sometimes isn't enough, but I think most people are glad that I put them into my works, even the rattlesnake people, like even a bad mention is better than not being noticed, what? I know that some things have been written about me and, the more gross and untrue they are, the better I like them. It's funny.

10. The critics in print are pretty fair. I get bad-mouthed by people who have never read my work, and by some who have but have read things into it. I am supposed to have an evil tinge (tindge?) about me, strangle babies in their cribs, walk about in underwear a month gone unwashed and so forth and so forth. Some of my stories are about lunatic and criminal people, therefore I am lunatic and criminal like that. The most ridiculous charge is that I'm a sexist pig. If one will read the body of my work, they will see that where ridicule or attack falls, the male receives just as much as the female. There are shitty women just as there are shitty men; the fact being, that I have lived with women, and some of them have been worse than shitty. I reserve the right to state that fact if I find that it fits into the flow of some work I am into. In American society about the only one you can safely attack is the white male, preferably if

49

he's a Nazi. And I don't want to sit around doing that night and day.

11. Oh, I see I overlooked a bit. No, no more readings. I never liked to read but I feel that when they got their money up I gave them something to remember. On promotional tours I got sucked into *one* of those, never again. One morning in Paris they shook me out of bed, beastly hungover, got me into the patio at 9:30 a.m. and interviewed me. Before the day was over I had given 6 interviews. There's just not that much to say. It's all in the writing. But people need that. They need to poke. They can poke you to pieces.

12. The recent Bukowski "exposés" in little mimeo editions of 500 are sad.[1] People who have met me at one time or the other and think it's a big thing. But again, it's curious when I hear what they were thinking at the time, things like: Bukowski was afraid I would steal his woman. Bukowski was afraid some young writer would take his place. Many other things like that, which I never thought of at all. It's only that *they* would have thought that way if they had been Bukowski, and that's why they weren't Bukowski.

13. Christ, that's enough. one thing: I'm glad *you're* interested.

[To John Martin]
October 11, 1983

[* * *] Linda appears to be getting worse. I don't know if I'll ever be able to write that novel. People who think I have it made and that I live in peace and glory, they just don't know. I've lived with so many insane women. I believe that Women's Lib has contributed greatly toward pushing some of them over the line. It makes them so concerned and conscious of their own identities and needs that they fail to consider the feelings

---

1. Perhaps referring to David Barker, *Charles Bukowski Spit in My Face* (Salem, OR: D. Barker, 1982) or Jory Sherman, *Bukowski: Friendship, Fame & Bestial Myth* (Augusta, GA: Blue Horse Publications, 1981).

of the men they live with. I'm certain that not all women are this way but many who are on the edge of hysteria because of aging, because of failure in what they individually wanted to do, to be ... that the easiest out for them is to take extreme umbrage and revenge against the man or men they are living with. This eases their consciousnesses [?*consciences*] and gives them the needed scapegoat, the needed excuse for their diminished lives. And if a man fights back against their in-fed railings, then he is a male chauv pig. And if he doesn't, he becomes a podosperm and/or a spiritual eunuch. The streets and the universities are full of them. The ladies have their balls in a bag, and the women are beginning to look and dress and act like men and the men are doing themselves in to appear to be all things ladylike. What it comes to is that each man must save himself, even if it means living alone, which, with conditions as they are, doesn't seem at all a difficult thing to do. I am still beset by erections but after the battalions of harpies I've lived with I really fear to engage said stiffness upon new females because of the terrible price attached. As I get older, if I get older drinking away my sorrows, I'll most probably need a nurse more than the other, and then will still probably still get sucked off upon the stairway or trapped and strapped in my wheelchair. Ah well, or not so well, we can't change the workings, we can only attempt to avoid them as long as possible. And John, I know you will never use this paragraph as a New Year's greeting but you are forgiven.

Listening to Bruckner, and it's a beautiful and magic night anyhow,

---

[To Larry "Ratso" Sloman]
November 11, 1983

[* * *] Jesus, I'm hobnobbing with the jockeys' agents and horse trainers now. Got drunk with some of them the other night. I now got Turf Club parking and owners and trainers stickers all over my car. I park right up front free and have passes to turf club and box seats at Santa Anita and Los

51

Alamitos. I play the day meet at Anita and then drive over the bridges and play the night races. Fuck writing.

I'm a better horseplayer than all of them. They tried to get my system out of me while I was drunk but I layed them some fake leads. Let 'em find their own way home...

Got my photo taken in the winner's circle at Anita, in color, man, it's hanging on my wall. Big thrill. Pincay up. I bet the horse that finished 2nd. [* * *]

●

• 1 9 8 4 •

[* * *] There's no New York publisher who can buy me away from Black Sparrow. Let alone these jack-offs with their mimeo machine souls. You do decades of work to publish me in fine format that has allowed my work to go world-wide and they think I'm just going to say, "All right, go ahead, what do you want?" Where were they when I was in the Post Office? Where were they when things were so impossibly and maddeningly awful? You were there. With help. Now they think I'm just going to offer over a bit of work, like that.
  They make me sick. It's an insult to me and to you. [* * *]

[To Suzy ?———]
March 1, 1984

Hello Suzy:
  Yes, there are many people out there who dislike my work, but for me, it's the same: if I met these in person I would probably dislike them too, so we're even. On the matter of women, many women are bitches and killers and I've slept with a few of them. If a black or an oriental or a midget is a son of a

53

bitch I will say so. People are offended because they are offensive. About the only person you can write badly of in literature and not hear about it is the *white american male*. Which must tell you something...

In this country, the male is dominated by the female, they went completely under to the Woman's Lib movement, so much so that most of them almost look like and act like women. About the only difference between them is that the female has breasts and her ass is bigger. Sexual parts different, yes, but I think some of those guys stick their dicks up their asses hoping to have pussies. And the worst male(?) is the one who is worried about Female Rights. This is nothing but open beggary, trying to score points in the most demeaning fashion.

I don't look at the female as inferior to me, only different than I and there will always be problems because of this difference, along with the joys. The best thing any person can do is to be as much the way as he (she) wants to be rather than being moulded by mass dictate, style, so forth. Of course, most people are completely wiped out by the educational system, church, country and the need to survive. And they will be offended by anything that goes against what they have been stuffed with, and they are *stuffed, stuffed turkeys, stuffed sausages, stuffed bags of shit.* Even death doesn't do them honor because it just takes meat, not soul, not true gut, not anything interesting at all. I say some of this here because I get weary of my work being attacked by moths... Christ, I'm almost forgetting to laugh at them... ow...

The movie *Tales of Ordinary Madness* was ridiculously bad. Gazzara looked like a satisfied dullard. Oh boy, holding to that girl's legs down by the sea and moaning out one of my early poems about the atom bomb... But almost all of it was worse than bad. And Gazzara always hitting on the wine bottle but never getting drunk. Water, what? I sat through that movie drinking bottles of wine and screaming against the whole atrocity. I wasn't mad but what a *disgust* I felt.

Luck with your novel. I dislike rules, they are made to be broken. But I'd say the best thing to go by is—never write unless you really *feel* like writing, it has to come out like hot turds the morning after a good beer drunk. So, listen, I'm going

... going to crack open a new bottle of vino and play with this machine, I hope to die upon this motherfucker ... o.k.

[To Al Berlinsky]
March 15, 1984

No, Hank Malone is wrong, I'm not dead as per report of his friend just back from the West Coast. Every four or five years somebody announces that I'm dead. Why they have the need to do this, I'm not sure. It's usually done by other writers and writers are a fairly ill breed. Then too, I live as isolated as possible because I feel better that way, and if I don't answer a letter or the phone, then I'm dead, you see. Some day they'll be right and it will be one of the few times they were ever right about anything. Don't consider me bitter, just accurate. [* * *]
Have been reading *The Passionate Years* by Caresse Crosby. All these people did was travel about, eat and party, and knock upon the doors of the famous. They also abused the peasants without realizing it. Caresse published one of my first stories and I always wondered why. Now I know. It was about a man with delicate hands sitting in a jail. Shit. [* * *]¹

---

1. At the end of this letter Bukowski types out his poem "The Lost Generation," published in *You Get So Alone at Times That It Just Makes Sense* (1986).

Douglas Goodwin is a Los Angeles poet, author of Slamming It Down *(Santa Monica: Earth Rose Press, 1993).*

[To Douglas Goodwin]
March 15, 1984

I don't know why they sometimes compare me to Henry Miller. I always had trouble reading him. He'd go on all right a while and then he'd get astral or fluffily literary and I'd get discouraged. Comparison will happen and I suppose it's better to be compared than ignored.

On Hemingway, I suppose it's the simple line but the man had no humor. As simple lines went, I preferred Saroyan's to Hemingway's. The early Saroyan, I mean. But Saroyan was too sweet, too optimistic; it worked well in his stories of the depression but when things got better it really sounded out of key. Then he changed too, for the worse. The paragraphs fattened and it made hard reading.

You're right on Fante and Céline and James M. Cain, each had something that helped me. There was also a Russian, Turgenev, who wasn't bad. And Sherwood Anderson, he exulted and exalted in the short and simple line, maybe a little too much so.

As for the attackers, I have been accused of "slipping" ever since my first chapbook came out when I was 40 years old. Many of the professors don't like it that I don't consort with them, and they don't like where I came from. It bothers them. For centuries these literary slickers have been fooling the people and they just pass the palm on down. They don't want anything to upset their doll's house. The best way a fake can cover is to call somebody else a fake. Their attacks on me are an affirmation that I'm doing things right. I just go on with what I'm doing. [* * *]

Gerald Locklin's 1984 books were The Phantom of the Johnny Carson Show *(Los Angeles: Illuminati),* The Case of the Missing Blue Volkswagen *(Long Beach, CA: Applezaba Press), and* Fear and Paternity in the Pauma Valley *(Detroit, MI: Planet Detroit).*

[To Gerald Locklin]
June 22, 1984

[* * *] Well, there are women and there are women. Mostly women. Some will reach under a table and squeeze a stranger's balls when you go to the bathroom to piss, then if you catch wind of the act they'll accuse you of "jealousy." But *reverse* the act on them, they can't handle it, not at all. Shit, I don't *mean* grab a guy's balls! You know what I mean...

Hey, I've submitted to you a proposed foreword. 2 copies. If it works for you, please send on to your man. If it doesn't work, then I'm glad the Celtics did it to your boys.

Sucking on the wine. Should work out with a few poems now. Habit, you know.

Thanks for all the books! Some I haven't seen. Have had some great reading.

you big fucking bear of grace, keep going...

p.s.—When I speak of "undiscovered talents," I mean a vaster fame, if not a la Mailer, maybe S. Bellow or who the hell have you...

[*Enclosure:*]

June 22, 1984
Gerald Locklin is one of the great undiscovered talents of our time. For decades now, I have enjoyed his work. Whenever one of his little chapbooks have come out or I have gotten hold of a magazine with some of his work in it, that day, especially, has been a good one for me. I say "day" because I read his work right off, prose or poetry, a couple of pages or many pages. I have never been let down. I have been picked up, lifted up, tossed into that rare area: excellent writing, writing with verve, writing

57

that laughs, writing that reads easy yet says something. That's a good package.

Locklin often attacks himself, or anything or anybody else that needs it, but always with grace and sometimes with wonderment and most always with a humor that I can only describe as most admirable considering the conditions he writes about. He is quite good at writing about the man-woman relationship, or, if you will, non-relationship. His ear for dialogue between the male and the female have [sic] not been so well done since, I'd say, the days of James Thurber. And with Locklin there is no side-taking, no preaching. He just tunes us in and lets us have it the way it is. And that takes courage no matter how easy he makes the writing seem to us.

He can write about sitting at a bar and drinking beer or shooting a game of pool, or he can talk about basketball, and it all fits together, it's all there: defeat and victory, fixations and traps, the daily going-on until it ends for us.

It has been my pleasure to speak very well of this man and now I think it will be your pleasure to read him. Fine then. Proceed.

Charles Bukowski

[To William Packard]
July 13, 1984

I like your sample rejects. They're funny but, lo, the recipients wouldn't laugh. I was a magazine editor twice (little mags) but happily for only a short period. But during those stretches I learned how precious and nasty and self-assured these poesy-dispensers can be. And the worse they wrote, the viler they were. I made the mistake, in the beginning, of sending out personal two or three page rejects explaining what didn't work for me, what I thought writing could and should be (with some luck). I remember one night writing a 5 page reject.

One lady sent me (in return) many pages of burning pink reply in which she listed all the magazines she had been published in and the names of the editors, plus all the places she had read her poetry (with dates) and she also told me she was in *The Blue Book.* She also called me a drunk and a letch.— Now you know that anybody who calls anybody a "letch" is fundamentally fucked in the backwoods of their mind. She also asked me, "Where have *you* been published, Mr. Bukowski? It seems to me that..." blah blah blah...Being married at the time and not feeling too good about it, I opened a pint and answered this lady with a 6-pager. She did not respond. Again.

There seems to be a lot of snobbery with people who write, even those who write well. What I consider special is a good plumber or auto mechanic, or a jock who can come through on the rail to get it at the wire when I have a few bob riding.

So, when you reject yours, it's always going to be a problem, they are going to believe it's for a wrong reason. There is hardly such a thing as a modest writer. Especially a modest bad writer. But if you only have to deal with them through the mails it's not so bad. It's the personal visits that are repelling: since you write, since they write, bingo, and therefore they expect something like a brotherhood or a sisterhood. I prefer cats as companions. I see enough people every day and the best thing about most of those is that they don't write.

Anyhow, a sample reject enclosed.

[*Enclosure:*]

This is a rejection slip, and most of what we receive must be rejected otherwise our magazine would be ten miles long and nobody could afford to buy it even if we could afford to print it.

We too have been rejected and will be rejected again and again. In this business you must expect it. And when it happens you can either quit or write better or try another magazine.

It's true that sometimes a rejection is unwarranted. Our opinion is neither final or anything else. It's only our taste or lack of it. But we can only proceed as best as we think we might know how.

It's good that you did try us and allow us to read your

work(s). From what arrives in the mail is where we must go. Without submissions we would be hapless and helpless. This rejection does not mean that we will not look at further of your submissions if you so desire to try us again. So this rejection is personal and yet not so personal, and if you do try us again and we find we must, once again, reject you, perhaps at least by then we will have a new rejection form to send you so you won't become too bored and unhappy with us, or perhaps there will, at last, be no need for a rejection, which will please you, which will please us and which, we hope, will please our readers. Otherwise—

Stephen Kessler was editor and publisher of Alcatraz, *and a book reviewer for the* Los Angeles Times.

[To Stephen Kessler]
September 10, 1984

Sure, run *Traffic* as a broadside in some future, if it suits you.

This poem has had some butt kicking and some traveling... First accepted by *New York Quarterly*, which then folded and now has returned.

The "Mailbox" broadside is all right, I guess, but when I read it in broadside form I felt it a bit cruel. The writer talking down the not-so-lucky ones. But my nerves jumped and I was goaded into writing it. No excuse, I know. But I'm not an editor or a publisher and my mailbox gets heavy with "works" of art. I drown in paper here. Plus the letters. Mostly from young girls who think I might be interested. Young girls develop into large problems. Nothing's free. Once in a long while I do get a good work and I try to suggest a place to submit it, and I've been happy to see some of this get into print. I don't think I've made any great discoveries, except maybe John Fante, and H. L. Mencken found him first almost 50 years ago. [* * *]

[To Al Fogel]
September 27, 1984

[* * *] Well, maybe you need woman trouble to keep you stirred. I used to feed on that. But women don't understand the gambler, and if you write on the side there's a battle for time with them. You know, sitting in a movie is one of the biggest wastes for me. I like to create my own action. Watching those monkeys on celluloid getting all fucked-up over commonplace nonsense, well, it de-balls me. I like the popcorn and the large Dr. Pepper, though. But it's no match to that bottle of wine next to the typer when it's running hot: 6F: I:07 4/5.

The track, at times, is a big zero too. When you're scoring heavy, there's a certain sense of rhythm, a music, you step light, you glide, and it carries over into other areas of your life. Winning is not detrimental. We're only here for one whirl. But when you run into a losing day or a couple of them, you're back in the factory again, it slugs you, drains ... There will always be trouble enough ... No need to tear up money and substance. Anybody can be a professional loser, most are. So, I work to alter that. The car runs better then, the sun shines better and that m.f. death doesn't get as big a bite. Yeah. Still, it's *War All the Time*.

[To John Martin]
November 22?, 1984

Well, I read *War All the Time* and I think the poems hold up the pages. You made a good selection, placement and balance of poems against each other. As they run off, it's almost like a story form. You know what you're doing. It takes instinct and time to make such an arrangement. Even though it's work, you like what you're doing. That's one reason why Black Sparrow Press continues both as a business and a pleasure.

I'm sure there are many others who have thought that since you did it, they could too. No way. You could even tell them what to do, they could still use the same writers and they would fail. They all want it the easy way. They want to sit on couches and chatter and roll joints. They pose, they don't do.

It's the luck of my life that both you and Carl Weissner took an interest in my work and at a time when there wasn't much. Carl too works like a fury. You might as well: if you're going to do something you might as well do it. And you've both done it.
[* * *]

[To Stephen Kessler]
December 28, 1984

Thanks for sending review of *War* from your column. Your words are kind and, let's hope, accurate. The Bukowski-haters are still out there and for this I am grateful. When these stop gnawing at their syzygies I will know that I'm finished.

I write the BMW poems to piss off those who hated me when I lounged upon the park benches. If I get my American Express Gold Card you can damn well bet I'll write a bit more to spoil their sated evenings. I like to play. Not that I write for them, more—from them. Then other times I forget them entirely, which is more than they can do with me.

Actually the poems 1981-84 are only about one-sixth of the output. I'm not saying that the 5/6th left out are all very good but there's a chance that a few are. John Martin has quite a buildup of unpublished material from a couple of decades. There's a very good chance, if the world is still here, that John Martin can publish a new Bukowski book each year for a good 5 or 6 or 7 years, maybe longer depending upon how long I continue to drink this good wine. Of course, that will all be beyond me: I'll be down in Hades playing the Horses.

Overseas fame while having limited fame here is the best, the gods are looking after me: I can walk through a dozen supermarkets or up and down the main drags of major cities (American) and nobody will bother me. This allows me to live a normal life which only I can despoil. Most indents upon me are made through the mail. An occasional rare and real letter deserves an answer. But to the young ladies who want to crawl under the sheets with me—I shrug off to the next. Sex is nice and serves the libido (or however you spell it) but all the rest spells overprice for value given. Fuck it. Not.

And there's always agony enough to keep comfort from setting in. I wish there weren't. I don't want to feel bad to write good. I really write better when I feel good. I am not afraid of happiness. But the deck keeps coming up with bad cards. Well? [★ ★ ★]

●

• 1 9 8 5 •

[To Stephen Kessler]
January 15, 1985

[* * *] Got your letter. Yes, I know you are an Ace. And
can handle such matters such as interviews much better than
almost anybody. But I've got to say "no" because I'm just
burned-out over such things. Went through an experience—
twice—of talking my ass off for hours to people who were going
to do a biography on me. Nothing happened. Not that that is
important, it's just the energy of the hours wasted. Then did a
film bit with some Italians and one other guy and they all got to
squabbling, stealing from one another, threatening lawsuits, all
that... the cans just sit there full of hours of my babble...
Finally did another film bit for another group and it worked,
was shown full blast... Then talked *for sixty hours* for a video. I
believe it began showing on National TV in France, prime time,
this Jan. 7 or 8. It is supposed to run in segments of from 3 to 6
minutes for a great many nights, depending on how long it
takes somebody to bomb the station.

What I'm trying to say here is that *I'm sick of talking about
myself.*

I need some relief from that. 8 or 9 times a month I turn
down interviews and readings. Some of these interviews are
from European newspapers. Or mags. Supposed to coincide
with the bringing out of a new book in translation. I have to tell

65

everybody the same thing—I can't do it for a while. It just has to rain some more to fill the dam.

The main thing about writing is to write, not to talk about writing.

I remember, maybe a couple of decades ago, every time I opened a mag it seemed as if there were an interview with Henry Miller, A. Ginsberg or Burroughs. Miller sometimes said something but G. just ranted on in hot air and Burroughs was bored and boring. But they didn't know how to say "no" and so here they continued to appear here and there, just saying *anything*. [* * *]

[To William Packard]
February ?, 1985

Got the *new NYQ*, the bird has arisen! Long may it flay and fly and fuck and fling and feast! [* * *]

What I liked best was the James Dickey excerpt (on and almost done with 2nd bottle, forgive typos ... typoes ... potatoes ...) about writer's blocks ... What he says is very true: not enough time to do it. What he means is not that he is torn away by the Superbowl Game or waxing his horse, what he means is doing all the damnable things we are forced to do or the fuckers will come get us: paying the bills, singing to the IRS and Franchise, keeping tires properly inflated, getting birthday and Xmas presents, seeking Christ or the Devil, getting your license plate tabs, teeth cleaned, new shoes, intestine check, arguments with the opposite sex; 90,000 empty faces at a sporting event; death, sickness, why go on?

I once wrote a short story about a man who decided to do nothing about all these things, and it ends up with him crawling under his bed (alone) and pissing into his hanky as they gassed him and came in with their guns to kill him ... The editors said it was "unrealistic" so I tore it up.

A month later a black woman, one B. Love, was shot to death over a matter of an unpaid gas bill.

Then there are always some people who need us for one reason or another. Sometimes the reasons are right or other times the other. But it's hell to be a final judge.

o.k., let's say we swept verily everything out and concentrated on *writing*. What would we be then? Proust in a corklined room? Nicely insufficient. If we are to put the word down well we are going to have to realize the rights of rats, roaches, bores and Parking Meter girls. If we don't get the whole flex we are fucked right up the twisted typer ribbon. I am not saying we must do the proper and taught thing but we should do the instinctive thing.

The human and the word can't be separated. Do anything else and the lie will come through. It's just one of those god damned laws. And a good one.

James Dickey always bothered me because he seemed to be writing from a position of comfort. I am prejudiced toward those who rise from the gutter. But being *down* doesn't necessarily preclude goodness either. It is possible to come from any area and still produce a substantial and entertaining art. Like some, no, one of your writers talks about writing upon yellow lined paper in the morning. Although I am usually puking my guts out about this time, yellow lined paper belongs too, according to the lightning it brings ... Let us be friends together, but not gather. The lice roam the dome of Buddha. See us helpless now, pretending.

[To John Martin]
4-late day-night, 1985

For me, the same taste is still there when I sit down to the machine as there was when I was in the factories or the post office or starving it out trying to be a writer. If anything the words now seem to arrive with more luck and order, less waste. It comes from doing and doing, I suppose.

I can't see getting older as anything but a benefit in this arena. Death gets closer but even that seems a good thing—I've

67

always enjoyed the ends of parties better than the beginnings.

The knockers have always been there, first because I came from the streets and later because I escaped them. Also, I have never consorted with the practitioners and I believe that this has pissed them. For me, I always thought writing meant to write.

Others become angry and edgy because they think I live a happy and contented life. They think that things have become too good for me, therefore, they formulate, I can no longer type.

Actually, they know very little of what is occurring in my life, and hoping for signs of decay, they invent them. Poor darlings, if only they could put their energies to a more generous use. No wonder there is so much room for me.

[To John Martin]
May ?, 1985

[* * *] All kinds of crap tumbling down here. I have at my fingertips one of the wildest novels a man could ever write. If you think the Father-scene was a mad laughing howler, you just don't know. This has 40,000 layers. But I believe in kindness toward those who really need it, it's far more important than any literary exposition.

Also, the lack of royalties of any kind is what a writer must expect. I remember once reading a Sherwood Anderson book he wrote about his life: "There I was being taught at all these universities and I had to borrow money to keep going."

All this reminds me of years ago when 2001 pulled in its horns and Carl and Montfort passed the message on to me, "The Bukowski boom is over."[1] Now, once again, there seems this withdrawal of support, and that's all right except I feel connotations of cowardice in other men I'd rather not see.

------

1. "2001" is the German publishing company Zweitausendeins (Frankfurt), which published four Bukowski titles between 1974 and 1980.

At the same time, I have this odd feeling that my writing is getting better and better, that each word placed seems to fit exactly where it belongs in humor, grace and with some fine luck.

I know that you are having your troubles too and plenty of them. This is the way it goes. You can't fool me—often times after busting your ass all day long in the office you want to come in for a breather and you find walls of yowling over nothing when all you want to do is inhale and exhale, just a moment. One thing you've got going: Barbara really helps Black Sparrow fly with her book design work.

Anyhow, Dillinger would laugh at both of us, especially me.

[To William Packard]
June 13, 1985

Just got *NYQ* #27, Jesus Christ, you gave me a spread! This has to be my finest honor, photos, craft interview, poems *and* there I am spread throughout your editorial. Like I said, it took some guts on your part, glad you've got them, but you're going to hear some croaking from those tender frogs upon their lily pads.

What I liked best in #27, though, was the editorial. You took the whole game apart and held it before them, saying, this is what you are and it's hardly very much. Your phone is going to be ringing and your mail is going to be singeing with that indignant and hysterical hatred that only the truly guilty are capable of.

I've got to mark you down as the first man, in your position, to move things around more than a bit. Old Ez woulda been proud, and it's well you used him too, a la editorial. [* * *]

p.s.s.—and today rec. your acceptance slips for the *five* poems. This is about all the good luck I can handle. They better not drop the Bomb for a little while yet...

69

Much strife on the home front, and so I escaped the screaming by going to the night quarterhorse track over the bridge, pulled in $150, came back, and I suppose to console myself further, I opened *NYQ* #27, re-read the craft interview, holding Whitman in the palm of my left hand, I found:

"... first thing I remembered writing was about a German aviator with a steel hand who shot hundreds of Americans out of the sky during World War *II*..."

Ow! one with Céline!

I feel that it's safe to say you've caught plenty a dung for running this interview, especially from the prim, the soft and the entrenched. Now they'll say you're hiding a Nazi under your rug.

Sorry, Wm Packard, I must have typed it up wrong—I meant world war *one*: (1914–1918). see Wilfred Owen and so forth...

You see, when I wrote my aviator-with-the-steel-hand bit, I was about 13, say in 1933, laying in bed with the worst case of Acne Vulgaris on record, or so the medics gleefully informed me. Adolph was around but he was still just moving his pawns on the chess board. Shooting those Americans out of the sky was my childish revenge for the boils which festered me, along with a brutal father and an indifferent mother. Rebellion is often caused more by reaction than by reason. I think I explain this all fairly well in my novel, *Ham on Rye*.

It appears that I've always been the victim of rumors:

"He beats his women ..."

"He doesn't pay child support ..."

"He's a child-molestor ..."

"He died, just the other day ..."

A couple of years back I happened to be reading an interview of a local poet in one of the papers and the poet asked his English prof, "What do you think of Bukowski?" And the prof answered him, "He's a fucking Nazi. He'd sell his mother out for a nickel."

I don't know *what* causes all this crap but some of it must simply be envy, and that's worse than sad. I only wish my fellow scribblers had just a bit more class.

Anyhow, it was World War *one*. And if I were a Nazi I would be the first one to come out and say so.

I hope you haven't caught too many outrageous arrows.

[To John Martin]
June ?, 1985

You've made a living at it, and mostly have published what you've wanted to, perhaps not so much at the beginning when you tended to listen more to "literary" voices who wanted to point you toward "prestige," but more and more you've become the gambler, one who gambles but still tends to win—out of style and knowledge, instinct. What sells is not necessarily good and what doesn't sell can really be bad, rather than a misunderstood Art-form. There are all manners of this admixture. Running a good show takes an Eye which can separate the bull from the bullshit. You do your work with an energy which boggles the slack, lackadaisical wishes and dreams of those who think things might arrive without the good fight.

They talk you down for making things work when they can't make things work; their envy is wrought out of their pitiful weakness. You simply go ahead, continue, while they rail at their seeming misfortune which is only brought about by a gross laziness and a licorice stick-like backbone.

You are the publisher, the editor, the script reader, the bill-collector, the publicist, and Christ knows what else, while you listen to the so-called Great Ones moaning and groaning over the telephone about all manners of trivial animosities, the tender two-bit troubles that trouble every living creature but which *they* feel particularly set-upon because of their very sensitive and chosen, so-called, God-given tenfold genius.

71

You do your fucking work and you do it well, very well, but what bothers me, even if it doesn't bother you, is what I consider your almost lack of recognition for what you do, have done, continue to do, relentlessly and with force. I dare say you've published a body of literature for almost three decades that stands unsurpassed in the history of publishing in America. Yet, what is said about you? Not that you need it, only that I need it for you. I prefer Champions not to go unnoticed.

Your problem is that in doing your work you have forsaken the time to go to all the cocktail parties and to kiss the asses of the media and university creatures who would boost you into the circle of their dull and death-like prominence.

Don't worry, the Bomb will be soon enough and if not, the record of your accomplishments will be there, Black Sparrow, you foolish wonderful kind son of a bitch.

[To William Packard]
July 3, 1985

glad the typo didn't bring on a bevy of Nazi hunters, I was getting ready to pack it away with Céline and Ezra, and Knut Hamsun. You're right, the reader doesn't read that closely—unless they really hate you and are looking for something and everything. I once wrote something about e. e. Cummings and in print it came out "e. Cummings." This bit elicited a two page ranting attack on me: "Everybody else calls him e. e. Cummings but Bukowski, no, he calls him 'e. Cummings'! Who the hell is Bukowski?" ... Two pages of this stuff, asserting that this was the key to the weakness in my character. Of course, it was a printer's error. And I didn't respond to the attack, figuring anybody that dumb was best left to slide on away. Even met the fellow at a house one night where I was drinking. He sat in a blither of hatred but I still didn't tell him that the whole matter was a typo. Didn't matter that much to me and the fellow has long since vanished.

Hot as Hades here tonight, woman with back and mind-problems, cat with broken leg, and I myself feel fitful, star-crossed, near useless. But... *here's the bottle!* Such a good companion, tonight I start with this bottle of cabarnet sauvignon ... Soon the earth will seem to be not such a bad place. ah, give a man a bottle and give a man some walls! [* * *]

[To William Packard]
July 15, 1985

You gave intros to the poets in the 1950's at the readings at YMHA Poetry Center? Jesus, William, how old are you? Not that I have anything against *age*—the longer a man lives and still keeps his senses, the more amazing it is. Just somehow, in my mind, I had you around 38. Dumb of me, I know. Here you mention those now gone: Eliot, Frost, Capote, e. e. Cummings ... Cummings could really cut the ice. What a fucker, he laid the lines down like slabs of sizzling bacon.

Well, I'm still here, though went to see my Chinese doctor today—easy on the drinks and smokes. Asked me if I could still get it up, told him: no problem. Also, met my old doc at the track Sunday—my body used to stiffen like a rock of pain while I worked the Post Office and I got dizzy spells, so he used to write me my little excuse notes for the P.O. He always let me sit in his office and drink beer while I waited my turn, he'd stalk in and say, "Shit, that woman has cancer of the ass, her whole ass is eaten away and she won't die!"

Anyway, he was drunk at the track, as per his custom, and I went up to him and said, "Looky, here, Doc, I want some free medical advice ..." and I showed him arm and asked, "Is this skin cancer?" And he looked, said, "You gotta get that cut off." And I told him, "I just wanted to know what it is, not what to do ..."

"The other day I only had 7 patients," he told me, "and the following day I only had one. You come to see me, I'm a cheap doctor."

"How do you select your horses?" I asked.

73

"The bartender selects them for me," he responded.

I knew then that I had to get away from him but he kept talking, then they were at the gate.

"Pardon me," I said, "but I have to watch them run."

He hollered after me as I walked away, "Why the fuck do you have to watch them run? It won't make any difference."

He was right, of course. [* * *]

[To William Packard]
mid-July, 1985

Is it me or is it them? I've met backyards and blooming top-floor ladies blossoming against the sun, I've been hacked and deterred and made more than glum by their ripping complaints, usually in the early morn as if, night-stored and energized, they are released upon me at the opening of a new day.

Is this what we live for and with?

And—even altering all considerations—considering ourselves guilty and at blame—would we even get to the point of this constant harangue, endless, dementing, vengeful?

Sex, love, duty, God, family are not to be bargained with against happiness, and we don't even ask happiness, just a little less pain.

Sometimes after listening to days, years of the female screaming face I wonder if I am really guilty of the cause of these dark, morbid and ever-continuing circus acts. This might be an unkind description of the act—but, if I have a weakness, it's kindness. And, that traps me in. No matter what the female rails.

I've met them of all sizes, stations, educations and experiences and their most central energy has seemed to be a constant anger against anything around—the slightest hinderance against their wants bringing forth all manner of cursing and vindictiveness.

So, it's not only me, it's everybody and everything, and Christ knows, I am discouraged enough by general and ungeneral happenings.

but *where* does this constant fidgetry come from, galling against any chance of a decent day?

PMS, indeed, PMS forever.

Men, too, have problems, most of them which they head right on into without the flap of aplomb and excuse of gender and championship or the lack of it, they hold up the corner bank or just drink themselves quietly to death. Or whatever they have to do to get done what must be done. And when they are smashed in the loss of their gamble, they know that that is the workings and that is it. That's not macho, that's simply guts.

Anyhow, hell, it's been a long night around here and so I type this manner of thing. Lucky, for all of us, male and female, there are other things about, other sights, other scenes, something to get us away from all this, and when death comes it will hardly be a task—not unless they follow us, programmed into their unhappiness.

[To William Packard]
near august ending, 1985

Glad your book[1] finally found a printer, it's amazing that in our age such a censorship exists. Yet I've known other cases where the printer has refused on basis of content. Most printers I've met are smug dolts and also fairly unlived. Censorship exists due to the fact that our educational institutions don't educate and the Church is still around dragging its feet one thousand years behind the times. False morality is the disease of a people who are told what to think and how to act from an early beginning; few ever use their own thought processes to question what they are taught. Talk about the living dead, they crawl like flies upon this turd of an earth.

---

1. Packard's novel, *Saturday Night at San Marcos*, published in 1985 by Thunder's Mouth Press, New York and reprinted in 1987 by Grove Press.

About getting married, if this destroys me as a writer then I deserve to be destroyed.[1] Christ knows, some of those shack jobs tried hard enough to put my balls into their purses. Also, drinking was long ago supposed to have destroyed me. I have been drinking heavily for 50 years and I feel fine. Also, gambling was supposed to have destroyed me. Not so—I gamble and I win. What these suckers are trying to do is to apply standard formula to me and it just doesn't work.

Anyhow, long live the *NYQ*! And keep those editorials going! You're going to miss some invites to literary tea parties and even some of the established poets are going to look at you with askance, but doesn't it feel *good* to shake that rotten structure just a bit? [* * *]

[To William Packard]
late October, 1985

[* * *] Got into a giant speed duel with some asshole on the Pasadena Freeway, this morning, the 3 bottle of Gamay Beaujolais hangover rising from my balls and out of the top of my Villon head, I got it up to 85 on the Devil's Curve where meat and bone are often separated in a flash of flaming nothingness and he fell back gasping, shifting down from 5th to 4th and flashing his front headlights in surrender. That'll teach 'em to fuck with a Suicide. [* * *]

---

1. Bukowski married Linda Lee Beighle on August 18, 1985.

[To John Martin]
December 11, 1985

Sometimes I wish I were this old guy sitting on the mountaintop subsisting on berries, grasshoppers or whatever. I wouldn't have to deal with the glazed eyes and lying dullness of my fellows, but I've got to admit I'm a sucker for modern plumbing and the racetrack.

Well, I've built my own little dungheap and here I sit flinging the shit about. There are minor and major regrets. And it's a hell of a thing to say but—I never met another man I'd rather be. And even if that's a delusion, it's a lucky one.

●

• 1 9 8 6 •

[To Al Berlinsky]
January 8, 1986

[* * *] my home life here has developed into nightmare proportions. I'm unable to write about this portion of my life now and may never be able to but if I ever get the space to, I've got a novel that will make *Post Office*, *Factotum* and *Ham on Rye* look like kindergarten stuff. Some people seem to envision me floating in an easy dream world now … If they only knew …

Well, the damned gods have always liked to play with me … I'm one of their favorite toys.

[To William Packard]
January 28, 1986

You took five poems, and no matter how long I've been in the game, it was a lift to me, a *high* lift. And it came when really needed—other factors in my life have been fucking me over (you won't get a list here, I imagine you get enough dirty laundry from the poets).

… I went back to that hotel not too long ago and it's still there, although my buddy the desk clerk is no longer about, I can see the window that I hung out of one night by my ankles, I

79

can still see it from the alley, and looking up at that fourth floor again, I can almost feel the same mad young rush of blood that was there, up and down the arms, and the whirling in the brain, I almost feel young again, like when closing the bars each night and sometimes coming out of them with a drunken female gazelle seemed the ultimate meaning and the ultimate victory.

Now they hustle drugs out of that place, it's murderous and dark and the cops don't go in there anymore. [* * *]

[To William Packard]
February 23, 1986

Thanks for your good letter. I don't know what the hell has happened to me of late: I used to tilt with adversity with a little more class than I have been showing. I think it finally becomes a matter of *wear*. Part of what is left of me has this odd dream of peace, not a total peace but bits and pieces of peace. It just doesn't happen. So I'm just going to have to toss out the dream and just work with the remains.

I think we all have to juggle and adjust our concepts as we go along. I just had a hard bad run of having to wade through shit that hardly seemed of my making. Although one can't always be sure of this. Just being alive seems to qualify us for whatever is about.

Anyhow, things seem better now. I'm on keel. And that's fair and good. I've always been one of these souls who is generally just about at a gentle ease under all the sundry conditions. It doesn't take much to make me happy and it takes very little, maybe almost nothing, maybe nothing, to make me contented. Small things please me, and at my worst I seldom feel anger, only disgust.

And the writing, like an old buddy, always seems to be there for me. When I'm down the most I get one kind of writing, when I'm contented—another. And when I'm happy, still yet another kind of writing.

The writing isn't everything but it counts. I also use

80

racetrack therapy. Yesterday I pulled in $313.00. It's not the money but the money, I'll admit, is a balm when the royalties are slow. The track is more for forgetting and for working magic tricks. To get your horse to come in first is much like controlling part of the universe—like you have an inside hand on the forces. And you tend to forget a lot of petty shit that is whirling in your brain. We are eaten up by the hundreds of trivial things we have to do daily. Of course, you can just stay in bed and damn well get away from much of that, and I do *that* sometimes too. [* * *]

Everything is a matter of knowing, calmness and pace. Betting the horses lends me the ability to put a line down the way I like it..., want it. Each race is a war, a crisis, a finality, a result and a readjustment. The typer is the clarifier. I can understand why Hemingway watched the bullfights: it was the working of the scene. We seem to have to remind ourselves.

When I hear some people talking I am confounded with how far away they are from anything. Most of them speak what they have been taught, not what they have learned. And what they lack most are two things: gamble and humor. Especially the poets. The poets are the worst. But hell, I suppose if I were mainly a painter I'd say that the painters are the worst.

Anyhow, I feel pretty good tonight, sitting here drinking this wine and listening to Bach, and I think I've bailed myself out of the dark for a while. And my 5 cats and my wife and the walls soothe me, smooth me. That Bach, he was a motherfucker, what?

[To John Martin]
Late June, 1986

Whether my writing gets better or worse—
You are my first hero and you remain that.
We both started hard and low and we kept fighting.
Never worry about my loyalty.

81

And please realize that any last word about anything *except* Sunday trivia—is *mine*.

I'm so happy that you're taking Julie[1] to Santa Rosa.

Please tell her that she can't fool me: I *know* she's *wonderful*!!

[To John Martin]
July 21, 1986

Well, it's not up to a writer to tell a publisher-editor how to run his business but since I was the one who brought Fante out of obscurity by continuously pointing to the neglect done to him ...

I am now the one to tell only *you* that the way you keep bringing out books of his found under the mattress or wherever the hell are a great disservice to J.F. (I note a new Hemingway book out now, 25 years after his death.)

To publish the bad writing of great writers is much like beating the shit out of a man when he is totally drunk. It just ain't fair, baby.

Joyce Fante wrote me recently about a Fante book you had published. She wanted to know what I thought of it. As kindly as possible, I had to tell her.

Well, business is business, I suppose, and if a name moves a book it will be published.

and, Christ, like in Fante's awful screenwriting life, I too will be absent from the general wars for a while. There are certain re-write problems with *Barfly*, I mean, I have to go over it and fix it up, one total character in particular, but I think Barbet has a good eye and I don't want to leave him in the lurch. At least I'm working on my own shit....

But if you don't hear from me for a while, understand, I am propping up the *Barfly*.

And I look forward to the release of *You Get So Alone*. The

---

1. Julie Voss, Black Sparrow Press publisher's assistant from 1984 to 1991.

more I think of the title the more it works for me.

Hope this letter hasn't spoiled your day. Writers can get awful bitchy. Bad times on the homefront here make me a little edgy. Just want you to know that you are the greatest singular force that has kept me going. And how.

[To John Martin]
August 12, 1986

Thanks for the good letter. I don't think it hurts, sometimes, to remember where you came from. You know the places where I came from. Even the people who try to write about that or make films about it, they don't get it right. They call it "9 to 5." It's never 9 to 5, there's no free lunch break at those places, in fact, at many of them in order to keep your job you don't take lunch. Then there's *overtime* and the books never seem to get the overtime right and if you complain about *that*, there's another sucker to take your place.

You know my old saying, "Slavery was never abolished, it was only extended to include all the colors."

And what hurts is the steadily diminishing humanity of those fighting to hold jobs they don't want but fear the alternative worse. People simply empty out. They are bodies with fearful and obedient minds. The color leaves the eye. The voice becomes ugly. And the body. The hair. The fingernails. The shoes. Everything does.

As a young man I could not believe that people could give their lives over to those conditions. As an old man, I still can't believe it. What do they do it for? Sex? TV? An automobile on monthly payments? Or children? Children who are just going to do the same things that they did?

Early on, when I was quite young and going from job to job I was foolish enough to sometimes speak to my fellow workers: "Hey, the boss can come in here at any moment and lay all of us off, just like that, don't you realize that?"

They would just look at me. I was posing something that they didn't want to enter their minds.

Now in industry, there are vast layoffs (steel mills dead, technical changes in other factors of the work place). They are layed off by the hundreds of thousands and their faces are stunned:

"I put in 35 years ..."

"It ain't right ..."

"I don't know what to do ..."

They never pay the slaves enough so they can get free, just enough so they can stay alive and come back to work. I could see all this. Why couldn't they? I figured the park bench was just as good or being a barfly was just as good. Why not get there *first* before they put me there? Why wait?

I just wrote in disgust against it all, it was a relief to get the shit out of my system. And now that I'm here, a so-called professional writer, after giving the first 50 years away, I've found out that there are *other* disgusts beyond the system ...

I remember once, working as a packer in this lighting fixture company, one of the packers suddenly said: "I'll never be free!"

One of the bosses was walking by (his name was Morrie) and he let out this delicious cackle of a laugh, enjoying the fact that this fellow was trapped for life.

So, the luck I finally had in getting out of those places, no matter how long it took, *has* given me a kind of joy, the jolly joy of the miracle. I now write from an old mind and an old body, long beyond the time when most men would ever think of continuing such a thing, but since I started so late I owe it to myself to continue, and when the words begin to falter and I must be helped up stairways and I can no longer tell a bluebird from a paperclip, I still feel that something in me is going to remember (no matter how far I'm gone) how I've come through the murder and the mess and the moil, to at least a generous way to die.

To not to have entirely wasted one's life seems to be a worthy accomplishment, if only for myself.

[To John Martin]
September 2, 1986

September? Where did it all go? Now the tax man wants his quarterly payment and I see the first fangs of Christmas. Last couple of days even my horses have been falling to their knees, and if not, losing all the photo finishes. Well, a certain amount of defeat is necessary but when it becomes habitual and something to wallow in, that's bad. There's this poet I know who brags about all his defeats. He loses at everything and is really not too bad a writer but everybody avoids him because he always has the hand out and screams and rages because he's not as famous as he thinks he should be. It bothers him. That's one loss he doesn't want to take. If he typed as much as he complained maybe he'd be luckier. And he badmouths the work of others. He finally got lucky and was taken in by this lady who attempted to fix him up. Fed and clothed him, got up a brochure for him, lined up a string of poetry readings. He decided to make it. Get it straight. An editor I know wrote to me, "I hope he doesn't blow it..." This poet is *loud* and over-demanding.

Well, he blew it. Last I heard he was heading toward San Diego and he looked like hell. Stopped here in town, got some money from a bookseller and wanted to know my phone number. Said bookseller was wise enough not to give.

Maybe I'm too hard on this poet. He could be a mental case. I've been to the track with him. He bets 99-to-one shots and after it's all over he says, "Well, fuck, you can't beat the game."

You do more work in one day than he does in a year.

It's true that the fates are unkind and will finally make mush of all of us, but there's nothing more tiring than the good, immortal loser. The secret is that anybody can lose, it's the easiest talent.

I'll have to say that the best thing that happened to me this year was something that never happened: picking up the phone and hearing his voice. I may be my brother's keeper, but not on *demand.*

[To John Martin]
September 26, 1986

Still hell on the battlefront and the poem is still the easiest way out of hell but went back to the story in spite of it all. After all, too many excuses can be made for not doing things, for not doing anything, in fact.

And still, I feel the itch and need to do another novel but don't quite know how to land on the material. My god, I may still find a circular way.

I note the good luck on the recent check, and also of the news on *Women*, which is certainly good. I realize, that on the contract (I haven't read it) that there might be a certain percentage due you, due me, on all this. Since you have negotiated and worked hard on this matter, of course, you will get the agent's fee. And if you think there should be more (I mean, agent's fee *plus* what it now says in the contract), please let me know.

We've always had a marvelous way of getting along; I don't think we've had one bad argument or a disruption of feelings in our two decades together. Whether we realize it or not, I think this has made you a better editor-publisher and has helped make me a better writer.

I must guess that you've caught plenty of shit from the poets and the critics and the poet-critics for publishing me but you've gone ahead anyhow.

And from my part, I've gotten plenty of anti-John Martin flak at this end. You should hear some of the bitter and bitching stories and opinions I get at this end. Most of this, I don't respond to. To the few I say, "Even if true, whatever he did, he did for a reason and the reason wasn't against me, it was for his survival and he needed that."

They don't realize how many publishers have gone under, how each edge must be fought for constantly and daily. They don't realize that you must be a bill collector, a book collector, a reader of manuscripts and often a shipping clerk and a truck loader, and a cheer-leader to your own small staff. And they don't realize that each book you publish is a gamble on your *own* survival, your continuance. Also, they don't realize the many things you have done for me which have kept me going when I might have not kept going. By this, I mean the monies given outright, and the mass of work and arrangement done to submit my crap to the various university archives.

And all the work done on the archives, the hours and hours, the order, the perfect letters to the librarians, the fitting of the pages in order, the shipping of such, and all the other attendant worries. And all this without *any* financial reward to you. (financail?) (never could spell) (make it financial)

I guess I'm saying all this because of my age: being 66 lends some doubt; I'd hate like hell to be running in a one hundred yard dash.

The writing must slip, surely has, although it feels better than ever to me. But the seas of booze I have consumed must leave their mark, plus the attendant years.

So, I want to say these good thoughts I have of you while I am still able to. The way I drink on certain nights of unhappiness might take me out or lead to stroke, so I better say a few things now.

But, all and all, I figure I'm just going to get better and better at writing, right up to the lip of the grave. It's just a feeling.

Of course, there are other things more important than writing. But it's all I know. And what a glorious hell of a "know," what a crazy grand way to face the impossible.

Long live the Sparrow!

[To John Martin]
near Thanksgiving, 1986

Well, yes, we've got to be thankful that somewhere our words were finally heard and that we didn't have to dilute them to get the luck. And maybe we've fought where others might have quit. It's hard to know. I only did what something drove me to do. Take a pit bull: once he clamps those jaws you've got to use a megaforce of total unbelievable, non-measurable

87

searing leaping hell hell hell to make him let go. Yet that pit-bull is not doing anything exceptional, he's only doing what he was set-up to do. He has no other way, no other choice.

There are no brave men. There are only men who pretend to be brave. Or women. Or hawks.

I have regrets. Like, even now, as the luck might hold tenderly, there's never any real peace. Things keep gnawing, grinding, looming. Death I've long been ready for, somehow she seems a sweet Bitch. But—I get soft, maybe always have been, still yearn for that ultimate magic that could be there in some *other* person. I think that's the saddest of the sad, but maybe I've got it coming. The non-connect, I mean. Maybe the gods figure that anything near-pleasant might destroy the concentration on the pit bull grip-within this game.

Sounds like a lot of crap and probably is.

With the writing though, I always feel the same: I am beginning at a beginning and moving through, against and with it. I am the same now as I was when I first started writing. It's a grand show, no credit accepted, but the sound of this machine like the sound of all the others, it's a functional joy that doesn't seem to relent, and accidental, meant or just irrational, I'll take it, take it, take it.

[To Gerald Locklin]
November 21, 1986

Thanks for fine poem in recent *Wormie*, I mean the one explaining to the disclaimers why I might do as I do. Actually, I have heard bitchings and wailings about what I do or don't do or what I should do since about the time I wrote my first poem. I think since my writing is open-mannered, people feel freer in discussing it and me. I've long grown used to this and feel that without the rantings and complaints of the sometimes envious I might even feel let down.

In *Barfly*, Mickey Rourke and Fay Dunaway are to play the leads. And when the lead actor gets 750 times what the writer does, there might be a tendency not to listen to the writer but I speak anyhow and will continue to suggest basic things. One thing I *do have going* is that not a line of the script can be changed without my O.K. This, thanks to Barbet Schroeder, director. I've made certain revisions for the camera's eye but all in all the whole bit runs too long and cutting is just like cutting off parts of your body but I suppose it must be done.

Mailer works for Cannon also. Met him at his place and we had some drinks. "Norman," I told him, "Hollywood scares the shit out of me."

He just looked at me like I didn't quite know what I was saying.

Oh yeah, when I met him we shook hands and I said, "The Barfly meets the Heavyweight Champ." He liked that.

Shooting starts sometime in January and I've already told the people that I won't be able to be there on the days the horses are running. Actually, I will be glad to get back to the poem and the short story. I've turned down a couple of screenplay offers. The money is there but I dislike the media much; most movies repulse me and I remember what happened to Fante: Hollywood killed him. I don't need that kind of money—the old BMW is at 130,000 miles and running fine. Had it since 1979. The main thing is to get the word down the way you have to. Lose that and no bankroll in the world can get it back for you. [* * *]

Actually, the best thing to come out of this movie thing is *The Bukowski Tapes*. I felt sorry for Barbet because he paid me to write *Barfly*, wrote it in 1979 and felt like he would never get rid of it, so I got drunk for many days, many hours, many nights and talked with the camera on me. He got *four hours* worth of tapes which he is going to bring out in video. I think I babbled pretty lucky and pretty wild and have enclosed a list of the tales from the wine bottle for your bemusement.

But, as you know, the typewriter is the only place to work from. These poets who call themselves *performance artists* are only trying to fancy up their petty vanities. The whole reading circuit is a mass of dismal dull crap. [* * *]

[To John Martin]
December 19, 1986

[* * *] On *Barfly*, there's still to be more tinkering with the script. Minor technical changes, also cuts because it runs too long and they don't have that kind of money; also cuts because too expensive and complicated to shoot certain scenes. If I had known this from the beginning I would have set the whole thing up in the bar, a la stage play. Of course, then they would have said, show us something of his life outside the bar.

What they are doing is *worrying* the thing to death.

I told Barbet, if they had just shot the thing as I originally wrote it, they would have had a better thing than what they have now.

"Oh no!" he said.

What they are doing is thinking of other movies, of standard ways and processes. That's bad. What you do is shoot the raw material as is and people feel and appreciate that. The last thing they want is finesse. The natural fibre is what invigorates.

Well, supposedly, they begin shooting Jan. 19 and I'll be free of their strictures. And I hope, of course, that the money comes through. [* * *]

●

• 1 9 8 7 •

[To John Martin]
February 8, 1987

It's strange that others think that if you gave their works more attention, millions could be made. All you can do is publish a work in book form. If that book doesn't move, there is no way you can print more copies. That would be suicide. You've made it because you haven't given way to pressures and demands. You've had to decide what to do. And you've made a living out of doing something that costs most other people money to do.

I'm truly astonished by the greed, pettiness and short-sightedness of the writers and/or their heirs.

You are not God. You are like I at the racetrack: you either select the proper moves or you stop moving...

By the way, I've watched some of the shooting, seen some of the "dailies" and Mickey Rourke is doing an *excellent* job—so far. He brought a rep in with him, well-earned, I'm sure, of being a complete bastard and hard-to-handle motherfucker. I've liked him both on and off camera. Much of it is Barbet's doing. He takes a very low key approach. You feel this joy in him, that he just wants to do it and it doesn't matter whether he's there or not, he just wants it done. And when he makes a correction, it's in a low voice, with very little criticism, more it's in the form of *suggestion*, as if he were asking: can we do it this way?

91

Well, a good start has a hell of a lot to do with it.

As it's going, this could be a very interesting movie, perhaps a great one. What I like best is that they are doing it as I wrote it—kind of a mad truth saved by a comic edge.

So, we'll see ...

[To John Martin]
March 29, 1987

Well, I've seen all the cuts of the movie and in some ways it doesn't work and some of that fault is mine: in some ways I gave over too easily to suggestion, like, "we should have a love interest ..." "We should show that this man is a writer ..." I didn't want the love interest or the *writer*. I think that the only way a great movie can be made is for the same man to write it, direct it, produce it and maybe even act in it—although the last is hardly needed and too often impractical.

The main thing wrong with movies is that there are too many hands on board. And the interest too often becomes seeming victories for seeming individuals but there can't be anything near victory if the final product doesn't have joy and daringness and inventiveness and just a lot of laughing luck.

And for all of it, in *Barfly*, the most came from the one who came in with the most damning reports: Mickey Rourke. The stories, the warnings, the rantings and railings against this actor were more than enormous. It even made one hate the name, and for a long time I had a mental block. I mean, even against the *name*.

"Who's playing the lead?" I would be asked.

Couldn't think of the name.

Rourke did it wondrously.—The eyes, the body, the voice, the spirit, the guts, the inventiveness, the gamble, all that—but never cheating on the reality of what I meant or what it was, at its best.

Mickey did it. Would only that he had some help from the others.

92

And not only that, but off camera Rourke appeared the most human of them all.

I don't understand where all the shit reports come from.

What is it, that in this world, the more rare and forward and good an individual becomes, the more you will hear the mocking tales and the lies?

Ah, John, it's like I said in an old poem like ago [*sic*]:

> Humanity,
> you never had it
> from the beginning ...

[To Gerald Locklin]
June 22, 1987

Well, I've always been a sucker for the simple, bare line because I've always had this feeling that Literature, that of now and the centuries, was largely a put-on, you know, like the wrestling matches. Even those who had lasted the centuries (with a few exceptions) gave me the odd feeling that they were fucking me over. Basically, I feel that with the bare line it could be harder to get the lie across; besides it reads easier, and what's easy is good and what's hard is a pain in the ass. (That comes from factory and woman training.)

So Fante gave me the line with feeling; Hemingway the line that did not beg; Thurber the line that laughed at what the mind did and couldn't help doing; Saroyan the line that loved itself; Céline the line that cut the page like a knife; Sherwood Anderson, the line that said beyond the line. I think I have borrowed from all of these and I am not ashamed to admit it. I only hope that I have added, what? If I knew what I were doing I could no longer do it. [* * *]

[To Louise Webb]
November 14, 1987

Good to hear, it's been almost two decades since I saw you and Jon, but as you know, it was a very magic and wonderful time for me—those great books and the faith you both had in what I was typing. I almost spoiled it with my drinking but you both forgave me. And published me when nobody else would touch me.

I hope you're alright, but like I remember you always wanted to move on—no place was right and it always seemed like the next place might be better. Except you folks had to haul the dogs and the printing press with you. What a crazy time.

Yes, I wrote a screenplay. This guy got after me and pressed me until I did it. I think it's all right. But think of all the terrible things you've heard about Hollywood, then multiply that by at least ten. I'm away from them now and it feels so good to be back in this room, typing at my old stuff.

But I remember the Arizona and New Mexico and Louisiana days best. I think I liked New Orleans best, living around the corner from you and Jon and coming over with the poems. You and I always got along so well. Linda just walked in and said, "Give her a warm hug of love from me ..." Consider it sent on. [* * *]

[To John Martin]
November 14, 1987

It's strange that you're finding all these old works of the past. In some of them you'll find that my style hasn't changed at all. When I'm going best I keep it simple and clear and whatever is said is said from that.

I think much of that comes and still comes from the heavy reading I did during my early youth, haha, like Christ, I was really young once. I was, I was. And now I'm old but I feel the

94

same. Maybe everybody has that? I think so. Age is a reality and yet it is a delusion.

Anyhow, most of the reading I did was little help to me as a form of entertainment or saving grace or even relaxation. It's hard when you're starving and mad and trapped and maybe physically ugly (although I no longer believe that in anybody) to find something readable. So, I worked in my own way of telling it, of putting the line down. I liked Hemingway's clarity, I loved it, yet at the same time I didn't like the *literary* feel of it—for it all, there was a upper snobbishness attached—for me, that is. I felt that. When you come in from the factory with your hands and your body and your mind ripped, hours and days stolen from you, you can become very *aware* of a fake line, of a fake thought, of a literary con game. It hurt to read the famous writers of my day. I felt they were bullshitting it, I felt they were soft and fake, and worse that they could not laugh through the flame, and worse than that, that they had never felt the flame. Sure, I'm drunk now as I write this, but that's what I felt.

So, maybe in the old stuff there was some revolt against this type of writing and maybe in the new stuff that revolt is still there. The gods have been good to me, I think: they keep stacking new shit around me to keep me from dozing off. I believe in the gods and I don't.

Anyhow, I rather share your looking back at the old stuff and even caught your genuine excitement as you talked to me over the phone about old lines, old ways. Because, let's admit it, I was bug-eyed wild and trapped, feeling about, hardly knowing, guessing, but, I think, hardly faking it too much.

I still think I'm standing on one foot on the dime in the ever-blizzard. It's unduly hard forever but I think I bite into that, go for the sad flavour, am the street kid of the 30's forever, and if you don't show at my funeral, motherfucker, I'm going to rise out of my grave and piss all over you from my bones.

[To John Martin]
December 1, 1987

Yes, nice article on Fante in *Vogue*. How strange. There he was just sitting there in the bookcases of the libraries for decades. Suppose I hadn't pulled his books out of there and read them? Even you thought Fante was just a name I made up for my writings. Of course, if you hadn't published him the critics would still be sitting on their hands instead of mentioning him along with Hemingway and greater than Faulkner. What a curious thing that you and I caused some literary history to happen. Some longshot. And poor John just had a little taste of the beginning of it all. And that I was able to visit him near the end, that almost seemed like an act of the gods. I think that when I pulled that copy of *Ask the Dust* out of the shelves of the old L.A. Public Library, that day the walls of the place trembled.

[To Gerald Locklin]
December 10, 1987

Yes, there were many interviews, too many, and *People* was the last. I never believed it possible but I did get quite tired of talking about myself, my ideas, all that, because, you know, a couple of years ago I talked about 64 hours for *The Bukowski Tapes*. After a while there isn't much left to say and you have to wait on a *refill*.

Now some of the boys are going to think the movie is going to kill me off, but they've always hoped something would: drink, the BMW, marriage, a house, 5 cats... Those fellows worry so much about my death (spiritual and otherwise) they can hardly do their own work.

Actually, 2 of the things that keep me in the clear are my drinking and my gambling. These can be rather consuming, almost all-consuming, and leave me little time to wonder and ponder on such things as fame or possible fortune. I'm lucky that way. If I sat around the house all day with a scarf around my neck and concentrated on writing I'd drown in the normal shit of the way soon enough. (bad sentence there, but I still like it).

Anyway, I've been on the battlefield a long time and I seem (?) to know when and how to duck. Like, I went for the *People* thing because I think it's corny and funny. So many jerk-offs are in there and you see the thing in the supermarket line. It is to laugh. I did turn down invites to *20-20, 60 Minutes* and the Johnny Carson show. You've got to instinct [*sic*] what will suck you dry. There's no chance to be normally real on those shows, they'd cut you off. I found out on that Paris program: there's a certain way you must behave. And that's what I like about typing things on a piece of paper: you behave any fucking way you please.

Always good to see you at gatherings, you always have a certain calming effect on me, like you can see through the bullshit. That after-premiere gathering was one of the worst. I felt mutilated and de-balled. There was a heavy nothingness in the air, black, stuffy. Barbet described it best when he walked up to me and said, "God, these people are horrible! I feel like my whole body is covered with shit!" That cheered me, and soon after that I talked Linda into getting out of there. And when I leave a place with free drinks, Lock, you know that place is minus zero plus zero = a nothingness worse than can be described.

Barfly is not a great film but it kicks along. I've seen it 2 or 3 times and it always makes me thirsty. I mean, to down a glass. So there must be a link to some realism there. [* * *]

●

• 1 9 8 8 •

Jeff Weddle was a graduate student at the University of Kentucky who was planning to write a thesis on Bukowski.

[To Jeff Weddle]
January 26, 1988

[* * *] Yes, working on novel, *Hollywood*. Should take a couple of years to write. My last novel? Who knows? The way I feel now...maybe so. Have had the flu twice running this month and really feel low, still not right. I hope it's not something major. Anyhow, I hope to finish *Hollywood*. What I've written so far seems solid.

On the novels, I'm afraid they're more fact than fiction and in the real sense I suppose they can't be called novels. Sometimes in the short stories everything is entirely fictional, other times not. The poems are hardly fictional.

I don't believe I'll write another screenplay. But then I never thought I'd write the first one. But Hollywood is the Death Pit and I try to stay away from it.

The Sartre and Genet question is a sad one to me and I'm not sure I can answer it correctly. Let me begin like this. Let's take an editor and call [him] X.[1] It is in an earlier part of my

---

1. Jon Webb of Loujon Press, publisher of *It Catches My Heart in Its Hands* (1963) and *Crucifix in a Deathhand* (1965).

99

life. X is publishing me in his magazine and bringing out a couple of books of my poetry in editions very beautifully done.

And for these books he came out with blurbs. Something like: "The best poet in America ... Genet and Sartre."

So I asked editor X about this. And he said, "Somebody read Genet your poem, 'Old Man Dead in a Room' and Genet said it was a great poem."

"But that's not the same as the other. He didn't say I was the best poet in America. I don't want you to use this blurb."

We were drinking and he just stared at me.

Then I asked him about Sartre and he claimed he had actually said I was the best poet in America in an article. I never saw the article. But my present editor at Black Sparrow claims it is true. I don't know. When I was in Paris I was told that Sartre wanted to see me but I was drinking heavily and passed. Sartre died soon after. So who knows what the hell. I think it's all horseshit and wish those blurbs had never been used. I don't need them and I don't want them. I hate that stuff. That's all I know. So if you're working on something on me, I wish you'd leave out the Sartre-Genet bit because I'm not sure that it's true and even if it is, I don't need it. My work is my work and that's it.

Thanks for the good words on *Barfly*. Actually we had fun on the set, it was lively, maybe because we used real barflies and maybe it was good because the stars didn't want to act too uppity around the real people.

The book by Locklin that Bukowski is here acknowledging was published by Slipstream Press, Niagara Falls, N.Y.

[To Gerald Locklin]
March 2, 1988

Man, thanks for the 2 copies of *A Constituency of Dunces*. I read it right through and as always it lifted me. Thanks for the inscription. I met N. Mailer, shook hands, told him, "The barfly meets the champ." He liked that.

Your books always seem to arrive when something has me by the throat you are a real saver, boy. What timing! Thank you. [* * *]

[To John Martin]
March ?, 1988

I'm out at the track every day but don't worry, I'm not losing. But the track gets sadder and sadder, there are less blacks because they go the lottery, they are the ultimate slick dreamer-losers—but worse are those that are there now, the old dumb whites hardly realizing that they are getting nearer and nearer to death, they stumble blank-eyed, the track is someplace to be and they bet $2 to show on 60-to-one shots, it's like a madhouse for the mentally slipped, not the crazy just the slipped. But *worse* are those from Central America and the islands and from wherever the else hell is and they have gotten away from, this is a little better, a *little* better, they are young and old and in-between and can barely speak the language, have an awful time at the windows attempting to tell the tellers what they want as the *old whites* scream at them: "*Come on! Come on! Move it! Move it!*"

These poor people who have seen murder up and down the streets like it's nothing but some kind of sneezing as the *left* fights the *right* everywhere and all the little people lose, are tortured and jailed and mutilated, the *left vs the right*, and both sides call their people *freedom fighters* but there's no freedom for anybody, and some of them get out of their countries, some of them get away from the *left*, others from the *right* and there they are at the track, stunned, still alive, half-alive, trying somehow to make 2 dollars into ten dollars, into a million dollars but it can't work and they are worse off, they go to a small room shared with a dozen others and to a can of beans or whatever the hell. They bet all the sucker bets, the daily double, the exactas, the pick-6, the pick-9, 2 dollars to show, two dollars to

101

place on a rat with four legs that died in hell one thousand years ago and has come back to put one more shadow across the death in their life—old clothes, sad bent bodies, hollow eyes like in the pumpkin, John you have no idea as that toteboard turns out there how many lives it chews to shit and spits out. But it's all right because the State of California gets its cut and there are those in the Turf Club who can afford to lose, to laugh it off. The suffering of the many has very little to do with anything. It's what's up top that counts. Counts its money and looks: the other way. The racetrack is just not where the horses run.

[To John Martin]
April 21, 1988

[* * *] Went in to the doc today. Will know more Monday when the blood breakdown is computed. If something's wrong, maybe we can take the proper steps. Just don't have the old drive and go. Took an EKG, heart is normal. Blood pressure 180 over 110, so the problem is elsewhere.

On the novel, I'm going to have to change some of the famous names further away from where they are. Like Rickey York as Mickey Rourke is too close. No use just asking for a lawsuit, let them work harder for it.

Carl wrote that he read the novel excerpt in *Interview* and said, "It sounded a little strained as if you had to force yourself to write it..." Actually, I think I enjoyed writing that chapter more than any of the others—the bit about the hotel of Peacocks and the frantic and mad Junky. Well, I must trust myself, I always have.

[* * *] Well, Monday we'll know more. One thing I found out while in the R.O.T.C. Man said, "If you have a problem, don't worry about it. Make moves to correct it." Right.

[To William Packard]
May 10, 1988

[* * *] Yes, the price of "cute ass" is exceedingly high, and it's not only their complaints but their criticisms. Women have a strange way of chewing men to pieces and down. They keep at it, while the man pulls in wondering what the hell. When they first meet you you are a golden knight; 3 months later you are a big piece of shit that clogs the plumbing. Then there are her friends and her parents and there are her ideas of what to do and where to go—a devastating drain on the senses and the spirit. And don't forget PMS which sometimes lasts 31 days in a month of 29 days. I have never seen a man with a so-called "fine dish" on his arm that I haven't felt sorry for. [* * *]

[To John Martin]
May 13, 1988

Well, with the arrival of all the good checks, followed today by the arrival of *The Roominghouse Madrigals*, I just have to allow myself to feel good, very damn good, I think I have some space to allow that to enter.

I read the *Madrigals* right on through, fine read, there are some good slicing and fiery lines there. Bad jobs, bad women can add up to some lucky things. I think it's a very good book, yes yes.

Wow! Where did you get the photo? It fits right on in.

Anyhow, this has all been a *gigantic* lift and couldn't have come at a better time.

None of this would ever have been possible without your support and your work, the way you've dug in from the beginning against all the little critics and groups, it's been miraculous. Don't think I don't realize what you've had to hear from all the literary pressure groups.

You are a tough guy, John, a hero and a buddy.

[To John Martin]
May 15, 1988

Well, as I typed these tonight, there sat the book *The Room-inghouse Madrigals* to the left of the typer.

Everything feels very odd.

You know, those small rooms were great places. You closed the door and there you were. The factory was gone, the warehouse was gone. There was just the dresser and the bed and the shades and the rug. It was a cave, it was total escape—for that time, and that time was crazy and wavering and fearful and wondrous. What they had ripped out of you, came back. At least, some of it did. Sometimes they took a great deal—just getting your shoes off was about all that you could do. Sometimes the dark killer of *quit* would come and sit inside of me. It would say, "Fuck it! Give it up! They've got you! Realize it and cough it up!"

But there was another voice in there too, it said: "No matter what they take, try to save *something*, no matter how small, save one tiny bit, hold onto that, even if that's all there is."

I went with that.

Although what I wrote I felt was good enough for me, I never felt I would have any kind of literary luck. All I was doing was swinging back after the 8 count; my idea was not victory but a continuance against the odds. In essence, now, it remains the same.

I am again in a small room with the door closed. People know that I don't want to sit with them and chatter about what they chatter about. I am pleased that they leave me alone. I see plenty of the world, it roars through me like a stinking wind. I know what is there and what is not there, at least, for me.

I still need words and the sound of the machine. I still think a good plumber is much more valuable than a good writer, but I don't have a taste for plumbing and I have the bills to prove it. Anyhow. Here I am, still. Moving toward 68, drinking red wine, and babbling.

You and I, John, we've had a good time while hardly knowing it. And that's the best way: steady, lucky and saving that tiny bit.

[To William Packard]
sometime in May, 1988

I am in the skin cancer game now. Got this dermatologist, jolly fellow, he burns lumps off with a hot little torch, tells me, "It's like arc welding. Same principle."

He tells me of the biopsy reports: "Lucky we got that fucker."

"Hell," I say, playing macho, "could be worse, what?"

"Oh yeah, of all the types of cancer, say ABCD, you've got the least, I'd rather have yours."

"I'd rather you had it too, doc."

I go to the track now with these big white patches turning purple (body serums escalating) and scare hell out of the mutual clerks.

When I lived in east Hollywood I went to this doctor (for something else stupid) and he let me sit in his office instead of the waiting room. I sat at his desk and read the med books and drank beers from the little refrig he had there.

Walked in one time, furious, cursing. Him. He.

"What is it, doc?"

"Son of a bitch, she's got this cancer of the ass, *horrible*, worst I've ever seen and *she refuses to die!*"

What can I say, William? I hang around doctor's offices, racetracks and madwomen. Everything wobbles and roars in a kind of curious green-purple light.

The only cures I have for the ills of life are to move constantly north and to sleep. But you run out of north and you wake up.

No cure. Just wait for the garbage man.

[To John Martin]
June 15, 1988 (income tax time)

Please don't worry too much about Neeli. If I can be destroyed by Neeli then I deserve to be destroyed.

What you have to do is to trust more what I am. I don't want to bring up minor bad moments, most of ours have been anything but that, but *long long ago*, oh my, we are getting *old*, John...

Anyhow, long long ago I was setting off for one of my first poetry readings across country and you were trying to coach me, "If they say this, you say that. And if they say that, you say this"... and on...

Finally, I had to say it, "John, which of us is Bukowski?"

I am never careful. I say what I think and I think what I say.

I am not afraid of some mud in the face.

John, just because we've lapped the field a couple of times and are running charmed and mad through the darkening sun, let's not get extra careful now, let's not forget how to roll the dice. Death is coming soon enough, we will not even back down to that motherfucker.

Here, in spite of some scenes on premise [*sic*] that are almost like a rolling lava from hell, I'm sure that many men have faced far worse than I, but the typer's still here, the bottle is still here, the walls hold up the ceiling and you and Black Sparrow were there when nothing else was and you're *still* there, and no matter *how* the hell, *how* big or *how* new or *how* hellish, it's even GOOD in hell, why not?

Don't worry about anything. I've got control, even when I'm spinning in the putrid muck, amen.

[To John Martin]
June 1988 burning down...

I think that the days of thinking of oneself as a writer are over, if those days were ever there.

As the years move on we move into stranger and odder times where I think even the literatures and philosophies of the past fail to adhere.

Suddenly we have rushed forwards or backwards and

things that were once ageless in their wisdom just no longer apply.

If I may make a raw comparison, it's like awakening in the morning and you look at the woman in bed next to you and it is no longer your wife. You get up, walk around and it is no longer your house. You go outside to look at your car but it's no longer your car, it's an animal of sorts with three horns and one blue eye and other other eye a color that you have never seen before.

They've switched the fucking deck on us, John.

There's something wrong with the sky and the old modes, the old dependables no longer exist, they've all run off somewhere.

But we move on, doing what we used to because habit bites deep.

Then, maybe too, I've just got the itchy jumps. It could be that people back in the 13th and 14th centuries got the itchy jumps too.

But what I'm talking about, since 1920 and now, things have gone into rapid shift and tilt, I believe that I really sense it. I mean, shit, we could go on for another ten thousand centuries but there's a definite stink and wildness in the air, the place, the time, the thing of it.

It could be that I am just moving closer to my own death but this never gave me the jumps, only a sense of peace.

I just don't know what it is.

But it's good to be in it. The new shake-up. Hell ramming through the Heavens of nowhere.

Things here have had excessive sharp teeth lately. Maybe I am overthinking.

Meanwhile, enclosed poesy.

[To William Packard]
ate 12 ate ate

I have automographed [*sic*] *NYQ* numba 35 alongside ye Stafford. Once when I was still working the boards and the

107

broads, I hreadeavy [*sic*] no light (go to single space) as a duet with Stafford and he was first and read away and then stated, "I don't write like Bukowski but I know you want to hear him … so I'm going to just read you 3 more poems …"

"Oh no!" galled by this, wailed the little birds. "Oh no, William, *please* keep on reading!"

They were afraid that those big boogers I was going to roll out there mkg poems would crush their mental vaginas.

I am happy I got the broken typer poem past you, you're a natural gambler, thank you.

On MacDonald Carey's book manu,[1] I just read first half of poems, phoned him, told him I need read no further, delightful read, he had his paragraph. I will read remainder at my own pelican pleasure. I just wish more writers knew how to play the line like Mac does, there's very little to read in the world. A fellow like that just naturally adds a couple of years to your life because no matter what happens it will never be quite as dark as it was.

Have had some health problems, all my fault, keeping dumb company, mixing too many drinks in one night, bad hours, feeling sick and still going out in a blithely fix, gambling. … I just broke down 4 or 5 days, fever, coughing continually, but the good wife there with the lemon juice and the 5 cats, and tonight for the first time, I feel the old pep kicking back in. I have a basic problem: when I drink with other people, I feel and get sick; when I drink alone, the next day I don't feel so bad. So therefore … Yes, I will … Drink alone … where often as a bonus … sheets of paper follow each other off of this machine … ah … ah … ah …

Luck with the auto novel. The youth bit. I got lucky with mine: vicious father, more than vicious, and also the medics sticking my rosy outbursts of flesh with these hot and whirling drills … tended to make me ponder the mathematics of existence … I think I pondered it pretty good, except the thought that a guy as ugly as I would never get a woman. It all turned out to be by far too many women, a flood of bodies and

---

1. *Beyond that Further Hill* (Columbia, SC: University of South Carolina Press, 1989).

bouncing springs and screams and little and big days and nights of horror and a few of pleasure. It's a world full of lonely women and some of them deserve to be. [* * *]

[To John Martin]
August 26, 1988

[* * *] You know, I've always had a certain routine, even when I was a bum. I still have a routine, maybe call it a rhythm? And I am always astonished at how people like to *visit each other*. I just don't mean relatives but also strangers and half-strangers. They can just loll away the hours with the damnedest chatter you've ever heard and somehow it *fills* them but it strickens me, sickens me, I can't get the least bit out of it, but one tries to be a good sort anyhow. Hell, maybe I'm a space creature and I'm stuck here. To me a closed door is one of the most beautiful things on earth. Their door or mine. When I was a bum it was easier, nobody knocked. And I loved it. "I have to fight for the minute," I told somebody not too long ago. She laughed. She had no idea what I was talking about.[* * *]

[To John Martin]
Sept. huh? 1988

Well, Neeli has come and gone, the Danish have come and gone and I have written to *Life* magazine about "*Why are we here?*"

Enclosed a very short chapter but I think it tells what has to be told. Besides there has been *heavy bombardment.*

I try to console myself that almost all my writing life has been under conditions of war, slipping in a secret hour or two in spite of all and maybe because of all. But, damn, I'm so much older now. Death is beginning to wink at me. There is always the dreamer in man that wants that hot blaze of happiness, just sun and singing, you know? It must be there.

But then I am beginning to sound like the complainers who complain almost as a matter of habit and who blame the world for everything that they are not.

Ah, the dogs of war gnaw at me, baby.

Yet, for it all, I consider myself very lucky. I am tuned toward happiness. It takes very little to please me. Often nothing at all.

It feels good to write. It feels good to sit at this machine. What a friend it is. It's like some secret magic warmth heats the inside of all the typewriters and my fingers get the feel.

Of course, there is another novel to write. There will always be. I like this one. I like the roll of it. It's getting near the end now and I have no idea of how it ever got written... I am getting help from somewhere. The gods are kind...

[To William Packard]
October 22, 1988

[* * *] Finished my novel *Hollywood* one Saturday night and awakened Sunday morning with a fever of 103. It lasted for over a week. It would drop a couple of degrees then come back to 103. Couldn't eat or sleep. One night I started freezing, shivering and flopping, the whole bed rattling like an earthquake. Pure neat hell. Lasted 2 and one half hours. Went to 2 doctors, neither knew what the hell. I lost 23 pounds.[1]

Well, I did the novel, I thought, and I'm not on skid row and I don't mind dying... But I got better. I returned to what is it? 98.6 degrees. [* * *]

The *Hollywood* novel is not so much a condemnation as a laugher. I think it reads well.

Anyhow, my energy is still limited, just wanted to off this to

---

1. In the summer of 1989 Bukowski was finally diagnosed as having tuberculosis.

you ... I read that T. S. Eliot's first wife died in a madhouse. You can never tell what goes into the makeup of a writer. It seems the more shit a man swims in the better the keys bite into the paper.

I'm swimming.

[To William Packard]
November 6, 1988

Your good news letter arrived ... well, let's say it arrived on a day when it was needed plenty ... I had once again returned to whatever my malady was and was burning up at 104 degrees ... the doctors still can't find anything ... but I loved the news and allowed myself to feel damned good about it. I mean, all those poems in 36, and if we can let ourselves feel good now and then without really getting the fathead, I think that's fair. One thing I've learned from the years is, anytime happiness comes your way, don't question it. When I was in my twenties I felt that if I felt bad all the time that that was a sign of knowing something. You know, born to die, born to be pissed upon by the snappish female, born to work the factory, born into a nation of presidents who one after the other all seemed somewhat like your father, born to have the talentless famous rammed down your craw, etc. No matter—a man can be happy in a private way, without braggadocio, and that's how I feel now. Also, my fever is coming down and I'm still weak but in a couple of weeks I will be burning the town down ...

On the poem "240 pounds," I was sending this batch of poesy out to a little mag when I eyed "240" again and decided to try you with it. Sometimes I really get to like a certain poem a bit more than others. It was one crazy time in my life and took place while living in two different courtyards. I suppose it was a totally mad and unhealthy way to live but in another sense I was one of the *freest* men about. After decades of being told what to do by others, I was on my own. One of the ladies told me, "You're one of the first men I've ever seen with a row of rusty razor blades around the edge of his bathtub." I hadn't noticed. "My husband had the tv on all the time. He even had to have it on when we made love. You don't even have a tv." So, you know, the poem was a kind of sentimental one for me, so I sent it on. And I'm glad you saw whatever there was there. Thank you

[* * *] But here I am still on the weak side and am wavering a bit—fingers not quite hitting keys as they should, eyes refocusing on page, I've got to close down now, just wanted to let you know about your lucky letter. I believe I'll be all right. I think the gods are just playing with me, using the fevers to burn off all this shitty fat from me. Christ, I have my high school figure again, I don't know who the hell I am. [* * *]

[To William Packard]
late November, 1988

Yes, there's no rest at this end now. And the mistake was that, in a way, I thought peace of some sort might come with an older age. But the tides are relentless and unchanging. The snappish female continues to snap and the garbage man throws the can lids out in the street where they are run over. The dreams are the same: of being lost in the same area of the city that is in my brain, in my somewhere. The streets all run east and west and I have to go south to get home. There are no south streets. I walk south anyhow, going in between people's houses and climbing their back fences and walking on up the driveway of the next house, always searching, going south. Last night I had the dream again, only this time I was walking through a large university, students sitting on benches, walking about, and the buildings there, some trees.

"Where you going?" a student asks me.

"I'm trying to get home. There are no streets going my direction so I must cut through this way."

"Oh, I see," the student says.

I keep walking between buildings and more buildings but I

sense that where I want to go is very far away. In my dream I walk and I walk, I seem to walk for hours but I am still on the grounds of the university.

Finally, I awaken. Same god damned dream, I think.

Something else bothers me. It's how people mutilate their leisure time. It's as if they do the dumbest things possible to destroy their brain and spirits. It's like they club themselves to death.

What do I do? Well, often I don't do anything. Stretch on the bed, think of nothing. It is better than being caught in the gears. I used to think that many women was the secret. That was just a mirage, a waste.

Also, there's nothing to read. After I reached 25 nothing that I read interested me.

Yes, the doctors know very little. This last one that I think of as The Hatchet, I was sitting on his table and he told me in a voice of regret, "Your temperature seems to be a bit better ..."

"Do you mind telling me what it was?"

"98.6."

"That's normal."

"Yes, but you've been taking Tylenol."

"But let's look to the light. 98.6 is not a bad thing."

"There's your weight loss, it's too drastic."

"Hell, I haven't eaten in 6 days. Besides, you weigh your patients in your outer office when they are clothed. When I was first weighed I was wearing heavy clothing and carrying a clipboard. Today it was warm and I had no coat, no clipboard and lighter clothing ..."

"But you're still sick. I want to hospitalize you. We can run tests there that we can't run here ..."

"Let's not get too hasty. Sometimes these things cure themselves."

It's too damned bad when you have to tell a doctor how to handle you. Why pay him? All those bastards just run an assembly line of in-and-out patients, rush them in and out, and hope they stay sick so they can keep making money on them.

Yes, your letter was right. I am still probably paying past debts of a past that I wriggled partially out of, one way or the other. It's all reflected when I see a repeat of the same thing in

113

another person. It's like a large section of the human race is just locked in a chamber of hate, bickering and ultimate nonsense. Somehow they manage to bring me down. I can never accept the way they are. I should, and if I can ever reach that, I'm in or I'm out or I'm different and maybe then I won't have those dreams of looking for south streets when they only run east and west. Yeah.

Thanks for letting me stretch on your couch.

[To William Packard]
December 3, 1988

Yes, I got #36 and Mac is as good as ever but the best thing is your editorial on writing. It's right there and if they can't hear it and or figure it when you lay it down in front of them like that, well, it's too bad because all they want to do is be among the rich and the famous and the real itch to write is not there and never will be.

By the way, "Dante For Beginners" rolls right along in fine comic flash, reads easy, certainly seems right and makes one feel better for reading it. The last being the ultimate test of the good or great poem.

We need things to read and there aren't many things to read. Like at the track today, the parking lot attendant said to me, "You know, when I get those suicide feelings I read your books and it helps me."

"Thanks," I told him, "but what the hell am I going to read?"

He laughed, which was a good answer. [* * *]

On people taking swipes at me, that's going to happen, and I said decades ago that unless you get certain factions railing against you then you will never know you are doing something good. That's a lousy sentence. Unless you get certain factions railing against you, you will never know that you are doing anything. Still not right but almost. It's the beer and the Indian cigarettes, they joggle the frontal lobe.

Editors, writers, women can embrace you wholly for decades then overnight are apt to change their minds—not because you have become different but because you have not engaged totally in one of their trivial whims. Refuse to suck breasts. Or give poetry reading. Or write a forward to a pamphlet. Or. May the devil help us: something they heard.

Then too, they try to dissect the writing because it looks so easy they figure that there must be something wrong with you. Also, because I remain isolated from the gatherings of the poet ant tribe that I must be unjust or dippy, say even inhuman. So, call me a crank: I dislike poets. But then there are a hell of a lot of non-poets I am not fond of either. I find pelican pleasure often in my 5 cats and often in my wife and often in the bottle and often in myself being in a room alone. I wrote a long poem about my proclivities called "The Mole," but no longer remember where I sent it.

Well, on my dreams of being lost, your idea of it could be it but whatever it is, it's there and it's still there. I am often lost right now and here, often often getting the feeling that everybody and everything is cleaner, smarter, more noble than I, braver, nicer, prettier and so forth. Sometimes I even feel inferior to a fly crawling across the table. A fly is a real challenge because it just doesn't give a fuck about you and here you are focusing on it, wondering whether it will shit, fly or die or not do any of those. Sometimes fear jumps all over me from somewhere and nowhere. I look down and one of my shoelaces are in ungainly order, one long string sticking out. But I can't *do* anything about it but record that and feel as if I were an asshole.

Trivial things wear me to shit. All the trivial things. Gas bills. Dental floss. Looking at people standing outside a church. Going to a gas station to pump gas into my car. Standing in any line. Looking in the mirror. Combing my hair. Shards and shavings of half things that must always be done or they come and get you and lock you up. Or the other things. Overhearing conversations of other people while you are eating at a table or in some stationary position. They say no words at all or words and things that others have said, stale ideas, old farty chewing words and dull mechanical laughter. It wears me like a club to the head or a punch in the gut, only worse.

115

And fears, cowardly fears about nothing. Crawling all over you as you wonder what the hell. You are an idiot. You might eat your own snot. Even suicide is worthless upon one.

Then in a flash, a tick, a blink ... it's over and you're brave, you're handsome, you're intelligent. You're tough and strong yet still you're kind. What a bundle! You tell your wife, "I can't think of anybody I'd rather be than me," smiling at that, like a joke, only it's not quite a joke.

Damn, you can stride across a room!

Outside, in the world out there, in places of business and non-business you say bright crazy things and people laugh, they laugh true laughter. You fear nobody. A big guy glances at you and you stare him down. You can take that fucker. He looks away. You could leap one hundred feet into the air if you felt like it. Women look at you and smile. Animals follow you down the street. You consider holding up a bank. You see 3 winos broke, red-faced, dying, dying for drink for their dry tongues. You walk up, hand them a ten. "Don't use this for food," you tell them.

Ah, it's up and down and all around. Don't try. Never try.

Well, I do try. I try to never think of myself as a *writer*. Blank that. You are just a body moving about, doing things. You are only a writer when you see the typewriter and some-times the typewriter is there and you don't see it. Sometimes, but luckily not too often, I am recognized. The person will say, "Aren't you ...? Listen, I really like your writing ..." And it's a shock to me. I have to pull myself around, remember. I am a writer. "Oh yes," I tell them, "thank you." What they don't understand is that nobody is a writer until they are at the typer and the lucky words are forming.

It's all fairly garbled. But I think writers who are constantly writers wear themselves away. I have seen it happen to many. They become statues in the park. They can't move anymore.

Damn this beer is good. And Gershwin is on the radio. He's usually hard to take. But tonight at one a.m. he sounds good.

Whenever I see a funeral I think of the present state of American poetry. ah, I really don't. Thought it would sound good. But next time I see a funeral I will.

[To Gerald Locklin]
December 15, 1988

[* * *] I don't have it on hand at the moment but one of my favorite poems of yours is about the female libber. Christ, how I've heard that bit: "Men find me too much of a challenge ... Men are afraid of me ..." These are the worst, they ask for Liberation yet go around with this superiority complex and they chatter endlessly, endlessly, thrusting their frustrations all over a guy. It feels so good to get away from these types, man. But you handled the poem nicely, without bitterness, actually with understanding. Nice go ...

Yes, I don't like readings. Those vanity warblers are un-believable. But if those people read as well as you, with the same bright and real material, I'd go to the readings. But they don't, oh no no, they don't.

Here, well here I've finished the novel, *Hollywood* ... about a month ago. It waits Spring publication via the Sparrow. I like the book. We'll see.

[To William Packard]
December 30, 1988

[* * *] I am all right. Of course, various forces are always fucking with a man and if you live through these, here comes another new set to test you. Test for what? I thought I had graduated Cum Lord long ago.

Once in a while I turn into a raving piece of meat but most of the time I think I handle most of the shit straight on and the craziest thing to me is that I'm still here. When things get the worst, I think that if a man can have a room of his own to get into alone with something to drink and some walls to look at he can then overcome just about anything but death itself. Outside of quiet isolation, a couple of good nights sleep can also buy you through a lot of hell.

Then there are days, even a week when all is warm and cool

117

and easy. This is when we mend for the next assault.

Then too, when you get near 70 you realize that some night, any night, you could go to bed and in the morning not awaken. Which is all right, except the next time you sit at the typer you think, maybe I better get it down good because ...

Listen, I found that bit by Steve Kowit that was in your last letter.[1] I had lost it somewhere. Read it the other day. Not bad. Except I think Kowit romanticizes the sex bit about me, writing about it, thinking about it. Much of that came from the past when I made my living writing for the sex mags. Not that the writing was bad or that I didn't enjoy tapping it out but it *was* pointed in the direction of sex because that was what the eds paid me for. Also, I seemed to be on a roll with many women, trying to catch up with what I thought I had missed out on. I hadn't missed out on a damn thing but a lot of sick trouble.

Well, I hope you keep on guiding the *NYQ* through the poetic seas. You are creating some type of history. It's needed, needed. Seems for decades now that *Poetry* (formerly *Poetry, A Magazine of Verse*) has paled into a restrictive and careful whisper.

You make 1989 look hopeful and mighty to many of us.

●

---

1. Steve Kowit edited *The Maverick Poets: An Anthology* (Santee, CA: Gorilla Press, 1988).

118

• 1 9 8 9 •

[To William Packard]
March 12, 1989

[* * *] Actually, I haven't typed much of anything for months. Came down with 3 sets of fevers at spaced intervals. After that, and of late, a great sense of weakness. In 4 months or so came down from 217 pounds to 175, where I am at now. Doctor to doctor, none of them knew much. Went to hospital and was tested by various machines, many machines and devices. They ran me through, stuck tubes, lights into me, photographed. On and on. They were looking for something. Found nothing. I had a low hemoglobin count of 9.3 and they were attempting to trace the reason. Nothing.

Much bed time. Often felt too weak to brush my teeth but managed. Bed time. Ceiling and walls. Silent typewriter. Nothing. Nothing in me, nothing on paper. For an over-prolific fellow such as I, it was strange.

I get about more now. Make the track but come in fairly tired A few poems but I'm far from where I was. Going to see the doc tomorrow. Another blood test.

This is boring, ah, I know. But you wondered where I was.

At best, I look at this as a transformation. I look up, take the bright side. The gods are reshaping me. They took 42 pounds of ugly fat off of me. I am 68 years old and have the body of an 18 year old boy. And maybe the mind too. I've remained at 175 for weeks. I think that the fuckers are

119

preparing me for a good hard run. Much more typing until I am 80 or 90 years old. Couldn't do that, packing all that fat. Also, the gods are forcing me to take a breather, let the buildup build. This is is the kind view I like to take. On the other hand it could be something not so good ... Well, any way it goes, I am ready for it ...

I am glad to see MacD. Carey getting some attention. I hope he can handle it and all those readings he's giving. Time will let us know. The long haul is the killer and few come out the other side of the wall. You have to know when to duck and when to swing and how to say "no." I liked Robinson Jeffers' way of going. He wrote a lot of letters that rather sucked at one time or another but he finally tossed all that, got behind his rock and carved against the impossibilities. By this, I don't mean we should take our work as a serious or holy thing, but more as just the best thing to do that there is to do. So why not do it?

All right, I'm going to make a comeback, you'll see.

you keep pounding,

[To William Packard]
March 31, 1989

Thanks your fine letter, it was a boost that was needed.

I'm still at low ebb, going back to doctor Monday, another blood test, another angle, he went to a seminar last week and maybe found out something?

By the way, during the worst of one of my fevers (104) there was a 6 part bit on tv called *The Singing Detective,* put out by the BBC.[1] This guy was fucked up in bed too but I didn't relate entirely on that score, the whole matter was so well acted by all, had so much pathos, humor, reality, juice and fire that I almost cried several times. I guess I'll never see it again but it is something to be remembered. People are still able to do powerful and miraculous things, sometimes. At rare times. Out

---

1. Television drama in several parts by Dennis Potter.

120

of all the shit, here it comes, and one is very grateful that the world has not been *totally* wasted.

Thanks for the list of backlog poems. I am honored. Please don't worry, I'm not going to do the precious poet thing and ask for them back or to be dropped or anything like that. It sounds like good stuff. Thank you.

Jesus, to get your nose cut off and put back on, that's a soul-shaker. Wish it had happened to me, it would have made a great poem.

Yes, the absence of fear. Dying is not bad at all. It's sickness, weakness that is the impossibility. I have this hacking dry cough, have had it over a month. The doctor just looks down my throat and smiles. Doctors see too many patients. They are over-rushed, no time to focus in. They have to keep hustling to support their lifestyles and their wives' life-styles.

No, I haven't received my compl copy of *Beyond that Further Hill*, but I suppose they'll get around to it.[1]

Short letter here ... Haven't been drunk for a week. This is just to get this off and to thank you for the great booster letter. I hope some day soon to send more poems for consideration in an attempt to add to our good old backlog, yes, yes, yes,

---

[To John Martin]
April 11, 1989

It's going to be a longer fight than I ever believed. Still low on hemoglobin count, iron, plus I have a weak pulse. The hacking dry cough is what really wears me out, though. Finally went for a batch of herbs (Finally). Linda cooked them up, a real potent brew. There was *some* relief from the cough, which really felt good. Thursday afternoon I'm going in for acupuncture. A man gets desperate; when the regular docs have no answer you go elsewhere.

Meanwhile, the few poems I have written have been

---

1. See letter to William Packard of August 12, 1988 ("ate 12 ate ate").

121

accepted everywhere, which shows the talent is still there in spite of my afflictions. The editors even claim that I am getting better. I feel this too but I'm so used to turning the poems out en masse, that the space between them now is not exactly exhilarating.

Well, I'm still here, in a sense. And then there's *Hollywood* on the horizon. All is not lost, uh uh.

[To William Packard]
August 21, 1989

[* * *] The docs couldn't find out what was wrong with me. I went through all types of hospital machinery. Hundreds of photos and lights and look-ins. Only thing is they left one thing out: chest x-ray. I was coughing and losing weight, no appetite. They didn't know what it was. I was going to 2 docs and they both dropped me out of their appointment books. Well, one of them passed me over to another doc who gave me herbs and acupuncture. No good. Finally, I went to one of the secretaries and had her set me up with a chest x-ray. Hey, hey, they found these markings. Ha! Now tubes down the lungs, tubes with little lights and little snippers. Crap for the lab to look at. Ha! I had TB. Good.

I've been on antibiotics for 3 months. 3 months to go. I hope that does it. I've stopped coughing and have gained a bit of weight and some of my strength but the antibiotics are hell on the writing. They do something to the brain. Couldn't write for months. Can't drink. But have finally begun to tap out a bit or two. Stuff seems all right. But it comes slow. I feel like Lazarus. Did he die again? Think of that: dying twice. What a fucking dirty trick. [* * *]

[To John Martin]
labor day 1989

It's good to know that you are working on another book of mine. Lucky we had some backlog when this TB struck. I'll tell you that it was a very strange feeling when I couldn't type for a couple of months. Just being in that bed, or getting down the stairway and going out and sitting under the walnut tree, trying to breathe.

I'm slowly working back into shape. I'm not all the way back yet but I've come a long way from the first part of the year.

As we go on with our lives we tend to forget that the jails and the hospitals and the madhouses and the graveyards are packed. [* * *]

[To William Packard]
October 2, 1989

In your bulging acceptance file there is a poem of mine entitled "escape." Would you be a good fellow and take this one out and tear it up? Reason is, I think a certain lady would think a certain line is about her, even though it isn't. Said lady has not been feeling well of late and I don't want to push her over the edge with such a misunderstanding. Please help me here. Let it be your good deed of the century. What? And thank you so much ...

I am still on the recovery road. TB. Antibiotics and *no drinking*. Ah, I have *suffered* and the writing has lessened—just as good, just not as much of it or as much fun writing it. But if all goes well, I should be cured Nov. 14 and that first drink will be so *marvelous*. I have been holding at 170 pounds for some months and it's a good weight for my height, age and temperament. I can't believe I was once around 240. What a fart-kicker I was. And it's going to be so good to be drunk and *mad* once again. I'll soon be 70 but I don't wanna do without my bottle, no no no ... Death means nothing. Only life.

123

Last issue of *NYQ* the best yet, pumped full of good poems. You and your staff are getting better and better. Got your joke in contributor's column: "Bukowski likes visitors ..." I've got a doormat that says, GO AWAY. But my wife hid it. Afraid her mother would come around and not understand. Uh uh. We always gotta worry about the non-understanders but they don't worry about us, or if they do they worry about the wrong things about us. Well, we have to live with the people. As little as possible but we have to live with them. And the longer I live with then the more I realize that there isn't much there. Maybe there isn't supposed to be.

But mainly this letter is an effort to get you to rip the poem "escape." Don't return it to me, just rip it. Thank you. Thank you, Prince.

I still get the idea that there isn't as much kicking around as there used to be. I mean, when Ezra was here, and T. S. Eliot and e. e. Cummings, Auden, Spender and the like. I don't know but they seemed to rock out great lines. great lines ... And there was a sense of discovery and excitement going on. Maybe we've discovered ourselves dry. Or maybe when you're starving and looking up, the game looks better to you than when you've been in it for decades and begin to recognize the poetic tricks and ploys and replays that go on and on and on. Maybe I do need a drink. [* * *]

[To William Packard]
Oct. what 15?
one nine ate nine,
moving toward 2,000 and the
tombstone

[* * *] Yes, I'm on the mend. 2nd big handshake with mr. Death. I'm ready when he is. I don't think I get 9 like a cat, although I have 6 cats. Sometimes when I feel real bad I just look at some of the cats and it cools me out. Such eyes, such fur, such a casual amokness. What's that mean? It means

something. Window sills mean something, bottle caps don't. Strange, isn't it?

Not too long ago I could hardly make it from bed to bathroom. Weak, dizzy. Feet go flop flop flop, no motivation. Dick dangling like dead sunflower. But what an excellent excuse not to see anybody. No faces entering the brain like a horror movie. *Bukowski likes visitors. Umm* ummm ...

Knew I was getting better when I got dressed and crawled to my car, drove to the racetrack. I was typer paper white. Hardly a voice. "20 to win on the 6." It was a whisper. The clerk said, "what?" Then, "is it you?" Couldn't stay the full card. Got too weak to walk. Won money. I'm a pro. Made it back to car. Once you're in that fucker it balances. Nobody knows. I drove on in like a 16 year old, *zoom*, rear view check for heat.

I'm almost back now. Missed some typing. The machine almost wept without me. Writing is a sick habit to break. Propped myself on the pillows and got to notebook and pen. Not bad. Strange stuff but not bad. Crawling through the antibiotics. 6 cats on the bed watching me write in a yellow notebook. Me not wanting the soul to quit. Come on, lad, show me something. Even the last dance can be a good one.

I'm still not where I once was. You can't drop 60 pounds as fast as I did and get away with it. Got back 15 and am stronger each day. Soon will be normal. Puffing on cigar and sucking at beer and wine and feeling knowing, very knowing again, and at the same time, as per usual, utterly stupid and lost and a touch demented.

But I could have died ten years ago and still felt lucky. The writing came pounding, late, but good, I think. Good enough for me. You can feel that particular bite of the key into the ribbon when you're running at full grace. Hail Mary. And hail Henry too.

Yeah, that Catullus was too much. He was more modern then than the moderns now. [* * *]

[To William Packard]
end October, 1989

[* * *] Yes, I get strange mail, a lot of it just dumb. I mean without the least bit of vigor or light. Flat. Much in pen on lined paper. May the devil help me that I have such readers. Of course, my days of being drunk night and day and being in jail, in fights, fucking away at will etc., these days are about over. Shit, in a few months I'll be 70. I am now mostly a quiet chap and when I begin drinking again it will be alone and mostly at the typer. I know that there's nothing out there in the world. The walls are beautiful to me. But I still get letters from ladies who want to suck my brains out. And from guys who think I could go it with Mike Tyson. I can't help what people think. I just go on writing what I want and mail it on out. But there are no longer any poems about finding shit-stained panties under my bed and no knowing whose. There's always plenty to write about. You know, just staying alive and not going crazy takes a lot of wisdom, or maybe it's not wisdom, maybe it's just practice.

I'm doing some painting now. I paint right out of the tube. Acrylics. Hot time. I like to lay it on thick. Got a lucky one of a big bird eating a berry.

Will have a new book out in the Spring, Black Sparrow. *Septuagenarian Stew.*[1] Admixture of poems and stories. Editor chose many of the poems I wrote during my illness, which again is fine luck for me. I didn't write as many poems during that time but the few I did seemed to be on target. The years help teach us to write the way we want to. That's good. We hope not to lean on tricks or fabrications. Invent, yes; fabricate, no. The idea is to hone it up to the last breath, to die on the typer, hopefully after the poem or the story is finished. Not for fame. Just for the roll and inner laughing glory of it. That after all they put in front of us, we knocked it down and found a minor clearance. That's enough.

Keep the *NYQ* going. It's got guts and style and gamble. It's needed, needed, needed.

---

1. *Septuagenarian Stew: Stories & Poems,* published in May 1990.

Eric Lyden was editor of Moment, *a "randomly published L.A. journal of the arts" from Shelf Life Press, Woodland Hills, CA.*

[To Eric Lyden]
Nov. one, one nine ate nine

[* * *] Yes, I've heard about the agents-for-poets bit. One quite famous poet, who will remain nameless, phoned me and told me to get an agent, he had one and that it really "helped." I told the gentleman that I didn't want an agent. "They do all the work for you," he told me. Did he mean the writing? I hope not.

Ah, poetry readings. There is so much push and vanity and self-promotion. I've seen almost the same pack of poets giving readings at little hand-out places for decades. They go on and on with their tiny readings. A few times I have been talked into attending readings. Somehow I always felt a sense of shame, being there. It felt like a gathering of idiots. Are these our creators? These *things?* These bellowing, vain, stomping, self-pleased creatures? Are these the ones? And some of these even give classes to others on *how to write.* 15 dollars an hour or whatever the hell.

A writer's job is to write, not to prance his ass on stage, not to hope to get laid by the few idiotic groupies who also think that they are writers.

You can have these. The last thing I want is somebody standing at my front door who claims he or she is "a *poet.*"

[To John Martin]
October, no, November 8, 1989

Thanks for the Sutherland video. I liked it. I liked *Bring Me Your Love* too.[1] Linda didn't seem to care too much for either.

---

1. Bukowski's story, *Bring Me Your Love*, published as a book by Black Sparrow Press in 1983, was filmed as *Love Pig*, directed by Chris Innis. The "Sutherland video" was another short film based on his work and directed by Starr Sutherland, with music by Larry Ochs.

127

But I think if I like the works, that's most important. After all, I wrote them. And we can't get Marlon Brando to act in these things. They should be viewed as good, sympathetic efforts. I really thought that Sutherland caught the admixture of humor and madness that both of those works possessed. Right on.

More *Hollywood* contracts. Jesus, I don't think I've ever seen a rush like this one. They want us. Good. It's a good book. I was right in the middle of all that shit and yet somehow I kept my distance. Which helped me write about it later. Right. On.

Norse. Well, he's going to bitch. Writers do too much door knocking and socializing. They like to reassure each other. The best assurance a writer can get it to get it down good at the typer. All else is nonsense.

All right, I'll try to remember to date my poems as per your request. Like I said, though, a great many of the poems in the new book were written during my sickness period. Maybe I should stay sick? X-rays of chest clean. I'm cured. Still will take antibiotics through Nov. 13. After that back to normal. Thank you for bearing up so well while I was on my ass. Your quiet words were a great tonic. Let's go on until 2010, then I'll concentrate on painting, or maybe fucking.

[To Patrick Foy]
December 10, 1989

I read your *The Second World War and its Aftermath*. A fine work. But where can you place it? I can think of no journal with the courage to publish it. After all, our journals too are part of our duped past. A century long barrage of propaganda seeps in everywhere. Well, almost everywhere.

Thank you very much, very, for allowing me to read your work. A refreshing rush of truth.

●

• 1 9 9 0 •

[* * *] Great news on the raise. Almost unbelievable. But please realize that I will understand necessary cutbacks if sales don't hold up. The whole matter is a bit dizzifying. I never wanted to write for money but rather for a bare survival. I don't think either of us ever realized anything like this would happen when we began at that gritty but wonderful bottom so long ago. But there's no use letting up now, let's give 'em a good run down to the last breath.

And now, Happy New Year, we have a problem. My fault. Maybe we can straighten it. If not, well we'll let it run. First of all, I cleaned up this typing room, really went mad and tossed paper out. I'm drowning in it. And one of the things I tossed out was the typewritten manuscript of *Sept. Stew*. I figured, well, the book will be next. A foolish move, because you would know more of what I am talking about if I could refer you to an exact page and an exact poem title.

Uh uh. Ow. Go to "The Dinner." You see, I wrote this poem about going to dinner with Sean and Madonna. Linda and I did. And I footed the bill. It rather pissed me because here were two millionaires. So, I wrote a poem about it. Now, *since then*, Sean has sprung for meal after meal and also sent a couple of limos and did some other good things.

If you could somehow locate this poem and pull it, I'd be

129

damned grateful, although I know it's somewhat like looking for the old needle in the old haystack. Think the last line read, "I'm at least that…"

Then too, Sean may do *Women*. And when the book comes out he'll see the poem. I don't want him hurt. We could run some other poem instead? Well, I messed up, jumped too soon. So, if you can't locate the poem for one reason or another, let's let it run and I'll just have to take what is coming to me.

[* * *] Well, 1989 was a rough year for me, some months on my ass, null and void, but during all that I thought about Fante, what the gods ran him through and he still went on writing, a true champ. Of course, what pleases me is that I've had such luck with Sparrow from the beginning but the next thing to please me is that you located and brought Fante back into the reading world—all those movies and he has fame in Europe. He finally got what he always wanted but, of course, he never knew it. Joyce is going to have to live it for him.

Got rid of the short story (recent) called "The Other." *Arete* took it. They pay a grand. Then they asked that I might illustrate the story. I sat down and flipped out 3 or 4 drawings, took me maybe 5 minutes. They accepted. 400 dollars. Everything is very strange. From a total bum to all this. But something is watching me. I am always being tested. There is always the next day, the next night. I began late and I'm going to have to keep pounding. I missed a hell of a lot of years. But the luckiest thing that ever happened to me is that I didn't get lucky early. And you didn't either. We know what it means to work for it and it's not behind us yet.

[To William Packard]
January 24, 1990

[* * *] Sure, the Xmas season is enough to give anybody the flu, at least. All that jolly fake goodness on cue could make a man puke up his god damned soul. I get so tired of lonely stale people who are stuffed with standard concepts—and they fling

themselves through the doorway at you. Damn scabby subnomals, lost in their hours and having no idea that they might be mutilating yours.

Happy 40th!

The whore gods shouldn't place you in a position, after 20 years of suffering through endless masses of useless manuscript, that you still have to scrabble for monies. No, poetry readings are not a sell-out if the $$$$ are truly needed. It's those slime who do it out of vanity and ego and do it badly at that, then that's the sell-out. They hope the little girls will wash their socks and their balls. But, actually, the little girls will put their balls in a bag.

Robert Burns, well, I have trouble solving the tongue it is writ in. Lazy, I guess. When I was a laborer, I remember some fellow telling me, "hey, you oughta read Robert Burns, he writes dirty stuff." So many people read writers for the wrong reason. But it's strange to me that people still do read. I guess reading the daily newspaper keeps them in the habit. And they'd forget their math if they didn't have their grubby little checkbooks to balance.

I don't know about the Scots reading me but I get a few letters from Belfast now and then. A lively place, I'm told.

Have been a bit hung up on drinking and gambling lately. Rather feel a bit in a dream-state, death squashing a bit in my shoes. I don't press on the writing. I let it build like a pus boil until it breaks and squirts out. Dare push the Muse and you end up with the old limp pecker.

Won $500 at the track the other day so took my wife to the boxing matches, ringside. I don't know if the horserace crowd or the boxing crowd is the lowest on the life-scale. And then I wonder what I'm doing mixing with them. But anything is better than running with the poets. Those old maid gossips, those spirochetes, those peccaries. The hex of hyposodia upon them all! [* * *]

[To William Packard]
January 28, 1990

So you've got a talking cat. I mean, that's hot bananas. And he listens to the answering machine. I've got 6 cats and not a damned one of them speaks even pidgin English ... You ever thought of putting that cat on the poetry reading circuit? think of him doing *The Inferno*. Or maybe he writes his own stuff. Is he fixed? The ladies just love to blow and screw the poets. We know that.

Yes, you've caught me out, I phoned in, and even *while* I was phoning word on the poems was sitting on the coffee table, god damn it. I'm ruined. Caught me weak. Just like any other jack-off. Please don't tell anybody or my book-sales will fall off to a titmouse's shadow.

Cool daddy Bukowski, pacing the floor, waiting on a manila envelope.

There goes another dream. Exposed like a flasher in a park full of kindergarten girls.

I've listened to enough poets over the decades, weeping about imagined wrong. Now I am in the same tent with them, doing the circle-jerk.

Or maybe that person on the message machine was somebody pretending to be Bukowski. There are those. I see them almost every time I open up a little magazine. And once I was reading a throwaway sheet that said that I had attended a poetry reading and had gone up and down the aisles smiling and shaking hands. I put a corrector on that one, hasty-like.

So, all right, #41 looks good, thanks for chancing me on a fistful. It will piss a lot of poets but I've always pissed a lot of poets and non-poets too. I was born to piss people off. Half my writing is a dig at the overpeopled universe. The other half is self-entertainment. I mean, you can't go to the movies. Well, you can go but there's nothing there.

After 9 months on my ass was pronounced cured of my TB Nov. 13, 1989. Got down to 155 pounds. I'm back on wine, beer, cigars and cigs from India and to leaving piteous messages on answering machines. Typer feels good, though, sound of keys, little words biting into the paper. I was supposed to be dead a long time ago. Each drink is a free one. The guy in the house next door is 95 years old. I'm going to let him go first (maybe?) and then I'll follow him. No more driving the crowded freeways. No more wiping my ass. Or maybe that's all there is in hell: those two actions. "Hey, Harry, all they *do* is drive the crowded freeways and wipe their asses! Honest injun!"

Well, there's a bottle of Pinot Noir (Firestone vineyard) (1984, Orwell grapes) to my left and the night is the youngest and oldest thing around here and maybe I'll reach into it and luck onto a couple of poems. Even wrote a story the other day about the night I saw somebody standing in the bathroom and this fellow looked like me. I took it from there. Some magazine took it from there. Told me it was "a real page turner." Let's hope so. It's when you write something that's really on your mind that it comes out best. Push at anything and it falls apart. Better to wait. Don't try. It's just that tonight I know that the poems are in the Pinot Noir. Or so I say now. [* * *]

[To John Martin]
January 31, 1990

There's always something to get in the way of the typewriter but it's been that way as long as I've been at it. Maybe it's best that these things get in the way of the typewriter. It holds the water in the dam.

I think that overambition kills. I think that *trying* to be a writer kills. Writing simply has to be a sickness, a drug. It doesn't *have* to be, it just is. When one thing or another cures your sickness, that's it. And, of course, there are no guidelines.

I've been lucky. For decades now I haven't had to force myself to write anything in any particular way. Black Sparrow had been a great help with this. But even before I had too much luck, even when I was starving at it, I seldom wrote anything that I didn't want to write. There were the stories for the sex mags—early—but I even fooled them with these because I just tossed in the sex and built a real story around that.

133

If you slant your writing it means you want to make money, you want to get famous, you want to get published for the sake of getting published. I think that only works for a while. The gods are watching us. And they`extract their toll. Without fail.

When I dim, if I dim, it will be because drink has addled my brain or natural senility takes over. If I somehow stay lucky, I may even avoid these things. Maybe the gods like me.

And even if it should stop, it's been a great and magical run. But I only want what is next, not what is past. I may have lost a step but I'm harder to fool on the curve ball.

Or so I think. Now.

A writer for Europeo *magazine sent Bukowski a list of questions to answer. I have interpolated the questions among his answers given in the following letter.*

[To Luciana Capretti]
February 6, 1990

(I presume you have your questions before you).

[*Hollywood* is obviously the tale of the making of *Barfly*: the characters in it are disguised under very recognizable pseudonyms. Weren't you afraid of being sued by any of them for what you reveal?]

Question # one I'd rather ignore.

[Despite your reputation of being irreverent and unconventional, reading your book you seem extremely sober and restrained: do you think you are? And why do you appear so different here than elsewhere?]

In *Hollywood* I was not the central character. In other books, in short stories, in poems, so forth, I often have been. I find it easier to attack myself, to be irreverent to myself than to others. I can take it. In *Hollywood* I was mostly the observer of others. And I found these others to be not too uninteresting and sometimes even heroic. And I wrote of them in this manner. Of course, I also found fools, knaves and assholes and I hope that I recorded them as such. But since I didn't have so much of myself to play with as fool's bait, the book might appear to be more balanced and restrained, kinder. I don't mind that as long as the total sum is not dull and I don't think that it is.

[When Schroeder approached you with the challenge to write a screenplay didn't you feel you had to study the form before doing it?]

Not at all. To study screenwriting seemed repulsive to me and I think that it would have taken away some of my natural impulses, my instincts. I prefer the rough to the polished.

[What do you read and who do you like most?]

I no longer read. Everything falls from my hand. I once read almost everything. My influences are Dostoevski, Nietzsche, Schopenhauer, Hamsun, Céline, Jeffers, Hemingway, Sherwood Anderson, Gorky, Turgenev, Fante, the very early Saroyan, and a few more others that I can't think of right now.

[What made you want to become a writer?]

If I knew this then I probably would no longer be able to write.

[You started writing early but became a writer after you were 40; what do you think of this new generation of writers who become famous in their 20s? Have you read any of them?]

I am afraid that I haven't read any of the new writers. I am sure that many of them are quite good. Or that at least some of them will be quite good for a little while. But the ability to *go on* turning out first rate work doesn't come to very many, old or new.

[Did it take a lot of guts to quit your post office job to be a full time writer?]

No. You see, at the age of 50 I was approached by the editor-publisher of Black Sparrow Press who told me he would give me $100 a month for life if I quit the post office and, then, even if I failed to produce any good work that the checks would keep coming. Backed by a faith like that it didn't take all that much guts to quit a job that was slowly killing me, mind and body.

[You say in your book that you like Norman Mailer because he is the last of the macho writers, but you seem to have quite a democratic and appreciative relation with your wife. What's your attitude toward women?]

My attitude toward women is the same as my attitude toward men: it comes down to the individual involved.

[You write mostly autobiographically: isn't it very narcissistic to think that people can be interested in your life? Don't you have any interest in imagining different situations?]

I can write more truly of myself than of anybody that I know. It's great source material. I've lived some strange and wild years, days, nights, moments … Some of them have been brave and humorous. Others have been something else. I have been told by quite a number of people that by reading of the hells that I have been through that it has made it easier for them to go on.

And, of course, I have an interest in imagining different situations and I have done so in some of my short stories, poems and even in some of my novels.

136

[Do you know who are your readers? You said once you were pleased many inmates liked your novels ...]

Yes, men in jails have written me that they liked my work. One of them wrote me, "Yours are the only books that pass from cell to cell." This, to me, is the highest praise. Who needs the university critics?

I went to visit a person in the madhouse once. I was recognized by one of the inmates. "You're Charles Bukowski, aren't you?" he asked. He had read my books. Perhaps that was why he was in the madhouse.

[You certainly know that the Italians like your writing very much, while the Americans don't have the same enthusiasm: do you know why?]

I would have to say that the Americans are now showing more enthusiasm over my work. Things have fairly evened out between countries. The bloody royalty checks show this. Why it took the Americans a little longer to get on to me, I'm not quite sure. I don't think about such things.

[You write in the company of wine and classical music: why not jazz or rock and how much wine do you need for inspiration?]

Jazz and rock simply do not lift me to the extent that classical music does. There's more of the edge of centuries in classical music. There's more blood, more style. It's just up and out and gone. Jazz just jerks around. Rock music is more sound and pretense than an actual and venturesome entrance into the grand gamble.

I drink wine slowly as I type. It may take me two hours to drink a bottle of wine. Good work only continues to about a bottle and a half. After that I am like any other old drunk in a bar: a repetitive and boring fool.

[You write that alcohol, horses and your typewriter are your ways to escape reality: what's so terrible for you about reality? What hurted [sic] you so much that you now want to avoid as many people as possible?]

Reality can be pretty terrible for any of us. Most people's lives are not very happy lives. Most lives are lives carried on without much reason. Or they borrow reason from sources and places and institutions. There are very few individual and natural souls.

I am a loner. I mostly avoid people because their concerns are often limited and petty and they tend to be mean-natured and hardly interesting at all. Animals, on the other hand, are fine creatures. Note the beauty of their eyes and their movements. Humans hardly look and act as well, or as truly.

[And if you want to escape reality why most of your works are autobiographical?]

Why are most of my works autobiographical? Why do I put my own shoes on in the morning instead of somebody else's? Why do I dream my dreams instead of my neighbor's? I only want to escape *common* reality that is distorted by false needs. My reality is not your reality. There is nothing wrong with life because there is nothing else we can compare it to. It is only what people do in life and against life that is distasteful.

[Drinking has ruined the careers of a number of American writers (O'Neill, Faulkner, Hemingway, London): are you worried about meeting the same end? Have you ever thought about quitting?]

I am not at all sure that drinking ruined the careers of the writers you mention. Maybe something else destroyed their careers. So many things can destroy a writer. They can be large things or just a series of small things. Or things that we know nothing of. The source of creativity is very mysterious. We know nothing of it.

138

No, I have never thought about stopping drinking. I have found it to be a pleasurable and sensible and creative function. I am almost 70 years old and have drunk more booze than most people have water.

[Is Hector Blackford Paul Verhoeven? And what happened anyway to his project to film *Women?*]

Hector Blackford is not Paul Verhoeven. On *Women*, Paul Verhoeven keeps on buying new options. He may finally do it or maybe somebody else will.

[You certainly saw the movie that Marco Ferreri made from your book *Stories of Ordinary Madness*: what do you think of it? After these experiences with movies will you be involved again in any others?]

I didn't like the movie made from *Tales of Ordinary Madness*. It was all out of focus. I hardly recognized it as something taken from my works. The whole thing was just dumb.

I stay away from the movie world as much as possible. I don't like movies, I seldom go to them. You talk about drink. Now the movie world is what *kills writers*.

[Has fame changed your life?]

If I have fame, it hasn't changed my life. I do the same things I have always done. If a man has fame he must tear it from him like a mad dog at his throat. He must simply continue his work. That is the joy and the miracle, the good sun, the singing in the gut.

[What do you look forward to?]

I look forward to the next piece of paper in my typewriter, the sound of the keys, the radio on to the classical music, that fine bottle of wine to my left, red and wondrous. What could be better? What could be luckier? Nothing could. It's everything.

[To William Packard]
February 26, 1990

Got the latest *NYQ* today, haven't had time to go through it all but it looks like you're still hitting on all cylinders and *congratulations on your big 40!* Like you said, "40 more ..." Will they send me a subscription in hell? I hope so. In 40 years I'll be 110 and burning in water, drowning in flame.

If I were interviewing you I'd ask:[1]

What have you learned in reading all those poems that have come over your transom? Or did you know that already?

Why is it that so many poets can be so explicitly wondrous, at times, on a piece of paper while in actual living, as people, they can be such obnoxiously hateful beings?

Why do poets consider themselves more elevated than the garbage man, the short story writer and the novelist?

Would you name your cat after a poet, even if it ate a goldfish? I mean, the poet.

Why do people go to creative writing classes? Poetry readings? Why do people give poetry readings?

Why does the word "poet" make you feel as if you've slept all night with a penny in your mouth?

Anyhow, and in spite of all, what you've done with 40 issues has to be one of the remarkable feats of our time. That's simply all that there is to it...

Yes, the New Criticism. I remember reading the *Kenyon Review* and the *Sewanee Review* in my starving park bench days, coming into the libraries of the cities with my empty belly and my itch to get the word down and admiring the fine language they tossed about. The critics were tall dark gods of power, telling us where it was at. They made it *seem* something but in reality the more you read the less you felt about it all. They talked a strong poetry game but when you looked at the poesy published in the same issues you wondered where it was. The

---

1. Issue no. 40 of the *New York Quarterly* contained a Craft Interview with the editor, William Packard by Dion Pincus. It included a hostile account of the New Criticism.

stuff was light, bland air. Puffed wheat. Finally I got the strange feeling that these fellows were just hiding out at the universities, soft and safe, shooting their polished darts. I wanted blood and song and dancing girls—on the page. I was starving for my ideals and just getting thinner to the bone. Down to no typewriter, just pages of Allen Tate and John the Crow and C. Brooks and the heavy dull thunder of some of the other boys. That's all I had, those pages and I couldn't eat them. Then their game went further, if I remember. The New Criticism was replaced by the *New New Criticism*. I dropped out there and followed my own nose which led me to further rejection and horror. The gods just didn't want to embrace me. The gods know what happens to people who are embraced too often and too early. See D. Thomas. See countless thousands. Anyway, I babble.

Again, happy 40th! Tyson is gone, you're still there! Bravo, indeed!

[To William Packard]
March 12, 1990

Hello Wm Packard:

Even the "new Bukowski" understands the nature of spoof and the ridiculousness of all. Slices of the Buddha remain embedded.

I am honored that you read parts of my letter to the poetry-blowers at the gathering but it will do little to change their need to prance for smatterings of applause. Weakness is weakness. You can oil it, spit on it, laugh at it, tutor it, but it remains.

And you're going to catch a lot of manure, attempting to ram Bukowski down the minds of that special breed. If, like me, you came up from the other side of the tracks, they put a special mark on you. And if you drink and are not particularly open to various overtures and invitations, that makes you a dog. Also, if you write in a style that almost anybody can understand that means that you must be pretty fucking dumb.

141

Also, I am anti-university although I went to a city college for two years. I feel that those greenswards breed softness and alliance with like rather than teaching one the basic reality of where life is really at. I've seen the bright stars on campus and I've told some of them, "Sweetheart, when you hit the streets it's all over for you."

What I'm saying here is that I've never played the game-game and it's really resented in some parts. One almost major poet was found out. He was at dinner with a lady who arranged poetry readings. He told her, "Don't let Bukowski read, he is a terrible man." Not that I would have read anyhow. And I am a terrible man. At the age of 70, if I run into him I'll knock him on his ass.

There are other stories that I won't land on you. The stories don't matter anyhow. I wrote for 15 years while starving to death and not having any luck and I still wrote because it came out and because it wanted to come out and because it was the only thing I wanted to do. Women be damned, automobiles be damned, telephones be damned, all I wanted to see was a sentence running across a piece of paper. I still feel that way. And I read what was being printed then and I didn't like it and I read what is being printed now and I don't like it. And I read the stuff that has lasted the centuries and I think, what the hell is this? Is it some giant hoax? Where is the life? Where is the fire? What has *this* got to do with anything?

Anyhow, like I said, you better be careful reading a Bukowski letter to the poetry-blowers. It joggles their sheaths of armor. They'll run bleating to their mothers and their uncles and their municipal judges and their bank clerks and their ministers of finance and the makers of their safe and buttered dreams. Protect yourself at all times. Look both ways after you open your doors. And if some sweet thing says, "Bukowski sent me," beware, she'll have a bomb in her purse which she will attempt to slide between your buttocks during love-making. You have been warned. And remember: *scribendi recte sapere est et principium et fons.*[1]

---

1. Horace, *The Art of Poetry*, line 309: "Wisdom (or knowledge) is both the beginning and the fountainhead of good writing."

[To William Packard]
March 23, 1990

Of course, it you would care to use my letter of 3-12-90 in a future *NYQ*, that's good, good.[1] Like I say often about other things, I am honored. Once more. But if you have other thoughts and in time don't care to run the letter, I will not bridle you with sundry and unsavory accusations. Me, I have changed my mind a few times, even. Especially about the female.

Lo, there is a danger in running a letter of this sorts. You will hear from other *poets*, letter-wise, how they too struggled in the murky and unkind waters, a very running sewer of impossible opposition: how their mothers kept them in diapers until age 4 and how they wanted to go to Harvard but instead had to settle for Stanford and how their sex operations were botched and they have tits for balls and the other way around, and etc.

You have been warned.

Sometimes I wish Ezra were still around to slap the shit out of these fondants.

Ow, you know, sometimes just words and paper don't seem enough, that's where the drinking comes in, it's like trying to crack through the walls. I tried painting once, painting and drinking. I was smoking cigars and drinking whiskey and I painted out of the tubes, thick fat reams of color. I was in an Art class once because my first wife dragged me there. The instructor held one of my paintings up and said, "Now here is a man who is not afraid of color." But that's all he said. Anyhow, the paint got on my hands and on the cigars as I drank and listened to the music and I got paint in my mouth from the cigars, and talk about being *sick* in the morning .... ah. Anyhow, I made 50 to 75 paintings and I stuck them up on the walls one by one (it took me maybe a week to do this) and I ran out of space on the walls and hung the paintings on the ceilings. So one night I went to a bar and picked up a lady and brought her

---

1. The letter was printed in facsimile in issue no. 42, Summer 1990.

to my place. I opened the door, she walked in, looked around and said, "Holy shit!" "You like them?" I asked. *"I'm getting the hell out of here!"* she screamed and ran off into the night. A couple of nights later I took all the paintings and put them in a bathtub full of hot water. Then I took them out and painted over them. In the morning I looked at everything and threw the mass of it, totally, into the trashcans out back. And went back to writing the dirty story.

Who cares?

I must be sick. Yes, run the letter if you want, now I'm going back to the good old poem-form tonight. Like they used to say when I was a kid, "See you at the circus." The circus is still here ...

[To Paul Peditto]
April 19, 1990

You're going to think me a prick. But I've seen far too many people lately. All sorts and for all reasons—except my own. I'm giving myself a break and not seeing anybody for some time. No reflect on you, babe. Various people want to see me at least a couple of times a week and some of them get pretty fucking persistent. Some I have to block at my very door. Lots of odd horror stories. What I don't want you to think is that *you* are being singled out. You're not.

Yes, Pinter does some strange work. You have to be in the mood for him.

On punching out critics, no don't do it, unless you do it in play-form. It's all viewpoint, you know. And most viewpoints are pretty damned standard-form. And how does one become a critic? You know somebody in power who gives you the job.

Sure, the fix is in. Always has been. But if you've got writing on the brain and mixed in with your shit, you're going to go on with it because that's all there is and the success of fools and jackoffs is just going to sharpen your line and your style.

I don't know about plays but I do know that you need

144

actors and that's the bad part. Those vain prissies. I don't like the way they talk, the way they look, the way they walk. I don't like their eyes or their clothes or their shoes or the way they breathe. They dehumanize and devitalize the best of lines. I wish monkeys talked. There would be a better chance.

Well, all we gotta do is die. And after living, that's a break.

7 come eleven,

Buk

Bukowski is responding to an expanded book-length version of Foy's The Second World War and its Aftermath.

[To Patrick Foy]
May 31, 1990

Thank you for sending me your *The Unauthorized World Situation Report.* I am into something of my own right now, about a week's worth and then I'll get into reading what you sent. Great, that you have expanded on *WWII and its Aftermath.* I peeked into the beginning, read a few pages and it sounds right there. I look forward to reading the whole thing, as I say, in about a week. Will let you know. But I already know, ahead of time, that it's a fine work because I know where you're headed and what you are talking about.

It takes quite some courage to do what you have done. You are going to meet incredible opposition and also some hatred from those who are unable to face up to what really occurred because it will mean that their lives, their ideas were wasted; it will mean that they took and swallowed the obvious bait and there is no way that they will ever admit that they were that dumb. And they are too dumb and fear-filled to get smart.

Again, congratulations on your courage.

[To William Packard]
June 11, 1990

Coming off too many visits from people I really didn't want to see. Well, there were a couple ... not too bad ... but all in all, too many people, sitting on the couch saying words. Looks like I'm going to have to get mean again and just shut all the fuckers out. I drink so I can stand them and have been sick for a couple of days. It's my own fault if I let the world chew me up.

Anyhow, I'm glad the I got the two poems past you— "Poetry Contest" and "The National Endowment for the Farts." Great.

The only time drinking is good is when I'm getting lucky at this machine.

I hope your production company works out. I don't know which is harder to take, actors or writers. I think the writers are harder to take when they're not writing and the actors are harder to take when they are acting.

Anyhow, you are on a great energy kick and I look for you to make it all around unless there is some crazy woman or women to chew holes in your time and your mind-frame.

I am still trying to set things right around here after the invasion of the hordes ... Almost every day I get a letter something like this: "I am going to be in L.A. at the end of the month and I thought I might drop by ..." They all have some angles: projects, interviews and the sundry. And it's all nothingness.

These people are lonely, depraved and not the least bit interesting.

Always remember, be kind to yourself first.

[To John Martin]
June 29, 1990

Thanks so much for the great box of *Stew*! My bookcase once again sparkles with the luck.

I still can't help looking back again to that shack in Atlanta, that was truly bottom, freezing and starving, the oil lamp gone out and me writing words upon the edges of dirty newspapers on the floor with a pencil stub. All the other rooms and no rooms, the used women, the used me. All the roominghouses, locked behind a door, 5 cents for food, a Payday candy bar. No steak more glorious than a small nibble at that. And the rejects from the *New Yorker* and the *Atlantic Monthly* and *Harper's Bazaar*. Those lovely snob pages. I read them over and over again in the public libraries, these famous writers and my eyes dug into the print and I wondered what it was. It seemed nothing, a trick. I felt no anger. I did think of killing myself and I worked at it, came close. But I didn't give it the total effort, thought maybe the booze or some big bastard in a back alley might help me to it.

Now I've had some luck and that's good, I mean if I had to choose between good luck and bad, I'm only human. I now drive a car that starts every time I get into it and I live in a large house and sometimes outside, people recognize me. That's just crap in the wind, that is what sometimes happens. I'm still a freak, all I want to do is get the line down on paper. I've always had this desperate screw in my brain. It's there.

And let that be the end of celebration and the continuance of continuance. Poems enclosed again. And again and again. Until the finish line takes me. Until, until, until.

What a joyous battle, what a fist into the eye of death. This machine I sit at. Rolling sevens. It's all there is.

[To Gerald Locklin]
July 1, 1990

Thanks for sending *The Conference*.[1] It reads well and I enjoyed it. But like you said, some ain't gonna like it. The putzies always seem to get their hair rubbed the wrong way.

---

1. Gerald Locklin, *The Conference* (Felton, CA: Minotaur Press), 1990.

147

You did some drinking, ah. Congratulations. On a drinker, if he can quit before 4 a.m. and sleep until noon, he will make it. You've got to have until 12 p.m. If you get up one minute before 12 noon, you'll die.

I remember once, so long ago, when I was scrabbling for pennies, I signed a contract that I would appear, the next morning after the reading, at eleven a.m. at this English class. It was somewhere in Oregon or Washington. I just stood in front of them, looking at all those even white faces, nary a ripple upon the lake of all of them and I asked them, petulantly, I'm afraid: "Jesus, hasn't anybody here ever had a hangover?" They were silent, the prof was silent, the sweat ran down my palms and spiders were spinning webs in my throat. The fuckers extolled their price and their price was cheap. anyhow ...

So you knew how to get through a conference. I loved your little conversation with the black activist or whatever he was. What they will never realize is that we are less racist than almost anybody or thing. What we don't like is hearing the same old obvious things. Especially from men or women who are failing at *something* and are constantly, agonizingly, angry about it. Fucked-up humans like to blame what they can't do on anything but themselves, their lack of talent, generousness, or just plain simple humanity.

Anyhow, thanks for the book ... [* * *]

[To the editors of *Moment*]
July 7, 1990

Of course, the last Moment is something we all have to face ...

You will be missed. You played it loose and with a certain lack of self-importance, something that I would call style, and style counts, I think. Good game, good show, and you got to meet a lot of *poets* in person, you poor piss-shits. ah. Well, you might have learned a secret: there's often much difference between what a person writes and what he (or she) is. That's a hard lesson but once learned, a good one.

Your offers of $$$$ for poem and drawing is gracious, but if what I have sent you works for you, forget the $$$$, buy yourself a batch of good booze. I am driving a 1989 Acura Legend and if I took $$$ from you when you are upon hard times, what sense would that make?

I've had a good crazy painful lucky life but if I have any regrets it's that we haven't had a good new and explosive voice in poetry for decades. It seems that between world war one and world war two we had new wild spring-ups of style and manner and gamble in poetry but that after world war two, everything just dwindled off and away and it has stayed that way.

The new geniuses are the dull whispers of nowhere.

So? So, well, hell, the starting gate is still there ...

[To John Martin]
early September, 1990

Well, the war's out there, the bomb's out there, everything's out there and there isn't much we can do. One big flash can solve it. If not, the national debt can just about destroy the economy. Nowadays nations fall apart over night. I really have to almost laugh when I look back at those who called themselves the *lost generation.* All those poor idiots were moaning about were ants in the picnic basket.

Yet I can't feel silly about sitting at this machine and typing out lines. I may be foolish at times but I don't think I am the fool. The fool comes in a bigger bundle, ever righteous about misconceptions.

It all could have been so much better. We just pissed it away. We were good at technical knowledge and we stopped there. Maybe there isn't an answer. Maybe there wasn't supposed to be.

149

There's time yet but for what? Minor adjustments. The major ones have gone by us. I feel strangely like I did when I sat on that same barstool for 5 years cadging drinks. We can only make slight moves within the fix. But never to quit within this darkness. We are still here. The slightest dent against impossibility is the miracle. That is why as these keys bite against this paper, I even feel good. Joy is not gone even in the face of reality. A good poem, like a good drink, is still worth something, like a cat walking across the floor toward you, both of you feeling and knowing the shining of yes.

[To the editors of *Moment*]
September 6, 1990

Thanks, surely, for the *great* bottle of wine for my 70th and my wedding anniversary. Linda no longer drinks wine so I took care of it. Four lucky poems in that bottle.

I still make the racetrack. It gets pretty damned dull out there but I can't think of any place else to go. If I ever get too senile to drive I guess I'll have to stay home. I've got a plan for when that happens—if it happens. I'll just lock the door and smear paints on paper all day. At night out will come the bottle and the poems.

If I've learned anything through the years it's that people don't change very much. Of course, that's bad news. Of course, of course.

And they kill faster now and with less reason.

Looking back, I'd have to guess that the best group of the decades was the group of the 30's. People talked less then but when they spoke it was fairly direct and honest. Well, that's enough of that.

Thanks again for the very good tasting vino. You give good Moments.

[To William Packard]
September 16, 1990

Luck with your autobio, sometimes that mirror flashes back strange signals. As per family, I've always said that the family is the last hiding place of the ultimate fool. Your own family is a total house of horrors, then marry somebody's daughter and here comes a whole new swarm of nightmare creatures. And under some strange code of humanity these are always supposed to be welcome through your door. And you end up forced to consort with people that you would never seek out under normal conditions. Just another hell on earth.

Thanks for the *NYQ* editorial #43. You're right, I got most of the baseball questions, although I detest the game. There are too many long moments of nothingness and I can get that on my own without watching others. On the modern writers, question #19, "style is the answer to everything," I liked that one. Sounds like somebody has got his foot a little bit into the door.

I am lost in the daytime now, major tracks closed, nearest track miles away, a hot long drive to get to ferris wheels, 2nd rate jocks and people walking about blinking their eyes and their lives away. I take comfort in my approaching death so long as none of these follow me.

When my wife goes out to get the mail and comes back with an armload, I ask her, "Is there a *New York Quarterly?*" And she always answers, "No, there isn't any *New York Quarterly.*"

So you see, we are always looking for you and yours. There's just not much motion anywhere. I wait for you to put a buzzer to the devil's ass or better yet to God's, if He's there. Hurry up, the tongue of my soul is hanging out.

[To Paul Peditto]
December 7?, 1990

You write a letter like a writer, maybe you ought to save your juices for the creative act? Hell, be selfish. Anyhow, sounds like your whorehouse trek filled in some holes. New York? All front and hard-ass. They like to play at humanity but that's a shield.

You're young, so nothing happening with the people is still a let-down, yeah. Let some decades pass over you and you won't be let down, you'll know the scenario is fixed and the let-down will change to wear-down, like just putting your fucking shoes on each morning is like climbing an icy mountain. Icey? Icy. Icey shot, shit.

People have faces, hands, feet, voices, etc. but it might as well not be there. Once in a while somebody rises up and lights a small flame but that somebody can't keep it going because he's sucked up by the traps—women, money, fames, parties, and worst of all, over self-belief.

Sure I laugh. When I'm alone.

[To John Martin]
December 27, 1990

I find out that more and more people expect to be respected simply because they are there. They've done nothing, are nothing. I mean, one way or the other, they have simply floated on through. And if you don't evince an interest in their carbon copy souls they anger, pout and blame you as the one who is lacking in humanity and heart. It's wearing and it never ceases.

Well, hell, what else is new?

●

152

•1991•

Patrick Foy had sent a letter to the International Herald Tribune, *replying to columns on the Gulf War by A. M. Rosenthal of the* New York Times.

[To Patrick Foy]
January 15, 1991

Fine reply to the Rosenthal bullshit.

If there is a good fight you are fighting it.

Yes, it looks like this country is in for another one. The idiot concepts of our leaders are endless. It all makes me sick straight on through.

Nothing has been learned from the past. Just new bodies, new waste, new hell.

Always a new excuse for a new war. And the family structure, religion and the daily newspapers leading us on in.

Yes, I am sick with it all. It sits in my gut churning, and they go on ahead.

you ... keep going,

plenty best,

[To John Martin]
January 15, 1991

Well, here are a few more. The time will come when I'll no longer be able to type on an electric typer.

Tonight is a strange night. (7 p.m.) I just turned on my radio for some classical music and got a man talking about how we are going to do it. First the bombings via air, then the etc. I look back at all the wars in my life and it's all just so much crap.

I think as far as you and I are concerned, we just have to go on doing what we have been doing. Only better.

[To John Martin]
January 22, 1991 11:41 PM

Well, the electrician hooked up the computer and a small lamp so we're at it again. Not for long, the light is bad but by tomorrow night we should be back to normal, unless there's a last minute screw-up. I'm still getting the feel of this thing but I think all in all, it should make the work luckier. Of course, the computer can't create but I like the look of the line as I go along and I think it all aids in the way the words flow and play around.

We'll see. But so far I feel good about it.

I hope all is going well up there. Dropped in on Either/Or Bookstore, Hermosa Beach. They stock an astonishing display of Bukowski books there. Gave me the old chills. All right,

---

[To Jon Cone]
January 31, 1991 11:59PM

Glad you found the two poems. About the one poem, well, Sandburg got off some nice-sounding lines but he was also somehow somewhat underhanded. What I mean is, I never quite trusted what he said more than how he said it. "The People, Yes" never went down well for me because it never coincided with what I had experienced in my half hundred jobs and the people involved thereof. And now and then, every ten or twenty years or so I'd write a poem about how, I thought this particular Sandburg poem to be a con. But it was always passed over by the editors. And so here I wrote another poem about the matter and you have taken it.[1] Now I can rest on that one. There are two votes in anyhow. That's the great thing about writing: you can keep hammering at it until you finally get it right enough. That is, if you have the nerve and the durability to keep bucking the ingrained backlash. What the hell, what else is there to do? Piss into the darkness. Nicely.

[To John Martin]
February 1, 1991 11:20 PM

Strange day. Came in from track, waved to a kid playing basketball, ran over the mailbox. About that same time a plane crashed at LAX.

Other things here are about the same.

Except the computer still seems like a new toy and I can't stay away from it.

I'm sure it will get to be old stuff after a while and we'll get back to normal.

---

1. The poem is "The People, No," as yet uncollected.

155

You know, I can get an addition to this thing and if you have this other thing up there I can send the stuff up to you at the moment I type it. But we don't need that unless the mails fall apart.

The world gets stranger.

[To John Martin]
February 15, 1991 12:27 AM

Thanks for sending the many copies of *The New Year's Greeting* books with the poem "in the morning/ and at night/ and in between." You're right, I liked it. Some good rolling lines. I'm glad I wrote it.

Things are calm and easy here, for the moment.

I see where Barbet was nominated for the best director group for the upcoming Academy Awards. He has his own office now, plus secretary at Columbia. I hope he steers a good course and doesn't get swallowed up by the bullshit. He should do all right.

And I see where Barbara is having her own Art Show. Great!

The only thing to do for all of us is just to push on and get better. Why not? Let's reach for the sun until it takes us out. Sure.

Oct. 27, 1976

Hello Big John:

here are some more.

not to hex myself but anyhow
I think after Nov. 13
I'll jump into this novel I have in mind::::::
WOMEN.
whether it works or not.

I don't think I'll ever be able to do #the
childhood bit. ⊘yee, maybe when I'm 70
but you know some woman is going to kill me
before I reach 60.

your boy,

5-3-79

Hello John:

Well, here's some more.

your boy,

Lean McHungry

10-25-79

Hello John:

It takes about two weeks to get over one of those readings.
I don't understand how the poets can go on reading, some of them
giving two or three readings a month.... Yes, I know how they
can do it: vanity. And also, lack of energy: when they read
they sound as if they were lisping into teacups.

Back at·the track, trying to forget all that nonsense. I
play the horses like the average man plays chess or maybe like an
extra average man plays chess. I know all the traps, bad plays,
panic plays. I've only had time to attend the meet 6 days, won
5,lost one day. I bet moderately. I've averaged about $90 profit
a day. I suppose if I were a desperate man playing for the rent
and the baby food I would lose. But going to the track, making
my bets, following my knowlege, this teaches me movement. A
cutting through the fog. I can# understand why Hemingway went to
the bullfights. There is death at the track too and there is life
and sometimes victory. All the women I have known have been incensed
with my horseplaying. They think it is very foolish and when they
attend the races with me they become angry because I usually win
and they usually lose. The problem is that they don't put any
effort into the game, they are listless and distracted. And it's
strange that most of them believe in some kind of God. That doesn't
take any effort either. At the track one must overcome a 15 percent
take.

Well, it's been about 20 years since my first book, FLOWER,
FIST AND BESTIAL WAIL was published when I was 40. I think it's
been a good twenty years of creation and I think it's still coming.
And even if it should stop now, I'd feel particularly ####lucky.
And I was lucky when the Sparrow came by and you printed my stuff
when it wasn't particularly literary, you know what I mean. I'm
sure you've heard plenty about it from some quarters. So it's been
a good ####show. Let them rage, let them weep, let them bitch.
o.k.

Poems enclosed.

your boy,

1-17-82

HELLO BIG JOHN —   GENERATION

GOT THE "LAST GENERATION" AFTER
COMING IN FROM THE TRACK. (WON
($ 122). PERHAPS DRUNK NOW.
SIGNED ALL. HOPE TO GET OFF
TO GREY IN MORNING.
        GRAY MORNING.
        IT'S PACKED.
I LOOK FORWARD.
    MEANWHILE, TRYING TO GET
THESE NEW POMES OFF TO
YA.
        THERE IS NEVER ENOUGH
TIME TO DO EVERYTHING,
AND I AM LAZY.
    LISTEN, CAN YOU READ
THIS?
    I'm ALL OUTA SOFT BOUNDS
OF DANGLING,   (FIVE)
    COULD YOU MAIL ME 5.?
SUBTRACT FROM MY TOTAL
COLUMN?
    I LIKED SIGNING "LAST
GENERATION" IT MAY NOT BE
A GREAT STATEMENT BUT
THINK IT'S O.K.,
        YR BOY, Hen

I2-I7-88

Hello John:

I'M NUTS
TONIGHT.

CAN'T
SPELL
THE
WORD.
REFUSE
TO
LOOK
IT
UP.

    Thanks to you and Barbara for the tremendous and healthy and beautiful
Xmas gift!

    Also, it was great to rec. the almost corrected version of HOLLYWOOD,
it looks so fine and I allow myself to feel good, it's a great moral and
morale boost, especially when the fiery winds of full hell are blowing full
blast around here, and it looks like it's going to be continued, around here,
so I might as well adjust and say, that's the way it is, and that's the way
it's going   to be. It's just what the gods have arranged for me,
those fuckers. #b#But, on other counts, they have been very good to me.

    On HOLLYWOOD, of course, there are some errors in there that the eye just
can't see until the printed version comes out, then something just jumps at
you, but that can't be helped. We do what we can.

    Meanwhile, enclosed some poems and a bit somebody asked me to do on Fante.

    Linda's mother coming after Xmas. We should celebrate New Year's
together!! You have a good one.

                        yr boy,

                        Hank

THE

DOGS

OF

HELL

6-29-90

Hello John:

    Thanks so much for the great box of STEW! My bookcase once again sparkles with
the luck.

    I still can't help looking back again to that shack in Atlanta, that was truly
bottom, freezing and starving, the oil lamp gone out and me writing words upon the
edges of dirty newspapers on the floor with a pencil stub. All the other rooms
and no rooms, the used women, the used me. All the roominghouses, locked behind a
door, 5 cents for food, a PAYDAY candybar. No steak more glorious than a small
nibble at that. And the rejects from the New Yorker and the Atlantic Monthly and
Harper's Bazzar. Those lovely snob pages. I read them over and over again in the
public libraries, these famous writers and my eyes dug into the print and I wondered
what it was. It seemed nothing, a trick. I felt no anger. I did think of killing
myself and I worked at it, came close. But I didn't give it the total effort,
thought maybe the booze or some big bastard in a back alley might help me to it.

    Now I've had some luck and that's good, I mean if I had to choose between good
luck and bad, I'm only human. I now drive a car that starts everytime I get into
it and I live in a large house and sometimes outside, people recognize me. That's
just crap in the wind, that is what sometimes happens. I'm still a freak, all I
want to do is get the line down on paper. I've always had this desperate screw in
my brain. It's there.

    And let that be the end of celebration and the continuance of continuance.
Poems enclosed again. And again and again. Until the finish line takes me.
Until, until, until.

    What a joyous battle, what a fist into the eye of death.   This machine I
sit at. Rolling sevens. It's all there is.

                yr boy ,

6/27/91 12:59 AM

Hello John:

Remember when Joyce wrote "Finnegan's Wake," not everybody took to it right off?

Whatever or however, the words are pouring out of me now and I like the action whether it be low level or otherwise.

But being a wise punk, I rather look behind the push that is pushing and I figure that somehow some part of me knows that the whole part of me is going to die very soon and I am playing with these last damned toys to my total enjoyment. Then too, that could be wrong.

I don't care. Shoot the fireworks up.

If Jane were drinking with me now she'd laugh her ass off, as beautiful as it was.

yr boy,

10/13/91 1:20 AM

Hello John:

Thanks for the great note. It's all strange, the older I get the more I seem to explode with words and I believe they are lucky words enjoying themselves. I am aware that everything can shut off in a moment. I don't mean death as death but death in life. I can only run back to centerfield and catch just so many over my shoulder. And I can't say I'll take it kindly when they sit me on the bench. I love the action.

I look behind me and in the bookcase are stacked masses of pages of paper of things that I've written since Jan. 18. It's like a madman was turned loose in here. I know that some of those pages are pretty bad but I like to go with the roll of things and let fly. It's been some interesting year. I keep getting stronger like some beast trying to work out of a cage. I know that death is a stimulant, a kick in the ass. It has something to do with it. But I was always crazy for writing. You and I know the story of freezing and starving in that Atlanta shack. The railroad track gang. All the rotten jobs, the crazy women. The 13 and 1/2 years in the post office. And before that the dozens of small rooms, living on candy bars, getting the word down, thousands of pages returned and thrown away. You know all this. And being a bum and an errand boy in a bar, a punching bag. I can't even believe it. I wanted to write. I was sick with it. I think this is what Neeli missed. The hollow bottom of nowhere. Writing with a pencil stub on the edges of newspapers. While starving, mad. I don't think Neeli could face where I had come from and he wrote around it. He never knew.

This is why it is so strange to me now. I laid down my guts and the gods finally answered. That isn't supposed to happen. And now that it is, I am digging in and swinging from both sides of the plate because it's such a crazy joy, the toteboard flashing the longest odds possible.

Even if it quits now, it's been great, my friends the rats and the roaches will know, and you will know, you had some inkling, you got me out of the post office, you promised a lifetime income whether you were right or wrong. You are a gambler, John, and you met a gambler. And we've jammed through literary walls they said we couldn't. I realize the abuse you took and still take. The literary darlings wanted to be me, not in the manner of creation but in the manner of being recognized. Screw those darlings, we are going into our last years, or I am going into mine, and the fireworks are exploding and the best is even yet to come.

sure,

yr boy,

3-14-93 (HOSPITAL)

Hello John—

Correction on entry in "Letters of the
60's" about Francis Smith (enclosed.)
She has many problems—(one of them
is her need to get close to me)
to go with the old description.
So, let's change it to:

"Francis Smith, mother of my daughter
Marina. We were unmarried."

I think that's better.
Lots of action at this hospital.
Linda is here almost continually.
She's a good girl.
    Some rough days ahead in
chemotherapy.
    You hang in, kid.
            yr boy,
            Hank

The following letter was sent in answer to a series of questions submitted by the editors of Beat *magazine, published in Norway. Here the questions have been interpolated among Bukowski's answers.*

[To the editors of *Beat* magazine]
February 23, 1991 1:18 PM

[*Septuagenarian Stew* was recently published in Scandinavia ... and is doing well ... You've mentioned your liking for Norway's Knut Hamsun ... what drew you to Hamsun's work. Are you familiar with Norway's playwright Henrik Ibsen? The painter Edvard Munch?]

Well, I was a starving writer when I read Hamsun's *Hunger* and so it seemed very real to me. His other works are very strange and very strong, a dark strongness. And the content of each work really varies. It were as if he had lived 100 lives. Ibsen? Well, Ibsen is harder to get into. I had trouble flowing along with him. Don't know the painter, Munch. Great name, though.

[Last time we did this interview ('84) you said there would always be good writers because it was "hard to hold down that thrust." In "Nowhere," a poem in the new book, you say there aren't any new writers to match the old masters ... a loss of "natural force." What does this generation of writers lack?]

Good writing in the U.S. seemed to stop dead when World War II began. Since then we've had half a century of dead writing. Everybody is too practiced, too precise, too lacking in gamble. There's no fire, no excitement. Why? I don't know.

[Did Jeffers, W. C. Williams and John Fante have that thrust ... natural force? Why?]

For me, W. C. Williams was and is overrated. He got off a few good ones. His ideas on how to write were quite fine but the idea seldom resolved into the act.

157

John Fante was a natural force when he was on, which was about half the time. Jeffers? He just laid blood on the paper. Unbelievable.

[You've said in our last interview that Hemingway was much better when you're young. His stuff doesn't hold up as well when you read it at an older age?]

Yes, Hemingway read better to me when I was young. I lacked life experience and he seemed packed with it. After I got to be 40 or 50 I had my own little knapsack filled with my own crap and his stuff didn't read so tough then. Also, he was a crank. No humor at all. Hell is really a laugh sometimes, you know.

[What about the late Raymond Carver? He once wrote a poem about you ... do his stories interest you?]

I met Raymond Carver one time, long ago. We drank all night. In the morning we went out for breakfast and he couldn't eat. I ate his breakfast and mine. I remember him telling me, "I'm going to be famous now. A friend of mine has just been appointed editor of *Esquire* and he's going to publish everything I send him." I never got much out of Carver and still can't quite see what the fuss is all about. Now, you asked, so I told you ...

[In one of your early stories "All the Assholes in the World and Mine," you nearly bled to death in the charity ward of L.A. General hospital. You were warned the next drink would kill you. That must have been over 30 years ago. You're still around, writing at the top of your form and, presumably, taking a few drinks. What's the Bukowski secret of endurance in the ring?]

The secret of endurance is to have so many things bothering your sensibilities that you have no time to think about quitting.

158

[You share a dim view, in the new book, of those who go to A.A. meetings—fake alcoholics. Your drinking seems to, for the most part, [have] worked for you ... enabled you to write and live through the boredom. Drinking seems to have kept depression at bay. Any words about this—or words on a life of drinking at age 71?]

Drinking is another way of thinking, another way of living. It gives you two lives instead of one. Twice as much to write about and two ways to write about it.

[William Carlos Williams once said, in his later years, that it was women that kept him inspired. All kinds of women. What role do women—or a woman—play in your life now in your seventies?]

I'm married now and I suppose that my wife has more to do with keeping me alive than I do.

[It there any real drama left on the American scene? In the boxing ring? At the race track? At the movies? In the bars?]

The bars are finished. TV took care of that. We used to be the performers. Now everybody sits and stares at the tube. Yes, the boxing matches are one of the last places of drama left. The racetrack is dead. I go there. And I study death. The movies? Unbearably bad, even the best ones. [* * *]

[To William Packard]
March 3, 1991 1:37 AM

I was just clowning, I'm sure you know. A computer is nothing but an instrument. It has no idea how to write a poem, a novel, etc. And most people with computers are at a hazard, most computer people have been gulped away by something awful. I resisted a computer for a long time for fear of going with this death gang. In fact, I didn't get the computer myself. It was an Xmas gift. Blame Santa Claus. [* * *]

On those darlings who worry because accepted work has not been published, these are the professional word-pushers. They ache more badly to make it than they do to get the next word down. They are not mad, glad or stricken enough. They are soft farts in a dead wind. Regard these as a giant nowhere. Then forget them.

[To Clive Cardiff]
March 8, 1991 11:33 PM

Thanks for the 20, it will be angled toward an excellent libation. The better the stuff, the less the hang over. I don't have any photos I can find right off. I don't like cameras. Not so much the camera as who is standing behind, with it. Photos, poetry readings, groupies, door-knockers, other writers, car salesmen, world leaders, joggers, professors, possessors, processors, presidents and betting to place is just so much dung with and on top of the dung. Ah, what blather—a rip-tide of wordage. Forgive me. All I had to say was, I don't have a fucking photo.

I know what you mean about a writer saving your ass. There was this fellow, Céline, *Journey* ... I read the novel straight through, actually laughing out loud. He lent me some guts to go on with. It's like a blast of roaring light ripping right through you. Afterwards you walk across the floor a little differently. The walls look better, the shades, even the toilet looks better, every thing—you are lent the courage and the laughter. The drinks taste better, you notice your hands, your shoe laces. Céline, the dog, he bit me back to life. Of course, there there were others but I remember that time best.

Yeah, jobs, just for the rent and some food in your belly so you can come back and let them rape your hours, your life, you. Then after the job you have to sleep, there's transport,

160

shopping, bills, laundry, automobile break downs, health break-downs and the hundreds of trivia and minute things you are forced to do just to slide along, barely existing. I figured out once, that in 24 hours a man had only 20 minutes of pure free time to play with. (I was working 11 and 12 hours a night at the time.)

For me, drink saved me from madness. It allowed me to evolve into another form, another feeling. It was the only friend I had. Sobriety was the evil.

And what was the most unbearable was how the other workers quit the light. Gave in. Went with it. Zeroed. I remember a guy sitting next to me once. He said, "Well, at least we get our 3 squares. That's important."

It passed through my mind that I should murder him but I let it go.

I began to barely have a little luck with my writing when I was 50. But even if I hadn't, I would have gone on. I had to. I still have to. The world and the people of the world are still here and they are a hard take. I'm 70 now. It doesn't matter. I could be 30 or 90. I get it off with the word. Shit-sackfuls of words. No woman so glorious, no luck as great.

You keep it going. Chop through the pages with gamble and fire. Death is nothing, you can beat him every day until the final day. He will know that you were there.

Maxwell Gaddis was editor of The Nihilistic Review *from Sioux City, Nebraska.*

[To Maxwell Gaddis]
March 23, 1991 11:1 3 PM

I could be unappreciative and self-centered but a "cock-sucker," I ain't. (See your last letter or your grandma's dirty underwear). But, I took a second sighting on your babbling and figured, in manner or speech, you were just coming on as a so-called tough to impress me. I am not impressed. It's a dangerous word, baby, that one, and if you use it against somebody standing in the same room with you there is a good chance you are going to get your lights turned out. So be careful. Unless you are a black belt man. Then still be careful—anybody can be had.

On your calendar and letter, I might have gotten them. I just didn't jump through the hoop, lala. I get lots of calendars and letters, and manuscripts, and photos of parts of women's bodies. I get threats, I get praise, I get dullness, I get garlands of self-pity, I get a mass and a mess of stuff. I can't respond to all these. I can't smooth and soothe all these, I can't flagellate them. There's not enough of me. I get toothaches, flat tires, the falling shit of darkness, etc., just like anybody else. Please understand, I am an isolationist but not a prick. Well, not always a prick.

You asked for something. It is a poem (enclosed). If you don't like it it means that your balls are tangled in your shorts and it's cutting off the blood supply to your brain. S.E.A. enclosed for your usage. And, of course, if you do like the poem it means that you are a fine fellow, acute, and riveted to the flow of the gods.

The Nihilistic Review, eh?

Can you back that?

I don't use calendars. I just ask somebody, is this March or mayhem ?

There may be flies on some of you guys but there's vultures on me.

John Martin came across a copy of an early letter from Jon Webb, who was to publish two books by Bukowski in the 1960s. Martin sent Webb's letter to Bukowski and it is printed here, along with Bukowski's interesting response.

[To John Martin]
[March 25, 1991 8:08 PM]

THIS LETTER IS NOT A PLEA FOR PUBLICITY
PLEASE READ IT, AS WE'RE DESPERATE

Jon Edgar Webb
11 Abingdon Square
New York 14, N.Y.
Feb. 23, 1947

Dear Mr. Winchell:

My wife and I are stranded without a cent in a rooming-house in the Village and we may be evicted by the time you get this, but please let me make it clear at once we are not writing this to ask you for money. Our hope is that you may know of someone who would be willing to gamble on the security I have to offer.

I have a novel scheduled to come out in May, this year, through Dial Press Inc. Our home town has been New Orleans for a number of years and that is where we came from in December. The book was completed there that month, but I was called to New York by the publishers to make some revisions.

On arriving here I learned the revisions were considerable, partly because of the Hearst campaign against "indecency" in literature, and partly because I had gone off the deep end into a too-honest book. I enclose a copy of the book's announcement now in the Dial Press Spring Catalogue. You will see by it that I am a former prison inmate. (I got in a jam 15 years ago while a reporter on the *Cleveland News* and served 3 years in the Ohio State Reformatory, during which time I was editor of the prison paper.)

Well, I got busy making the revisions, meanwhile

getting some extra advance from Dial beyond the $500 my contract called for. (Got the $500 last year when I got the contract, in January.) I worked on revisions for six weeks, only to discover in the end I could not possibly revise the copy as was, in the last third on which the revisions were being made, without getting into a sensational, typically corny prison novel. So I junked the last third of the book and, with that move I lost out on spring publication. The book now cannot come out until early fall.

I have three months work to do on it, in the direction it must go in now, and until two weeks ago had no worry about the money problem. There was someone we knew who was going to loan us enough to keep going until the book was done, but very foolishly we let that person see a copy of the book's announcement in which I am described as a former prison inmate. The patron at once withdrew, and then began our troubles. After working a few years on a book we had already had help from every possible source. Most of our friends, anyway, are poor writers and artists. (Not bohemians.) Dial had given me a total of $250 more than the contract called for until the book was completed and in, and that was their limit. So ten days ago we began living on coffee and bread, our only food since.

We have tried our best to borrow. No luck. Before coming here we'd raised money by pawning or selling what petty jewelry we had, my best suits, phonograph, radio, etc. We have nothing to pawn now. I haven't even a suit for a job of any sort. Besides it's not easy to get one in my profession with a record—though it was only one offense. (Got into the jam while drunk, and have touched whiskey only twice since.)

The help I hope from you is that you might know someone who would be willing to loan me some money with the book as security, or on a percentage of royalties. Dial plans to push the book to the limit, though I will not say it will make any money as I refuse to write it sensationally. There are no machine guns in the book, no riot, no mass break, no typical cop lingo, nothing off the regular prison beat of monotony, etc. Nor is it bitter, as the blurb hints. I leave spouting of brutalities to the hacks. Nonetheless, it tells a story.

164

Or you may know someone who has a place they're not living in right now and could use a caretaker. I'd do that, anything so that I could write during the next three months and get this job done. My wife knows I could turn this thing into a piece of book-club crap, but she's with me on my decision not to. If it makes a book club we'll be amazed, though Dial Press say it might make Book Find.

However, here we are, broke, a little dizzy and weak from no eating, a thousand miles from home, and expecting eviction any moment. Please try to do something for us, will you? You may check up on me at Dial, though I would be grateful if you did not embarrass me too much. They've been swell to me, especially on my not revising for spring deadline with the book scheduled. And they've gone their limit on dough for the moment. My situation is not their fault, nor anyone's except my own. The book will bring in at least several thousand dollars, so anyone who helps us out can't possibly lose. I will sign necessary papers assuring them of first claim on royalties, or from the advance coming upon completion of the book, plus a percentage. Editor at Dial is Mr. George Joel.

We have a hall phone here, four flights down, so in case (miraculously) you want to contact me at once the number is Chelsea 3-9714.

Sincerely,

Am not just a former prison inmate writing a biographical book. Am a writer outside of that, with many short stories published.

Also, please don't confuse Dial Press with smaller publishers using the name Dial. They are a big house, publishers of *The Foxes of Harrow* and *David the King* and many other best sellers and they usually accept a book that has a pretty good chance, though sometimes they accept one on its literary merits alone, hoping the writer in his next book will write a money-maker.

From: DIAL PRESS BOOKS SPRING 1947
A Novel of Prison Life—by a Former Inmate
The Glass House

A Novel by
JON EDGAR WEBB

The author of this penetrating novel of prison life is himself a former prison inmate. Writing from bitter personal experience, he has told the story of John Ditto, the convicted murderer, who became the official czar of the prisoners.

Through the eyes of John Ditto the reader is shown the day by day life of the prisoners. Ditto, as editor of the inmates' newspaper, has been given exceptional privileges, and he is free to move around as he pleases. Only one thing is denied him—actual freedom. Time and again he listens to the plans being formulated by prisoners who are considering making a break, but he will have none of it. He feels that by using his influence plus that of the chaplain, who has befriended him, eventually he will be paroled. Only one thing hinders him in his plan—his wife, on one of her visits to the prison has been permitted to be alone with him and as a result, she has had a child.

This is a grim book, it is true, but its vignettes of prison life, of solitary confinement, of the mental breakdown of the prisoners, of the brutality and venality of the prison system have been rendered with a freshness and penetration that will make *The Glass House* widely read and widely discussed.

342 pages May, 1947 $2.75

Thanks for the Webb letter to Walter Winchell.

As you know, Jon Webb put out a great magazine and some great books but he still had a lot of con and bullshit going. He was always crying wolf. And he felt that as a writer and editor he deserved monetary support from anywhere and everywhere. I have met many others in the field who felt the same way, in fact, most of them do. For them to get an ordinary job and to live in an ordinary way was an impossibility. As Artists, they deserved support, they had a direct line with the gods. I think Henry Miller had much to do with this attitude. Early in his career he squeezed the juices out of many patrons, and, in a sense, demanded it. Of course, Miller was preceded by others

166

and followed by others. I always felt it was easier to get a job than to hold out the hand. After all, maybe you weren't a genius. Maybe you just thought you were a genius. (God or the devil or something knows that there are enough of those.)

The Webbs were always hit by fire, flood, robbery, so forth. There was always a new horror story. Of course, there is horror in everybody's life. But I know that the Webbs caused many of their own troubles. Louise, especially had a way of getting to hate the city they lived in, she demanded a move elsewhere. And so here would go the heavy press and all the materials, packing off, the dogs too, to some new location. Only to have Louise again hate that new city and off they'd go again, press, dogs and all, often back to the same place they had left. This was expensive. And they had troubles with the rich who became their benefactors and then wanted Loujon Press to publish their own works. Nothing is ever free and it never will be.

In the letter to Winchell, Jon claims he can't get a job because he is an x-con. This is not a truism. I had a record and it was on the books (see Moyamensing). I got dozens of jobs after that. I only lost 2 jobs because of my record. One with Yellow Cab who send out a criminal check on their employees. The other was when I was working as a shipping clerk somewhere and they had to let me go because the Bond Company would not bond me because of my record.

What I am getting at is that many people in the creative world are full of bullshit. This is why I stay away from them.

Now, I am not saying here that Jon Webb was not a great editor-publisher. He published beautiful books for me. But there was a lot of crap and subterfuge going on. To not admit this part of it would not be telling the whole story. The letter to Winchell brought much of this back to me. The long run of sob stories. The handout blues. Of course, I did not accept royalties. But after some time, more and more of the Eternal Tragedy Script really began to get to me and I gradually broke it off with Jon Webb. "Bukowski doesn't write me anymore," he once said, "but Henry Miller still does." Of course, Henry taught him how.

I don't think that The Artist as Beggar is romantic at all.

I prefer some son of a bitch, say, working as a fry cook and

167

getting it done in his lone, clean free hour or two. That's the way to break steel with your bare hands.

hell yes.

[To Henry Hughes]
March 28, 1991 11:28 PM

Whatever happens, I will always remember your seeming particular delight in accepting my poems. You showed a warmth and humanity that I have seldom noticed in the University area of publishing. And your courage in accepting certain poems can't be doubted. You stuck your neck out and maybe your job out to do what you felt should be done. You enjoyed clashing against those stale concepts of literature and life. You showed guts, baby, and they don't like that. They don't like their dusty cobwebs shaken, and deep down, even as limited as they are, even they know that they are charlatans. They don't want to be uncovered. They've grown used to the unchallenged comforts of their drab and deathly ways. There are too many of them in that stinking tribe. They want to kick your ass back somewhere where you won't trouble them. They are strong in their entrenched weakness, they are full of falsity, decay, shit, boredom and fear. Universities are not places of learning to them, they are places of comfort to them, they are the Eternal Ostriches with their heads in the sand. They are turds who teach turdism.

Be proud that you fought against these, no matter the price. You are alive. That's rare, that's rare. Rejoice.

Bruce Woods was editor of The Writer's Digest.

[To Bruce Woods]
April 3, 1991 9:27 PM

Good of you to offer me a column to espouse my views upon what is wrong with poetry today, and, for that matter, throughout the centuries. And lucky for you, I am not accepting. Lucky for you because in a very short time that column would be dragging its ass. It's all right to bitch, now and then, about what you think might be wrong with anything but to continue on about it, especially about the same thing, well, that verges into the area that qualifies you for the shrink's couch. The best way to prove one's point is in the arena itself, that arena being the poem. That's where I work out, for better or verse. Ugh. That's where I work out, take the 8 count and come in for more. I don't think that poetry can be taught, and theory is the playground of the comfortably self-assured. The only way to learn writing is to write and write and write, and want to write so badly that if you don't you'll go mad or rob a bank or drink yourself to death or run your car off a cliff. Writing grabs you, there is no chance to do anything else and there is nothing else to do. All other approaches are useless nonsense. That's all, that's it and that's why it works or doesn't work.

[To Bruce Woods]
April 13, 1991 10:54 PM

Thank you for inviting me to your Poet Circus but I must decline. Why? Why oh why or why? Well, it made me slightly sick to think of doing it, this explication of the workings of a poem, the mechanical outlay and all that. After I write a poem I forget about it. Gladly. The first thing to avoid is preciousness, the second is not to wallow in it. Poetry, most of it, is so dull because it's so practiced. People sometimes corner me and begin to talk about something that I have written and, except in a very vague way, I have no idea of what they are talking about.

You see, when I write a poem I have no idea of what I am doing. The poem writes *me*. There was a poet (I have forgotten his name) who when asked, What "did that poem mean?" answered, "When I wrote that poem only God and myself knew what it meant. Now, only God knows."[1]

I think that you will find many darlings who will happily detail the meanings, ramifications and justifications of a given poem. These are the same ones who love to get up on the boards and warble their works to an audience for that instantaneous applause and adulation. The job of a writer is to write, all else is a nonsense that weakens mind, gut, ability and the natural state of being. Give most poets even a minor touch of fame and like moths they will fly into the flame and burn off to rot.

Is it any wonder that the poets are so drab?
Is it any wonder that nobody wants to read them?
Is it any wonder that there is no wonder to them?
enough, and not enough.

[To Gerald Locklin]
April 17, 1991 9:46 PM

Thanks for the biblio. You've compiled quite a backlog of lively and readable work, to say the least. Thank you.

On *Hank* by Neeli, since you asked, and *this is between you and me*: well, I might be over-touchy but I felt that he sloughed it off. I gave him plenty to work with on tape, hours and hours, and to me it seems he left out most of the wild and strange parts of my life—especially the down and out, starvation and mad areas, the women coming and going, the jails, the drinking episodes of hellish order, the suicide attempts, all the hard and woolly crap. I gave him a run-down of a time in Atlanta when I

---

1. This story is told of Robert Browning and his poem *Sordello* (1840).

170

was living in a tar paper snack, freezing, broke, no water, no light and how I found a pencil stub and wrote words on the margins of dirty newspapers—I had no paper, toilet or otherwise. I recounted for him other scenes of pure dank ultra darkness. But he watered it all down or left it out. Instead he gave space to a couple of meetings and trivial happenings between N. and myself. It's like he took away my balls and left the skimmed milk.

I got a headache trying to read it and finally just couldn't read certain parts. The writing is choppy, doesn't flow, doesn't jump, doesn't laugh; it flips out half-truths and dull inaccuracies. Of course, I haven't told him this. Hell, the book is done. Let it lay. I don't even have a copy. I gave mine away. And he gets things mixed up. He has me "threatening" Linda King with a frying pan. When, in fact, she attacked me in a dark kitchen (I had thought she had left) and I grabbed the pan with both hands, during which time she clawed my face to ribbons. Which happened and was told to him on the tape. There are many other mixed up sections of the book.

Neeli's problem is Neeli. He's got Neeli on the mind. During all the tapings he held the microphone directly at his mouth and boomed the questions at me. Then he'd play the tape back and say, "I can't hear you." Linda, my wife, told him, "Neeli, you are talking directly into the microphone and Hank is sitting 3 feet away. Of course, you can't hear him."

"Oh," Neeli would say, push the mike halfway toward me and begin again. But it would only last a moment and then he'd be gripping the mike and mouthing into it. And he had a hundred photographs, and with an exception or two, chose the most uninteresting. There are even misspellings, one of a cat's name.

Maybe I'm picky but it looks to me like he flattened everything out, diluted it, strung it out in boring scraps of nothingness. He completely missed the horror of the childhood. He mentioned things, but they were just stated as if my viewpoint were a prejudice and that something else really happened.

I could go on and on, Christ. But the mistake was mine in letting him do it. I read the bit he wrote about me in *Whitman's Wild Children* and thought he might give the biography the same slant and run. He was only good for one run. It was a fluke. The fault is mine. I should have been more perceptive. I wasn't. People will read this book and wonder where I went because there is nobody there.

Well, you asked what I thought and there was no other way to answer.

I can't even laugh at this crap. It will certainly give the Bukowski critics plenty of solace.

I'll just have to write my way out of this shit. I should have seen it coming.

[To William Packard]
April 21, 1991 12:55 AM

Glad you found the 3 poems to be all right. On any bio note, please go the fantasy fact route, like "Bukowski prefers frogs to people," and/or etc. Although preferring frogs to people is not too much of a fantasy.

I get from the tone of your letter that you are wearying somewhat of publishing these literary micros, but, you know, for it all, your last issue was your best, many of the pages jumped as I turned them. A delightful roar, William, take a bow and then a drink. Yes. Yes. Yes. Poetry should be exciting, it should upset the grandmothers and make strong men puke. Make the spiders laugh and the sea shit back. Now.

You tell this psychiatrist that if an editorial can "discourage" people from writing then these people aren't writers, they are childlings still clinging to the mother-breast. A good writer is always stronger and weaker than anything about him. And on his strong days he can parlay damned near any obstacle into the miracle of the flailing line across the page. This shrink, like almost all shrinks, needs another shrink. Writers are different, they never need another writer, they'd just as soon kill one.

About being an editor, sometimes I feel like one. I get two or three packets a week containing letter and poem. First they tell me how much my work has meant to them and then they toss in some bit about their wife or their life, how they just lost their jobs at Wells Fargo or McDonald Douglas. I do sympathize with the life horrors that fall upon all of us, but then come the poems. And they are comfortable and flippant and bloodless. I don't know what to do with the poems. I can't save them. I'd have no place to walk around finally. So I trash them. And I somehow feel guilty. But I don't know what else to do. Maybe I should turn them over to this shrink who wrote you about not "discouraging" people from writing. But he'd only charge them a fee. That's always been the funny thing to me: get a person who is crazy or helpless, then charge him a goodly sum of money, which will only make him more crazy and helpless.

Oh. And then I get the Potential Invaders. There are many of these letters but they seem written almost by the same person. It goes like this, after some opening praisology and buttering-up: "... and anyhow, I'm going to be in your town in about two weeks and I thought I'd stop by for a beer. I won't bother you. Really. What's your favorite brand? I'll bring a couple of six-packs ..."

I used to write frantic letters of response, listing in a kindly fashion as possible all the reasons I didn't wish to see them. These didn't work, there was usually a followup letter saying that they understood but were coming by anyhow.

So I began resorting to the simple but steady rejoinder:

NO VISITORS!

This got me results: violent, insulting, rabid letters, rancorous and vengeful pages, and once, even two 8 and 1/2 by 11 pages smeared in shit.

The last fellow was more gentle, he simply said, "Well, you know, I was thinking that when I was interviewed in the future and they asked me, 'Did you ever drop by and have a beer with him?' But since you feel the way you do, I'm simply taking you off of my computer."

Interviewed about what? Here is another fellow who automatically thinks that he will be famous in some future. No chance at all. Fellows who are busy knocking on doors will never be busy cutting through the steel ...

Thanks for the Li Po translation. Sounds good and clear,

173

scratched in granite. What a great wino that lad was.

Well, my head has to be fairly clear for the racetrack tomorrow.

Yes, *The Brothers Karamazov*. I only wish that the brothers weren't divided so exactly into their partitioned selves. The intellectual, the Christ man and the drunkard-scoundrel. It was too pat for me. Of all of F.D.'s works I preferred *Notes from the Underground*.

But, like I said, the racetrack tomorrow. The worst horror show in town and I'm right there with them.

And you've got your poets. Well, it's all horseshit.

hang in, on, and tough,

[To Gerald Locklin]
May 1, 1991 10:06 PM

Have changed my mind. If you care to show the letter I wrote about Neeli bio to somebody, fine, or if you wish to quote from letter for some reason, o.k.

I don't see why I have to hide my feelings in order to protect N. He gave it his best but his best wasn't very good.

Anyhow, if a writer is to be judged, his work is where it should be measured. But, anyhow, we don't write to be judged, we write to get it out of us so we won't do something worse.

At this moment, I am strictly into the poem, have written hundreds since January and they are still popping out of me. A shitty gushing effusion. So many, the problem is where to send. Who knows? See something listed somewhere … try it. I've always been hooked on the "littles" but not so much on who and what they publish.

keep it going,

[To David Reeve]
May 3, 1991 11:55 PM

I seem to be getting more and more mail as I near the lip of the grave, not as much as Richard Geer or is it Greer? Anyhow, I'd rather sleep than get to answering most of it but you were clever—you baited me by making up this sucker Robert Gold and his wife. Never met him. Or his wife. Or did I have lunch with him.

I get a lot of this crap lately. One woman told somebody that she had been married to me for 2 years. Never saw her. I read throwaways and find out that I was at some poetry reading, walking around talking to people and shaking hands. Not me. Somebody else. Another time, I died. This N.E.A. lady stepped off a plane and told these poetry freaks, "Bukowski is dead. Our Rimbaud is dead..." Magazine came out with a page, black border, date of birth, date of death. Lots of women claimed to have fucked me. Well, lots of them have. But those who have don't talk about it much. I'm just not that good. Not many sweaty horse fucks in my bag. I could go on and on. People who claim to be my friends. People who claim they have gotten drunk with me. People who claim they have beaten the shit out of me. Well, there are plenty of those, but those who really have done it know that it's no great thing. Well, I could take a punch but so can a timeclock. People will say anything. About me. Or you. People lie out of their dribbling brains. I don't. That's what's so refreshing about me.

On Henry Hughes, I sent him some porcupine poems but he just picked them up with his bare hands, placed them in the magazine. Took guts to do that on that calm sleeping greensward. I think he just liked the poems and thought, what the hell, I'll just take a chance. I think he's been in trouble ever since. So, he's 25? That's where the guts came from. I don't even know if he's with S.R. anymore or not. You can bet that the powers want his ass out of there. Universities love the sleepwalk they go through. They've got the soft touch going, they don't want it busted up. It's strange, isn't it, that our places of learning are, in the arts anyhow, at least a century behind? I don't want to press Hughes with any more submissions, he's made the good fight, let him breathe a moment.

Oh yeah, Malcolm Lowry, I had trouble with his writing, a bit inbred fancy for me, but I loved his life style. I still drink and I'm still here. Told somebody just yesterday, "I'm afraid to stop drinking or I might get sick."

I don't give poetry readings any more, that was for the rent and survival, plus all the worthy little dolls who thought being a poet meant somebody to go to bed with. Stupid. As soon as I got enough money to make it writing, I dumped the readings and the groupies. I don't have the rock star mentality. I am happiest just being in a room by myself. I needn't hear the applause, I needn't step out of bed and get my feet tangled in the panties. Best thing I liked about the readings were the long air flights, harassing the stewardesses for more drinks, *more drinks!* And flirting with the professors wives after the readings, really turning on the two bit charm, saying daring and philosophical things to them, I was Sartre, Céline and Li Po, all holding the same drink. But that crap pales, loses meaning. You want to get back to carving the word into the page, like you began, where you blasted through the hell of life with your own hell. A writer's job is to write. And it's a joyous wild job. The best.

So, I don't do any more readings. I don't see people. Not many. I keep it down, down, down. When the phone rings, ten times out of eleven its for my wife. I love it. I've made it known that I don't want to be fucked with. I'm 70, but if they come around and persist, I will knock them on their asses.

What am I doing writing you?

All right, listen, stay with your writing. Be your own judge. Slam it down as you want. You can't beat death but you can sure let him know that you were here, fully, giving it the go, blazing, goofy, banging the drums and breaking the furniture, the best show in any town anywhere.

[To David Mills]
May 13, 1991 8:50 PM

I liked your story in *Revolt* but not the way you ended it. [* * *] Even if you feel it, even if you mean it, when you get into moralizing you are begging off. Always stay beyond good evil, just photograph the action and leave the reader on his own. He'll probably come up with something like, coke has no conscience and that you are a son of a bitch. Better always to have the reader believe that you are a son of a bitch. He'll remember you longer. Always better to leave people pissed off, they deserve it. I think. Just be kind to the caterpillar and the moth and the gods will smile at you.

[To William Packard]
May 18, 1991 10:30 PM

[* * *] I know what you mean about the Craft interviews, you might be reaching down into the bottom of the Bards. Too bad Li Po isn't around. He'd give good one, probably quite brief, like, "The saying is in the doing."

I've always been quite surprised how the poets can write long books on what poetry is and what it should do, then sit down and write dead crap. Well, crap is dead, isn't it? Only, it stinks.

Yes, issue #43 was the best, you're going to have to go some to top that one and it's possible that the material is just not available. It's a tenuous game for all. For me too. Like I said once, I think I said once, "You can go to bed being a poet and wake up being nothing at all."

And for you, you might be burning too many candles: teaching, editing, writing books, writing plays. You probably need a space to do nothing at all. Sometimes you have to get on the phone and tell everybody to go to hell, all the women, all the so-called friends, everybody—sweep the boards clean and breathe again. There is nothing quite so pleasurable as doing

177

nothing at all and being aware of that. Pace is a must. The divine secret. One needs solitude, solitude, solitude. Being alone within 4 walls is immortality upon the earth. Yeah.

Me, I hope you keep the *NYQ* going. I'm selfish, you've allowed me to kick around quite freely there. I think it took guts to run "The National Foundation for the Farts." Also, it might help loosen up some writers. It's about time we left the 19th century…. [* * *]

[To the editor of *Explorations*, Juneau, Alaska.]
June 27, 1991 11:41 PM

Thanks for sending *Explorations 1991*. By the way, it's hard for me to believe that it's 1991 and that even that year is half over. I never planned to be writing in front of a computer with the 21st century and my death racing to the wire to see who gets there first. I was once actually a young guy, reading Auden, Spender, Jeffers, e. e. cummings, etc. And trying to drink myself to death. Yet here I am beastly hungover writing to some university in Alaska. There is a wife and 7 cats downstairs and my fingers itch more than ever to get at the keyboard.

Forgive my lateness in responding. A wrong address was attached to the envelope the magazine and your letter arrived in, so there was a delay there, and then again your letter got mislaid within a mass of papers until I found it again tonight. I'm no literary snob, I just got lost in the shuffle of life and my sloppy desk. So? Thank you for inviting me to be a judge of the best that has come along for you. I'm honored but I must duck. I'm into beginning of a novel right now, called *Pulp* and right now it's running hot and I want to stay on it. It's a detective novel which I hope will end all detective novels forever. Of course, it won't. But I've got to go with it anyhow.

It was good to land in your pages.

Maybe the ghost of Jack London trods [*sic*] Glacier Highway.

Thank you again for the invite to judge. But right now I'm a

Los Angeles detective, cigarette dangling, bottle of scotch in my coat pocket.

May the gods of the Word be kind to you and your students.

[To John Martin]
June 27, 1991 12:59AM

Remember when Joyce wrote *Finnegans Wake*, not everybody took to it right off?

Whatever or however, the words are pouring out of me now and I like the action whether it be low level or otherwise.

But being a wise punk, I rather look behind the push that is pushing and I figure that somehow some part of me knows that the whole part of me is going to die very soon and I am playing with these last damned toys to my total enjoyment. Then too, that could be wrong.

I don't care. Shoot the fireworks up.

If Jane were drinking with me now she'd laugh her ass off, as beautiful as it was.

[To John Martin]
June 30, 1991 1:33 PM

Sitting in front of this computer I realize that it's a long way from Atlanta when I wrote with a pencil stub along the edges of old dirty newspapers. The word wanted out of me, it was there, it didn't matter.

I remember one freezing night stepping outside of my shack and looking at the warm lights of the big house of my landlord. I saw his fireplace blazing inside. For a moment my damned soul wanted that, to be that. Damn the word, nobody was reading my Word even when I managed to get it out to those New York and Boston magazines. Those magazines which I

179

read in the libraries and was confused by the seeming dullness and trickery of the writing. I think I was right, the magazines were publishing well-written crap by people who understood the formula. or by one or two fairly good writers who were getting a bit of it down. One was Irwin Shaw, he started well, he was raw and open. Then I noticed that with each of his succeeding stories he began sliding, writing more what *they* wanted instead of what he believed. Some consider this professional writing, I considered it to be a method of eating shit and getting paid for it. One guy who held up was James Thurber. And yet, even with his stuff there was the slightest sheen of comfortable snobbery.

All that went through my mind as I stood in that yard, freezing and starving. I had dedicated myself to the Word and there I was up against the wall. I was an idiot. All I had was this feeling that there was a better way to write than what they were doing. *A Bell for Adano.*[1] Holy Christ, what a horrible novel! And I was without women, without anything and I stood and watched the tall flames in that man's fireplace.

I'm glad I didn't quit. I'm glad I didn't toss it in. I still have the *word*. I work with it, play with it, it consumes me as it did then. I think the gods were playing with me. They still are. I'm going down to the last burning ember. The fire is hot. I have a small smile and the words leap onto the computer screen and I'm as young I was then. There's no vanity attached, no wish for fame, just my guts pumping with the Word, one more, some more, the way I want it, the way it should be. I am laughing with the gods. What a wonderful joke we have! No man on earth is luckier than I. Atlanta, you were glorious! San Pedro, you still are.

---

1. Novel by John Hersey, 1944.

[To the editor of *Explorations*, Juneau, Alaska.]
July 12, 1991 6:25 PM

My wife keeps telling me "Go on, go on, do it." Be a judge, she says. Well, I've been before a few judges of my own. Pleaded guilty, not to what I had done but to all the things I hadn't done. So. all right. if you're still with it, I'll judge the poems, but the reason I hedged off at first was because poems are so difficult for me to like. Poems of the Ages, Poems of now, poems of tomorrow. I'm a crank. The stuff just doesn't go down for me. I always seem to feel an ultimate lack of gamble and I sense the writer attempting to con the reader. Also, I like my serious poems cut through with an edge of madness so that I know that it's coming from the gut. I could go on and on ... I won't.

After finding the best poem or the best of the worst, I might add my thoughts. I don't know, it's all too far away.

So you have your judge, the park bench kid turned gray, We'll see what happens. You asked for it.

[To John Martin]
July 14, 1991 9:29 PM

Just a short chapter [of *Pulp*] here to stay in the ballgame.

What happened was that I wrote two fairly long chapters and then lost them off the computer. But rather than repeat those chapters, I just forgot them and began somewhere else. To have attempted a rewrite would have shot the joy out of it. I'm not here to do hard work.

I think that I now know how I lost the two chapters. But in searching for them, trying to find them again, I erased the whole of the novel that I have written so far. I wanted to put it on a disc. Things happen. I've checked with 2 computer experts so far on how I managed to erase everything. Or how I could get it back? I am now waiting on some word from a Super Computer expert. I doubt he knows.

Anyhow, a computer easily beats a typer in spite of the accidents. You just jump back in and let it roll again. I love this thing. It's a mad, magic fountain.

p.s.—As time goes on, computer errors will decrease to an extent which will be almost non-existent.

[To John Martin]
July 17, 1991

Well, they broke my hitting streak by taking away my computer and now I have to learn to type again. The keyboard went out and the thing has been in the shop for two days and they haven't touched it yet. God knows how long they will take so this is my first practice on the old machine. If I don't get the computer equipment back tomorrow I am going to use this machine. Equipment. So I want you to know that I haven't died, they just took away my favorite bat and I might have to swing from this thing.

God, those guys are slow! I suppose they have a backlog and there's only one mechanic, and so since most repairs are on warranty they take their time. Forgive the typing, the positions on the keys are ever [so] sightly different. Slightly. Jeus, Jesus, I am having a hard tide—time.!!!!!!!!!

Am I giving you a headache? I am practicing on you. Forgive.

Got some poems from an 18 year old kid, who enclosed his photo. I send on to you. The photo. Said he wants to be published by Black Sparrow. But first he is sending the work to me. I read it. Utterly bland and false stuff. These chickadees have no *drive* to write, it's not roaring out of the ears and brains and guts, it's just a dribbling of weak piss. They've been reading their things to their mothers and friends who tell them it's good, of course. Then it comes back from the regular publishers and they don't believe it. So, the next thing they do is to send it to some old writer who has had some luck. They think that the old writer will see something there. The old writer

182

doesn't. And the old writer remembers that he never sent his things to other writers. He sent it out to places where he got his regular printed reject and threw it away and wrote some more. The old writer didn't believe in politics or covering letters or even other old writers who had gotten lucky.

I hate these creampuff boys who've never lived badly enough or well enough or originally enough to have anything to write about.

Understand, I am practicing on how to type again and must write about something.

I didn't send the creampuff's poems on to you nor did I answer anything for his s.a.e. Why tell him he doesn't have it? He won't believe it. And then he'd write about how the old writer really didn't understand.

I get a lot of unsavory mail but somehow this guy gave me a very unpleasant feeling about it all. The photo certainly didn't help. It's all yours now and you have suffered enough as I have practiced on this IBM at your expense.

But, God, it works slow this way! On the computer I'd be on page 9 by now!

I'm a spoiled lucky old writer.

[To John Martin]
August 5, 1991 9:18 PM

Hard to believe but I wrote a chapter 21 and lost it. I have no idea how I did it. It was all there, then I touched something or other, the lines turned blue, the delete key locked and trying to work my way back to a clarity, I hit something wrong and the whole works erased. Trouble was, I felt it was a very good chapter. So, I had to rewrite it from memory and that never works as well as the original but it beats giving up ...

The money keeps coming, strange ... Was I once really in Atlanta, half mad and reaching toward that dangling and frayed light cord? Poor Neeli, he missed all the wild and crazy aspects of my early existence. Even though I told him. The lad led such a protected and sheltered existence that I think his mind subconsciously blocked out what had occurred in mine. He had never gambled with his life and simply didn't understand that aspect. Oh well...

[To Cyril Humphris and Kevin Lygo]
August 9, 1991

I read your script of *Ham on Rye* and liked it. You have certainly stuck close to the book version and that pleases me. It's seldom done that way. Usually the adapter's ego gets in the way and the screenplay hardly resembles the book it was taken from. You've allowed the book to transform into the script without diluting it in any manner. This shows that you respect what I have tried to do. Thank you very much. Have you sent a copy to John Martin?

The only changes I'd suggest are minor. Actually, I was "Henry" in the book until I entered Jr. High School. Then I became "Hank." It happened that way. "Henry" is rather the name of the child who becomes "Hank" later on. I don't know how you can bring this about naturally. Maybe just let it happen. But it's not normal, doesn't sound right to call this character "Hank" from the beginning. Is it possible to make this change?

Also there is a place where I hide in a "closet." You have it "cupboard." Perhaps this is the English way of saying "closet"? over here, a cupboard is where we might store dishes or clothing...

And then there is the base6all game. In our game, when we attempt to steal a base, say from first base to the next base, that base is called "second base" not "home plate" or "home."

All these are minor or technical matters. I like the script. yes, yes. Glad you worked in the hospital and the time my grandmother jabbed that crucifix into my back—that, especially, would make a great scene in a movie!

I think that you are right onto things. Great job. I can't see any flaws. I feel useless. Let me hear from you on any possible changes you might consider...I wouldn't play with this too much. Seems you are there.

[To William Packard]
August 15, 1991

I'm glad you found all the poems I sent to be o.k. I know that you'll never be able to publish all the work you've accepted but the *NYQ* has been very good to me and I can't help sending along another submission or so now and then, just for the hell of it.

This is the night before my 71st birthday and I'm a bit down. I really don't mind marching toward death too much, it's that doing it by the numbers seems oppressive. Well, I shouldn't even be here—the battering I've given my body and still do—I should have long ago coughed it up and out.

I'm glad writing came along for me and that I've had some late luck. But I would have kept going, no matter. It's all stuck inside of me and has to keep coming out.

Thanks for enclosing your play, I'll get into it at a better moment.

By the way, we have 8 cats. There is much to be learned from them, the way they cool it out, sleep it off. I just look at a cat and I feel better. With humans, that reverses.

I'm going to lift a few with Li Po tomorrow night.

Thank you for allowing me on the pages of the *NYQ*. You've printed some of my rife and wild stuff, made me feel good, good. I try to feel good, William, it's a good trick if one can work it.

185

[To John Martin]
August 21, 1991 12:00 AM

Enclosed the deletions and changes in *Pulp*. I am not as crazy about this thing as when I started but at least I've dumped some of the worst garbage. Stuff that got in the way of the roll of the lines. I really don't know what I'm going to do with this thing. If it continues to roll along by itself, then all right. If I finish it I'll probably do a rewrite. We'll see. Right now, I don't even like the first page ... but have left it for the moment.

There are some chapters that click nicely and I hate to see them just vanish. So, we'll see. There's still always the poem. But I have an idea that this novel (?) will pick itself up again. If it works, and on name changes, etc., we'll work on that later.

Still I feel good having removed what I considered to be the sloppy lines. Good thing the computer broke down ...

All right, we'll see what happens.

[To John Martin]
August 23, 1991 12:05 AM

Rewrite of chapter 3.

I do what rises to the top for me first. This seems it, so far. I should run right through the whole thing. As long as the fun lasts. When that stops, forget it.

First version of *Pulp*, up to where it had gotten, I found too flip. Obvious exaggerations of the obvious, overplay upon sexuality, etc. I felt like I was watching Saturday Night Live. Bright talents there, but just blowing it away, pressing obvious keys to tickle a public that had never been quite alive to begin with.

It's all right for your main hero (?) to act goofy and mixed up but only if this is caused by actual life pressures. People cop out because they are frightened and want to huddle together under certain symbols, known names, causes.

Hell, I've been drinking ... forget the speech making ... this stuff ...

Pressures abound for all of us.

186

A hypothetical question, has nothing to do with anything, of course. And don't *respond* please. *No way.*

But what would you think, if you left a person in the morning and this person were totally raving mad? And full of the most terrible and unreasonable´ hatred that you had ever seen or heard—then to return and have same said person act as if nothing had ever happened?

Anyhow, you might guess what [?*why*] such a thing as *Pulp* is such a pleasurable outlet, great literature be damned.

Yes, I'm drunk, I'm the drunk at the end of the bar, spilling it. Bad form.

Just to say, it has been so wonderful that the Sparrow has been there.

Looks like my old age is going to mean nothing but running straight into the sawmill, generally, but all and all, we've had a grand show, you and I, and we haven't spit it out yet.

no, no, no,

yr boy

p.s.—on the last page, I think, of what I have sent you, I use the word "brisking." It doesn't exist. But seems the perfect word for that. Why are we so structured? Why are

we ... ha, ha, ha ...

p.s.s.—did Hemingway rewrite? Probably all too much. Gambling with the gods always beats looking for the ultimate perfection.

[To John Martin]
September 8, 1991

Well, I saw a good poem by Clayton Eshleman in *World Letter* number 2. it's called from "Under World Arrest," stanzas 37 through 40, a touch of Whitman, maybe, but the stuff rolls off real well.

Most of his stuff just slips off the page for me but he got good here.

on the home front, lots of shrapnel ... Christ, sometimes I

187

can't believe it. She could be going through a mid-life change. Thursday her older sister arrives for 4 or 5 days. I almost welcome it. A buffer ...

I know that you are handling everything up there. Read in the paper today where hundreds of thousands are running out of their unemployment checks and Bush fails to sign for an extension but we ship billions to Israel and everywhere else. Many of these U.S. people have had the same jobs for 20 or 30 years. They are in absolute terror and they should be.

I guess we're lucky. I surely am, the way you have guided me through the years. Everybody wants to have it happen to them like you made it happen for me. But they want fame. To them, writing is only a way to get there, writing isn't a mad need, a craziness. They think it's all a trick. To hell with them.

[To William Packard]
September 12, 1991 9:56 PM

Thanks for sending the foreword to *The Art of Poetry Writing*.[1] Like Shapiro said, it's odd that I'm in the company of Plato and Yeats, and certainly the boys I used to work with in the factories and warehouses and in the post office would think it odd too. Or the boys in the bars. I don't mind it, although I don't write for recognition, I write to keep my poor ass from getting totally ground up by this life. It saves part of me, although why I'm trying to save part, I'm not sure. Perhaps some grubby instinct at work?

When you've lived as long as I have and written as long, you realize that none of us has done enough or very much for that matter: Socrates, Descartes, Hume, Kierkegaard, Sartre, Wittgenstein. We are all brought down finally because there's little we can do about existence or non-existence (death) but think about it. We are locked in. Sometimes we kill each other or

---

1. Packard's *The Art of Poetry Writing* was published by St. Martin's Press in 1992.

ourselves, it's about the only movement we can lend ourselves to.

Poetry? Well, it's not much, is it? A lot of posing and prancing and fakery, wordplay for its own sake. Somehow poetry beckons the worst, the weaklings, the cowards, the pimps, the pushers. Reading a book of poetry puts me to sleep. There's no fire, no gamble. I keep waiting for some *arrival*, some *explosion*. Or, I used to keep waiting. Now, I don't. I just stay away from it. There's no light at the end of the tunnel, there isn't even a tunnel. The best thing I can do is get drunk and listen to classical music. Or sleep and wait for death to get closer. Leaving this will not be a horrible thing. Yet I'm glad, somehow, that I threw my few words into the air: confetti, celebrating nothing.

[To Paul Peditto]
September 14, 1991 1:21 PM

Well, so the play is on. I think that the way you have culled and splattered my crap in there, it should make a sound. You never know. I always write for myself and not for them. Still, sometimes they get it.

Mickey Rourke? Yeah, well, that's the way it works. He doesn't drink, he doesn't act. But there's no need for acting nowadays: the public can't tell the real from the rancid. People are dumber now than they have been for centuries. Maybe it's the pounding of Time against the genes.

Listen, on horse racing you need an edge. A method of play that beats the percentages. Most people lose. First, because of the 18 percent take. But they lose more than 18 percent of their money, they lose it all. Who is picking it up? A very small group, say 2 percent of the crowd. You must have a method of detecting where the good money is going and the bad money is going. All public handicappers, *Racing Form*, tout sheets, newspapers show a loss. To beat the horses you must do a lot of work, not on handicapping but on anti-handicapping. The real drag in going to the track is that you have to look at the people. And then there's that long wasteful 30 minutes between races. And sometimes after you wait that long, some longshot just wakes up and comes in at 30 or 40 to one. And maybe they'll follow that race with another one like that. That's when most people fall apart and just start betting anything. The other day I lost the first 5 races. But I remained with my play, got the last 4 at fair odds and walked out a nice winner. The racetrack tests a man in dozens of different ways. Few pass. But what I hate to see is all those poor people taking a beating. They have this dream of scoring but they just get picked off. Sure, it helps pay taxes, what the hell.

Don't let those 17 year old bodies worry you. There's nothing to these, they didn't earn it, they were born with those bodies and it's their ace card, for a while. But start living with these and all you get is an empty vessel, a look-machine, a fuck-machine and a crass spoiled empty mind. You want real hell? Try living with a so-called beautiful woman. It's a mirage that changes into a total nightmare. If you have to have a woman, look for kindness. a sense of overall reality. In 15 years they are all going to look alike. Play for the insides, the suckers will line up for the outside facade.

And now that I've told you all this, reverse it and you'll probably do fine.

[To Evan Russell]
October 7, 1991 11:54 PM

I don't want to nurse you or to engage in a correspondence, but a word on the stories you sent. Once or twice a week I get the works of some writer, either in manuscript form or in chapbook form. Most of it is pretty poor and much of it is total crap. There are people who want to be writers and people who have to write. Most of the people are people who want to be writers, who want the fame, the name, the pussy or whatever they imagine comes with that. I don't know which type you are;

190

I sense an admixture of both. The years will sort you out.

I found your stories good, high level stuff. Witty, intelligent, real enough, and touched with a wash of agony. On the fellow from the *Sewanee Review*, well, that's no place to try anyhow. That inbred snobbery has languished there for decades. Places like that and, say, the *New Yorker* think that good writing should be dull and tedious, and the less it says the better it seems to them. Creating boredom, to them, is a sign of class.

Where to send your stuff? Well, there isn't any place. There hasn't been and there never will be. Check the best short story of the year collections and it's worse than the dry heaves. In fact, the best so-called writing of the centuries is mostly dross and put-on. We've been sold down the river in a basket of shit.

When I was (am) rejected I sometimes got the urge to get a look at the guy who said "no" to me. I mean, get in a room with him for an hour, see how he acts, talks, dresses, mimics, breathes, walks. Then I would know that what I think is true.

Your work could be better. It's good but it can go up further. I think it's the line, you need more briskness, madness, gamble in the line, in the manner of telling, putting it down. Your content is fine and believable but there's a little kick missing in the way you lay it down. I don't know quite how to say this, maybe it is that now and then you must find a way to kick the reader in the ass, that what you are writing is truly you and to hell with all else. The best knew how to do this: Hamsun, Céline, Dostoevski, Turgenev. Say it wild, kick down the walls.

You're young. The older you get the more there will be to write about. The word is the magic which keeps us from killing ourselves. There's no better way. There is nothing else. Go get it.

[To John Martin]
October 13, 1991 1:20 AM

Thanks for the great note. It's all strange, the older I get the more I seem to explode with words and I believe they are lucky words enjoying themselves. I am aware that everything can shut off in a moment. I don't mean death as death but death in life. I can only run back to centerfield and catch just so many over my shoulder. And I can't say I'll take it kindly when they sit me on the bench. I love the action.

I look behind me and in the bookcase are stacked masses of pages of paper of things that I've written since Jan. 18. It's like a madman was turned loose in here. I know that some of those pages are pretty bad but I like to go with the roll of things and let fly. It's been some interesting year. I keep getting stronger like some beast trying to work out of a cage. I know that death is a stimulant, a kick in the ass. It has something to do with it. But I was always crazy for writing. You and I know the story of freezing and starving in that Atlanta shack. The railroad track gang. All the rotten jobs, the crazy women. The 13 and 1/2 years in the post office. And before that the dozens of small rooms, living on candy bars, getting the word down, thousands of pages returned and thrown away. You know all this. And being a bum and an errand boy in a bar, a punching bag. I can't even believe it. I wanted to write. I was sick with it. I think this is what Neeli missed. The hollow bottom of nowhere. Writing with a pencil stub on the edges of newspapers. While starving, mad. I don't think Neeli could face where I had come from and he wrote around it. He never knew.

This is why it is so strange to me now. I laid down my guts and the gods finally answered. That isn't supposed to happen. And now that it is, I am digging in and swinging from both sides of the plate because it's such a crazy joy, the toteboard flashing the longest odds possible.

Even if it quits now, it's been great, my friends the rats and the roaches will know, and you will know, you had some inkling, you got me out of the post office, you promised a lifetime income whether you were right or wrong. You are a gambler, John, and you met a gambler. And we've jammed

192

through literary walls they said we couldn't. I realize the abuse you took and still take. The literary darlings wanted to be me, not in the manner of creation but in the manner of being recognized. Screw those darlings, we are going into our last years, or I am going into mine, and the fireworks are exploding and the best is even yet to come.

[To William Packard]
October 13, 1991 1:33 AM

Regarding your health, I think it's most important to do what your mind tells you to do and then consider the doc's advice afterwards. Like, why am I telling you something you already know?

Me, I'm selfish because along with John Martin you seem to have a sense of the whatever it is that I am playing with. You are pissing off a lot of holy cows by having published me in every issue of the *NYQ* since #7. Some believe that you can only come up through certain sanctioned avenues in order to be one of them. Whoever they are, those fat soft bellies of life who consider their dull and ponderous lines as the ultimate way. These snob-sucks have not only relegated and dominated the Word in our time but in centuries past. It's a power play now and it was a power play then. We can now romanticize the gathering of some of those in the Paris cafes and other places throughout time, but it was all crap and blathering, a clasping of assholes. So we have a half-blind James Joyce dropping into Sylvia Beach's Bookstore. Or Hemingway and his buddies getting drunk and getting upset because of what women or writing does or doesn't do. Or the poets of old marching down the streets singing their madrigals. This is all crap and will always be crap. There is only one way to do it, if there is anything to be done, and if there is anything to be done it must be done by one person in a room alone. This is the clean branch, the trembling of the lightning, the fist in the face of death.

193

When the so-called creators met, talked together, rubbed together, they forgot what they were doing. They jollied up their insecurities, they jacked-off their individualities. They became famous together and they died in their own gizmo.

On the Shapiro poem on Lowell, which took a bag of guts to write, to take on this *Lord Weary*, some of the essence of what I am saying is spelled out here. It's like the poets who are ultimately accepted by not only by the establishment but also by a bevy of mother-in-laws, or just about anybody who comes along and is not used to thinking, then we have the rot which not only fosters dull text books but dull students and a dull humanity. Democracy fails to work for the same reason poetry fails: it's seldom truly presented as to what it could actually be. It's dead before it's served. And as the dead ingest the deathly there's nothing left to do but shoot at heads through windows or yawn into sleep.

Well, I said I belong with Plato and Yeats. Well, hell. You ever read any of Yeats' early stuff? It could have almost been written by somebody's grandmother. Wasn't it Pound who came along and told him to can some of that stuff? Plato I always get mixed up with Socrates anyhow. And on Pound, he had his bright tough period. He had some great value as one of the editors of the old *Poetry, A Magazine of Verse*. He sent on some lively poet-types and although this was in the asshole-clasping mold. As per his *Radio Speeches*, if the fascists had won, these would now be part of our world literature. Cleaned up, more clearly translated, honed. And the United States Congress would be delving through madhouse walls. And dead by now, as they are.

As for myself, I can't see any future for poetry, I see it as a house of snobs who pretend at delicacy and insight, who continue to dole it out in a diluted form without any roots in reality, joy, gamble, light or love. Thus it has been and will continue to be.

Do you wonder why I lived with the worst whores I could ever find? Do you wonder why I poured drink into myself until I burst like a balloon spilling red? Do you wonder why I still pour at the age of 71? No matter, I go to the racetrack, pick numbers, drive back, then face this machine. Somehow, I think,

194

we have missed something that is very clearly here. Maybe not. Maybe we just don't have it. Who can we compare ourselves with anyhow? The ant-eater? Death seems the kindest thing, the best whore. Just wherever it leads us, please, no more poets! Give us plumbers, geeks, idiots with mandolins, bakers of bread, onion growers, but no more poets, no more poets, please, those cowardly chipmunks gag my brain cells, make me want to run to the kindly distant hills.

Let me die without poets and more importantly, live without them. Let me never see any poets at my door or lisping their precious inanities upon the stage. Or find another poetry magazine in my mailbox, unreadable and rancid with the lie.

Enough. Too much. *Finis.*

[To Paul Peditto]
October 16, 1991 8:11 PM

Thanks for the poster, looks good to me. No, it doesn't glorify alcohol or alcoholics, it indicates subject matter. The lady who claims that you're "in denial" sounds like she's been playing ping pong with her shrink. As to the fellow who claims he doesn't understand what a man means when he says, "I feel like a can of sardines" well, he's just never felt like a can of sardines or even opened one and looked in there, or if he did, his only response was that there was something to eat. Sometimes I feel like a lamppost with a dog pissing on it. Maybe he would understand that one. Maybe.

You are always going to get people chewing on you because they only understand what their mothers told them or what the books told them or what their bosses told them, etc. These people are flattened into a strict nothingness. They talk but they don't say. They project their dullness. People walk away from them but they soon find somebody else and they begin their lifeless chatter all over again. The world is full of boring, identical and mindless people. They vote for the mayors, the governors, the congressmen, the president in their likeness—

195

that's why there's no leadership, no hope, no juice, no life, no understanding.

Sorry you lost your job at the bar. Having a boss is like having your head in the guillotine. You just don't know exactly when but it's never a surprise when your head rolls. And the worst thing is when you get a look at the guy who replaces you: a subnormal boot-licking patsy. I had problems too. They told me, "It's your attitude." What was I supposed to do? Feel joyful because they were buying my life-blood for pennies? Well, I hope the Live Bait catches some fish. I thought you put together a good script. It runs and bounces and screams and says some things. And you pulled it together in a sensible fashion. It should go well. The fact that it's being put on the boards shows that somebody somewhere had some guts. Thanks for your work and struggle with this. I am honored. May the walls roar and pour it to them.

[To Maxwell Gaddis]
October 22, 1991 2:44 PM

I have been having some problems. I knew your letter was there, somewhere. Today I found it. I can't keep up with my mail mainly because I'm hooked on straight writing.

You're right, I had problems ingesting Kerouac. But I'm an ironhead, I have problems with most writers. So I have to write the stuff myself and after I've written it I can't read that stuff either.

Kerouac I didn't meet. I never ran with the writing crowd. Did meet Cassidy [*Cassady*] (Neal) though, he came by *Open City* one day when I brought in a column for "Notes of a Dirty Old Man." John Bryan introduced me to him. Neal's best days had gone by. He was standing there with his head against a radio that had a speaker missing, loud jazz blaring. He was burnt-out on speed. It was a rainy day and I guess Bryan wanted to scare the shit out of me. Got me in a car with Neal driving in the rain. Mostly Neal scared the shit out of other drivers. One thing I will say, he had a good perception of speed vs. distance. I have some of that which I use in my freeway driving but Neal had it down about as good as I have seen. Still, I didn't find him too interesting. I think he was working too hard on being the character he was supposed to be.

I don't remember where I read in the past. I was always astonished when somebody invited me to read at a university because I knew I would blaze a drunken path. Maybe that place in Nebraska was where I walked through the women's dorm in my underwear, terrorizing the coeds. I did it, I think, with humor though. Playing the fool and loving it. Then too, it might have been some place else. I no longer read. That was for the rent not the vanity. Now I've got the rent. Let somebody else expose their soul's genitals.

In New Orleans I was in a lot of bars but don't remember all the names.

I note the photo of me at racetrack. I'm glad whoever took the photo didn't come up and talk to me. At the track, well, that's a different art form. No place to jolly up and chatter, have some laughs. No place is.

Ginsberg, well...I think he started in the right direction then got too fucking fancy and wordy and sucked too much to media events, the self-love spilled out too much, it all just ran away and died.

[To William Packard]
November 3, 1991 10:29 PM

Glad you liked the last batch of poems I sent. Great. You've got a stockpile now of my stuff like nobody anywhere. But I liked the two bar poems and thought I'd try them with you anyhow. Great. Certain poems just take over the page and enjoy themselves. You've written them, you know how it feels.

I've felt like hell for about a week, reminded me of the year I had TB and just sat at the typer with a hollow head. I feast on words, they run through my bloodstream, they jump about in

197

my brain. Sometimes at night I can't sleep, sentences will be running through me in the dark. But I know if I get up they will be gone. If the words don't hit me by 2 a.m., I close the bar. I'm sick with this thing but without it I'd be sicker.

Old guy next door fell down and broke his hip last night. I watched them load him into the ambulance and drive off. He's 96. His wife died last week. They've been married 47 years. Me, the pain in the top of my head is almost gone now, my throat has about cleared up, feeling better but it will be a couple of days before I smoke or drink (booze). I know that this interests you. Sure.

Thanks for sending the autobio by MacDonald Carey.[1] Frankly, starting off, it seems a little dull. Now that he's A.A. and back with the church, I fear a bit for him. A man can't take too much cover in life, it's debilitating. Carey wrote me a letter sometime back and since he seemed to be just getting started in the poetry game, I offered him a bit of advice, mainly to stay off the reading circuit. I told him that it was a form of vanity and had nothing to do with creation. But, look, how are you going to tell an actor not to act? I should have known better.

Here in this town we have the same group of aging poets reading week after week in every little poetry hole. Mostly, they read to each other. It is one of the saddest, threadbare acts around.

Well, I hope you exposed a few backsides in your autobio. If you fail to make anybody hate you, then you haven't done your job.

About lawsuits, I worried about them when I wrote *Barfly* but still couldn't resist calling a turd a turd. Then too, I thought, well, if they take me to court I'll write a novel about it. Material, material!

all right, slam it to them,

---

1. *The Days of My Life* (New York: St. Martin's Press, 1991).

198

[To William Packard]
November 8, 1991 11:29 PM

Got the advance copy of editorial for #47. Thanks. I feel that you have fully defended your position. You have a right to. You are the one who has to read the manuscripts. Should you turn your head away and say that everything is all right?

I believe what we have to fear is the feeling of the general public toward *poetry* and/or *art*. They have no idea what it is but they have the thought that anybody can do it if they feel like doing it. They feel that way too—they can do it, after Jill and Bobby finish college and the mortgage is paid. In fact, many of them already label themselves as Artists. "Oh, Bobby paints... Jill writes..." And they even might have little stacks of listless and off-hand work about. They may even have attended classes. They are the piddlers in the field and most of the field are piddlers. These won't lay down any blood to get their work done, they won't gamble with madness, starvation in their need to get the work done. They don't feel it that way. They want fame and name but they won't give up their comforts and their securities. They just claim to be Artists and somehow feel that it will all come together for them. Meanwhile, they might live on hand-outs from relatives instead of having the guts to score for an ugly 8 hour job and to try to break the walls from there. The public has this big soft toad concept of Art, they see it as being done by nice scrubbed intelligent pretty folk with French, German or especially English accents. They have no idea that it can be done by a bus driver, a field hand or a fry cook. They have no idea where it comes from. It comes from pain, damnation and impossibility. The blow to the soul of the gut. It comes from getting burned and seared and slugged. It comes from being too alive in the middle of death. It comes from... new and awful places and the same old places... It comes...

Damn them all! We are wasting our time talking about them! And with them. Let's get back to where it's at, if it's still there, and let's hope it is because without it then they become truly monstrous! Indeed.

[To David Reeve]
November 13, 1991 1:24AM

Burned-out tonight. Took my wife to Disneyland for her birthday. She likes that place. All right, I dragged along. But the types I thought would be there were there. These humans who had found a way to survive the economic squeeze. They weren't rich but they weren't hurting. Placid, mostly. Totally placid. Like photos of ice cream cones. They didn't even terrorize me. They were just there. With their intestines and their ears and their etc. Lining up for the fake dream. The little tickle. The soft prod. Mickey Mouse is the safest thing ever invented. Anyhow, those hours and those people worked their drain and here's what's left, writing to you.

Sylvia Plath was the lady who stuck her head in the oven, gas on, unlit, to out herself. Her poems never sent me but many women abide by her, relate their sufferings to hers.

On Malone, I don't send to him anymore.[1] He's gotten too picky but I feel that he is picking wrong. As the years go on I see him more and more printing the comfortable poem. They are well written but have no edges and after you've read them you have no memory of any of them. I've had some good years with him. He probably has some of my poems on backlog but after they run out, that's it.

Mailer, yes, I met him. He's more easy going in person than when he's pushing his product. All those x-wives have him nailed to the typer. We had both worked for the same producer at one time. Like good boys we went to the producer's birthday party. And I sat at a table pouring the drinks down as fast as I could. I had the waiter running madly. Finally, instead of bringing me drinks, he started bringing me bottles. At one time during the evening I caught Norman just staring at me. I winked and laughed, then went back to the kitchen to tip the bus boys. When I came back my wife said Norman had spoken to her, had said, "It was nice of Hank not to say anything about my writing." Somehow, he sensed what I thought about it. I thought that was funny.

---

1. Editor of *Wormwood Review*.

Don't send any more money, even if it did get you a letter. I was going to send it back but the good wife said, "No, don't." Being weak, I didn't ask her why. But now—don't.

On the *Sword of Shaharazad*[1] I sent some poems to the original address you sent me. Haven't heard from them and somehow don't expect to. I've always had trouble with so-called geniuses. Especially those who earn that mark by scoring high on exams and shit like that. Too many of their brains have computured-in [*sic*] answers. I knew a kid in highschool who was the super honor student. It was his mother. She forced him to put his nose into the books from the moment he got home until he slept at night. Maybe not that long. But 5 or 6 hours a day. Actually, he was the dumbest kid in school. All that you learn in the books must be forgotten or ignored. You start over again, building from what you see and feel. That's all there is. And, also, stay away from Disneyland.

[To ?—— Kelly]
November 27, 1991 12:04 AM

I can't really tell you whether Alaska is a better choice than where you're at, it depends more upon how you feel than I feel. All I can tell you is that when I was a young guy and even not so young, I had this idea that if I could stay in motion I could avoid a lot of the traps. Keep the wheels rolling under me forever, I thought. Find new cities. Move on. I was on so many cross country buses I felt like a driver on a route. But it was rough on the finances, the drinking and the bowel movements. And I found out on buses that you were trapped with other people. Also, each city was filled with more of the same. And there was the need for a job or it was the park bench. I don't know how many jobs I went through or how many cities or how many women. Not too many women at first. And it didn't matter all that much to me. But I don't know if the moving

---

1. *The Sword of Scheherazade*—not identified.

201

around did me any good or not. Then I lucked it in this bar I found I could survive in more or less. The drinks came and the days and the months and some years went by. Now and then I'd get a straight job to buck up some room rent money. But I didn't work for long. Until the fucking post office. What I am saying here is that I don't know if travel did any good. And I think it was easier to get a factory or a warehouse job in those days. Now the economy doesn't allow as much motion and gamble with your life.

Man, I just don't know. You have to sense and feel your way with each move. Humanity is a hard take and it isn't going to go away. If it does, it will be almost at once and almost everybody. I think the largest illusion I went through was the thought that a man had to have a woman, almost at any price, to be a real person. It took me a lot of women to realize that was nonsense but by then the years had been pretty well used up. As a writer, or as a guy who finally turned into a writer, I suppose that all the drinking and all the women and all the different places lent to material to be used but I hadn't meant it that way—something was eating at me and I didn't know what to do.

So, Kelly, I can't say what's best for you. Like you say, "in a world of shit." With everybody quitting, selling short, playing it dumb and safe and cowardly. It's unsolvable. The only thing I came up with was, "Save what you can." Meaning of yourself. Don't let it all go. One spark can start a forest fire. I conned myself along with this ... In a sense, it worked. After 5 decades I got a little lucky. But the same old thing was all around me. And different traps appeared. The fight never stops. But it's a good one. So when you die you'll know you haven't gone the route of the many who are dead long before their deaths. I don't know, man, I don't know. It's yours. And luck. Yes.

202

Howard Fredrics has set many Bukowski poems to music, including Inevitable Conflicts, *his Master's thesis composition from the University of Texas at Austin in 1991. A tape cassette of* Bukowski Songs *was published by Aurӓcle Music, Austin, Texas in 1994.*

[To Howard Fredrics]
November 30, 1991 10:35 PM

ow ow ow, you don't know how many letters like yours I get and I have to tell them all, "no visitors." Each thinks they are the exception and many want to come: guys getting out of jail, college profs, sexpots, bartenders, etc. And so, I keep losing readers and so-called admirers but I've always been a loner, all my life, and I see no need to change now.

Thanks for enclosing the cassette, I'll listen to it on the way to the racetrack. Were you the one I told that the human voice, the piano and the violin were horrible instruments? Well, at any rate, most of the time, they are horribly used. Happened to go to a musical recital—long story—of modern music and was delighted to find the fellow at the piano, playing his own composition, did so using the piano in a different manner, almost percussion-like, with spaced strange notes, it gave me wonderful chills to see this breakaway from the staid and the standard. Just thought I'd tell you. And thank you again for your interest in my work. I always write while listening to classical music and now maybe the music that goes into the poem is now coming out again. Strange. Especially since I prefer to keep my writing close to the bone—like Bach.

best to you,

[To Paul Peditto]
December 3, 1991 12:20 AM

You're right, it's the toughest of Ages, man drawn dry. The Atomic Bomb and AIDS arrive within 50 years of each other.

203

Nobody can think of ten years ahead of time. It's just today, tonight and hope you make those.

Yeah, it was easier to be a bum when I was a bum. You more or less chose that and now it chooses you (or me). You just got to be lucky. Talent has little to do with it. Many fools are making it because they fell into the right place. That's all. They are interlaced into the sections of our society which haven't fallen apart—yet.

When I was a bum I tried to stay in the warm weather parts of the country but I miscalculated once or twice and almost went under, notably in a place called Atlanta, Ga.

But you've got some hope going. Your day work may be sickening but at night, lo, you become a Prince, watching the work you helped create unfold. That's some magic, Paul, and not many men get it. Concentrate on that part and the other will not close in so badly.

Thanks for enclosing the fine reviews. I think we got something over on them, they picked up. Our simple language to the gut of the matter. My notes, your arrangement. On technical facts of things, those people naturally screw up. Like I don't have TB. Did have. Other matters. But who cares? Some people are going to get what we are saying and they won't feel quite so alone in the world.

Well, I've got a bad hangover, turning in early. Old farts like me have to pace themselves, right up to the edge of the fucking grave. It's been a great fight, Paul, and I intend to fight some more. You will too. Oh—tell the cast and the set designers and all attached that I thank them plenty for their great work. Yes, yes, yes, oh yes!

204

[To Robert Patterson]
December 10, 1991 11:38 PM

Thanks for yours. I hear from others who say I give them something to go on. So? Well, some get it from soap operas, some get it from the current rock star, some get it by torturing animals. The great wash of humanity doesn't interest me but it sure as hell almost ingests me in its horror show. I fight back with little tricks: the typewriter, the bottle, hiding out, ignoring the consensus. I write to save my own ass, to shove the grip of madness away from me with words. If I save anybody else's ass in the process, it's extra purely coincidental.

It's raining tonight and I'm sitting by this open door, curious that I am still alive. And I'm lucky too that death is now standing very close behind me. It gives everything a new focus, a new color. Most of my life I rushed toward death, mocking it, trying to find it. Now, it will find me. It's easier. And I still have my little words to play with for my old ass still needs saving not from death but from life, as always.

Great rain tonight in the dark. I am not on the park bench. Chances are I might die in my own bed. Or at the racetrack, or in between.

You? Well, stay away from writers and work your way.

[To John Martin]
December 29, 1991 11:26 PM

Well, there went Xmas. Now New Year's night. It appears there will be a gang here. I can't deny Linda her friends, her mother. If it were for me, there would be nobody here. I can't believe the babbling of the crowd or their gnawing little niceties. But life never changes, it's a matter of overcoming and living through the obstacles. Our moment will come, our day will come, our night will come. It's worth waiting and fighting for.

205

Thanks for sending on the new Black Sparrow spring titles. I am pleased that you are republishing *Birds, Beasts and Flowers* by D. H. Lawrence. I remember how surprised I was when I first read these poems so long ago. D.H. got it so right. I don't think anybody has gotten into the nature of these things like he did. And, of course, there's the "snake" poem...I suppose that's the one that gets at most of us. I felt the snake, the shiver of reality when I read that one. It's fine to revive a classic like this book. I'm sure that many people are not aware of it. Good then...

[To William Packard]
December 30, 1991 10:30 PM

I've sent in for *The Art of Poetry Writing*. I hope those bastards remember to send me a copy when it comes out. On teaching poetry writing, I think there are things that can be taught, perhaps, but mostly what can be taught is how not to write very awful poetry. But, of course, you and I know that's about as far as you can go. Anyhow, like you said, you can steer them clearer than most and that counts. With your long editing background, if anybody knows, you know. All those issues of the *NYQ* are surely some barometer. Yeah.

Out here, I've fought past Xmas and there's only that revelry of ignorance, New Year's Night to get past. January 2nd is always one of my favorite days. All the bullshit is past and the masses crawl back into their holes where they belong. As they become depressed and embittered, I move forward into the light. Or what light is left.

You keep going strong.

206

[To Jim Testa]
December 30, 1991 11:18 PM

Thanks for the invite on the music video bit but I must duck out on that one. Besides being one a them thar classical music freaks, I am also beholden to gambling, drinking, the poem and at the present, a novel. I'm just eaten up by my own crap, man. The trouble with most rock performers is that they create it before they live it and they sound more like children trying to get away from their parents than anything else. And their audience is the same. But I guess it's all needed like needles on a pine tree or a gopher hole for a gopher. Thanks for the Jersey Beat. I used to take in the boxing matches at Camden around the mid-forties. A lucky 1992 to you. And to me too.

[To David Reeve]
December 31, 1991 12:42 AM

I tried the *Indiana Review* some time back. Got the old standard reject. You know, many of the university publications like a certain type of poem:

> I husked the harvest
> burnished
> bulked at the sun's edge
> the ants of heaven at my
> feet,
> Oh, Tamberlaine,
> Tamberlaine!
> come home to
> me.

I mean, either you write that way or you're not in and if I have to write that way I'm going back to that end seat on the bar. I sent the *Midwest* outfit[1] a batch, we'll see. It doesn't

---

1. *The Midwest Quarterly* published Bukowski's "The Crowd" in the Fall 1992 issue and "Depression Kid" in Winter 1993.

matter all that much. What matters is a candy-striped wheel barrow in a sandstorm.[1]

Then too, anybody can be an editor. Say you get a rave letter in the mail, guy says he's starting up a mag. He tells you you are God. So, what the hell, you send him something. And then the "magazine" arrives with your stuff in it. It's just sheets of paper run off a mimeo machine and stapled together. Not even a cover. And the editor's poems are in there right alongside of yours. And I wouldn't even mind that so much but look... the editor has printed his friends also. And the writing is horrible, of course. The way these guys justify this crap is that they call their publications "zines" or something like that. And the guys in the "zines" print each other just like the guys in the staid literary magazines.

I've followed this game a long time. Strange thing. Take a guy who has been editing a magazine. You see him published here and there. Then he decides to stop publishing his mag. And devote himself fully to his "art." He then vanishes and is never heard from. He's no longer there to play you publish me and I'll publish you. And this happens as well with the magazines of more expensive format and a larger readership. What the hell does this tell you?

This stuff isn't even worth discussing but I've done it. It's this damnable Xmas season, it's got my brains pissed on and over. You ever read Sherwood Anderson? Don't miss.

I'm sleep deprived, going to turn it in early tonight. Got off one good poem and then the lights went out. So I practiced on you. Maybe you can sell this letter for a 6 pack.

Sometimes I think, I'm 71 years old. What the fuck have they done to me? Besides, I'm not supposed to be here. But I'm in direct line of fire now. Fine. Let's do it.

●

---

1. Parodic allusion to William Carlos Williams's "The Red Wheel-barrow."

• 1 9 9 2 •

Thanks for the word on the Pushcart nominations. Looks like *World Letter* scored with an enormous amount of work. Good, sure, hell yes. Good.

By the way, I received your letter suggesting that I might send more submissions but being screwed up in my way, I lost the envelope, and had no address to send to. Also, couldn't find my copy of *World Letter* #2. Lo, the other day I did and then your letter followed. It may be too late but I'd like to send the next batch I do off to you for a look. For better or worse. Should be within a week, depending upon the muse.

One of my main problems, after I write something is where or where or where do I send this? There are certainly hundreds and hundreds of magazines but it certainly doesn't solve the problem. You know what I mean?

I'll soon be 72 but I feel that I am still firing at full blast. Yes, I write some shit but, all in all, most of it isn't. Meanwhile, forgive my lack of organization. I am not indifferent, sometimes just fly with one wing.

hold,

[Addressee unknown]
January 4, 1992 12:37 AM

Hello Bullfrog:
Yes, I knew a guy once, called himself Red Strange. A sharp recluse. We drank at my place and he told me some good stories. Red had a good nose for detecting the bullshit in life. His way out was the road. I didn't want the road, I wanted to write so I needed some walls for that. But in our ways of thinking about things in general, Red and I were not too far apart. When I knew him some woman was driving me crazy and he must have considered me a real asshole for getting into such a fix. I was.

Anyhow, Red told some good stories. At the time I knew him he had a job cleaning rooms someplace. He sometimes brought me articles of clothing and so forth from people who had died. Red just didn't want to get into society. I didn't either so I was an almost starving writer. I stayed that way for some time then had a little luck. I live pretty fucking good now but the world looks just as bad to me, maybe worse. I'm 71 now and I still write. It's still my last hiding place.

By the way, I took a few of Red's stories, changed them a little here and there, and they became published. We had some damned interesting nights. But the energy was his. You see him, tell him I own my own home, have a pool, a spa, new car, young wife. He'll laugh his ass off. Anyhow, yes, he knew me and I knew him.

Take care of your leg and yourself.

[To John Martin]
January 6, 1992 12:21 AM

Well, we're into '92 and I can't expect another lucky year—writing-wise—as '91 but I'm glad the computer screen is still here and that I can play upon it. I'll be 72 this year—if I make it—and I don't feel any different than when you knocked on my door what?—over 2 decades ago. My health is probably better and that damnable urge to write seems to be worse than ever. I feed on this crap. It keeps me rolling. Some things really weary me more than before because it's a repeat of the same. I don't understand people, I never did. But what the hell, what the hell. It's raining now. That's good. I'm not on a park bench or a madhouse or a hospital. Not right now. I think of Céline, Hemingway, Henry Miller, almost all the writers ended up on the rocks. Dylan Thomas. The whole gang. Hamsun gave it a nice long run but even he got screwed up in politics. Pound. I want to write not to pile up books or pages but because it keeps me at a level, a place. The lights stay on. If I were to die at this moment, I'd have no regrets. You and I, we sprang out of nowhere. We did what we did and we still do it. It feels well to do so. Sane. Clear. Good. Why not? There's no better way. There wasn't then, there isn't now. And the last thing it is is *work*. *Not* doing it is work, madness, the end before the end. Pal, it's been great.

[To William Packard]
January 12, 1992 9:24 PM

Well, no, I didn't send the dead cow. I don't know who would do that. Think, man, have you flunked any students lately? Or have you rejected the advances of a poetess? Women are far more dangerous than men. Men want to get away, women want a thing called vengeance.

Thanks for the good words. I don't often hear good words. It's all right. Wasn't it Dostoevski who said, "Adversity is the main spring of self realism"? The problem being, how much adversity can we ingest? We need a breather now and then or else we crack.

A rough period for me right now. Too much drinking, plus other matters. Tonight I stretched out on my bed and looked back through my life and it was more than odd. Something was always plaguing me, pounding at me. I don't suppose that any person's life is different. You get past one horror and another just steps up and takes its place. I get letters from people who tell me that the things I have written has helped them get on through. This is all damned fine. But where can I look? Well, tonight, in particular is not a very decent night. There will be better nights. Let's hope so or else I'm going to toss it in. Or maybe mail myself a dead cow.

People who really think that they can teach other people to write poetry? Well, first of all they have a misconcept of humanity and after that they have a misconcept of their knowledge of what poetry is. They are air bags who like to spew it out. It makes them feel worthy. They need to feel worthy, it's their sickness. They write a hundred poems, get a couple of thin volumes of poetry published and off of that they then presume that they are able to teach others. No matter that nobody can read their books or that their writing is hardly exceptional. There are their books, see! They know something. They have been published. The poets are the worst. When I hear the word "poet," I cut and run ...

My wife just knocked. She dug my wedding ring out from the bottom of the swimming pool. I was drunk last night, swimming in there with my friend Barbet Schroeder. I told Barbet, who now draws enormous salaries for directing his movies, "Hell, man, I knew you when you lived in the ghetto and I'd come by and there'd be fresh bullet holes in your front door. Now you live in this huge home which I haven't even seen. Aren't you worried about your soul?" "Oh no," he told me, "you see, I don't have a swimming pool." I went on to other subject matter. [* * *]

Douglas Goodwin is a Los Angeles poet, author of Slamming It Down *(Santa Monica: Earth Rose Press, 1993)*

[To Douglas Goodwin]
January 13, 1992 11:41 PM

As usual, what one says gets a bit twisted. What I had said is that the magazines that I liked were overstocked with me and that I really had a problem sending to the others, you know, those who print poems like:

> Winter's haven bursts my star,
> the little feet of heaven thunder past,
> where are you, Dulcia?
> etc.

or:

> I stock of myself. you. blitz.
> the butcher's button.
> hold the take.
> the onion floors fallward.
> etc.

The *NYQ* has accepted 66 of my poems. How many more can I send them?

Actually, I don't worry about getting into magazines. It's just that after writing poems I like to get them the hell out of here. A habit. [* * *]

Listening to Schubert's 9th now, real bad reading, guy conducts like he's afraid a carrot will fall out of his ass. Fucking shame. The 9th properly played is a mighty work.

Don't let your fellow workers get at you too much. What I did was develop such a sharp lip that they steered clear. I put it all in the form of humor but I sliced them to ribbons so that they were just as glad when the final minute arrived as I was.

213

Ivan Suvanjieff edited The New Censorship: The Month-
ly Journal of the Next Savage State *from Denver,
Colorado.*

[To Ivan Suvanjieff]
January 13, 1992 10:59 PM

I'm glad you found the poems to be all right. And if you
want to feature some in your April issue, great then. Let me try
some drawings first, then if they don't work for you, then you
can try somebody else?

I'm also glad I am writing an editor who is a parking lot
attendant rather than some comfortable prof. Life keeps nip-
ping you at the balls to let you know where it's at. It's painful
but it might be worth it. The whole scheme operates on a
system of balances. Too much pain and travail can take you out
too. The gods give those they favor the proper dosages.

I can see you going on working in spite of the ankle. One
gets pissed at the fates. The overdosage. You see these fat
subnormals rolling up in their expensive cars, stuffed with their
subnormal women and none of them have the slightest idea
that they are where they are through pure luck. They've stum-
bled upon a product that the idiots buy or they are the product
that the idiots buy, or they fell into money, born into it. Few
decent minds there. They just fell through the slots and into
some golden shit. But it dehumanized them. So, who wins?
Nobody.

But now you have some time. And there is nothing more
beautiful than that. Breathe it in, swim in it. I broke a toe once
while working the docks in Oakland. I got some compensation
for it. Which gave me time. I made all the bars at night. Kept
going back to the doc who said, "I can't understand why this
toe doesn't heal. You been staying off of it?" "Sure," I told him.
(I meant while I was asleep.) And he kept putting on new
splints. Finally got real pissed and roared at me. What did he
fucking care? He wasn't paying the bill. He just didn't like me
sitting around on my ass while he worked.

All right, Ivan, keep it going. And thanks for your quick
response. I remember one place, a university mag, sent them

214

something, it sat there two months then somebody sent it back with an almost illegible note: "We don't read anything these 3 months of the year." Well, well, well, and what do they do? Must be something real hot and mighty. Bloody shitheads. Soft suck tits. Give me a parking lot attendant with a broken ankle any time.

[To Jon Cone]
January 16, 1992 10:51 PM

Great fast answer from you from my poems just born. Makes me feel like something's moving. I liked your choices. I've got a problem, the older I get the better I write, I feel. It comes out like chunks of hot steel. I get this natural power kick. It may be an illusion, it may not. Who cares? It feels good.

On Roditi, Mrabet ... well, poets get hunkered down into their own ways and other writers seem to be, well, false, prancing at it, you know. As we shake our influences and become more ourselves, other writing not only doesn't interest us, it often repulses us. Not only contemporary writing but the writing of the centuries. Soon we can only read our own stuff, and then only once because it's to hell with that and on to the next. The next is all there is until they pull down the shades.

Well, no, I don't send to *Poetry*, that's useless. Their days of cutting through the dung and allowing styles of gamble and openness have been over for decades.[1]

Thanks for the tips on mags. I'm into a detective novel now, *Pulp*, "dedicated to bad writing." This book may totally erase my thin reputation but I don't give a damn, I'm having fun. But if I should come up for air and do a few poems I'll remember those mags you mentioned.

---

1. Later Bukowski changed his mind. *Poetry* published his "fingernails; nostrils; shoelaces; a not so good night in the San Pedro of the world" in the September 1993 issue and "cold summer" in July 1994.

215

Long day at the track today but a good one. Going to drag out my detective, wind him up and see what he does.

Thanks for letting me enter *World Letter.*

Great letter. Don't you know that the man you saved today might be the one who gets you tomorrow? Don't give mercy, ask mercy. Just kidding. Been drinking for hours, playing with little words ... soothing my stupid ass ... much of the time battling this Macintosh who keeps giving me "System error ... etc." and then refusing to function. I have to go half way around the block to trick it, pretend that I want something else, then change my mind, come back to the original and very often it clicks in. And I can get on with my fucking business. I'd dump it and go back to the good old typer but it overwhelms me with its utter conveniences ... when ... it's acting right.

Your story reminds me of one of my own, only yours is much more likable and courageous. I mean, yes.

I don't know. It was decades ago. I was walking along somewhere in some city and it was about 5 a.m. in the morning. Somewhere during the night the laughter and good times had ended and I was walking along battered and beaten by somebody or somebodies, who knows? Let the good times roll. My clothing was torn, my face bloodied, I could feel something dripping, dripping ... not too much pain there ... still drunk and stunned ... now and then retching, my gut spewing nothingness toward this great morning sun ... my wallet was gone, of course. Again. The general idea was that I was trying to find my room. And I had lost track, somehow, of where it was or what city I was in. But I knew I had a room somewhere and the rent was paid for 3 or 4 days and that place, it was my only place, my only universe. Find that room and I'd live. Otherwise I would die. I mean, it was like that. I didn't mind dying, I only wanted to die more or less relaxed, memorizing a rented rug, footsteps

216

of somebody going by my door. Stupid sure but when you're tired to the bottoms of your feet and everything is clicking and clacking like broken sounds all you want to do is to chose a good corner to die in. Animals do that. Wounded cats. Birds. Fish. Even humans.

I walked along somehow sensing where my room was. I had even chosen the city. I was either in Philly or east Kansas City. I forced myself on through the voiceless morning.

Then I heard something. Footsteps like my own. Only more faltering. Disordered.

I was walking east. I think. And upon the sidewalk. And here, walking west, I think walking west was this man in the very center of the street, a main boulevard. It was a Sunday morning and there wasn't a car in sight. But he was actually in the middle of the boulevard. He was silent, except for the shuffling, haphazard, inept and helpless sounds of his shoes upon the pavement. He came toward me and I thought, Jesus, here's some poor fuck worse off than I am. How can that be? I was Suicide numero uno, I put myself in the greatest situations of hell, I challenged monsters. I slammed myself into death and now ... here was this number ... taking my play ... but as I got closer ... the sun was rising ... I saw his mutilated face and worse ... I saw one of his eyeballs dangling ... it was out of his head ... dangling on a thin thread ... it swung back and forth upon the thread as he walked ... a pendulum ... I had to help him.

But then my gut wretched. A whirling of white ran through my head, my brain. And I knew that in that situation that I was a coward. He looked so impossibly horrible that I imagined that he was horrible, that what had been done to him had become him. That he, himself, was beastly, instead of those who had done that to him. Those that were now laying next to their women and snoring, feeling vindicated, human, tough. Or worse, feeling very little. But there he was, the eyeball dangling. And I let him walk past. And I walked along still hearing his pitiful footsteps behind me.

I rationed it off that I was pretty bad off myself. But really, I just wasn't man enough. I was a cowardly walking through the morning sun. I hated myself but I couldn't change.

217

I walked and walked and walked and finally found my roominghouse. I got in and walked up to the second floor, threw myself upon the bed. I was safe, momentarily. I was in my cheap cocoon. But I couldn't sleep. I wasn't bothered with Christian morals, etc. I had always felt myself like F.N., Beyond Good and Evil. But it wasn't taking. I was nothing but a nothing nothing. I lacked kindness, I lacked reality. I was a bluff. When the chips were down, I ran. I didn't have it. There was nothing that I could do but lay there and accept the fact that I was hardly a decent human being. I was a fake. A pretense. I had no heart.

I stayed in that bed 3 or 4 days and nights thinking about that poor bastard with his eyeball dangling.

Finally, I got up and into motion, pretending that everything was all right. I would be the only one to ever know.

But one thing I knew, I was not what I pretended to be. And the closer I could get away from pretense, the closer I could get to dying straight on into the maw. And hell, that's what it's all about. Every time you put your shoes on in the morning, every time you drink a glass of water, every time you turn the key in your car and wait for what you want to hear.

God damn, I hope the next person found him. Chances are they knew what to do and that it was no problem at all.

[To John Martin]
January 24, 1992 12:19 AM

[* * *] On the matter of being photographed and appearing in the Madonna book of "erotica," I phoned her agent and told her, "no." Madonna acts like she has just discovered sex and she keeps hitting you over the head with it. Not for me. [* * *]

[To Teresa Leo]
January 28, 1992 11:59 PM

Thank you for the invite to the poetry reading but I don't read anymore, haven't for years. I feel that too often one who reads poetry does so for his own ego and for the instantaneous applause. I am guilty of giving many poetry readings in the past but I tend to cajole myself that it was for the rent. Maybe it was. Maybe I've known too many poets or too many poets of the wrong kind. But their mincing, posturing and prancing upon stage really gave me a gut feeling one gets just before vomiting. Anyhow, and still, thanks for the invite. Oh yeah, and to still further my point of not wanting to, not too long ago was offered an all expense paid trip to Amsterdam for two, plus 10,000 dollars to give two readings. Passed. I believe the writer's place is at the keyboard writing.

Thanks also for sending on the proofs of Louis McKee's "Thirteen Ways of Looking at Bukowski." Not bad, he's done some homework. [* * *]

Yes, Philly was one of my favorite cities even though I seldom moved out of a 5 block area. That bar I spent 5 years in was located at 16th and Fairmount and is no doubt long ago gone. It was a pretty rough area decades ago, it's got to be really under now. So hello to Philly and hello to the Painted Bride. What a curious life it was

and still is.

[To Ivan Suvanjieff]
February 20, 1992 12:03 AM

Glad the bullet missed.

I use a Macintosh IIsi. MacWrite II. Software [*i.e.*, *System*] 6.0.7. 1 don't know anything about computers. My wife got me one for Xmas '90 and I use it basically as a typewriter. Have gone to computer class, read some manuals, still an amateur. Lost quite a bit of work to nowhere, machine just erased it for

219

no seeming reason. But as time goes on I have learned little things here and there—basically ways to stop fuckups. Some so-called computer geniuses couldn't answer some of my questions relating to breakdowns and fuckups. The general answer from all of them was something like: "I don't understand it. Those things shouldn't happen." But they did. But by trying this and that and that and this, I found that by going around the corner instead of straight in the machine stopped coming up with these glitches—one quite major and related to the laser printer. I found a quite simple way to stop the laser from fucking up, a very quick and simple thing. *What I did was never mentioned in any of the books on the matter or in the frigging class.* Why not? It's like they are trying to hide information. Christ. Let them hide Christ, give me the info. Also learned another little trick so I would never lose anything again. *Again, none of this mentioned anywhere.* Well, I'm going to be like those fuckers: what I've learned I'm not going to tell anybody.

What the computer has done is to allow me to write *more*. Now, "more" isn't any good if the quality doesn't hold but with me (forgive this) it has not only held but increased. It's a bigger party now, more fun, more fire. I used to get drunk one night to write the stuff then get drunk the next night to correct it. Carbons, crossout ink, new ribbons, new erasing tape, etc. Now, I do it all in one night, correct the shit tight on the screen, run it off, store it for god damned eternity and mail it out somewhere. The keyboard sizzles and sings and laughs and there's even different typefaces to fit one's god damned mood. **Chicago is best when you're burned out and thinking of the razor against the throat or the car off of the bridge.**

YOU GET THE SHORT
BLOODY
POEM
AND THEN GET
OUT,
CONCENTRATE ON THE DRINKING
IN A ROOM BLUE WITH CIGAR
SMOKE AND
CLASSICAL MUSIC.

220

I generally prefer "Palatino" because it makes me look like a better typist.

For a guy who used to hand-print his stuff I've gotten pretty frigging fancy. But I measure the total work and how I feel about it. I never worry about editors or readers. Never have. I get it out to keep what sanity I have.

There is something about seeing your words on a screen before you that makes you send the word with a better bite, sighted in closer to the target. I know a computer can't make a writer but I think it makes a writer better. Simplicity in writing and simplicity in getting it down, hot and real.

One editor write me an almost snarling letter "All a computer does is to allow you to correct the composition of your work!"

This man understands nothing.

When this computer is in the shop and I go back to the electric, it's like trying to break rock with a hammer. Of course, the essence of the writing is there but you have to *wait* on it, it doesn't leap from the gut as quickly, you begin to trail your thoughts—your thoughts are way ahead of your fingers which are trying to catch up. It causes a block of sorts. Indeed.

Well, enough of this.

Luck with your painting. The first stroke leads you. Don't overstroke. Better to leave underdone than to lard it on too much. I have spoken. Oh yeah. Oh yeah. Oh yeah.

yes,

p.s.—it is to laugh. [*Remainder of letter in bold face*] Just after bragging that I had this machine by the balls and after writing your letter, it vanished in spite of all my learned precautions. Couldn't find letter to you anywhere. Went to "Find File." It told me that I had written the letter and when. It also suggested that it might be lurking in one of 3 places. I found it in the 3rd place. Somehow the machine had stuck it into the "MacLink Plus Bridge" folder. No damned good reason for this. I never sent it there. Dragged it out of there and printed it on the laser. Ivan, if I live, if I somehow eke out another 5 years, I will have this thing by the balls. Then you can attend my computer class. For free.

[To Jon Cone]
March 2, 1992 8:41 PM

It's been raining too many days and nights, the people can't control their cars and the sirens are going continually but at the track they load those four-footed animals into the gate and they're off, as usual. Me, well, I have moments and times, long times that seem to run together when nothing seems more nothing than ever. I mean, I can't shake it—stuff hangs on me, gloomy stuff, black ... and to exaggerate the point, I feel like the Xmas tree from hell. I know from the practice of the years that waiting is the only thing, wait, wait, wait, not on death but on life and it usually returns and then, at once, you feel pretty damned good. For a time. But, it's the waiting that galls, the waste ...

I know what you mean when you speak of disorganization. There are too many trivial things to attend to and left unattended these trivial things will mount into one large mass that will kill you. I mean, I once wrote a short story about this condition but nobody understood it so I threw it away.

Yes, well, you have *World Letter*. You gather them in and if you get some good work, it's surely worth it. The problem, of course, is that you're dealing with writers. For this, you have to keep a *distance*. Meet them and it's over. Giant suckerfish. Wailers. Bitches. Gutless seekers of fame. Not a human in the bunch. They just troll out words. Words, words, words and most of them come from the worst places and for the worst reasons. I could machinegun the whole gang of them and not drop a tear.

Now just waiting for the fights on tv tonight, 12:30 a.m. I always wanted to be a boxer but I had these scars on my back which I figured would scare the hell out of the audience. So, I passed. Became a drunk. Still am.

222

[To William Packard]
March 5, 1992 11:47

Strange that your letter came today. It was just last night that I put a poem in an envelope to submit to you and the editors of the *NYQ*. I promised you that I'd send any piss-burner poems to you in spite of the backlog you have. Well, I slept on it and then in the morning I took it out of the envelope, reread it, decided against it and sent it to *Mountain & Plain Motorcycle News*. Editor there thinks the bikers might like my stuff. But I don't think this poem, "The Cigarette of the Sun,"[1] was a pissburner, just half a piss-burner. Working on a novel now, *Pulp*, but the piss-burner will arrive one day and when it does I'll send it on, not necessarily to be accepted but because I like the damned thing. So, you're on my poor mind. In fact, even dialed your number the other day to listen to your message but you didn't have any message on and I thought, oh oh, Packard is tired of hearing from everybody and I don't blame him. Every time the phone rings here, I feel invaded, a chill runs through me and it's mixed with anger and I don't anger often. Disgust is my thing. And I hear from the plain and the famous. One guy said, "Why don't you answer? Did I do something wrong?" Others just keep leaving messages. I'm no snob, Mr. Packard, just a loner, always have been. I made up a special message or so for these and I thought they were funny and effective but my wife didn't like them too much, except for one, they upset her mother who just doesn't understand, nor do some other people. In the old, old days I used to just take the phone off the hook for a week or so and then the people would come, mostly women, and throw rocks against the window. And then the phone co. phoned and said I couldn't take my phone off the hook that long, it violated some code or other. So, I took the back off of the phone and stuck rags around the bell, then screwed the thing back together. Sitting there one night, nicely drunk and alone and here came this loud *loud* new sound through the phone. It was the phone co. An emergency, a Mr.

---

1. Collected in *To Lean Back into It* (Black Sparrow Press, 1998).

So and So was calling. "Yeah," I said, "what is it?" And here was this lonely, drooling, vicious and sick person—not even a woman—and he said, "I couldn't get you on the phone, I wanted to talk to you ..." "*Jesus Christ!*" I screamed and hung up.

Yeah, I know how it gets, they are days, weeks when everything falls apart. Sometimes I have to lift one foot and deliberately place it in front of the other just to move around. Everything seems stiff, repetitive, black, useless. And everything stupid falls upon you at *once*, it's like a scenario dreamed up by the hell gods. I keep thinking, wait it through, wait it through ... but meanwhile, you can't *do* anything ... pick up your stockings, read the newspaper ... even walking up to a gas pump and sticking the nozzle in the tank is like moving a mountain. All those things, all those things ... Things most people do without thinking, you have to force, to plan, to push. I used to call it being *the frozen man.* And usually about this time your wife or whoever you are with becomes hypercritical and unreasonable. You're just on earth. You think of yourself dying nicely in bed, waiting on the sweet blade but even that doesn't happen.

Thanks for a good issue as usual except for the lady blathering about teaching poetry. They get caught in this thing. They think there are certain rules. Also, they think they are hot shit. They get out 2 or 3 books of safe poesy and latch onto some university for some reason or other (totally unknown to me) and then they start telling you how to do it even though they've hardly done it themselves. That's one of the big problems of poetry, it's dehumanized by those who teach it for a salary and are afraid to lose that salary by doing anything outrageous or even just a little bit different. Great Art, if there is such a thing, is created by the gamblers, by those who are at the very edges of their minds, doing it without knowing it, and certainly without intent or instruction, doing it or else jumping off the bridge or setting themselves on fire or and etc. God damn anything else.

About the other matter: There's nothing makes me sicker than lawyers and lawsuits. It churns and turns my gut. The language of the lawyer is the language *of the trickster. It's an inhuman language, a sub-language. And justice is hardly ever*

224

served. Justice is just forgotten. Our court system are just swamps of dark and devious jargon. It's just a wash of dull, crippled, masked wordage put before a jury of 12 imbeciles or a bored judge. Luck with your mess there. There is only one *NYQ*. And long may it be. And long may you.

[To Maxwell Gaddis]
March 14, 1992 12:21 AM

Well, it's nice that you know a lady who steals your books instead of your money.

On Richmond, he has a right to defend himself. He has run his Rubinski piece elsewhere. If you want to rerun it, fine. What he needs to do, he needs to do. The piece never bothered me, hence I have no comment upon it.

If you want to run excerpts from my letters, fine, if they have the juice and the dance, good.

Regarding *Who's Who* and my advice, "don't try." Well, it means if the stuff doesn't jump on you and make you do it, forget it, in writing and in everything else. I liked best what Ferlinghetti told them when they asked to list him in *Who's Who*. He wrote back, "Fuck you." Beautiful, beautiful.

Cassady, well my problem with him is that I usually spell his name, "Cassidy," but hell, that's o.k. Sometimes they spell me, "Charlene Rubinski."

Cassady had burned down to the end of the string by the time I met him. He wasn't the one Kerouac wrote about. But he was playing to the same old tune, only it had muted. Still, he was best at the wheel of an auto of anybody I had ever seen. The drugs had not altered his perceptions of time vs. space vs. speed. Luckily, I was drunk, damned, and in the back seat as he did his near misses in a drizzling rain. Still, there was an awful sadness about it all. Maybe he knew it. A month or so after I met him, he was dead.

Gaddis, I've got to get back to my fucking detective novel. I hope to finish it one day. Maybe not. I've got the guy in such a fix now I may never be able to work him out of it. I gave him my most fucked-up qualities. In fact, he may even be a bigger asshole than I am. Let's hope so ...

Marc Smirnoff edited a short-lived periodical, The Oxford American.

[To Marc Smirnoff]
March 18, 1992 10:37 PM

I received the copies of the first *The Oxford American.* Beautifully promulgated. Congrats. And thanks for setting up my poems and drawings in fine style. Have not read it all yet ... Back cover a charmer. Read the Kael. Good. But there is a time when one has seen too many movies. And since most of them are god awful, I don't blame her for retiring. On your "Declaration of Intent," I had to smile about your reference to the 3 poems. Your better readers will understand that you did not advertise for poems relating to this particular subject matter and that 3 good poems about crap are better than 3 crappy poems of a seeming more noble aspect. William Faulkner, if he could, would be the first to agree.

I am honored to have been a member of your opening cast.

[To William Packard]
March 20, 1992 12:20 AM

I'm glad I got the poem "it's a drag ..." past you. I like to send you what I consider my luckiest things—not that they can't be rejected, huh?—but anyhow things that I think bite into the page a little better than most of my *poems.*

Work that I send to motorcycle mags and horse racing publications ... well, it is to laugh at the gods, more or less. Big kick to crash into pages that usually don't publish poetry.

Shows anybody can handle a poem if you light the right fire. And I don't slant it to them. I think it's funny when they go it. But you know and I know that there is only ONE *New York Quarterly*. And I think that your publishing so many of my bits does show a bucketful of courage on your part, since Academia and various power groups only consider me a drunken slob and they're right there except I sometimes do things better sloshed than they do sober, staid and sinless. Or maybe I do? Or sometimes I do? Naw. Forget it.

Thanks for sending all the pages to read. I will. They look good. And for sending on table of contents for #48. *Five poems!* I am honored, truly, truly I hope they don't burn you out of your living quarters. Be careful, please. Ummm, umm, ummm ... Great. All too.

On the Belli sonnets,[1] thank you. I used to know Harold Norse (the translator). I've used a near facsimile of him in a couple of stories and maybe some poems. He believes I knifed him in the back with my publisher. Not true. Anyway, if I knifed anybody, it would be straight forward, just above the bellybutton. Ah, we literary freaks, a dismal bitching lot. Thank the gods that the first 50 years of my life were spent with the Blue Collars and the truly mad, the truly beaten.

I am still high, thinking of the 5 poems upcoming in #48. I am sitting here smoking cigarettes from India and getting a further fix listening to classical music on the old black radio to my right. At times things get more and more magic for me and for this I allow myself to feel good. Then I realize it's time to dig in and try to hit a few more over the wall. Maybe I'm the Li Po of San Pedro. But, for it all, I think it's important to attempt to remain human and easy outside of the creative act. If anything's important. Like the famed red wheel barrow. We've got to give it a chance. And still be able to laugh like hell when it all goes wrong as it does for each and all of us, until we no longer need those nostrils to breathe through or the hand that lifts the drink.

---

1. *The Roman Sonnets of G. G. Belli,* translated by Harold Norse, with a preface by William Carlos Williams (Highlands, NC: Jonathan Williams, 1960).

[To John Martin]
March 20, 1992 12:49 AM

Enclosed some letters. Blame the computer age for my re-
taining these, it's all too easy to do. When I had a typewriter it
was one copy and out and gone. Otherwise, I would have to
stick in a carbon which made it seem all too pretensive. This
way, not quite so. [* * *]

Michael Basinski is a poet in Buffalo, N.Y.

[To Michael Basinski]
March 24, 1992 12:00 AM

Thank you for all your work on doing the article on me for
the *Dictionary of Literary Biography*. You've done your research
and have done it well. On the aspects of your insights and
overviews of my work, I take no issue with any of them. You've
taken a look at the long haul, so your view is better than mine
because I'm engrossed with what I'm doing now and also I was
never quite sure of what I was doing then. Frankly it just came
out. Like a bird flies but doesn't know how it does it. Or maybe
we should say, like a snake crawls naturally. If there was
anything which directed me or gave me some impulse, some
drive, it was that I was discouraged with the work I saw my
contemporaries doing. I fired from both guns hoping to wake
up the show. An act of desperation against life and literature?
And ... something to do while I was drinking.

But I never expected the luck that finally came around. Not
that I thought my work was that bad, only that I thought it
would never be accepted. I expected to struggle on in small
rooms via a bare survival. Of course, I did have decades of this.
But what finally came around ... to be known world-wide and
all the rest, this I never never expected. And when it started, it

228

scared hell out of me. Am I getting soft? I asked myself. Will I lose my natural edge? My wild fling with the gods? The best I could do was to ignore this acceptance and to continue the work as I wanted to do it. The work was the joy the saving grace, keeping me from the madhouse. The work was the god damned function by itself. I wanted nothing to keep me from it. And the best of the luck was that the luck came late, very. And now death was moving in. Not that I minded that so much. But it put me into a new area: each drink tasted better and each line, I felt, roared out better, slammed into the page harder. Why not? Why not? I didn't fight this long to toss it in now. I hope I didn't. And that's about where I am now. Thanks again for your work on this article. From Chinaski and me.

[To John Martin]
April 1, 1992 11:27 PM

Some raise! Unbelievable! To think, you promised me $100 a month for life. You and I could never have guessed about this. Maybe all the young and not so young guys will be running to Atlanta to starve and freeze in a tar paper shack without light or water to get themselves started. The whole matter that has occurred is beyond miracle. And your energy has had much to do with it. And you've kept all the stuff in print and available for anybody who wants a look.

Still, I don't have to tell you it isn't the money, never was. But it's a curious signal. And I don't mind it in that way. It's not nice to say but many people make too much money for writing pure shit which tickles or soothes or fools the mass mind. So, in a sense, I can't feel guilty getting some money. Because we wrote it for ourselves, for the joy and madness of it. Great then and all right then.

And if there's a fall back, a cut back, fine. We'll accept that too. What we want to do is to keep going as we have since the beginning until sickness, accident, senility, death or whatever the hell, stops us. Right? Sure.

Us kids from the 30's are some tough sons of bitches. You know it.

[To Ivan Suvanjieff]
April 3, 1992 10:57 PM

Back from track, had some luck but still beastly hungover from last night. But on coming here, here was *The New Censorship*, 2nd Anniversary Issue. Beautifully done, thank you. You placed the drawings nicely and I reread the poems and I think that they still hold. This may be your swan song, I'm sorry, but honored to be along like this. There is a neatness and a warmth in the way you do this thing, these things ... Thanks, mucho, again ... yah ...

Christ, $200 a week, that's bare survival, no, you can't put out a mag on that. When you screwed up your ankle, literature, too, took a great fall. And typists don't get tips. I wish I knew what to tell you, my brain is not too good right now. And, yes, you're right, I'm surprised that I'm here right now. I did all the wrong things to myself and here I sit, my nights are numbered but that doesn't bother me. It just tightens up the structure. I still ache to crash the line down, that's still there. But I don't feel right talking about myself when you're the one in trouble. Yeah, you should get a grant and if you want some words from me, then I'll happily tell them. But you know how that shit goes—those grants go to the already fat and those entrenched safely in the universities. It's an in-grab, all those mother's boys know each other. And you sit there typing for 5 bucks an hour while hoping for the miracle. It's never been fair and it's not gonna get that way.

And for all your troubles, you are still a good enough guy to ship me this mass of magazines. Don't worry, they will go into the best hands that I know.

And thanks for the nice little editorial to open the mag with. I can take some of this. It won't melt me.

I don't know what else to tell you. I wish I had some bright and happy things to wing at you, to give you a lift. But whatever and whatever, it's a great mag you have put out with me in it or with me out of it. May the gods treat you better. Let me hear from you now and then. O.k.? Let me know, huh, Ace?

[To the editor of *Explorations*, Juneau, Alaska.]
April 13, 1992 12:03 AM

Well, I read the poems and it wasn't as bad an experience as I expected. Of course it could help that I don't do this too often?

I've broken up what I have to say into two sections, one about the poems themselves and the other about poetry in general.

Really, the poems I considered best and next best really surprised me, I mean, the writing was really good. Must be something about Alaska?

Well, I hope that my response to all this is suitable to you.

[To William Packard]
April 17, 1992 12:15 AM

Huh. Listen, I know that you can never print all the accepted poems on your backlog. First, it would freak all the good souls of the universe. And, second, there are other writers. Huh.

Yet, I can't resist, in spite of knowing all this, sending you a shit-balloon poem that might explode into the multi-faced reign of ultimate godliness. Huh. Huh, huh?

Still, some concern on "dumb night," for such a poem is considered anti-social enlightenment... such as a drunk vapid woman? Impossible and unfair. There are no longer any

231

drunken sluts. There are only stupid, mean white men. There are no vicious homosexuals or lesbians or bisexuals. And there are no longer any stupid, mean black men. Although there might be some stupid, mean yellow men or brown men, depending upon the political climate and the local of the moment. Each only deserves attack and derision in direct relationship to any force they might apply to our survival. Most successful commercial writers know what to attack and when. And even the Artsy-Fartsies who are touched upon with the Nobel and Pulitzer prizes, they too are screened for any dangerous signals of individuality. But how about … ? you say. How about them? They too sucked to the signal of the moment, the edict, the on-coming demand of thought control. They were only the forerunners of the obvious.

But getting back to small matters, it has always been curious to me that my writing has been attacked for portraying others as I have seen them, but my writing has never been criticized when I ended up as the jackanapes. This could be art, they say, he is calling himself a fucking fool. They like that, it takes the heat off of their frightened asses.

We are living in a terrible climate now. Everybody is waiting to be insulted. I think that I believe more than almost anybody in the right to be whatever you want to be. In fact, I have probably worked more directly from that premise than most and have ended up in any number of hells for doing so. But I did this from a singular stance, most alone, and not buddied up by a jolly group in safe chorus.

So often now, it is not so much a group demanding their rights as it is a group wanting more than their rights, it is almost a tribal on-surging, subconsciously or perhaps even consciously wanting to be top dog and screw all else. Also, there are those within each group who are simply psychotics who want to be seen and heard in parades or any other damned place or time.

As a writer, one must write what one sees and feels regardless of the consequences. In fact, the more the consequences the more one is goaded into going for it. Some call it madness, I call it near-truth. You know, there is nothing more entertaining, funnier than near-truth because you see it, read it so seldom. It hits you with a refreshing blast, it runs up the arms, into the head, it gets giddy, god damn, god damn, so rare, so lovely. I saw some of it in Céline, in Dostoevski, in Hamsun, I started laughing as I read them, it was such a joy

In our age, the only safe target for the writer is the white heterosexual male. You can make him a murderer, a child-rapist, a motherfucker. Nobody protests. Not even the white heterosexual male. He's used to it. Also, things like "White men can't dance," "White men can't jump," "White men have no sense of rhythm," etc.. What is happening here might be a near-truth, still it is mostly mouthed by white women and promoted by white men in the media. Am I racist? Tell me, how many non-whites have you had in your home or in your room lately?

Well, we go on and on. Probably a certain psychosis working here. I hope so. It seems to give one an edge in the working place. Still the poem "dumb night" got me to thinking about this and about the reaction you'd get if you published it. Yet, many of us have had nights like this one. It's just a place within a place, something that explodes into the air, and for all its grossness there is a certain demented glamour of two people trapped together in a world that has never worked for them and never will. There is no insult to man or woman intended but if there is some insult there, then fine, it belongs.

Well, I'm drinking, have been or wouldn't have gone on so long. Basically, only want to say that at this time it is tough for the writer who wants to put it down as it is, or was. The 90's have far more strictures than the 50's ever had. We've gone back, not so much in how we think but in what we can say. Each Age has borne its own contriticions [?contradictions ?contritions] but the end of the 20th century is a particularly sad one. We've lost our guts, our gamble, our heart. Listen, believe me, when we say it and say it true, the women will love it, the blacks, the browns, the yellows, the greens, the reds and the purples will love it, and the homosexuals and the lesbians and all the in between will love it. Let's not crap ourselves, we are different but we are one. We bring death to each other and death brings it to us. Did you ever see that flattened cat on the freeway as you drove by at 70 m.p.h.? That's us, baby. And I scream to the skies that there should be no way, no word, no limit. Just a roll of the dice, the tilting of the dark white light and the ability to laugh, a few times, at what has trapped us like this.

[To William Packard]
April 17, 1992 1:42 AM

Thanks, got your big fat return envelope, like those enclosures, will get at them next day or next, whenever I feel fat and sassy. I like your bits, they tighten my screws, hopefully keep me from wandering all over the place creatively. There is a certain tight line I haven't adhered to. My guts are lazy.

Drove in from track, had won $120 but my lady was in a certain snappish mood right off, and so I had to cut. The right-off gets me, if they'd only give a man time to inhale, o.k. But the jump is too quick. I mean, shit, man, let me scratch myself first.

Anyhow, drove to this skidrow sushi joint, just sat down and here some guy at the end says, "Hey, Hank!"

I looked at him and he said, "I guess you don't know me? Met you at a party at Paul's one night, you wanted to smash my face in..."

"Oh hell, forget it," I said. He was talking 25 years back.

A drink arrived, c/o Smashface. I thanked him.

Then guy next to me said, "Are you Bukowski?"

So, that started that. Another drink. And he laid his life down. Not bad. Educated.—Wife had been screwed by best friend. What else is new?

Anyway, wanted to congratulate you on taking poem "dumb night" so wrote you about it in *another letter*, enclosed. You're getting all these goodies tonight, William!

You know what? I think Auden got the word down better than anybody. Clipped and to the point and, at the same time, explosive. But you were never offended by his presence. Hemingway, ultimately, offended, you could always feel him saying, "Watch me. See what I am doing?" It finally shows. You

234

read him again and again and it finally shows. Read Auden and it's there. Clear. Even with Jeffers you feel the prancing. Or Shakespeare, especially. Or for me. Taste. I always preferred the old one in the chorus line to the new stripper she has replaced. No, that's bullshit, I'm just playing around....

Been reading this book, *The Thirsty Muse* by Tom Dardis. Good stuff, especially on Faulkner and Hemingway. I think they both drank more hard liquor than I ever did, mostly I couldn't get hold of it, had to settle for the beer and wine I could scrounge. But I really did the noon to doom trick for decades and how I made the rent and the sanity I'll never know. And the jails and the beatings, and the women who said they loved me and took my poor wallet when I was out cold. The loss of a wallet when you're right on the edge is damn near like losing your balls. Again and again. That nailed home my distrust of Humanity.

My god, how I warble on here! Trying to explain how I wrote the first drunken letter, I am drunker here.

For a fellow nearing 72, though, I am a tough nail. I will get out of bed in the morning, feed all 8 cats while my wife sleeps, go off to the track, handicap tomorrow's ten race card and probably win. Not for the money but for the hell of knowing something and following it through.

I know I am going to die, fairly soon, maybe. I should. It's mathematics. I get charts from life insurance companies telling me my life expectancy. Thank you, motherfuckers. But I'll tell you, there have been three miracles in my life: *Loujon Press, The Black Sparrow Press* and *The New York Quarterly*. Others have hesitated or said no, but these three outlets have been very strange, they've said, "Good, good, send us more. Do you have more? Send it."

Not to put the rust on the crap but for a fellow who has really grubbed it and been torn by the hyena and the powdered inane mother from the hell of everywhere, such an opening to my madness and my limping half-assed genius has made the impossible become the miracle. And yet I know that you will be just as gracious to the next. The next young. The next old. The next next. Always before death there will be one more sleeping tiger, one more frog leaping, one more Hemingway opening a

235

bottle of Valpolicella ... one more letter to write, one more time to think, maybe it's all right ... And the saddest thought of all, when I was in Paris and Sartre sent word that he'd like to meet me and I said, no. Horrible, horrible, horrible .... And I wasn't even young. I was drunk and maddened with nothingness. A good time for him. I didn't realize it. I realize it now and my whole life stinks of ugliness.

[To John Martin]
April 17, 1992 2:02 AM

Late. Have to get to bed to make track tomorrow. So, this is short. Except computer breakdown, which I solved in my own fashion, have eliminated many former trips to repair shop. Have tested a few computer geniuses on my method of cure. They look at me blankly, say, "Never heard of that." Nor is it listed in the manuals. Of course, I never told these so-called computer geniuses my answer, only hinted at it.

But I can tell you, any answer is very near and almost too simple to realize. Test the closet factor never mentioned and it will bring you in. Maybe. But it's worth a shot and it's sensible.

Letter bit enclosed. In case of a book of letters, probably long after I'm gone. You know what's really tiresome? Old farts babbling about their age. Well, this old fart has got to hit the sack ... take it easy, kid ... Hard to believe you were alive in the 30's but easy to believe so now.

[To Jon Cone]
May 8, 1992 12:07 AM

Thanks for the copies of *World Letter* 4, nicely done indeed. Good to be aboard with all that roaring talent. My favorite piece was the Irving Stettner novel excerpt.

236

I don't think you took too long to get your mag out.

If you want to publish my poem "screwed within the universe" I'd be honored. I haven't sent it elsewhere. I don't do that. But there might be some poems coming along soon. I have two sitting here from last night but I like to send them out in groups of 4 to 5, so I'll wait to see if more come along, then I'll submit for your look-see. There is a strange flavor to *World Letter* which fascinates me. Of course, I might send you some shit. If I do, well, you know how to handle that.

On the novel, *Pulp*, "dedicated to bad writing," I keep getting my detective into screwed-up situations and it's often hell trying to get him out. Most of the time he just rather blanks out and sucks on vodka or cold sake. It's not a literary work, not meant to be. But I can have him babbling any number of things about life and people and I can blame him for bad form instead of me. It's a nice escape hatch and if I can work him out of his dumb jams I might finish the bit. Would seem a shame to leave him dangling but that's the way most of us are: dangling.

all right, all right, all right, all right, all right, cheers to you,

---

[To Eugene Donders]
May 8, 1992 12:45 AM

I don't think there will be another trip to Europe. Death has me pretty much by the balls now and the time I'd take to travel would be put to better use playing my word game.

On writing, you're right, the simple word usually gets it better, it seems to carve it deeper into the paper and there is the manner of saying too, the easy roll of words as you get at something or try to get at something. Still, there are odd times when I like to throw in an almost awkward word that somehow becomes not awkward when it gets worked into a sentence. It's rather like a tightener, it makes the sentence jump into the air for a moment. But you must be careful not to overdo it.

I'm in a bit of spiritual funk now, frankly feeling shitty, there are reasons, or so I think, for feeling shitty and I also feel that the feeling shitty bit will end even though what often causes me to feel shitty will remain. And I am not the only person about who is getting slapped about by the stupid forces. What would Céline say? Probably, "Ah, hell, I knew it all along …"

Well, I've been lucky in my writing in that it's getting better as I get older. If I could buck up and live to be 82 my words would probably set off explosions or start barking like dogs. What I've tried to do, I have done. It's all the rest that is so tiresome, so wearing.

Yes, your cigars are still about. They go best with red wine and the dear old classical music. I owe so much to those composers. They pump me up when the crap closes in.

[To Jon Cone]
May 17, 1992

Thanks for sending some of the Céline-Hindus correspondence.[1] I have a special taste for Céline. His words exploded upon the page, Laughter from Hell. Poor Céline, Hamsun and Pound were politically incorrect: they picked the losers. But more out of obstinacy and contrariness. Good writers seldom go with the obvious, it's an instinct.

Anyhow, Céline, especially in *Journey* … really landed with an original force, far more so than Ezra P.

All right. The walls still surround us.

---

1. Milton Hindus, *The Crippled Giant: A Literary Relationship with Louis-Ferdinand Céline* (Hanover, NH: University Press of New England for Brandeis University Press, 1986).

[To William Packard]
May 22, 1992 1:17 AM

[* * *] Thanks for your notices of the poetry show. Yeah, I think poetry would sound better to *me* in another language. *On* language, you are probably right: "American" beats "English" and the others. It's a more brittle rock and it screams.

Say, you do keep busy! I like action too but find most of it outside the field of the Arts. Like the Horse and the Bottle. An old man's old habits.

Well, yes, I spoke German to begin with. Brought over here at age of 3. Soon had to rid myself of it and the accent because it was in grammar school where they hated you for it. Soon I could no longer speak it, only understand it when I heard it. Then after that I forgot it all. Strange though that most of my early luck in writing came through (early luck? I was about 55) the German translations of my work. I went back to Germany twice. First time read in Hamburg. Before the largest crowed, they joked, since Hitler. "It's good to be back," I told them. Saw my 92 year old uncle and the house I had been born in. For some decades I was told, it was used as a whorehouse. Fitting.

Yeah, the American language in poetry. Not much of it. e. e. cummings?

I only wished people, writers, could realize that poetry can be entertaining without losing any of its values or force. God damn it, what is the prissy show we are still putting on? Ow, ow, ow. [* * *]

[To Jon Cone]
May 22, 1992 1:12 AM

I am honored that you found so many poems acceptable for *World Letter* 4. I'm only too glad to wait for whenever #4 comes out. There is something about *WL* that reminds me of the old days when writing was exciting, a great act, an exploring flame—

basically from 1919 to 1936. After that, something happened to the writers and they wrote programmed and careful works to appease and fulfill whatever demanded to be appeased and fulfilled. So, yes, it's an honor to be with you.

Between us, the poem "the old literary chit chat" does refer to N[eeli] C[herkovsky] and one other fellow. Yes, that book company never would have published a line of mine but they can come in when it's safe with a safely-written book.

Regarding Harvey Pekar,[1] the bad health matter is truly a horrible thing. And all about you the idiots are chewing apples and farting their brains out of their ears. I saw John Fante slowly chopped away. And let me tell you, he just showed natural guts during the process. I mean, he didn't make a big show of it, he faced it straight, he was truly beautiful about it. I wish Harvey Pekar much strength and luck and the blessings of the gods, in spite of everything.

I've had a problem or two myself, nothing too awful, I don't think. But going to lay it down now and ease off.

Just wanted you to know I got your o.k. and that this city hasn't burned down again yet but there are one or two matters working now that could start it up all over again. I was also here for the Watts riots so many decades ago. Nero would love this place. All right, onward *World Letter*!

[To William Packard]
May 30, 1992 12:12 AM

Sorry about Maine getting on your case about subscriptions but you're not a salesman. Poetry is hard sell anyhow. There aren't more than two or three people in the U.S. who can make a living writing it. Please do send me some subscription forms and I'll try to place them where I think they might do

---

1. Author of comic book scripts, such as (in collaboration with his wife, Joyce Brabner) *Our Cancer Year* (1992) and the *American Splendor* series.

something. That's a slow process, though, and I'll have to wait for the good spots. Hope I can help.

Hard to believe you've been at the helm of the *NYQ* since 1969. And I must say that your backing of my work has been an amazing thing. What I mean is, you've published some of my things that took some nerve—I mean, on your part. You are not afraid of the gamble. Thank you.

I've been coming in from the track pretty damned tired, the game is wearing me down. Still, the writing comes along. Writing is like digging yourself out of a pile of crap but then the pile covers you again and you have to write your way out of it again. Shoveling shit with words, huh?

You say, send more poems. I don't know. Wrote some last night. One I think is much better than the others. I enclose. Of course, a writer is often the worst judge of his own work. And I've been rejected before. Don't worry.

Still can't see too well. 4 or 5 weeks and they take the stitches out of the eye. Should be able to see the ugly world real clear then.

[To John Martin]
May 31, 1992 10:20 PM

Yes, I'd like to join Hornsby, Cobb, Sisler, Williams, et. all but the eye is still on the mend. Operation was May 12. My man says it should be 7 weeks before they remove the stitches that hold new lens in place. Maybe I have an old-fashioned Dr., I don't know but whatever I've got, I've got to go with. He tells me that there are 3 stitches and that these cause the eye to basically "wrinkle" and that with the removal of the stitches I will see 70 percent better at first and then it will go on from there. He seems very precautionary and perhaps he should be. Perhaps those quick type recovery stories are from those who had a different type of operation. Anyhow, I am stuck with mine and really don't mind. I have the feeling that I have lucked it onto a fellow who really knows what he is doing.

241

Anyhow, this is nothing compared to the old TB party of—what was the year?—1990? Not much writing that year. I don't see how D. H. Lawrence ever fired up to create during it. The antibiotics really knocked me on my ass. [* * *]

[To William Packard]
June 13, 1992

I'm glad I got the turf club poem past you. Invited to another function there today but passed. Lost my money in the clubhouse.

I'd be only too happy to say something usable about the *NYQ*. If you can use it, fine.

Lemme see.

1 . The *NYQ* merely has the finest format and content in the land.

2. The *NYQ* is a bloody miracle. No more, no less.

3. The *NYQ* publishes the best in all schools of poetry and criticism.

4. Promulgated to go forward with guts and style.

5. Poetry is not dead. Only the idea of what poetry should be is dead. The *NYQ* gives us a new transfusion of the written word, something to astound, entertain and delight you.

Any of the above do? I tried to think about it at the racetrack but I can't think at the racetrack. This jockey's agent approaches me with a drink in his hand. He wants to talk. I'm losing and my fucking eye hurts. Phoned my doctor but he wasn't in. They never are when you're in deep shit. The jock's agent begins on me but I shrug him off with a few words. He always looks hurt and puzzled when I do this. And I do this almost every day. I used to be the other way, I used to suffer for other people, let them slobber their dullness over me. No more. I'm running short of days. I've become kind to myself. I can handle it. Don't get me wrong, I'm not brutal about things but I have a way of sliding off and vanishing. Like, I got caught at a party once, poets and guitar players and other general damn

242

fools. I took my drink, walked through the kitchen and out the back porch, climbed the back fence and walked through somebody else's yard out to the street, walked around the block to get back to my car, got in and drove off feeling wonderful. I'm a real loner. I never met a loner like I. There might be one? We'd better not meet. We'd run from each other.

Well, the computer has been in the shop, it's back now, I'm sucking on beer and maybe I better play with this machine and see if there's any juice left in it.

Approaching 50 issues? With the *same* editor? This is impossible. Sometimes I wonder what you *really* think about it all? I really have problems with poets, they are totally inhuman, I mean, in person, and all too often with the word.

[To Jon Cone]
June 14, 1992

Thank you for the good words on *Last Night* poems.[1] I feel my work is getting stronger also. Age needn't be a detriment: see Cervantes. *Last Night* poems were written in 1991. Maybe it's the luck of doing it for so long but I feel the words just grip at the page better. When I sit down I get a power glow and it just emanates. I was a very late starter and one of those old-fashioned starve-for-your-Art types. I lived the mad and the desperate years. I think it all fed forward to where I am at this moment. Yet, I am aware that everything can vanish overnight, I can just become a common old fart weakly tickling at the word. But right now I need it all—the words filling the page, getting me out of corners, explaining away the almost unexplainable. I don't see how people can do anything at all without writing or painting or something of the like, some excessive splash against the darkness. It's just too damned dumb to sit

---

1. *The Last Night of the Earth Poems,* published by Black Sparrow Press in March 1992.

and take it straight like most of them do. No wonder people look, act, are so awful awful awful...

Well, on e. e. cummings, he came at a time when I was reading everything and had many half-heroes. It was not so much his content as his tricky and lovely and easy and funny way of using and placing his words. That was it. No content, say like Jeffers. But somehow I had this strange Romantic feeling about him. And Auden, Spender, Pound. Sherwood Anderson, etc. These bastards simply gave me the old thrill. It didn't last but it was good while it did. And I look back at them and probably feel that they were much better than they actually were. But they did their work for me: they carried me along while I worked with my own madness and failure. William Saroyan also gave me a hell of a boost. He had this easy open style. His sugary optimism got to me at times. But some of his things were truly rolling great. Then he got to writing too much. And somewhere along the line his ideals and his originality vanished. His writing flattened terribly. I felt betrayed by him. I didn't expect him to melt away like other human beings. Some do hold though. Hamsun was a son of a bitch, he never gave an inch and he explored about every damned thing. Ah, well...

man the guns, they're coming, yrs,

[To Donald McRae]
June 23, 1992 11:58 PM

Linda located you for me, good, I've been wanting to write you to thank you for the great review in the [London] *Guardian*. It was an honor. And besides being accurate was written in a good lively style. Indeed.

Here I am still writing, poems mostly, dark but steady stuff, I think, and even one or two for small laughs. Slowly working away at a detective novel, "dedicated to bad writing." It's not exactly literature, which is nice and relaxing. And the detective is a mixture of the stupid with just a touch of the sublime which allows me to say things I couldn't ordinarily say. Only I get this dick into so many weird jams that it sometimes takes me a long time to figure my way or his way out of them. If I ever finish this thing it will be called *Pulp*. In the 30's there were many "pulp" magazines around in which the writer got a penny a word, sometimes less. The writers wrote night and day to make it, they just lived on top of the typewriter. Romantic, weird and horrible times.

I am sending the latest book by separate (and slower, probably) mail. *The Last Night of the Earth Poems*. Believe all of them were written in 1991 when I had a rush of poem gushings. I think that basically they hold.

Linda said you mentioned something about a BBC thing. The BBC had asked me at an earlier time, I think within a year, to do something. But feeling anti that sort of thing at the moment, I believe that I asked for 2 thousand dollars and scared them off. Which was my intent. You know, you can talk your life away. The only idea is to put words down on paper. The other things tend to detract, sometimes kill. I turn down 2 dozen requests for interviews a year. Recently turned down invites to appear on the Carson show (now-x) and the Dennis Miller show. These are talk shows and have nothing to do with what I'm doing. Actually I'm not even interested in selling my books, only in writing them. Of course, I hope they sell well so that I can live to write more but as long as they sell well enough I'm not interested in pushing them further. But I feel that with you at the helm of the BBC thing we might have some fun and madness. So, if the BBC boys aren't still pissed at me and if you can line them up, let's go ahead. Let me know.

Right now, I'm kind of stalled at the track, I stand on one foot, then the other and then it's all over, wasted and weary and dumbly sealed and doomed. I feel shit upon by the Fates. I used to do well out there, get into a kind of rhythm with life and then come on in and carry it forward onto the keyboard. Looks like I've got to shake up my system. I do that every now and then and seem to move into another area and it always works. So, tomorrow I'm going to shake them up and try this new insight I've been working on during some sleepless nights, just lying there next to Linda, all the various angles running through my brain. I think I've come upon a real good one. I call it The Law of Racing. That is, the horse almost has to win, it can't do anything else because when all the values are applied it almost has to happen—first at the wire. It doesn't work in maiden races because there's not enough background to feed from but I have a special play for those anyhow.

Well, take care of yourself. Who knows? One of these days we might be lifting a few across that same table. Remember?

well, all right and yes, and yes and all right,

Kevin Ring was editor of Beat Scene *and* Transit, *both from Coventry, England.*

[To Kevin Ring]
June 24, 1992 11:28 PM

Yes, I rec. *Beat Scene* #14. Very nicely done. Had forgotten I'd sent you the poems. Thank you for setting them up so well, you make me look good.

I don't know, though, the Beats somehow make me sad. It's like they just didn't come through. They hung together too much. And talked too much—about themselves. And they went for the media, the limelight. They slacked off on their work, their creation. It weakened. It's like they had no carry-through. Fame mattered more than just doing it. It's all terribly sad, Kevin, it really is. [* * *]

[To Terry ?————]
July 2, 1992 12:07 AM

Hello Terry:
Whether to use a comma after a parenthesis depends upon the construction of the sentence.

246

I believe it's unconstitutional to force religion upon patients in a State Mental Health facility. But I doubt that you are in a position to fight this matter. I had a similar experience when I was near death in the L.A. County Charity Ward. At 5 a.m. the Salvation Army Band arrived outside of our windows and began blasting us with Godly sounds. It was Easter morning. The sound (and message) were unbearable. After the band left they rolled out 5 stiffs. (Note the non-use of a comma in above sentence containing a parenthesis.)

Terry, you keep fucking up. You can't drink when you are medicated, you know that. It would also be nice if you showed some remorse for those you brutalize. Including your mother. I shouldn't lecture you. I don't particularly believe in morals but I do believe in kindness. It's a good thing.

The problem is that they just don't want to root out the cause of your problem, that's too much work. They'd rather keep you medicated and locked up. That's the easy way out, except for you. In some cases the patient must be his own healer because that's the only out.

Well, I'm tired. Got a few problems, none like yours but they wear on me. So, I'm going to close. Need an early night's sleep. That damned world is going to be waiting for me in the morning.

[To William Packard]
July 4, 1992 12:30 AM

Karl Shapiro sent me a copy of his *The Old Horsefly*, inscribed.[1] I feel honored. He still hurls the word nicely. A very good read. I read it straight through.

Here, I wait to live through the 4th. On these holidays the masses gurgle up out of nowhere and overswarm everything. Ant-roaches. I'm sorry, I can't love them. I know I should. I

---

1. *The Old Horsefly* (Orono, ME: Northern Lights, 1992).

should understand. But I always go more on what I feel than what I'm supposed to think. That sounds precious, doesn't it?

Just wrote a friend at the violent ward of a Texas mental hospital. His latest is that he pulled the hair off of a blonde girl. But he writes asking if it is proper to use a comma after a parentheses. Says Norman Mailer does. I told him that it all depends upon the construction of the sentence. I hope that calms him somewhat.

[To Miles Corwin]
July 11, 1992 12:23 AM

Thank you for wishing to interview me on the future of the city of Los Angeles. I have been here since 1923 but for the sake of my own sanity and decency I'd rather not join the soothsayers. All too many have taken the riots and adjacent problems as springboards toward their own publicity and aggrandizement.

A similar situation is taking place with the AIDS problem. Big Names have become Bleeding Hearts to the Cause. Why? Because it looks so great. It'll pay off elsewhere, the public will believe that you are a good soul and they will tend more to buy whatever particular talent you pretend to.

So much is said out of one side of the face. The history of humanity does not change. Nor do our leaders, our politicians, our entertainers, our businessmen, our etc.

Count me out. Again, thanks. And good luck to you.

[To Gerald Locklin]
July 26, 1992 12:30 AM

Yeah, a lot of roadblocks lately—spiritually and healthwise —a fucking drain. But looking back I realize that something was always eating at me and I worked around it anyhow. Now with death on the back of my neck, I should realize that change is coming anyhow. A new movie. Could be a worse one. Anyhow, there's an excess of wear working now, on me, so that's one of the reasons I say, no interview. Lock, I get calls for interviews about 3 times a month. I mean, I could be yapping about myself continually. Problem is, I'm just not that interested in myself.

On e. e. cummings, I don't think he was that much of an influence. He did catch me at a time when I was Romantic about those guys. So many of them working out of the 20's and into the 30's. It seemed a lively time to me. Like now, I don't feel like there's any liveliness in writing, nothing cutting, new, interesting. People just ... write ... but it's more like a task. On cummings I liked the way he placed his words on the page. He had a painter's eye, a gambler's eye. Others try it, it doesn't work. There was a joy, and a rareness in the way he placed the word. That's all. I don't really believe he said too much but the *way* he said it lit things up. High interest. It was good reading. That's all I know.

On *Hank*, well, I'm trying to forget about it. Maybe it will just vanish. It deserves to. I should have made a better character judgment. On top of everything, the guy lost a mass of irreplaceable photos and other items. It was just a real sloppy and careless undertaking all around.

On *Pulp*, I think it's coming along good. Lots of lucky dialogue. So far. I have fun with it between poems.

Too many ten race cards lately. And a 6 day week. Plus pressures which I won't speak of. Sometimes I wonder why I haven't cracked yet. I think it's writing the Word down. I need that. The ass I am saving is my own. So far.

[To William Packard]
August 4, 1992 11:54 PM

Sorry you've been down ... You are pushing too hard, they are expecting too much of you and you are giving too much. Back off a little and breathe. Please.

I too have rather gone bust. I measure myself by what comes off the machine and I've been too drained to even get at it. Got over the eye operation, then here came the old pains in the right leg and to make it worse I got in the jacuzzi the wrong way and twisted hell out of it, then got drunk the same night talking with an actor and a rep from a channel about a TV series, it all turned out shitty, nobody agreed and thankfully everything fell through. But next day leg was worse. Went to a doc today, he said it could be diabetes, better get a blood test. So, that's next. I'm probably all right but it's the pain, can't sleep, limp out of my car, crawl into track, have to leave early, come home to wife. So, that's enough crying.

I've probably got you some subscriptions—Blue Moon Bookstore—others—or so they claim to have subscribed by writing me about it. I still have the eye out and have the forms for the potentialities. One writer-editor misunderstood when I sent him subscription form with a notation that this was "a damned good mag ..." "O.k.," he wrote back, "I sent them a copy of the magazine and some of my poems ..." Ah, Humanity! He'll probably send a cover letter stating: "Charles Bukowski suggested that I submit my work to you ..."

Writers. Another one, he was supposed to be dying in a hospital, got these poems from him. They were fair. So, to cheer him, I wrote him a little line, something about him showing some courage. Ah, he didn't die. Time went by. And out came this book with my blurb on the cover, words changed just a bit so that they seemed to cover the entire contents of the book and his life. He'd also gotten something by Creeley. The poems were pretty bad. You have to be careful with anything you write to a writer. There was one fellow, decades ago, he was good and I wrote somewhere or other, "A great undis-covered talent." But something happened. His writing went flat. The years went on and more books came out with the

250

blurb, "A great undiscovered talent." Also in ads and also used by book reviewers, "Bukowski says that —— is a great undiscovered talent..." I don't "say" it. I *said* it, a long long time ago. Ah, the writer. It's all a game of push and shove to them. Tricks. Why don't they just keep writing poems and let the poems speak for themselves?

Also, Terrell[1] should understand that people don't subscribe to poetry magazines. Poets read them but only when they get a contributor's copy. The public isn't interested in poetry and you can't blame them. Most poetry has very little to do with their lives or anything else. Poetry has its head stuck up its own crotch. The old *Poetry, a magazine of verse*, had a quote, "To have great poetry we should have great audiences..." They had it backwards. The poetry should bring the audience. It hasn't. And your last issue was a lesson in how to get that audience. Truly astonishing work. But the masses don't know, they don't trust it, the centuries of it have done them in.

Long ago I brought out a little magazine, long long ago. 3 issues.[2] We had one subscriber. And we were very astonished and surprised to have our one subscriber. But even that didn't last. He wrote in and bitched about something we had printed, so we sent him back his money and told him to get lost.

I'm tired, man. You keep it going.

[To William Packard]
August 23, 1992 11:14 PM

Thanks for sending the inscribed copy of *The Art of Poetry Writing*. And that you used me quite often here and there to make a point. It felt very strange to be in with some of the big boys and girls of the centuries. Thank you, indeed.

I've been a bit weary of late, physically tired along with

---

1. Carroll F. Terrell, publisher of the *New York Quarterly*.
2. *Laugh Literary and Man the Humping Guns*, 1969.

some problems, and have also been spiritually dragging. So, it was good to lay about with your book although I used it mainly to read bits of poems and sayings, some of my favorites like Ezra's let's to war poem[1] and others. I think a poet should have a grounding in all areas of poetics and if he wishes to discard or not use some of them afterwards, fine. There is no such thing as knowing too much. I don't have a basic grounding in poetics, my lifestyle got in the way. Now I'm too frigging craggy and inbred to learn. Anyhow, it was good of you to send the book. It is needed and, better yet, it's quite interesting. Yes.

[To William Packard]
October 2, 1992 11:48 PM

[* * *] You know, I get many magazines in the mail, some of them with my poems in them, some without, and most of them have the same tonality and style, much of it influenced by my own writing style but they just don't get it right. And the liberated ladies with their sex poems, what a bore. Don't they realize that fucking can be a drag and talking about it, dragger? Anyhow, the poem, "Ah, Look!" allows me to air some of this out, thank you.

Speaking of magazines, got one in the mail today, *Chiron Review*, Autumn 1992 and on page 17 was a poem by one Antler called "Pussysmell Candlelight" which I believe was previously published by *NYQ* #47 page 32.

I used to know an old beatnik who came over and drank my booze and puked on the rug and borrowed (?) money. He kept sending out his already published poems for decades and decades and when I told him this was a nefarious practice he screamed at me, "There ain't no fucking law against it!" And I told him, "There ain't no fucking law you can't write any new

---

1. "Sestina: Altaforte," which begins, "Damn it all! All this our South stinks peace."

stuff either." I soon rid myself of this one. And for that matter, almost everybody else.

[* * *] Ezra. Ezra Pound. Strange, yet not so strange. Look at Céline, Hamsun ... There is something in the writer that likes to go the other way for the hell of it. That's why they write: what's closest seems the most unbearable: country, father, mother, neighbor, you name it. The writer wants more than there is and it's just not there, so most writers end up drained, deluded and fucked. But then, who doesn't?

[To William Packard]
October 3, 1992 11:32 PM

Thanks for the test questions. I'm afraid I'd flunk your course.

And thanks for enclosing the cover letter you received from the person in Scottsdale, Arizona. Pretty amazing, they think they can push through by methods they have been taught in Salesmanship and Business Administration. So many people think it's done by trick and push. Such a letter is, at the same time, humorous and sickening to one who might read it. And thanks for not sending on the poems of "peace and calm" which came with the cover letter.

[* * *] About a month ago I was bitten by a spider. Or so presumed the doc. There were 3 bites, large lumps on the left arm. Doc said spiders usually bite in 3 bites, they walk along and go bite, bite, bite. Got on the antibiotics and some other pill. For about a week. Really felt mind dead on the stuff. Just to try while I was in that shape I sat down and faced the machine. Absolutely nothing. Not even a bad poem. Just nothing. I thought, this is what happens when it leaves you. What will I ever do if this happens? The answer came quickly: you just drink yourself to death.

I'm all right now, though. I think.

[To the editor of *Zyzzyva*]
October 6, 1992 12:46 AM

Hello Editor Zyzzyva:
Glad you liked "The Bully." The incident took place while I was working at the loading docks of The Biltmore Hotel, Los Angeles. Nice job.

Thanks for enclosing the bit from *Poets & Writers Magazine*. No, I don't know Ed Ochester. Good of him to mention me. 1957 a hell of a time ago and I wasn't young then but just beginning to write poetry, began more or less at age 35. (born 8-6-20). 1 do remember *Epos*, down there in Florida, a bit on the flowery side, lady named Thorne ran it. I wrote some stuff for them, wrote hard poems but stuck in a poetic line here and there. Later when I no longer did this, they sent the stuff back: "We are disappointed in you, believed you had the makings of a major talent." I went on writing anyhow and still am.

[To Louise Webb]
October 13, 1992 12:05 am

Well, I'm a louse. I've put off writing you not because I didn't want to but because I let other things get in the way, stupid and ordinary things, dull things and some things that had to be done just to do them. Life gets in the way but that's no excuse. So—*I hope to hell you survived the hurricane.* Please write, if you have. Or if you're too pissed at me to write, well, I don't blame you.

We've had a few happenings around here. Earthquake. Riot. I had a cataract operation on right eye. See better now even if I can't understand most of what I see. I still write. Working on a novel, *Pulp*. A detective story. I should finish it. Linda's o.k. and sends her love. We now have 9 cats. The strays arrive and we can't turn them away. We've got to stop. Damned cats get me up early in the morning to let them out. If I don't, they start ripping up the furniture. But they are wonderful and beautiful

254

animals. Cool. I know where the expression "cool cat" comes from now.

Anyway, enough of this. Hope you're all right. I'm 72 now. I should have been dead decades ago. Still go to the track everyday. And drink. But not as much. Pains in my right arm now. But basically I'm pretty sound physically but my fighting days are over. Except with the writing.

If you're there, hold on. Those days and nights with you and Jon were and are unforgettable.

[To Paul Peditto]
October 25, 1992 11:17 PM

Well, there has been a large anti-Columbus movement for several years now, or it seems I have noticed it for several years. I don't know anything about Columbus, for or against but I guess your piece came out at a bad time for you. I guess the movie will do all right but people on stage look too real. In fact, they are.

A writer is going to get resistance to his work always unless he feeds the mass mind the pap they want. The only thing you can do is to write the way you want to write and to hell with everything else. It's better to fail your way than to succeed their way. And so you know what that means: you've got to stay alive in another way, financially, than with your writing, and that's the killer, the gut-ripper, it can turn out all your lights. You just have to concentrate on the little time they let you have outside of the job and then there are traps within your own time: women, the weakening of your endurance, all that crap. But if you want to put the word down bad enough, you're going to do it anyhow. You can't expect a fast breakthrough, you should even be wary of one. You know what happens to those who get early success, the edge leaves and they fall away, they soften and vanish. You've got to figure what they have done to you they have done to many writers. You've got to outgut them, outwait them, slam the word down harder. I got lucky pretty damned late but I had decided even if nothing happened I was going to continue. I had to because when I saw what was said to be the great writing of our time, I couldn't believe it, it sickened me, I knew there had to be more than that, even if it was only for an audience of one: me.

What the hell, kid, it's a great fight. Don't toss in.

[To Jon Cone]
November 4, 1992 10:57 PM

I'm glad the big bird drawing worked for you. One never knows, I figured what the hell, it's just like writing: you do what you want to do or have to and afterwards if anybody besides you sees anything in it, that's just a free plus, So, good ... good.

I crashed down on the brick steps where I live, came in totally drunk, split head on right side, fucked up knee and back and right hand—tonight is the first night I've been able to use it—but am mending and going to start over again. Will try to keep my drinking to beer or wine from here on in. I have this tremendous thirst and I toss the hard stuff in and in and on and on ... That's what happens when I go out: I try to escape people by drinking myself senseless. At 72, I should make some adjustments, I don't want to be sitting on a bed pan somewhere with a roomful of people who are dead but not buried. [* * *]

[To John Martin]
November 4, 1992 10:40 PM

Great contract! Great!

This is the first time I've been at the computer in days. My head wasn't all that crashed. Right hand badly hurt but evidently no broken fingers. Bad back but getting better. I will step back up to the plate very soon ...

It's all so stupid. Rock doesn't mean that much to me. Lots

of noise and often a great beat but the word content not too great for any of the rock bands. Actually, the rock bands *are* the establishment. But for the very young I suppose it makes them feel as if they were fighting the parent. But they soon become the parent. Anyhow, I was very foolish and if I don't learn from this, I never will.

At least, you are holding your ground. You know that the meaning is in what you do, not in what the others try to do.

[To John Martin]
November 5, 1992 12:24 AM

Montfort asked me to do a thing for some show he has going somewhere, some kind of big shot deal. See enclosed. I screwed up the margin a bit, couldn't get it straight. I'm still on the road to recovery...

Well, I hope he likes it. He's helped us a lot.

[*Enclosed:*]

Something about the Photographer

It was some time well over a decade ago, my editor-publisher John Martin phoned me, "There's this fellow, Michael Montfort, he's probably the world's leading Bukowski collector. He wants to take some photos of you, photography is his trade and he's a nice guy. How about it?" The first thing I remember about Michael is his arrival. He knocked on the door, I opened it and there he stood with a case of wine on his shoulder. My kind of fellow.

Oh yes, and there were the German pretzels. Linda, my wife, joined us. We drank and talked and the camera made its sounds. It was all very gentle and painless. That was the beginning... We have been friends of Michael's ever since.

We visited his place and saw the Bukowski collection. It was in fireproof compartments under lock and key. Michael

257

had things I had never seen. The collection was unbelievable. We drank wine and looked through it. Montfort was with us on our first trip to Europe. His camera was ever there. I don't know how many thousands of photos he has of me, and of Linda and myself. And photos of my German relatives, including my Uncle Heinrich who was then in his 90's and living in Andernach the city of my birth. I doubt that many movie stars have been photographed as much. It was somewhat embarrassing. But utterly convenient. He has freely given me his photos to use in my books and elsewhere. In fact, one book was published, *Shakespeare Never Did This,* which is a group of photos of our trip to Europe and my hazy story about it all. And another book was published, *Horsemeat,* which are Montfort photos and Bukowski poems about the racetrack.

What does it mean? Only the gods know and they are silent. And the years have gone on and Michael's camera has just kept going and I am very honored that he has taken the time to lend me his talent. I am a writer who writes and that is the main thing, of course, but photos are often needed—ask Elizabeth Taylor.

But Michael and Linda and I have met without the camera, often, and these times too have been good. We often watch the boxing matches together or meet and eat at Musso's, sometimes stopping at the bar or going to Red's bookstore. If this sounds dull to you, it hasn't been for me. I have problems becoming friends with people but Michael Montfort is not one of them.

These photos you are about to look at come from a talented man, a good human being and my friend. I hope that you enjoy the workmanship, the style and the warmth of my German and American buddy. Thank you very much.

Charles Bukowski 11-6-92
San Pedro, Calif. U.S.A.

[To Marc Smirnoff]
November 12, 1992 11:57 PM

Thanks for the free copy of *Oxford American 2*.

No, I'm not angry at you. I just felt that what I write doesn't quite fit your needs.

Since you asked to look at more poems, here are 3 that I wrote last night. Don't feel bad rejecting me, pard, I can handle it. Being an editor ain't all just a jolly bit. I ran 5 issues of a lit mag long ago. Fellow sent me some poems that were technically good, proficient but I felt that they were flawed by their very special workmanship, that I would rather see more of a crazy heart pumping than all that polish. I wrote him as much. Here came back his letter: "Horseshit!" He was famous, I was not. But I was surprised that he replied. I think that silence would have been the best retort.

Regards your mag, I think the Faulkner ad, page 22, is a smile in the sky. Really funny. Only, he should be holding a bottle instead of a pipe.

[To John Martin]
November 19, 1992 1:17 AM

Thanks for sending the letter from the nut case. But you've got to realize that the more of these you receive the more you have arrived. I get them too. Not as many as you. My thought always is, what is the best way to handle this so that this person doesn't arrive at my door? I'm not sure but over the haul of time I think I've found the best method is simply non-response. Formality only enrages them and kindness never works. You just have to go about your business and hope for the best. Usually, though, with letters from the unbalanced, it is *letters*—that is, *more* than one, and with each preceding [*sic*] letter getting weirder and weirder, down to the point of ultimate sickness. There are people out there living seemingly normal lives who are completely screwy and nobody is aware of it—

259

except people such as you and I, and *they* always think that there's some trick to getting somewhere and they'll do anything but dedicate themselves, work at it or love it, they only want the cheap easy out and there isn't any. [* * *]

[To William Packard]
November 19, 1992 10:54 PM

Glad "Chicken Giblets" got past you. Thought you might be pissed because I spelled "Shostakovich" as "Shostakovitch." But then, I couldn't get a full take on that either. Anyhow, I sometimes write of my life in East Hollywood. I didn't realize then that I was so crazy and I probably don't realize it now either. [* * *]

I'll be glad to say something on behalf of Carroll Terrell for making it possible for *NYQ* to continue. I can submit something and if it works for you, fine. I presume there has been the good old financial aid to keep *NYQ* afloat and along with this an almost hands-off policy allowing you freedom of choice of content. Do I have this right? I will wait a while and if I don't hear from you, I'll presume that I have it right and will send on something for the better or worse, hopefully for the better.

Has been a stinging year for me, eye operation and various pains. Came in roaring drunk about 2 weeks ago and fell, cracking my head open on the porch steps, real bloody shit mess. Just recently had the cement porch replaced by bricks and so I kind of baptized the damned things. Anyhow, the writing has been going good and that's what I gauge most things by. I can handle anything if the words dance for me. Working on a novel, a detective novel of all things, actually gives me new ground to play with. This dick is part asshole (like me) so I can have him saying and doing some weird things. But the poems keep getting [in] the way of the novel...Why complain? And do you want to hear it? Hell, no. I have 9 cats now and make the track every day they're running. Waiting to live. Waiting to die. Sleeping on the half-rack. Thunder in my

bellybutton. Great to see Bowe shovel Holyfield out. Now Christmas aiming at me like rocket. I'm sick.
hold, hold, hold,

[To Carl Weissner]
November 19, 1992 11:50 PM

Thanks for royalty statements, strange stuff, all those books still selling.

Well, pal, my eye is all right, had a cataract operation, they dig out a part of your eye (the lens part, like a camera) and replace it with a fake lens. Seems to work. The old lens, the real one, gets covered with cataracts and you finally see less and less until you go blind. Main reason I have to keep seeing is to drive my car and to work this fucking computer. It was the right eye they worked on and it took some time to come around. They took the stitches out. Real freaky. The guy has you roll your eye into different positions and he cuts at the stitches with a little razor. Don't sneeze, fart or twitch or your eye is gone ... Lots of fun ... Will need the left eye done eventually. Have cataracts there but lens is peering in between them. Before operation it was all hell night driving, lots of guess work, just following the paths of other cars, etc. I was lucky.

Came in from U2 concert the other night—they announced to 25,000 people, "This concert is dedicated to Linda and Charles Bukowski!" and everybody screamed as if they knew who we were. Free drinks afterwards in place for the big shots. I slammed down huge double shots of vodka 7 for hours. Afterwards when I stepped out of the limo, I lurched forward, ran at steps, which are now brick, fell and crashed my head against them full blast. Blood, blood, blood, Christ. But, I'm still alive. [★ ★ ★]

I'm already depressed, thinking about Christmas already. Shit.

But it's been a good year for the writing. Hundreds of poems and the novel is slowly moving along. 150 pages. This should be the detective novel to end all detective novels, that is, if I end it myself. I get the guy into impossible situations and have to work him out. But it's all inventive. Good for me. I have to work it out. It's fun until I run into a wall.

Two people I knew at the track, a mutual clerk and a coffee girl died within a month. Both good souls. My own death I can handle. But I'm not realistic with other people. That stuff cuts.

Well, that's the way the war works: there's no winning. We do what we can and sometimes what we can't.

straight on, baby,

[To Marvin Malone]
December 3, 1992 12:51 AM

I'm glad I got so many poems past you. I realize that I run hot and cold.

Oh, please don't send any poets on to me. I get too many now, unsolicited, via mail and at the door. It's really a fight and not a pleasant one. I get so many poems, stories, novels, letters in the mail ... I could start a magazine. But the contents would be crappy. Those who send their works to other writers lack the ultimate courage to enter the arena straight on. They think there's an easy way, a short cut. They want any kind of yes. These are the writers who read their stuff to their friends and relatives, who try to give all the poetry readings they can anywhere, everywhere for anything. The weak will not come through. Talent and will are in the same bundle.

Don't let *Pushcart*[1] worry you. You publish a much fresher, livelier and more original work than the *APR, Paris Review, Kenyon* or *Poetry* ... You are needed. *Pushcart* could be pissed at me. Once was nominated. Packard of the *New York Quarterly* sent me the tear sheets and asked me to mail it to them. Hell, I just didn't feel like doing that. It didn't mean that much to me.

---

1. *Pushcart Prize,* the annual collection of the "best of the small presses."

I've read *Pushcart* and their compilation seemed awfully tame, almost dead.

[To Alfred Vitale]
December 3, 1992 12:12 AM

Got your letter asking if I might submit something. See enclosed. Of course, my "ranting" may not be your "ranting." That's all right, I've been rejected by the worst and the best. By the way, long before I knew better, I knew this other writer. Was at his place one time when he opened his mail to a reject. He went into a delicate tizzy of a rage. *"But they asked me to submit!"* He was a famous writer at the time and I was only a famous drunk. I tried to explain to him that a request for a submission is not an automatic acceptance. He wouldn't allow himself to understand this. Well, what I couldn't understand was how he got his fame in the first place. Well, he had knocked on many doors. Sometimes that works. But I think it's the worst way to get your shit spread. Anyhow, he went on raving, only stopping to pull a bit of celery out of his fridge and to suck down some carrot juice. I got out of there and stayed away from writers evermore.

Well, anyhow, this doesn't have much to do with anything. I write like this when I'm hungover. Like I am. Now. And so. Luck with your mag. There's a great one in New York City. *The New York Quarterly*. Give it a look, if you haven't.

They say it's going to rain tomorrow. But they didn't say what.

263

[To Douglas Goodwin]
December 4, 1992 12:16 AM

Thanks for the good words on the "Poems and Journals" section of the new *Onthebus*.[1] I haven't received my copy yet. The old story: the writer is the last. Same thing with a preceding issue. My copy arrived about 6 months after the fact. Editor wrote me, "It was stuck under some papers." Grapes is good to honor me with a section but he has a mental block on other matters with me. I suppose he wants me to write and ask for a copy. Not sure I'll do that. That's my mental block.

Onthebus fills a lot of pages each issue but I'm with you: there doesn't seem much there. Grapes describes the stuff as "good writers on their way to greatness." Hardly seems close to that.

Christmas and New Year's move toward us again. The old sickening duet. The masses coming out of their tv caves. The family gatherings. The gross dull nothingness, the fake drunks, the fake smiles, the fake people. May we live through this somehow, one more time.

[To Teresa Leo]
December 8, 1992 1:17 AM

Well, I'm glad I got the poem "piss" by you. Bio note? Working on a novel, *Pulp*, a detective novel, "dedicated to bad writing." This should help the critics in determining that I have finally lost it.

On the cassette to precede the showing of *Barfly*, it all sounds too dreary. Somebody else will have to introduce it. I can give you a few things about it for your own use. I preferred Sean Penn to Mickey Rourke. Sean was willing to work (do the whole thing) for a dollar but he wanted his own director, Dennis Hopper and I had to stick with Barbet Schroeder, so

---

1. *Onthebus* was a magazine published in Los Angeles, edited by Jack Grapes.

264

that didn't work out. Sean, at least, drinks. Mickey doesn't. And Sean is far the better actor. Fay Dunaway? Well, I think we could have done better. She really didn't play it insane enough. But I had very little input once the film got going. Some of the scenes I didn't think fit the reality enough, others worked. But to hell with the writer, it's just his baby.

You know, I wrote about most of this in the novel *Hollywood*.

One thing I didn't like, strange as it may sound, was Mickey Rourke's clothing get up. The baggy dragging pants, the hair in face, the filthy shirt and undershirt. Now, I was a bum but let me tell you, I'd often come into the roominghouse drunk and wash my bluejeans, underwear and shirt, shorts, in the bathtub. I'd take them back to my room and put them over chairs to dry. This took a day or so while I wore my other set of stuff. My clothing was wrinkled but clean. The Rourke get up went too far. And the bar room fights were hardly as brutal—with the exception of one night—4 or 5 good shots to head and gut and one or the other of the drunks was finished. Most of the time by the time we went out to fight we could hardly stand anyhow.

All in all, though, I'm glad the film was made. I was a barfly and a starving writer and I don't think that life style has been depicted too often. And all through that time I still had the idea that I could write better, with more life and verve, than many of the famous. Their work seemed very pale yet putrid to me. And I thought, well hell, if I can't get published at least I can get drunk and I did and I stayed drunk and now I still drink although I've gotten luckier with getting published. And somewhere now there's a young man reading me and thinking, I can write better than that. And he's probably right. I hope he is.

The Jacaranda Review *was published from the Department of English at UCLA*

[To Bruce Kijewski]
December 10, 1992 11:25 PM

Well, what do you know? My wife has taken and developed the photos of me. I wouldn't be surprised if she sent them off in a day or two.

Yes, you have a strange project: electronic books. It might well be the future as more and more people find that the computer is such a magic thing: time-saver, charmer, energizer. But, still, when that time comes I will still miss the old fashioned book. From the writers that I have known, their words have always been better than their actual selves. Meeting them visually and hearing them speak was always more than discouraging and in most cases sickening. So, I don't know. Your idea seems good but you're going to have to find artists whose personalities are not disgusting and that takes some doing.

Anyhow, I look forward to the *Jacaranda Review* ...

[To William Packard]
December 21, 1992 1:18 AM

It's been a bit of an off time for me: eye infection after a cataract operation, then some type of illness, stuck in bed. What crap, to get out of the action, no typing , no racetrack, no rhythm of any kind. I voted for the aid-to-do-yourself-in bill on the Calif. ballot but there were too many dumb fucking voters who believed in the will of God and that kind of crap, so it didn't pass. Anyhow, feeling somewhat better and much cheered by your sending me on the lineup of #51, wow, wow, I am honored, and also and besides it looks like a good lineup. Good you've plugged in so far ahead on issues and that you're still there! But I'll bet even you never envisioned over 50 issues!

266

You and the *NYQ* are granite monsters of glory! Growl on, kick more ass and shake them into life!

[To Jack Grapes]
December 28, 1992 11:05 PM

I'm sorry you've been up against the blade, these things occur when all goes wrong for you and everybody around you: accident, bad health, madness, the long run of gloom, you find yourself sitting in hospitals and in emergency rooms and it's either about you or somebody close to you, and then all the shit piles up and you are too locked in the moil to fight it off, to answer the letters, to counter the claims which are usually false and somebody else's error, and on and on it goes, including traffic tickets, car breakdowns, toothache, sleepless nights, just the relentless pounding of everyday and everynight hell. I know what you mean and I hope it clears up for you ...

But I did get the latest *Onthebus* and it's a fine honor for me, great display, and I think it reads well, poems and the journals. Old Jon Webb would be proud of you ... Thanks, Jack. The mag arrived at a good time, I've been swimming a shit river myself. Had a cataract operation, then recently eye got infected. Followed by a puking flu. Headaches that aspirin won't deter. Then an Xmas visit from an 82 year old mother in law who can barely walk or think but remains full of stubborn ways. So, it really helped to read *Onthebus* and feel that the work held, or god help me, was even better than ever. Thanks for the pages, Jack, for something shining in all this fucking dark!

●

267

• 1 9 9 3 •

[To William Packard]
January 2, 1993

Dear *NYQ*:
I am a native Albino who lives with a mother with a wooden leg and a father who shoots up. I have a parrot, Cagney, who says, "Yankee Doodle Dandy!" each time he excretes, which is 4 or 5 times a day. I once saw J. D. Salinger. Enclosed are my *Flying Saucer* Poems. I have an 18 year old sister with a body like you've never seen. Nude photos enclosed. In case my poems are rejected, these photos are to be returned. In case of acceptance, I or my sister can be reached at 642-696-6969.
sincerely yours,
Byron Keats

Adam Green is the author of Crazy Straws and Broken Hearts: A Cartoon Collection *(Chicago: Paranormal Press, 1992) and of* What Were You in a Previous Life? *(New York: Thunder's Mouth Press, 1993).*

[To Adam Green]
January 4, 1993 10:52 PM

I get 4 or 5 books in the mail a week, most of it self-published and unbearably, unbelievably bad. They fall out of my hands like the pieces of shit that they are. So, I opened your book and expected more of the same old ... And was delighted and shocked at the newness, the unique angle of thought, the humor through truth, what a ball! Thanks Green. It's been years, maybe decades since anything has astounded me. For Christ's sake, don't get killed by some woman or by the driving in traffic or by ...

Keep it going. You got it all. Don't let them take it from you. Don't let fame or dame mutilate you. If you're lucky, the former will arrive late.

I can't believe you are as good as you are but you are.

What a blast of light, motherfucker!

[To Marc Smirnoff]
January 4, 1993 10:20 PM

You were once my favorite vodka. Also, you must write the kindest rejection letter in existence. For that, my thanks. Also, glad you liked "on the banks," although after I wrote it I hesitated on sending it out because I thought a certain person might identify with the poem. However, I ducked and shot it out. I mean, I have written many poems about myself that were not favorable and I will write others of that vein in the future. What's good for me is good for them.

On drawings, I submit a couple. If neither work for you, please keep them. If you want.

270

I should try you again, soon, with some poesy. Right now I am trying to finish my detective novel, *Pulp*. I get this dick into impossible jams and have to bite some edges off of my brain to get him out. It's mostly play and con, and gives me an excuse to loosen some misanthropic rantings from somebody else's mouth. If I have any literary reputation this novel should hastily dissolve it. Which was one of the reasons for writing it. The others I'm not sure of.

here's Faulkner in your eye,

[Addressee Unknown]
January 5, 1993 8:27 PM

Hello Terry:

Christmas, ugh. People act on cue, doing it because it's there. They are afraid not to. I've had my greatest Xmases on the bum. Just locked the door of my room and didn't see anybody. It was glorious.

About Christ or what they call Christ: instinctively and forever, I've felt that He or what they call He or the Son of He, didn't ever exist, along with the Father. It's all too pat, too put together. I mean, if I am to believe that, how can I respect myself? I'm letting go to an irrational push if I buy that story.

I don't mind that others have Christmas and their beliefs; after all, they prefer many other things which also turn me away. But even I go through the Christmas act for their sake, I let them win that one and I say nothing, although I am saying something to you. Imagine the reaction of my mother in law if I told her, "Christmas and Christ are a bunch of crap." She'd think I was a madman.

Well, it's all over for a year and we can breathe more freely for a while.

On the matter of sports, I can do without all of them except boxing. I know that it's cruel business and stupid and crooked but something about a good boxing match appeals to me. In a sense, I relate it to other areas of life and living. Well,

271

hell, we all have our chinks and cracks ... boxing is one of them for me.

[To Jon Cone]
January 7, 1993 1:21 AM

[* * *] Have been crawling out from under here. Flat on my ass in bed twice during the month of December. Something strange both times, halfway between the flu and some type of draining weariness. Then, in there somewhere, an eye infection. But I'm up now, strong and only slightly depressed.

So, it's 93? Just a number. It's just time and you can't number it. Forget the BC, AD crap. Only good of the numbers is for filing purposes—stuff like history, income tax time, auto license renewal. The longer I live the less I buy of anything. I couldn't buy the game at age 2, still can't at 72. I exist in life more as a matter of orneriness than desire. Shit, I like that last sentence. Should have saved it for a poem. No, that's wrong, when we start saving stuff instead of just letting it fly, then we're truly finished. Most of us try too hard, we're too grim, we're too ambitious, we're too competitive and we stare too long at our turds. Millions of pages of literature and maybe only 4 or 5 thousand pages worth a damn. All the rest is waste and a great deal of that is revered and studied. That's one of the reasons there are so many dull boys and girls about, our minds are stuffed with holy nothingness. [* * *]

[To William Packard]
January 11, 1993 11:56 PM

Glad I got the poem, "The Game," past you. At least my women were something to write about and that was just about the extent of it. On the cover letter, I sent that as a joke in response to some of the actual cover letters you sent me. That is

272

why I didn't include a S.S.A.E. But if you think it is printable, fine with me. Extra fine.

By the way, one of those who sent you a cover letter, I met him once. He's a prof. I hear he underwent a sex-change, man to woman. But he may have switched back again, woman to man. To hell with it.

Thanks for enclosing the editorial for #50. A monumental issue. Remember when *Poetry, A Magazine of Verse* was about the only thing about? It even seemed exciting then. Now it's like something has run over it and flattened all the life out of it. You have to keep going! Oh, o, yes, yes.

Thank you for teaching me, I saw your sheet. Christ, I'm in with some names! Feels real odd. Oh, yes.

Was a lousy December, sickness and other things working their toll on me. But as long as I have my little words to play with, I'll probably gut it through.

[To John Martin]
January 15, 1993 10:37 PM

Thanks for the 1992 rundown. 19 books in print and available! What other author in the world can make that claim? You're probably the only editor-publisher to try this. There's always room for new ideas even after thousands of years.

I'm glad that I'm just about even with you. We lived through the recession and it's still here. To me, $7,000 a month seems an unbelievable sum. Just as that $100 we started with seemed a miracle. I'd like to think that anything you and I manage to earn is justified. But the most important thing is that I am still writing and you are still publishing and I think, at the moment, we are both at the top of our game. I may slip a bit in the future but even with slippage I will probably still be a good and a lucky writer. It's sometimes hard for me to believe I am still at it but its most of what I basically feel like doing, have to do, in order to endure all the rest. [* * *]

273

[To Jon Cone]
January 19, 1993 11:40 PM

I don't know about the price because I got them as an Xmas present, a Macintosh IIsi computer and a Personal Laser Printer. Once you get in to these things you'll hate a typewriter if you ever have to go back to it, such things as ribbons, carbons, white-outs and hand shifting, etc., will seem stupid and galling. You correct your copy right off the screen. The computer even corrects your spelling for you. And you can save all your work on disks which can be filed into a small space, any portion of which can be reprinted in as many copies as you wish. And the copy just looks so much better than typewritten copy. Everything saves you hours and those hours can be used as you wish sleep, drink, go to a movie, pet your cat, walk your dog, take a bath, muse. For me, actually, it has doubled my creative output and somehow strengthened it.

I'd advise you to go for a computer and a printer, doubt you'll ever regret. In the beginning there might be some minor frustrations but as you continue to go along these will vanish. Go for it, if you can. You'll be delighted, damned delighted.

[To Michael Basinski]
January 24, 1993 11:22 PM

Yes, you're right or your inference is correct: without our writing we would surely be howling mad. Writing allows us to continue even when that continuance is like swimming through waves of shit.

Thanks for sending on your essay. You've done your homework. And I must say it seems a selfless task on your part. So many contributors to *Sure* simply drop the name "Bukowski" and then go about flaunting their feathers, as if they might be discovered as extraordinary.

The time you write about was a strange time indeed. I had no idea of being a great or even an exceptional writer. I only

274

wanted to get the word down. But I was very fragmented. What to do about life really horrified me, the masses were a nightmare to me as were every single man or woman I met. I felt that I could get the word down better than those who were famous for doing so in the past and present. I knew I had rough edges but I wanted to keep those, they were part of existence. All I wanted out of writing was a bare survival. But the only thing which made me feel clear of all the crap was drinking, so I did that, and how.

An aside for you, about the Black Sun Press, don't know if you know about it. At one time I ended up in Atlanta, really about at the end of things. I was in a tar paper shack without light or water or heat and it was freezing. I was starving and out of funds. There is something about freezing and starving that is somehow unbelievable.

You figure, somehow, that it just shouldn't happen. Yet there you are and it's real enough. I had some paper, some envelopes and some stamps. Caresse Crosby had already published me. I don't know. I went mad. I wrote a letter to Kay Boyle and another to Caresse Crosby. I told them both that I was starving but if they would just send ten dollars or so—and *hurry!*—I would some day pay them back and double, triple, only I had to have it *now!* I don't know how I lasted on. I had a loaf of sliced bread and I ate a slice of bread each day. I was gone, out of it. Probably imbecilic.

I never did hear from Kay Boyle. Finally a letter arrived from Caresse Crosby! I ripped it open and looked for money! There was none. Just a letter. She said that she was now living in some village in Italy, in the hills, and that she helped the poor peasants. She told me how much she had enjoyed my contribution to her magazine but that was over now. And she wished me future success in my writings ...

Oooh, oooh, oooh. Ow. Caresse, Caresse ...

I finally got out of there by signing on with a track gang going "some place West of Sacramento."

Anyhow, thanks for all your work. Good, good things to you. Hold against the tide. Hold.

A magazine entitled Caution *was published from Richmond, VA.*

[To Tim Meinbresse]
January 26, 1993 9:37 PM

Yes, I received the copy of *Caution* you sent me. Not bad. Thank you.

I'm glad, of course, that you found all my poems usable. I think I've been on a hot streak lately, writing a lot of shit but hot shit. Always difficult to find a new outlet, so it was lucky for me when I heard from you.

Not much here. Sucking on beer, listening to a bit of classical music on the radio; waiting to die, waiting to live, waiting to sleep. One can't always be on fire. You have to learn to live through the lulls, the horrors, the impossibilities. Have to? Well, you just do while thinking of the butcher knife in the kitchen drawer or that huge span of bridge over the cold dark water. Yeah? Yeah. Talk about it.

[To Kevin Ring]
January 26, 1993 9:14 PM

Thanks for the latest copy of *Beat Scene* and the extra flyers. Going through the magazine, I notice that you are exposing me all over the place. You ought to be ashamed of yourself, but thanks, of course. I suppose that fact that I write and sometimes get published might mean I am not totally mad.

I've been having some personal problems lately so I'm not sure of many things. Like getting Zip Code, I can't recall, can't locate—although this place is a total mess. In fact, I have no recall of getting a copy of *Two Winos*, although I realize you didn't publish this one.[1] On the other hand, I could be totally

---

1. Charles Bukowski, *A Couple of Winos* (Seattle: Fantagraphic Books, 1991)—a comic book by Matthias Schultheiss.

wrong about all this. I hope to get myself together more but tonight was another bad night ... Some light has got to fall soon, though ... ???? Still, I'm still writing my stupid ass off, which is something. [* * *]

[To Stephen Kessler]
January 29, 1993 10:33 PM

So, you're not going to write any more about me until I'm 80? You sure you can last that long?

Thanks for sending on *Poetry Flash* which contains your good and long review. I won't curse you for it if it doesn't put a curse on me. Meanwhile, thank you.

With me, the whole matter has been a day by day, night by night journey. The words were put down, the drinks were drunk, and there still seems more to do. What I mean is, stopping now would be hell. The words have saved my ass, it's as simple as that. There's always something more to overcome, to live through. Death's coming, that's all right but it's not here yet. The BMW is now an Acura and there's a swimming pool and a jacuzzi. It's in my writing.

For me, the words seem to bite into the paper better than ever. A writer should get better as he gets older: there's more to work with, a larger canvas. But most writers get lucky too early, then get the fat head, get greedy, get dull, fall apart. They are short distance runners. Too bad. That's why we have so much crappy literature about, the slim volumes, the slight pages of Selected Works. It's disheartening: everything wilts away.

I've been lucky to have John Martin (Black Sparrow) as my editor-publisher. From the beginning he has allowed me to write anything I wish in any way I wish, never suggesting anything. What he has done is to select what should be published and what shouldn't. I trust him in this. Why not? Also, it gives me more time to write. And Martin keeps my books *in print* and available. I've been a lucky man to have such backing. I believe I would have come though without him but

277

not in this fashion. There is also a chance that I might have been dead or mad without Black Sparrow. This press has allowed me the strength and the resources to continue writing. Indeed ...

Luck with your novel. Good move to get out of New York.

[To William Packard]
January 29, 1993 12:16 AM

Just received *NYQ* #49. I am honored. All those poems of mine which you ran, plus the letter. Honor and madness, gladness, the weird roar of miracle. Thanks, man, I feel very strange. Will my head be able to handle it? I've seen real balanced guys, good souls turn to pieces of shit overnight on much less. Good thing I'm almost 73, maybe I can sort it out and hold. Meanwhile, I forget about my god damned soul for a while and just feel great. Yes.

Read right on through 49, one of your best issues ever. It doesn't even seem fair to point out this poem or that from the others, there's a feeling of crazy joy and gamble running throughout the entire issue. I don't see where you get all this stuff. The other magazines just aren't doing it. What a wild batch of pages! The world isn't finished yet, is it? There's a lot of kick and daring and newness abounding in #49. It's difficult to believe it, but it's there. Now, you sleep good, feel good, be good, you are. It's a great song. Death is nothing. We've kicked its ass. My man, my man. [* * *]

[To John Martin]
February 1, 1993 1:33 AM

Yes, it will be strange to see what I was thinking about in the 60's. (The letters). Linda has told me more than once: "You missed the 60's." "Hell yes," is my answer, "I was in the

278

post office." Indeed. 11 and 1/2 hour nights with only 2 or 3 days off a month. I was hardly a Flower Child.

Meanwhile, here in 1993, enclosed more poems...

[To Steve Richmond]
February 4, 1993 10:55 PM

Hello Steve:

52? Shit, man, you're getting *old!* The babes are going to be watching these young black guys walking the boardwalk. (Get you mad at me, you'll write some good poems).

Well, you've got to admit you didn't get sucked into the ordinary. You could be sitting in some lawyer's office (as a lawyer) getting pounded into imbecility by the demands of your station. You've held out down by the shore, it's your fort and you have your own individuality which I don't always agree with but at least it's *yours.* And I still have this vision that some day a large tome of thousands of Richmond poems will be promulgated and the young groupies will be banging on your door seeking your body and your new fame.

Keep it going. And when you're able to feel good, do it, don't fight it.

hold, and continue,

[To William Packard]
February 6, 1993 11:54 PM

Glad I got "fame" past you. You really want a straight bio note? All right, "Harper-Collins to publish *A Bukowski Reader,* April 1993. Also, I am about 2/3rd's finished with a detective novel, *Pulp,* dedicated to bad writing."

On *Poets and Writers,* I don't think there is anything to worry about from those flea-pickers. So you don't take time to

279

cultivate "relationships" with your writers? All your job is is to publish the best submissions. It's that simple. You are not running a lonely hearts club. You don't want to hear the sob stories, the complaints of the scribblers. Screw them. If they are aching, lot them get it down in the line, in the art form. You don't want them sitting on your couch chatting away. There's nothing to talk about, nothing to cultivate. This is not a matter of being cold, it is a matter of being sensible. Most writers outside of their work are very despicable and unsavory characters. Most of them are sublimely stuck on one subject matter: self.

You know, if I had a hero, an artist, a writer, a somebody, I would never knock on his door because I know that I would find too many things that would dissipate the dream. Usually the first look is enough to send everything smashing into the rocks. You must sense the same thing, hence you keep these far, far away, if possible.

You don't have to nursemaid these, it's just not right. It has nothing to do with editing and publishing. Personal matters should be left out. One of the main reasons that most literary magazines are so bad is because they do cultivate relationships and end up publishing friends, lovers, relatives, etc. And you get limp words and dismal pages. And this perpetuates some writers into believing that they have true talent, especially when said same magazines issue their little 12 to 15 page chapbooks.

I believe that what makes such as *Poets and Writers* angry is when you and your staff admit editorial-wise that most of the submissions you receive are unbelievably horrible. You know the old adage: every man is a poet. Nothing is further from the truth. Very few men (or women) are poets. Very few of them are anything at all. Mediocrity exists because of a failure to slap it down. It exists because there is so much of it that we get used to it and even deem some of it as valid, for lack of anything else to do, for lack of anything else around. I mean, if that's all there is, isn't it somehow something?

Whitman said, "To have great poetry we must have great audiences." No, we must have great poetry, then perhaps we will have great audiences. Nobody reads the stuff now because there's no juice, fire, adventure, dance and truth to it. You have attempted to do something about this and you have hurt the feelings of the darlings by calling a piece of crap a piece of crap. The inept want to be told that they are good or else they'll whine to the skies. Forget *Poets and Writers*, let their attack on you be construed as a signal of honor. Those want the mother's nipple, the baby's bottle. They just want a poet labeled as a poet, no matter what or how they write. Can you imagine a plumber coming into your place and not knowing how? You'd have shit up to your neck and that's what you're getting in the mails. Can they blame you for mentioning this? Sure, they can. They will. They have. Let them die. And you continue to publish the many good and great poems that you have been. That is your answer. And the gods hear you. And some of the great audience too.

[To John Martin]
February 9, 1993 10:21 PM

Good deal on selling the one time rights to *Bring Me Your Love*. We'll take the money. You never know in this life, things can happen. Catastrophic illness, accident, whatever the hell. Talk all you want about a nest egg, one thing it allows you: to continue doing what you like best.
Long live Black Sparrow. And Chinaski.
We'll not only go out with our boots on, but with our guns firing.

[To Kevin Ring]
February 9, 1993 8:16 PM

[* * *]On *Hank*, I am very disappointed in the book. It is virtually unreadable. Very bad writing. Dull, inept. I gave Neeli hours of tape, really good stuff, of wild and wonderful times, crazy times, deadly times but he put *none* of it in. He has lived a

very protective life, so subconsciously I guess he didn't believe the things I had been through. Also, various inaccuracies. There's one where he has me trying to hit Linda King with a frying pan. I never told him that. Linda King was the one, in a darkened kitchen, who sneaked up behind me and tried to kill me with a frying pan over the head. I got to Neeli over the phone on this. "O.k., give it to me again," he said. And I told the story over again. He read it back to me and he said, "then Hank tried to hit Linda King over the head with a frying pan..." "No, Neeli, no, you've got it backwards again!" "But," he said, "she might *sue* me!" What can you do? I gave up, hung up.

I shouldn't have trusted Neeli to do the book. He had done a good one, *Whitman's Wild Children*, in which one of the chapters on me was lively and well done. On the strength of this, I let him go ahead with the bio. What a mistake! It gave me a headache reading it. The book fell from my hands. Linda, my wife, tried it. "God," she said, "this is awful..." She couldn't read it either. And on top of that, none of the original photos and other materials were returned. Lost, I was told. Lost.

I'll just have to live the damned book down. Somehow.

[To John Martin]
February 13, 1993 12:03 AM

Thanks for sending *Selected Letters of the 60's*. Read a bit tonight. Strange, weird stuff but me, then. As I read each letter it really took me back. God, I was kicking and scratching—the old-young writer trying to get it rolling. This book should interest many and give them some hope. Strange, the lines in the letters sound much like the lines of the poetry I was writing then—kind of a tense madness. The type of writing Grapes prefers. I prefer the stuff I'm doing now. But the letters, I think, are great indicators of something bubbling on the burner. Book a great idea, I think. The 60's. 30 years ago. Where were you? Moving toward me...

[To William Packard]
February 18, 1993 12:17 AM

I remember you asked for something on Carroll Terrell. I don't know if it works as you want it to or not. Anyhow, I gave it a shot.

I'm still playing with the detective novel but can't seem to figure how to finish it off I get this dick into jams and I can barely get him out. And in between times he just sits in bars or stares at the walls and tries to figure what the hell. Kind of a cheap-ass philosopher but I can have him say things that I might not dare. Might not.

Some poems but not any really top grade stuff. Just working out.

Those two who wrote poems about me in last issue. Funny, made me smile. I'm not too sure who I am. Weary guy, maybe. Slugging on. Some journey.

Hope you're healthy, stepping jaunty. Don't let the world get too much on you.

[To Daniel Halpern]
February 20, 1993 12:26 AM

I'm glad that "musings" worked for you. [* * *]

Thank you for the thought of doing a book of "musings." But all my work is promised John Martin and Black Sparrow Press. He was there when nobody else was, I can't forget that. On the Harper-Collins book they simply purchased rights to rerun certain portions of work already published by Black Sparrow, crediting John Martin as editor. I am glad that "musings" worked well for you and I am still honored and look forward to seeing them in *Antaeus*.

On your issue on music, if I write anything relating to that I'll certainly submit it for a look. Music (classical) has helped get me through. I have never written anything without the radio on to classical music. (it's on now). I listen to from 2 to 5 hours of music a night. It's a grand habit, clears the muck out of me. And the magic thing is, that even after decades and decades of listening, I will sometimes hear a piece that I have never heard before and it's bold and marvelous and adventuresome, chilling, the chills run up my arms and down my back. There is an immense lore of awesome and startling music out there. It appears to me that, somehow, music has attracted the greatest souls. Literature, on the other hand, has only had a very few who could do it well. Or, so I feel. The painters, sculptors, are in between. But the musicians give us the true juice, the roar of life. It's all very strange but it is so.

[To Marc Smirnoff]
February 20, 1993 11:04 PM

A Faulkner room at the local McDonald's. That's really funny. I'm afraid if I lived down there I'd be hanging around that room waiting for him to show up with bottle jammed into a side pocket. (Yes, I know he's long deceased but ...)

I remember as a young man reading Faulkner down at the beach, there on the sand, the waves blasting behind me. The water was clean in those days. And I was reading *As I Lay Dying*. I liked it, I liked the style and yet the style bothered me too as if the style were doing too much of the writing. And then, of course, I'd go back to my room and write like Faulkner. I wrote like Faulkner when I wasn't writing like Hemingway or, the devil help me, like Thomas Wolfe.

Thanks for your kind rejection. The poems were all right but I can see now, probably too long in saying whatever they were trying to say and maybe too prose-like. Anyhow, a bit of rejection is good for the soul, it's much of what has kept me going so far into this night.

Long live *The Oxford American*. William is watching you, and maybe Ezra too.

hold,

[To Tom Chivens]
February 26, 1993 11:41 PM

Hugh Fox is a tiresome ... windy ... fake. He wants to be more than he is, which is a national malady in the U.S.A. You can have all of them. Take them away somewhere, please.

Yes, I read so many of these writers (mostly in the fifties) who try to write as I. They don't have the gut style to bring it off. Also, as they plunge into one of my territories, I have moved on to the next. I also have another advantage upon them: I am staring at death while they are still looking at their mothers. Anyhow, what happens is what happens and most just aren't very inventive and fear to gamble, either in or outside of their work. Who cares? I don't. Not a twig. Not an elephant's ear. Not a half-eaten corn cob.

Humanity is dead. The beauty of life is their absence.

p.s.—Forget the N. Cherry, *Hank*. Very bad piece of reporting. I gave him the juice on tape, he took the rinds. Outside of that, he doesn't know how to write.

Stiletto, edited by Michael Annis, was published from Lawrence, Missouri by Howling Dog Press

[To Michael Annis]
March 5, 1993 12:27 AM

Great the 3 poems worked for you. *Stiletto* is, indeed, a handsomely published journal.

But now I'm probably going to piss you off twice. Don't think I can do a full section/ signature bit for you. I'm into my novel now and the poems just aren't coming that fast. Also, at Black Sparrow, my editor, John Martin gets a bit upset when I do signature things. Martin was there for me when nobody else was, he was a great help financially and spiritually. I hope you understand.

Then, on the Fante, I don't think I'm the proper one to

illustrate his movie script, *Storm Point*. My drawings are too off-handed and lopsided to fit the Fante mold. I felt this right away when you asked. Then, just for the hell of it, I asked my wife, "Do you think my drawings would fit Fante?" She agreed that they would not.

Don't get me wrong, I am honored by both of your offers. Truly.

Suppose I just submit the next poems that come off of the typer if and when they do? I don't know how this fits in with your time element or when you're going to press.

Fante was a tremendous influence upon me. Not so much the content but in his manner of getting it down. I told him as much in my visits to the hospital. "You're really a nice guy, John, I'm the son of a bitch." He agreed.

By the way, he took it quite well, all those awful things they were doing to him in that place. Would that I had one fifth of that man's courage.

Again, you put out a marvelously beautiful publication. I am happy to be a part of it. Yes.

Peter Bakowski is an Australian writer, author of Thunder Road, Thunder Heart *(Melbourne: Nosukumo, 1988).*

[To Peter Bakowski]
March 5, 1993 12:55 AM

You have passed through the shadows of hell and have emerged. Salute! And congratulations! And on top of all this, you are still banging the poems out and having them published. This is no small matter. Many a lesser man would have wilted. The magazines you mentioned are all first rate and so are you. I'm glad your girlfriend is so good to you. When you get something so rare be careful of it. You will.

1994. Visit? Such things embarrass me, Peter. There is nothing to be talked about. I suppose you've been warned, I am a lone dog. It's inbred.

My wife just brought me a hot pretzel, said, "Put out that cigar, it's bad for your health." So, I have. I'm biting into this delicious hot pretzel and writing to you. It's the small things which keep us dancing.

I sent some poems to the mag you suggested down there. Who knows? Each editor thinks a poem is something else.

Well, you keep yourself together. You have a second life. It's like you've lived twice. You will be stronger for it. I'm betting on it.

[To John Martin]
March 14, 1993 [holograph]

Correction on entry in "Letters of the 60's." About Francis Smith (enclose). She has many problems (one of them is her need to get close to me) to go with the old description. So, let's change it to:

"Frances Smith, mother of my daughter Marina. We were unmarried."

I think that's better.

Lots of action at this hospital. Linda is here almost continually. She's a good girl.

Some rough days ahead in chemotherapy.

[To Jon Cone]
April 23, 1993 4:34 PM

The reason I haven't answered you is that I've been in the hospital for 7 weeks. Leukemia. I'm home for 2 weeks now, rebuilding, hopefully, for the last round of chemotherapy and the antibiotics. They say it looks good for me. We'll see. They just about blast the shit out of you, killing most of the blood cells and plenty of other parts. Some day a better way may be found.

Hope you didn't think I ran off with the literary suck-tits. Your last issue was great. Keep going.

[To William Packard]
April 23, 1993 3:03 PM

In from hospital, temporarily, maybe a couple of weeks here, then back in for the "consolidation." Leukemia, a rough motherfucker. Had 2 sets of chemotherapy, maybe 13 days. Not much hair on my head and fairly weak. At this moment, things look good for recovery, so you ain't seen the last o' my pomes yet. But like they say in the back room, nobody really knows. Couple of doctors in the place knew of my work, one from his 19 year old son. They hung around my room telling me their stories. That's all right but they went on so long I could only get a few of my own in.

A few nights of horror. Almost kicked in twice. One time, they couldn't figure it, the other time is was just human stupidity from one of the subnormal hired hands. Then other times, they brought the wrong food, food that could kill under my conditions. Other big and little fuckups which I won't fry you over with here. A few ever sneezing suzie nurses, nice girls but … Bitches were like that for 7 weeks.

Anyhow, I am here at the moment. My wife, Linda, has been a bulwark and a marvel during all this … Unbelievable.

And I hope you and the *New York Quarterly* are doing fine. I am so honored by all that Bukowski stuff you printed in your last issue. You've got to know you're pissing off the soft-gut toadies down to their last tootsie rolls. You stay with us, I'll do what I can.

[To Jon Cone]
May 4, 1993 5:32 PM

You're of good heart. And hardly "small fry." It's my belief that you put out the best literary magazine, along with the *New York Quarterly.*

I am resting up now, hopefully building up strength for the last round of chemotherapy and antibiotics. My thanks for offering assistance in contacting editors, collectors, etc. I am pretty much up on things now. I hope in a day or two or three I will be able to write the last chapter on my novel *Pulp.* Don't know if I told you, it's a detective novel which I hope will end all detective novels. "Dedicated to bad writing ..." I've had fun with it and it should surely kill off any literary reputation that I might have. But I've never given a damn about that or immortality. It's day by day with me and all I want to do is to play it loose and free.

All right, you keep it going, the gods are on your side.

[To William Packard]
May 5, 1993 8:32 PM

I'm not out of this thing yet. Nurses trotting out here, had to go to hospital today for chest x-ray, possible infection, high fever, all that crap. One day I feel pretty good, the next brings complications. If I get lucky might be able to stay home until June 1st when I go back to hospital for last round of chemo-therapy and antibiotics. If I get past that, then I've probably made it.

I wanted to send you the Harper-Collins, *Run With The Hunted, A Bukowski Reader,* but so far they've only sent me one copy. It's probably in the bookstores now. There's a special reason I wanted you to see it.[1] But I wanted to sign one to you

---

1. The book is dedicated to William Packard.

but too weak now to fight all this and haggle them for more copies. They'll probably send more, finally.

Sorry to hear the boys from Maine are chickening out. They might have gone along with you if you had printed pussy-foot poetry. I think you upset too many people by running strong contemporary work and pointing out in your editorials that the poetry game is more con than real. There's a large gang out there of bitter and resentful toadies who don't want their cover blown. Unfortunately, they wield a lot of power because there are so many of them everywhere. [* * *]

[To William Packard]
June 30, 1993 9:31 PM

I've been back from the hospital a week. Long road back, gathering strength. Still have various problems but—so far—the main one has been checked. 64 days in that place—chemo plus antibiotics and blood transfusions, etc., can pretty much take the life out of you while trying to save said. But, shit, here I am for the moment, hopefully crawling back inch by inch. Your missiles to me were a great help, your letters, guys like you want to make a man live 200 years.

I am honored that you are using *Run with the Hunted* in your class. That's a real booster through this hell.

The muse still has not appeared for me. I mean, since this thing happened. She better, I am dependent. Still taking antibiotics so not functioning as should—like trying to drive with the parking brake on. Man, I hope the *NYQ* is still there and that you are still there. This is my first time back at the computer, feels strange and good, but must stop for now.

Stay with us.

290

[To William Packard]
July 8, 1993 5:36 PM

Got the cards from Hugo, Zola, Wharton, Waugh, Wilde and Kipling. Thank you for forwarding these to me. Great cards.

I'm still at home, hopefully gathering strength. The cancer is in "remission," which is their way of saying, "Right now, you're o.k. but..." Anyhow, you've got to play the cards they hand you.

Great news on all those poems o' mine coming up in numbers 51 and 52. You've got guts galore but the poetry pretty birds don't like that kind of stuff, it rattles their golden cage. Not only my poems but the other wild and fresh material you shoot at them. Each issue you get stronger. Luck with a continued life of that... It is a god damned miracle.

Wife and I getting a free dinner tonight from a pathologist I met in the hospital. A very strange fellow, very.

Again, you being there has been a vast help in pulling me through this last little swim down the Stygian river.

[To William Packard]
July 13, 1993 8:38 PM

Glad, sure, that I got "they rolled the whole bed out of there" past you.

Yes, I know about hospitals and death-bed bits, seems like I've come close so many times. I'm going to makes it one of these tries: practice makes perfect.

Yeah, the nurses can kill you, the assistant nurses can. Main thing is, the patient must watch and guide and advise. Errors and misjudgments are commonplace. And to get the floor mopped takes some persistence. Where I put in my 64 days, the air conditioner was out of whack and it read far too cold at night. I slept under 3 or 4 blankets but I'm sure that they killed off many who were addled and out of it, froze them to death...

Anyhow, I've been home a while now and am feeling a little better each day and I should make it unless there's some unforeseen turnaround. I pace myself, physically and with the muse. Feet still numb from the chemo ... One doc says it may just stay that way.

Oh, I've been getting all these cards from these dead writers and actors. Interesting and weird. Their photos look quite self-imposing, a bit of a put-on maybe. But most of them had hard lives and should be allowed a touch of self-love.

I'm honored at the reading of my poems ...

And am delighted that you and the *NYQ* are still there.

[To Mr. Bohlke]
July 25, 1993 3:51 PM

Dear Mr. Bohlke:

I answered your last letter regarding your inheritance. Is your mail being intercepted? At that time, I believe I told you "no" you better give your inheritance to somebody else. But now, since you wrote again, I'll change it. All right, I'll accept your inheritance in case you die. I'm probably as worthy as anybody else. But I still find your offer very strange because you've never met me in person. I suppose it's my writing?

Well, all right, I hope that this letter gets through to you. Yours was dated June 19 and I received it yesterday, July 25. Does somebody mail your letters for you?

Well, don't die and then we won't have to worry about anything.

[To Daisuke Obuchi]
July 26, 1993 10:07 PM

You appear to be an innocent man who still understands his fellow man all too well. It will make for hard living but I think it's better to know than to not know.

I guess what bothers us is that we expect more of the human race. The potential is there but it's seldom touched or used by the billions of people. Just a few. We must understand that humans will never be excessive in their kindness, understanding and fortitude. That's the way they are and we should not be disappointed, we should not expect them to be what we want them to be. A plant can't fly, a fish can't sing and we shouldn't expect them to. And the human animal will go on grossly as it always has throughout the centuries. The only problem being is that we have to live with them, depend upon them for food, transportation, housing, etc. There's no way we can break away, we are locked in with them. So be it.

Yes, I was very ill, leukemia, but didn't die and am still around, feeling better and I should be able to play with my little words a little longer.

It's strange that I am heard of in Japan. By you, anyhow. Thank you.

I watch Sumo on channel 18 when they have tournaments. Sumo is one of my favorites. Each match is over rather quickly and here comes another. That Akebono (spelling?) (Akabono?) is tough. (Akibono?) Anyhow, he looks good.

Well, stay alive, stay well and don't fight against happiness.

[To William Packard]
July 26, 1993 10:59 PM

I'm glad you liked the poem the university boys got scared of. I should have saved their first letter to me, trying to beg off after accepting the poem but I was lazy, sent the letter back with note scrawled on bottom: "O.k., send the poem back and we will consider the contract null and void ..." They make you sign a little contract upon acceptance ... Anyhow.

Sounds like you have an awful lot of work ahead trying to keep the *NYQ* afloat. But if all fails, you've still made history. So many of us needed a place to go when *Poetry* (the magazine)

293

went soft and staid. May the gods send the luck to keep you going!

Leukemia in remission, feeling better every day. The doc has warned me, though, relapses do occur, especially in the first year following. I've altered a few of my habits but the chemo probably chewed away a great portion of my brain cells. Maybe I had some to spare?

Popped out some poems last night but I will save you from them, no real piss-biters in the batch. Sometimes I just like to write to stay loose. In fact, that's the way I work it most of the time and when a good poem just happens to arrive along with the others, I think, hey, what the hell, look at this!

Going to bed early tonight. Sometimes it feels good to just stretch out and forget everything. It's been a long battle. And there's more to come. But you've got to learn pace. Right? Sure.

[To Carl Weissner]
July 30, 1993 10:31 PM

You take care of yourself, what is this pancreatic stuff? Could be dangerous. Hope they snuff it. There's always some god damned thing slashing at a man, physically or spiritually, trying to take him out. Dying's not the problem, it's all the crap that comes along with it, of course: pain, total inconvenience and you are shoved aside like a filled garbage bag. Meanwhile, some guy is arguing about a button missing from his shirt that he picked up at the cleaners ...

I am still amazed that you came all the way over here to see me in my hospital bed. Strange, strange ... and thank you, hit man.

Here, the cancer is supposed to be in remission. Which means, so far so good but there is always a chance of it coming back. But so far, good. I go to see the doc now and then. Am getting stronger. Hair starting to grow back on head. Should go to the track some time this week. That will really seem like old

294

times. Only it won't be a 5 or 6 day week anymore. 2, 3, or 4 days...It's a grind. But need it to tighten up the forces. Not drinking. Could be finished with that. I hope so.

I drive past the hospital and look up there. What a time. 64 days. The hanging chemo bags, blood bags, antibiotic bags, the etc. bags...Something going all the time. Ummm, Ummm...

All right, stay in there, Carl...Love from the cats, Linda, me...sure.

[To John Martin]
August 2, 1993 10:20 PM

Montfort was over yesterday, took a mass of photos of me. You really ought to pay the guy something, he's broke and it's an expensive process, plus time, travel, etc. You ought to think about it. There, I've spoken.

Been feeling a little off in the past few days. Have made an appointment with the doctor tomorrow. Hope I'm o.k. I don't know if I can outlast another bout with that hospital. I'm probably all right, though. Yet, there's always the chance.

It has felt good being back at the machine, playing with words. 2 day breakdown over weekend. Problems. Screen went blank. At other times the printer just printed blank white papers. I worked with the machine, went mad. But after many hours, many, I've got it running again.

All right, keep the show going.

[To William Packard]
August 7, 1993 9:40 PM

Feeling somewhat off-feed, went to doctor, mixed signals, leukemia could be coming back. Will see my regular doctor Tuesday. If I have relapsed, I don't know what the next step is. Do they take you out and shoot you? Anyhow, I may not be one

295

with Job but some of his shadow has fallen upon me. We'll see.

Thanks for all the things you've been sending my way. The letters from your students were good, they seem nice folks, kind, gentle. Thank you.

The letter to you from the x-student is funny but chilling and a touch horrifying. She's crazy in an acceptable way, that is, to society. I needn't tell you to stay away from this one. Didn't you just get away from one who crouched in vestibules in order to glance at you. God, I've known some crazies, it's when they try to kill you that you begin to think that you might be able to do without any women at all forever.

I'm weary tonight but wanted to say, great on #53, I saw the table of contents you sent. 4 poems! I can't die now, I want to see them in print. I note you are going to run the one the university boys sent back. When they accepted that poem I wondered if they had really read it. I guess they finally did and figured out, "Jesus, this poem is about *us!*" Those featherbed souls, how can they stand themselves?

[To Jon Cone]
August 14, 1993 10:17 PM

Yes, I rec. the poem translated into the French. I don't recall if I wrote the gentleman back. Probably not. I've had some problems. But if you'd care to publish translation of poem in a future edition of *W[orld] L[etter]*, I'd like that, sure. Thank you.

I'm glad you are going to publish some poems by William Packard. This man is a very courageous editor, quite refreshing and remarkable.

I'm behind on everything here, so must keep this short.

So, you work in a hospital. Then you must know the enormous amount of error and indifference involved in those institutions. They kill as many as they save and they charge outrageously.

[To William Packard]
August 14, 1993 10:39 PM

This is between you and me. Private. Went to doc and leukemia has come back. "You've got about a year," he told me. Still, I'm going to try the Aryuvedic method starting the 25th—mind over matter, body balance, etc. What the hell, I've got nothing to lose with that. I'll still retain my regular doc and work with these guys as well.

You know, I'll be 73 on August 16th and the way I've lived I've beaten the odds but somehow I always figured I'd hit 80 and go on a few more from there. Kind of give me time to round out the writing. I really didn't have much luck until I was 50, so I figured the gods owed me a few years. Of course, what I figure has little to do with what happens. Anyhow, my luck with the *New York Quarterly* has been one of the most astonishing things to happen to me. So, I go out with a bang and not a whimper. But I'm still here. And I've fooled them before.

You keep it going.

[To John Martin]
August 21, 1993 10:41 PM

Still trying to hold the fort down here but they keep rushing in new troops against us. Well, you know, we still have *Pulp* sitting in the reserve tank, although you have a manuscript full of spelling errors ... and typos ... I'm sure these can be worked out. Meanwhile, here are a few more poems. I've found it difficult to write anything but what is at hand. Have tried to wait for other things to arrive but they have not, so ...

I feel strange. Getting a bone marrow Tuesday. Wednesday, starting in on Ayruveta (spell?). Who the hell knows? Some direction, some pathway, instead of sitting around waiting. The M.D.'s are not very upbeat fellows, they are too consumed with avoiding malpractice lawsuits, healing the patient is only an afterthought.

[To William Packard]
August 23, 1993 9:42 PM

I am truly honored to be selected for the *NYQ* award, March 1994. But, oh, the way I feel now I might not be here then. But am working on new angle and may make it...but won't know what shape I'll be in. I don't know of anybody in New York who might accept it for me. What the hell will I do? Ow, ow. Sean Penn, a friend, who was over last night hits New York city now and then but I don't know. Ow.

On death, it's all right for me but I just hate to leave my wife and 9 cats alone here. And it can be a painful process. When I almost went in the hospital the pain was unbelievable. I mean, I just didn't think it could get *that bad*. I hope when I go that it's easier than that. Also, I don't have the God-fix so I have to leave with a deck of unmarked cards.

Happy upcoming birthday to you. Yeah, 60 is a tough one. But after that, all the years are free ones, bonuses. Feel good.

You've shown such guts in backing my work. I know that it has cost you in certain quarters. All right, we've had a great time no matter what happens.

hold, then move forward.

[To Carl Weissner]
September 5, 1993 9:38 PM

Yeah, I got rid of the leukemia and it came back, we gotta hope for miracles now. Who knows, maybe I can outfox the Fates for a little while. It all seems such a waste, after all the chemo and crap. Well, I've written *Pulp* and it sits there waiting. The dick dies in the last chapter...

I got your birthday message, thanks, old pal. You keep boosting me.

I'm glad your mother pulled through. Yeah, the docs are plenty discouraging. I know this pathologist now, strange guy, met him at the hospital, he comes by here about once a week and he tells me some stories, hospital stories and others. He's a loner. But in his profession, he's one of the best.

Those 4 or 5 days you came were great, beyond all call. But never do it again. You take care of business over there. But thanks much, you have no idea what a god damned surprise it was to see you!

A bit tired tonight, not much energy but wanted you to know that I was thinking of you, old timer. Stay with it. Love from Linda and me.

[To William Packard]
September 11, 1993 5:40 PM

I'm glad I got the "gym co@ch" past you. By the way, my keyboard refused to print out the standard "a," so I went ahead and used the "@." I wasn't trying to be Gertrude Stein or any of those. I just thought, well, I'll just write it this way and if it's accepted I hope they print it as is, just to jar some people and to piss some others off. However, if you should get around to publishing the poem, either way will do. I mean, "a" or "@."

Thank you for all the enclosures. "Notes on Bukowski," well, I think you're right. Good of you to tell them.

I think one of the main problems of poetry is that it reads too much the way we think it should read, like, that's a poem, sounds like a poem ... It's structured instead of being free. I'd as soon somebody handed me a lead pipe instead of a poem, it wouldn't be as boring. I don't know how we got so far away from saying what needs to be said but we have, it all remains cloaked and slick and airy. Something is said but what is it, where is it? Ah, there it is! I get it! And the more obtuse and distant you get, the closer you get to the Pulitzer and other prizes. Everybody has bought the con and there are thousands feeding off of it from University to somebody's grandmother. We've been stuck with this mess and it runs centuries deep.

Well, the latest from the m.d.'s is that my bone marrow has "petered out."

There are days when I get pretty fucking depressed. It's not death, it's the stupid inconvenience, the faltering of the will and the way, missing the drunken nights and the days at the track. This sitting about, on the wait. Well, I'm not the first. The evening darkens. What a fix, what a fate, what the hell.

[To John Martin]
September 19, 1993 8:44 PM

You could be the last honest man on earth. On those checks, I believe I was in the hospital at the time. Linda says that she deposited all the checks I signed during that time. They were all put into checking at Cal Fed Savings, Palos Verdes branch. However, Linda does not make note of deposits or withdrawals when she makes transactions. I've checked my other banks and there is no indication of any deposits at this time. I can't judge what happened but my guess is that the checks just didn't go into deposit. Lost mail or whatever. If you haven't received the canceled checks by now from the May period, I don't think you'll ever receive them.

I don't know. Maybe you could send me some new checks and I could deposit them. Then, if anything came through on the old checks, I could repay you, no problem. Is this asking too much? It's the only way out that I can see. Unless you'd rather wait longer. Anyhow, total thanks for your honesty in this matter.

Not much writing of late, I suppose you've noticed. I should get lucky soon. Have been feeling a bit off lately. Got a blood transfusion last Wednesday, 2 pints. I am keeping on the Aryuvedic Program. Had my first TM session today. Going out to see a person Wednesday who has had some luck with his leukemia. He's 75. I'm rather curious as to what he did or is doing.

Linda is doing pretty good lately. Me, I won't feel good until some stuff comes off of this computer. Having you up there on my side helps a hell of a lot, kid.

[To William Packard]
September 22, 1993 9:13 PM

My TM instructress lived in the same town as Hemingway and the little girls used to think of him as "Santa Claus." She heard the shot on that morning. She is also a good friend of A. Huxley's second wife. Odd world, what?

I might well fool the doc (maybe with some help from him, like the blood transfusion I got last Wednesday) but what else helps is that I belong to the Stoics. I'm ready to go but I'm cool about it. Panic kills as quickly as anything else. I may piss you off and live to be 90. On the other hand...

Your fight for survival with the *NYQ* is one of the most amazing things going. And what has been utterly astonishing to me (besides your publishing wild and fresh poetry) is your taking on the University boys. Nobody has ever bothered to try to undercover the rot there. Too dangerous. Those lads are vicious. They cluster, sleep cheek to cheek and cover each other's asses. Their lives are all too soft and easy, no matter how false, and death to anybody who dare point them out. I mean, what the hell would they do if their soft and corrupt undersides were exposed? Work for McDonald's?

Well, I wanted to write you something to help keep you going but I'm already experiencing an energy burn-out. When I couldn't find out how to underline McDonald's I went limp. No guts. New keyboard. No guts, new keyboard.

I can't believe the number of poems you have upcoming from this Bukowski guy. I'll have to live just in order to see them in print. I hope they don't put a hit man on you. Well, it's good to write something here anyhow even though I dropped away after a few paragraphs. Have to get into the poem soon.

You stay there. You stay with it. You are being watched from the top of the universe. Valor noted. Indeed. Push through, push on...

301

[To William Packard]
November 3, 1993

Thanks for your great letter of last.
I'm too weak to respond. Going back to hospital.
Thanks for everything and everything.

[To Jack Grapes]
December 23, 1993 9:05 PM

Thanks for *Onthebus* 13. You've given me a nice show here, thank you. Honored to be on board.

Back from another long stay at the hospital. More chemotherapy, more antibiotics. I still have leukemia. You might say I'm hanging from a thread. But I said it. [* * *]

[To William Packard]
December 26, 1993 4:22 PM

Just got back from hospital. Couple more months, chemotherapy, antibiotics. No go. Still have leukemia. My time is up for grabs.

So, this is a hard letter to write. I was honored when you offered me the the notice of being one helpful to the *NYQ*, come March. My problem is that I may not be here then, or if I am, doubt if I could find anybody to come to NYC to accept award for me So, I think it's best the award be given to somebody else. I hope you understand this. Believe me, I only hope it could be otherwise. [* * *]

[To John Martin]
December 31, 1993 5:52 PM

It's good to have you rooting for me. I can feel it and use it. I'll do what I can, what the hell.

New Year's eve approaching. You've long known how I feel about all this. We've just got to duck and endure.

Just one poem off the machine lately. Enclosed. By the way, I actually dreamed I shook hands with Richard Nixon. That's close to nightmare.

[To William Packard]
December 31, 1993 9:26 PM

New Year's Eve. My wife has some friends about. I am still alive?

By the way, great last issue. I had it in the hospital and read it there and it was a big help, and how. You keep getting better ... you've got the magic working.

Also read my own book, *Screams from the Balcony* (letters from the 60's) and it made me realize that something or somebody has always been upon me.

How many days must a man be tested?

As many as they give him. [* * *]

•

• 1 9 9 4 •

[To William Packard]
January 5, 1994 8:36 PM

Thanks for the card. It threw some light into some dark corners.

Yes, I've heard that I lead in thefts from bookstores. This doesn't bother me too much. It's when they steal them from the libraries. That takes one book out of the hands of the many and a reader like this I'd rather not have.

Here life is strange, so many things have had to be altered. But look, for better or worse, I'm at the frigging computer. That, to me, counts for something.

[To John Martin]
January 5, 1994 8:51 PM

Feels good to be back at the machine, if for just a bit.

By the way, I am getting quite a few letters about *Screams*. Basically, the message is that the letters do them some good. So many letters from writers are far too comfortable and cloying. They self-congratulate themselves straight into a grade A boredom. [* * *]

[To William Packard]
February 24, 1994 4:28 PM

Got your letter and photos from the hospital.

Sure, the gods are testing you. You are a Leader and a Creator.

Remain in the fight. I can think of no other man as badly needed.

Stay. Endure.

I dispatch luck and love toward you.

[To Al Berlinsky]
February 25 1994

Hello Al —

Solitude gets sweeter and sweeter.

Once knew a guy who did time. They threw him in the hole.

When they asked him, "Do you want to come out now?" he said, "No."

So they pulled him out anyhow.

They thought he was crazy.

He was one of the sanest men I ever met.

Yes, yes.

Charles Bukowski died on March 9, 1994

Index of Principal Names

Gere, Richard, 175
Ginsberg, Allen, 32, 66, 197
Godard, Jean-Luc, 29
Gold, Mike, 33
Goodwin, Douglas, 56, 213, 264
Gorky, Maxim, 135
Grapes, Jack, 264, 267, 282, 302
Green, Adam, 270

Halpern, Daniel, 283
Hamsun, Knut, 13, 72, 135,
    157, 233, 238, 244, 253
Hardy, Thomas, 13
Hemingway, Ernest, 40, 56, 82,
    93, 95, 96, 135, 138, 158,
    193, 234–35, 284, 301
Hersey, John, 180n
Hindus, Milton, 238
Hopper, Dennis, 264
Horace, 142n
Housman, A. E., 10n
Hughes, Henry, 168, 175
Hugo, Victor, 291
Humphris, Cyril, 184
Huxley, Aldous, 301

Ibsen, Henrik, 157
Innis, Chris, 127n

Jeffers, Robinson, 135, 235, 244
Joyce, James, 179, 193

Kerouac, Jack, 196, 225
Kessler, Stephen, 60, 62, 65,
    277
Kijewski, Bruce, 266
King, Linda, 38, 171
Kipling, Rudyard, 291
Kowit, Steve, 118

Lawrence, D. H., 242
Leo, Teresa, 219, 264
Levy, D. A., 33
Li Po, 173, 176–77, 185, 227
Locklin, Gerald, 28, 35–36, 40,
    43–44, 48, 57, 88, 93, 96,
    100, 117, 147, 170, 174, 248
London, Jack, 138, 178
Lowell, Robert, 194

Lowry, Malcolm, 176
Lyden, Eric, 127
Lygo, Kevin, 184

McKee, Louis, 219
McRae, Donald, 244
Madonna, 129, 218
Mailer, Norman, 9, 41, 43, 89,
    136, 200, 248
Malone, Marvin, 30, 55, 200,
    262
Mann, Thomas, 13
Martin, Barbara, 18, 69, 156
Martin, John, 17, 25–26, 30, 38,
    50, 53, 61, 67–68, 71, 76,
    81–83, 85–87, 90–92, 94, 96,
    101–06, 109, 121, 123, 127,
    129, 133, 146, 149, 152,
    154–56, 163, 179, 181–84,
    186–87, 192–93, 205, 210,
    218, 228–29, 236, 241,
    256–57, 259, 273, 277–78,
    281–83, 285, 287, 295, 297,
    300, 303, 305
Meinbresse, Tim, 276
Mencken, H. L., 60
Michener, James, 43
Miller, Henry, 11, 18, 27, 56, 66,
    166
Mills, David, 177
Montfort, Michael, 68, 257, 295
Mrabet, Mohammed, 215
Munch, Edvard, 157

Nicholson, Jack, 16
Nietzsche, Friedrich, 135, 218
Norse, Harold, 227

Obuchi, Daisuke, 292
Ochester, Ed, 254
Ochs, Larry, 127n
O'Neill, Eugene, 138
Owen, Wilfred, 70

Packard, William, 9–10, 13–15,
    58, 66, 69–70, 72–76, 79–80,
    103, 105, 107, 110–12, 114,
    117, 119–20, 122–24, 126,
    130, 132, 140–41, 143, 146,

Printed March 1999 in Santa Barbara &
Ann Arbor for the Black Sparrow Press by
Mackintosh Typography & Edwards Brothers Inc.
Text set in Plantin by Words Worth.
Design by Barbara Martin.
This first edition is published in paper wrappers;
there are 750 cloth trade copies;
& 376 copies handbound in boards by Earle Gray
each containing an original serigraph
print by Charles Bukowski.

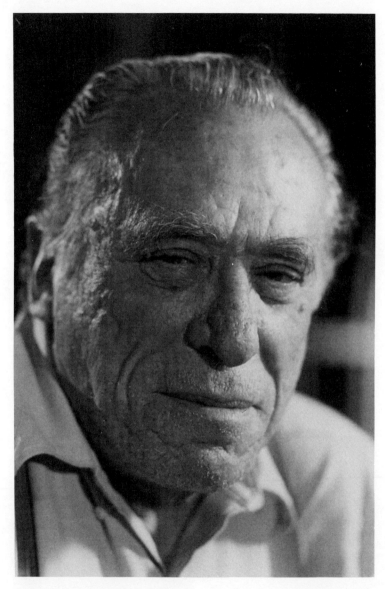

PHOTO: Michael Montfort

CHARLES BUKOWSKI is one of America's best-known contemporary writers of poetry and prose and, many would claim, its most influential and imitated poet. He was born in Andernach, Germany to an American soldier father and a German mother in 1920, and brought to the United States at the age of three. He was raised in Los Angeles and lived there for fifty years. He published his first story in 1944 when he was twenty-four and began writing poetry at the age of thirty-five. He died in San Pedro, California on March 9, 1994 at the age of seventy-three, shortly after completing his last novel, *Pulp* (1994).

During his lifetime he published more than forty-five books of poetry and prose, including the novels *Post Office* (1971), *Factotum* (1975), *Women* (1978), *Ham on Rye* (1982), and *Hollywood* (1989). His most recent books are the posthumous collections *Betting on the Muse: Poems & Stories* (1996), *Bone Palace Ballet: New Poems* (1997), *The Captain Is Out to Lunch and the Sailors Have Taken Over the Ship* (1998) which is illustrated by Robert Crumb, and *Reach for the Sun: Selected Letters 1978–1994* (1999).

All of his books have now been published in translation in over a dozen languages and his worldwide popularity remains undiminished. In the years to come Black Sparrow will publish additional volumes of previously uncollected poetry and letters.

SEAMUS COONEY was born in Ireland and educated there and in the United States. He now teaches English literature at Western Michigan University in Kalamazoo.